DEDICATION

Pain Unforgiven is dedicated to my children–Tiffany, Brantley, and Anna Grace–to my mom, Bobbie Pierce, and to the place I call home. *Pain Unforgiven* is also in memory of my dad and hero, Ralph Pierce, and in memory of a special young lady, Carli Michelle Brewer.

DONATION

Part of the proceeds from the sell of this book will be donated to the Greene County High School Drama Troupe.

Pain Unforgiven

by Randy Pierce

SH
STEER HOLLOW
PUBLISHING

PAIN UNFORGIVEN
Published by Steer Hollow Publishing, LLC

Cover and inside design by The C2 Group, www.thec2.net

ISBN 978-0-615-45932-5

Printed in the United States of America

table of contents

acknowledgments

There are so many people to be thanked for helping my dream of writing *Pain Unforgiven* become a reality. A special thanks to my publication team: Shawnassey Howell, Kamel King, and Jeff Christian for a first-class publication. Many thanks to Alan Huffman and Neil White for reading the manuscript and providing valuable structural recommendations. To my editor, Tylina Dunnam, thank you for teaching me so much. Thank you, Cheryl, for character wardrobe advice and thanks to Penny Lott for much-needed medical advice. To those who read the manuscript and provided suggestions–Stacy Wilson, Quentin Whitwell, Jonathon and Tiffany Rayborn, Brantley Pierce and Clint Pentecost, thank you! Thanks to Jeff Rimes for legal advice. To my daughter, Tiffany, the Facebook page was perfect. To my sisters, Shonna–my biggest cheerleader–and Cheryl, thanks for the encouragement. I owe thanks to Julia, Tara, Jennifer, Suzanne, Ryan and Roun for allowing our lunches to be dominated by this book (I am sorry!). I also owe special thanks to my late Uncle Lauvon Pierce who instilled in me the love of a great yarn. And to the many authors who have written for generations–I have been inspired by so many of you–thank you. To my parents who taught me the value of hard work and that everyone bleeds red, I owe you everything. To the countless people, including Gayla and the Smith family, who have encouraged me throughout the years–

thank you. And to the house at the end of that dead-end dirt road where I would lie in bed at night and dream myself to sleep–I miss you. Finally, I would like to thank the Lord for the many blessings that I do not deserve.

Faulkner introduced us to Yoknapatawpha County, and Grisham introduced us to Ford County. Both fictional places. For me, I chose to place a fictional story in my home county–Greene. Some of the places you will visit in *Pain Unforgiven* are real, and some are fictional. The people of Greene County have helped me achieve my dreams.

Mississippi is often at or near the top of *The Generosity Index* which measures the charitable giving of each state. Having traveled to many places, in my humble opinion, Greene County is the most generous place in the world. Thus, I owe a special thanks to the place I call home. For those of you that have never met Greene County, I invite you to come for a visit. When you arrive, you will be met with hospitality and an invitation to stay. There is indeed, "No place like home."

Part One:

The Phone Call

chapter one

GRANT HICKS ROUNDED THE FINAL TURN of his morning run, wrestling with indecision. After all, it had been nearly twenty years since he left that place—a place where people, though well-intentioned, often drew conclusions prematurely, a place where folks were quick to judge, a place where people sought understanding and forgiveness only when the dreadful, abhorred circumstances happened to them.

Grant did not hold a grudge against the people, only the place, the place where he learned that if one is willing to accept those who are different, there is indeed a heavy price to pay. Grant paid that price. Or at least he thought he had. The pain lingered. The payment was still being made. And now, as he opened the front door to his Marietta home, the question returned: Would he go back there?

Grant met Samantha Novy in undergraduate school at Ole Miss. She was from the small north Mississippi town of Hickory Flat. Her parents divorced when she was five, and her earliest memories of her family centered around conflict. Actually, *conflict* is a kind word to describe the events of her turbulent childhood. Neither parent fought for her custody. The fight was over who would take her. Her momma lost.

So for the next eight years she moved thirteen times in and around Hickory Flat. Too many men to count lived with her mother at various intervals. Her mom had two other children with different men. Samantha was lost in the shuffle. After a brief stay in a foster home in the custody of the Department of Human Services, she ended up with her dad's mother where he treated his mom as badly as he treated Samantha's mom. Samantha was not impressed with men. She vowed never to get married. Grant was okay with this arrangement, and they had lived together since college. Marriage was not in sight, nor were kids. But she knew Grant, and she knew he had been living with the pain of that place for almost twenty years. She knew he needed to go back there.

Grant entered the kitchen as Samantha was finishing her morning grapefruit and was about to leave for work. She had worked her way from a local television network to CNN where she was an assistant in the international assignment drama. Her ultimate goal was to be a foreign correspondent covering human rights and international relations in Russia or China. She was well on her way to achieving that goal. Both she and Grant were ambitious and worked well north of forty hours per week. They had plenty of toys to show for their labors, but they had precious little time to play.

"Good morning, Sam. It's Friday. Please try to report some good news today, Sweetie, if there is any." Grant kissed Samantha on the cheek and popped the top on a Coca-Cola.

"That's real smart, Grant. Run five miles and then drink a Coke."

"Baby, I'm not trying to lose weight. Just trying to keep the arteries clean." Grant indeed was in great shape. He was six feet tall and weighed 175 pounds with little body fat. He vowed always to have his ties hang vertically. He once had a psychology professor at Ole Miss whose stomach caused his ties to lie around his gut like a snake crawling over a mound. Plus, Grant was type-A to the max. Everything had its order. His personal appearance ranked at the top of his priority list. "What are our plans this weekend, Sam?"

Samantha knew they were supposed to attend a fundraiser for the local humane society that night and attend the wedding of one of her co-workers Saturday afternoon, but she elected to omit those details. "Nothing, just work." Samantha then looked at Grant and asked, "Are you going home?"

Grant's demeanor changed as he walked out of the kitchen. "I'll see you tonight. I have to take a shower and get to work myself. I have a very important Summary Judgment motion in federal court this afternoon. I love ya, Sam." And with that, he was gone.

"He is so stubborn. Ugh!" Samantha muttered as she disappeared into the Atlanta morning.

chapter two

As nursing homes go, Greene Rural Nursing Center is one of the best. Of course, like most nursing homes, its residents are not visited quite enough, but they are nursed, fed, and bathed by the people that know them. Local churches take turns providing ministry to the residents there, but the key to the occupants' hope in their last days is the staff. Led by a life-long Greene Countian, Becky Berry, the employees are pretty much local and take great pride in caring for their neighbors.

Former Greene County Sheriff Lauvon McInnis moved into Greene Rural two years ago at the age of sixty-five. Although sixty-five was young to be a resident at Greene Rural, an untimely stroke and partial paralysis necessitated McInnis' care. Divorced at the age of forty-eight, McInnis never remarried. His children encouraged him to live with them, but he did not want to be a burden; therefore, he chose to live at Greene Rural. He is a favorite among the staff and the other residents. He served twenty years as Sheriff of Greene County before being defeated by a man who would only serve one term. He lost that election by only twenty-four votes. Many said it was his own doing. Others said people just wanted a change. But, he knew why he lost, and he was proud that he only was defeated by twenty-four votes. In the same year he lost the election, his wife left him. He was quietly proud of the fact that he stood his ground, and thus he slept well at night. He never became bitter. He had learned to forgive.

Sheriff McInnis was especially fond of a young Greene Rural nurse named Jade Lott. Jade finished high school with his youngest son. McInnis lived in the Vernal community his entire life until he moved to Greene Rural. The Lotts lived in Mt. Pisgah. Both communities were located in Beat Four. In Greene County, one was defined by the beat or district in which he or she lived. More people lived in Vernal; thus, Vernal usually elected the Board of Supervisor for Beat Four. The McInnises and Lotts never voted the same. They were always political adversaries though no one quite knew why.

Jade was the picture of southern beauty. She had blue eyes that would turn to green when light caught them in the right way. Her hair was defined as blond but had a tint of light auburn. Her dimples lit up at the slightest grin. Jade was valedictorian of her senior class in 1992. She was offered scholarships from almost every college in Mississippi and Alabama. But Jade had a dream, and she had pursued it. She wanted to live on the Big Screen, so she had struck out for Hollywood. As evidenced by her current employment, the dream either died or faded away. However, that did not matter to Sheriff McInnis. She was like a daughter to him, and he loved her as such.

"Good morning, Mr. Lauvon. How is my favorite patient?" Jade was always cheerful. If she ever had a bad day, nobody knew it. The sheriff insisted on Jade calling him by his first name. Everyone else still called him Sheriff.

"Morning, Jade. I'm good. How are you?" The sheriff was watching *Headline News*. He still enjoyed keeping up with local, state, and national politics.

"I'm great. It's Friday, and I'm looking forward to sleeping late tomorrow." Jade handed Sheriff McInnis his morning regimen of medicine and poured him a glass of water.

"Well, you earned it, Jade. You work very hard around here." The sheriff took his medicine and handed Jade the glass.

"Thanks, Mr. Lauvon, but it's easy to work hard when you love what you do." The sheriff knew what it meant to love a job. He had loved being sheriff.

After Jade checked the sheriff's blood pressure, she told him she would check on him later in the day and left. She also reminded him about the bluegrass band that would be playing for the residents that night. Jade's brief visits were the favorite part of Sheriff McInnis' days at Greene Rural. He had no way of knowing, but his days, as well as Jade's, were about to get a bit more interesting.

chapter three

GRANT HAD LEARNED TO FORGET ABOUT that place. Almost. He swore he would never return. His bitterness had turned to hatred, his hatred to anger. It cast a shadow over him he had never escaped. But on March 16, 2010, a phone call opened the floodgates to the memories that robbed his soul of laughter and joy and peace. As he was preparing for a deposition in a case where he was defending an Atlanta doctor accused of medical malpractice, his secretary interrupted him despite his adamant directive to hold all calls. He was in the zone.

Linda Caldwell had been with him since his arrival at Rimes and Yancey as a hot-shot new attorney in the fall of 1998. Grant was the firm's most sought-after recruit that year. He finished number one in his class at the University of Virginia School of Law and was the editor of the *Law Review*. His academic resume included

Summa Cum Laude graduate from Ole Miss with undergraduate and graduate degrees in mathematics. Linda had been with the firm for fifteen years prior to Grant's arrival. She had become a mother figure of sorts to Grant, and she knew how he despised interruption as he prepared. But this phone call seemed important.

"I hate to interrupt you, Grant, but I think you may want to take this call."

Grant looked up at Linda with obvious disgust. Patience was not his strength. "Linda, I told you no interruptions! Damn it, you know I can't be interrupted when I'm preparing for a trial."

Linda, unfazed by his tone, turned to leave and said, "Fine, I'll tell her you will call her back. Sorry!"

"Well, since you've already interrupted, who is it?"

Linda stopped at the door and said, "I'll patch her through to you. Her name is Elsie Smallwood. She says she's from Leakesville, Mississippi."

Grant's heart fell, and his pen dropped to the floor. Just the sound of those two words, *Leakesville, Mississippi*, crushed him. He simply could not escape that place. It haunted him. And it had found him again.

Elsie Smallwood is a quiet woman whose husband died in his early thirties and left her with four boys to rear. Luther Smallwood was drunk more than he was sober, and the locals, too late, found him passed out lying on the train tracks near Little Creek in Perry County on a cold February night. The seven o'clock train had severed both legs mid-thigh. He bled to death before the Forrest General Hospital helicopter could land on Highway 98. The community raised money to plant him in the ground, but no headstone had ever been purchased. No one wanted to remember Luther Smallwood.

Elsie has been a cafeteria worker at Leakesville Elementary

School for over forty years. She also cleans houses after work and irons clothes for extra money. She has done the best that she could with a ninth-grade education and a very limited vocabulary. She lives in a small wooden house with an ordinary tin roof which had rusted long before Luther met his Maker. The home is heated in the winter by an old fireplace and electric heaters. In the summer, an attic fan keeps the place cool at night, but in the daytime it is almost too hot to bare.

All her boys were dear to her, but one in particular was her joy. Brandon was the third child. He was only four years old when his father died, and his memory of his dad was scant. But he loved his mother as much as one could love another. As a child, Brandon would accompany her to the houses she cleaned and even learned to assist her as she ironed. As Brandon began to mature, folks knew he was different. Brandon would often be picked on, but he never fought back. As he became a teenager, he began to notice that he was different, too. His two older brothers stayed in and out of Youth Court; therefore, Brandon thought that he would be considered normal if he took on a new image, a tough-guy image. So he dressed the part, but deep down inside, he knew who he was. He also knew that secret could never be revealed, especially in that place.

As Grant picked up the phone, his mind was busy trying to figure out why Elsie Smallwood wanted to talk to him and, more importantly, how she had found him. "Hello, this is Grant."

"Grant Hicks? From Greene County?" Elsie's delivery seemed tired and aged, but Grant recognized her voice immediately.

"Yes, ma'am, how are you doing, Ms. Smallwood?" Grant had not experienced this level of anxiety since he had waited for the results of Samantha's pregnancy test in college. When the results were negative, they celebrated with a few drinks. Before they knew it, they were sweating another pregnancy test. They were more careful after that.

"I've seen better days, Mr. Hicks."

"Please call me Grant, Ms. Smallwood." One thing Grant had never forgotten was his southern manners and his respect for elders.

"Mr. Hicks, I mean Grant, I really hated to bother you, and it was almost impossible to find you. But, Brandon wanted me to call you." Grant had not seen Brandon Smallwood since he lived in Oxford while attending Ole Miss. Brandon had been incarcerated at Parchman in Sunflower County in Mississippi's Delta region. It was just a little over two hours from Oxford, so Grant occasionally had made the drive to see Brandon. Grant's visits eventually stopped because each time he saw Brandon, the place to which he had vowed never to return would monopolize his thoughts. Grant's heart had been hardened by his bitterness for that place, and Brandon was a visual reminder of the pain. "Brandon is sick, really sick. He was diagnosed with cancer about three months ago, and I won't have him much longer." Elsie began to cry quietly, but Grant could sense that she was almost out of tears. Grant silently allowed Elsie to regain her composure, his mind racing to figure out where this conversation was headed. "He wants to see you; he's at home with me now on hospice. The doctor says it could be a few days or a couple of weeks, maybe a month."

Grant remained silent. He was not about to step foot back in Greene County. But the words that usually flowed off the end of his tongue were simply not there. He managed to get her phone number and vowed to let her know by Friday whether he would come. He planned to have Linda call her to let her know that he was simply too busy. Damn that place!

chapter four

THE SUMMARY JUDGMENT MOTION hearing did not go well. Judge Shonna Rayborn was tough and to the point. After Grant argued his motion, Judge Rayborn simply denied it without requiring the plaintiff's attorney to respond. She then called both attorneys to the bench and scolded Grant for wasting her time. This was not a good way to end the week, and it was Friday, which meant Elsie Smallwood needed an answer.

Grant arrived at the office at 4:00 p.m., 3:00 p.m. in Mississippi. He stopped by Linda's desk first. She was not there, and her computer was turned off as if she were gone. In his office, he discovered a note from her which read, "Grant, something came up, and I had to leave a little early today. Please don't forget to call Elsie Smallwood; she called again this morning. I told her you would call as soon as you got back in the office."

Grant paced a few minutes trying to convince himself that the phone call would be easy. After all, she was 350 miles away, and he had not seen her in two decades. Grant made his living with words, and he was a lethal adversary in the courtroom against the brightest lawyers in the nation. Elsie Smallwood did not have a chance. He dialed the number.

As the phone began to ring, Grant hoped he would reach an answering machine. Then, he would simply leave a quick message before anyone could pick up. Or, better yet, if no answer by the fifth ring, he would hang up and have Linda call on Monday with his regrets. After the fourth ring, Grant was about to hang up when a male voice answered.

"Hello?"

Ugh! Grant thought he was in the clear. "Hi, my name is Grant Hicks. Is Ms. Smallwood there?"

The man on the other end cleared his throat. "No, she had to run to the drug store to pick up a prescription for Brandon. But, she's expecting your call. Brandon is sleeping right now. The medicines keep him out most of the time."

"I need to leave Ms. Smallwood a message if I can. Will you see her?" Grant exhaled, relieved that he did not have to talk to Elsie.

"Yes, I'll wait here until she returns. She don't have a lot of help with Brandon, so I give her a break when she needs one. I used to be her pastor."

Well, this just keeps getting better, Grant thought. A preacher! The most narrow-minded humans alive. Grant had avoided them, too, since his escape from that place. He despised religion. "I've been looking at my schedule, and it will be impossible for me to make it down there. I was just letting her know."

"Oh, that's too bad. Brandon won't be here much longer. He's been a trooper, though. He has endured a very tough illness with tremendous courage. But he is ready to meet the Lord." Grant was silent for a moment, and before he could thank the preacher for taking his message, a feeling overwhelmed him which he had never experienced. He felt drawn to that place for the first time in years. And it scared him. "Son, there is one thing you should know before you go. Brandon had two requests when he found out he was dying. He wanted to die at home and for you to speak at his funeral. Elsie has been looking for you for two months. If you change your mind, let me know. My name is Lollis Clark."

With that, the pastor gave Grant his cell number and hung up the phone. Grant walked to the window of his office and stared across the Atlanta sky. Thoughts returned to him that had been dormant for years. The trial. His dad. The verdict. Brandon. Pain. And as he traced the path of a distant airplane hanging in the sky, he finally admitted to himself that he had to return to that place. He had to return–home.

When Grant walked into the kitchen, he found a note from Samantha telling him that she was attending a humane society event and would be in later that night. It further said, "Grant, I know you have been struggling about what you should do regarding Brandon. But I ran across this quote today from Joseph Bradsky and thought of you: 'No matter under what circumstances you leave it, home does not cease to be home. No matter how you lived there–well or poorly.' I believe in my heart you should go see Brandon. But I won't mention it again. I love you, Sam."

Grant then called Linda to make sure she was okay and to discuss with her the next week's schedule. She kept a copy of Grant's calendar at home because he was prone to call her on Sundays to see what his upcoming week held. It turned out that Linda had to leave work early to pick up her niece who had car trouble, and she reminded Grant that he had instructed her to clear next week's calendar for him to prepare for the medical malpractice trial the following week. He then told Linda that he would be leaving the next morning to drive to Mississippi and would return on Monday. She had several questions she wanted to ask, but she could tell Grant seemed preoccupied, so she left them for another day.

As Grant began to pack for the trip, the anxiety and nervousness began to turn into anticipation and a hint of excitement. For the first time in years, he began to wonder if the place had changed since he left it in August of 1990. Most people who were able to escape Greene County subscribed to the *Greene County Herald* to keep up with the happenings in and around the rural county. The *Herald* is the local weekly newspaper, much like every other weekly in small-town America. The most read portion of the paper each week is the arrest report which usually garners front-page coverage. The pictures in the paper often contain a shirtless soul holding up a catfish pulled from the Chickasawhay River, someone holding a dead rattlesnake by its tail, or a proud hunter holding a deer by its horns with its lifeless tongue hanging out. Grant never subscribed. The last thing he wanted was a weekly reminder of that place.

But, Grant's pending return had him in a nostalgic mood. He found his high school yearbooks which he had placed in the cedar chest he had inherited from his Grandma Hicks, now located in the guest bedroom. As he opened the 1990 Greene County High School Wildcat annual, he wondered where his classmates had ended up. Whatever became of them? One by one he looked at each face, recalling memories with each photo. Some pleasant, some not so pleasant. Grant had attended kindergarten through high school with most of these people. He was surprised by how many of them he had forgotten. But as he turned each page, memories that had been locked away for years began to peer through the cracks of his soul. There was one person, however, glaringly absent from the 1990 GCHS yearbook–Brandon Smallwood.

Grant then found the 1989 annual and located Brandon. Brandon was described by most as a boy that was a little strange and most likely headed for some kind of trouble. He was extremely poor and somewhat of a loner. He had dark, almost black, eyes with naturally pitch-black hair. As an eleventh grader at Greene County High, Brandon was rarely noticed. Most of his classmates did not know if he had started kindergarten with them or had moved to Greene County at some other time. Greene County High is a mid-sized school by Mississippi standards. Most students who attend there are taught by many of the teachers who taught their parents. There were 526 students in grades nine through twelve when Grant attended. Everybody knew everybody. At least everyone knew everyone who counted. Brandon Smallwood did not count. No one really knew who he was, except Grant Hicks.

As Grant started to put the yearbooks back in the cedar chest, he fumbled them, and a piece of yellowing paper fell to the floor. Grant picked it up and unfolded it to find the obituary. Grant read the obituary, and he silently began to cry. The tears could not come fast enough, and his chest struggled to push the pain out. His body ached. He could not control his emotions, and he fell to his knees. "Oh God! Oh God! How could this be? Why did all this have to happen? Why?"

chapter five

FRIDAY NIGHTS AT GREENE RURAL ARE busy. Other than Sunday afternoons, Friday nights are the most active. Once a month a local bluegrass band plays for the residents. They were there, the banjo, guitars, and fiddles in perfect tune. The residents enjoyed the monthly performances. Family members, who were absent during the week, would stop by for their weekly visits on Friday nights. All would gather in the common area where the occupants ate three meals a day and shared activities from bingo to tic-tac-toe.

Sheriff McInnis enjoyed seeing who came and went on Friday nights. But on this Friday night, he stayed in his room. His children had gotten very busy, and it had been some time since he was paid a visit. He was always cheerful, but tonight he was sad. And Sheriff McInnis did not want to be unhappy in front of anyone. If he could not cheer others, he kept to himself. Truth was, he was getting quite lonely.

Then Jade walked in. "Hey, Mr. Lauvon! Why aren't you out listening to the band?"

Jade did not work on Friday nights, and the sheriff was surprised to see her. It caused him to smile, though slightly, as she walked through the door. "I'm just needing some alone time tonight, Jade. How are you, dear?"

"I'm fine. I forgot my cell phone charger here today and stopped by to get it."

The sheriff was glad she did. "Now, why aren't you on a date tonight? A pretty girl like you surely has a date on a Friday night."

Jade grinned, then said, "To be honest, Mr. Lauvon, I'm tired of the old dating scene. My last two dates were a disaster. One guy took me to watch his cousin race at the dirt track in Citronelle, and although it was freezing, he wore a T-shirt so everyone could see that the steroids were working. The other guy took me to Ward's and then parked in front of the junior high school to show off his new Z-71. Not exactly what I'm looking for. You know what I mean?"

"So what are you doing tonight then, Jade?"

Jade sensed the sheriff needed someone to get him out of his melancholy, so she replied, "I would really like to go to a bluegrass concert, but I have no date. Would you be my date, Mr. Lauvon?" Jade smiled with those beautiful dimples, perfectly placed on her cheeks. "I'd really enjoy a handsome, slightly older man to take me. And I know exactly where there is a concert that is not too far from here. In fact, it's right down the hall."

The sheriff perked up. "Are you sure? I know there are hundreds of places you could be tonight, Jade. Plus, you just left here a couple of hours ago after working since early this morning."

Jade then walked over to Sheriff McInnis and grabbed his hand, "Mr. Lauvon McInnis, would you be my date tonight?"

With somber kindness in his eyes, Sheriff Mcinnis accepted the invitation. As he stepped inside the bathroom to comb his hair, Jade saw the picture lying on the stand by his bed. It was the sheriff and his former wife from happier days, surrounded by their beautiful children. She also noticed a *Greene County Herald* article from November 1991. It showed the election returns from the recent election. She saw that two election results were underlined. Sheriff Mcinnis lost 2,764 to 2,740. And State Senator Michael Hicks lost the District 43 Senate race after getting beaten in his home county by forty-eight votes.

When the sheriff had finished grooming, he grabbed his cane, and Jade held his hand as they proudly walked down the hallway and took their place among the residents enjoying the band. For the first time since she began working at Greene Rural, Jade could feel a sadness settling deep into the sheriff. As the band played, she spent the next hour by his side. And although the band was plenty loud, Jade's mind began to wonder. So this is life? Thirty-five years old, never married, twice heart-broken, dreams never came true. But she felt that the Grand Architect of the Universe had something out there for her. She wished He would hurry.

In the meantime, she decided that she was going to spend more time with this precious man. For the first time as she sat there and looked at him, she realized that he had become the daddy she never had. And a peace covered her spirit and soul like the morning dew covers a beautiful field of grass. She smiled, herself comforted.

After the concert, Jade slowly walked Sheriff McInnis to his room, kissed him on the cheek, and thanked him for a wonderful evening. She could tell he was much happier than when she found him. She decided to take the long way home as she listened to Supertramp's *Breakfast In America*.

The night was clear, and the stars were majestic. As Jade was driving, she saw a falling star burn into darkness. And as if she were the eight-year-old little girl she barely remembered, she made a wish. As often happens in life, the events that turn our world upside down are right around the corner. Jade was about to find that out.

chapter six

GRANT DID NOT SEE SAMANTHA AS SHE peered through the bedroom door while he struggled with his past. It was bittersweet for her. She hated to see Grant hurting, but she knew he needed to deal with the pain that had been bottled inside of him since they had first met. She quietly walked back to the kitchen, poured herself a glass of wine, then called out to Grant to let him know she was home. Grant regained his composure and looked into the dresser mirror to be sure that Samantha would not know he had been crying.

Samantha would not mention witnessing Grant's tears because she knew how prideful he was. One of his favorite movies was *The Outlaw Josey Wells*, and she knew Josey did not cry. Grant often repeated the old Indian chief's statement after the chief visited with "Abram" Lincoln's Secretary of the Interior: "Endeavor to persevere." Grant's life certainly was a journey of perseverance.

Grant joined Samantha in the kitchen. "Hey, Sam, how was the fundraiser?" He attempted to portray as much normalcy in his voice as possible as he entered the kitchen.

"It was fine. We raised a lot of money tonight, which is always a good thing." Samantha loved animals. She was on the board of the local humane society chapter and was the proud owner of two dogs and a cat. She would own more animals if she had the room.

Grant then picked up the note she had left him and told her what she had hoped to hear. "I'm going to Mississippi in the morning." Sam looked surprised. "I called to tell Ms. Smallwood that I was too busy to come and ended up talking to this old preacher who was sitting with Brandon while Ms. Smallwood ran an errand. Can you believe that Brandon wants me to speak at his funeral?"

"Really? Hmmm. That's interesting. What did you say?"

Grant poured himself a glass of wine and joined Samantha at the table. "Nothing. I sat there and did not respond. I told him to let Ms. Smallwood know that I could not come."

Samantha then looked puzzled. "Does anyone know you are coming?" They both took a sip of wine.

"No. And I'll keep it that way in case I change my mind. Would you like to go with me?"

Samantha thought about her weekend plans and the long drive. "How long will you be there?"

"Not long. I'll come back Monday."

Samantha's schedule was racing through her mind. "I can't. I have to attend that wedding tomorrow afternoon, and I need to work in the morning. I also have an appointment Monday morning." Samantha had not told Grant that she was interviewing for a foreign consultant's position on Monday. She had been let down too many times before and decided she would keep the interview to herself.

"Okay. I plan to leave around six o'clock in the morning."

Samantha tried to convince him to take her Range Rover instead of his Porsche Cayman. Grant refused. After all, Samantha's Range Rover would stick out in Leakesville about as much as his

Porsche, especially with Samantha's left-leaning bumper stickers plastered all over the back. More importantly, however, Grant did not want to fit in. He had no plans of staying long, just long enough to visit Brandon and head back to Atlanta soon afterwards. He certainly had no intention to stay for a funeral. He packed enough clothes to last four days in case he had trouble of some sort. His type-A personality planned for everything. At least, he thought it did. Some things of the heart and soul defy man's plan.

Grant pulled out of the driveway at precisely 5:58 a.m. His trip to Mississippi could not have been on a more beautiful day. The forecast through Monday was exceptional as well. March in the South is simply gorgeous. With spring bringing to life thousands of acres of forest land, it was the perfect place for new beginnings.

Grant merged onto Interstate 85 en route to his life's destination. Reconciliation sometimes must be nurtured, cultivated. But for it to bloom into forgiveness, it needs a place. And for Grant, that place was home.

Part Two:

The Return Home

chapter seven

BRANDON HAD ANOTHER DIFFICULT night, and he opened his eyes on Saturday morning to find his mom sitting by his bed. She was listening to the recorded sermon from the previous Sunday's service at Cedar Grove Full Gospel Church. As if he thought the congregation would understand him better, the pastor was screaming as he preached.

"Momma?"

Brandon's voice was getting weaker, and it broke Elsie's heart all over again each time she heard it. "Yes, baby. How are you feeling this morning?"

Brandon knew his mom was heartbroken over the events of his life, and he tried his best to be strong. "Oh, I feel good. Better today than yesterday." Brandon would respond in the same manner each morning when his mother asked, but she knew the truth. It was written all over his shrinking body. "Have you heard from Grant?" Though Brandon did not say it, he knew his time was drawing to an end. He wanted so badly to see Grant. Brandon's life was soon to end at thirty-seven years old. It was a tough draw when this life was assigned to Brandon Smallwood. However, he did not question it. In fact, he expected it. When the doctor gave him the news that his cancer was terminal, Brandon's reaction was unlike any the doctor had ever seen. Brandon simply thanked the doctor as if the news he had been waiting for had finally arrived.

"I haven't heard anything. He was supposed to call yesterday. If he does not call by tomorrow, I'll call him first thing Monday."

"You know, Momma...." Brandon adjusted his body in the hospital bed in which he would remain the last few days of his life. "Grant was the only person, other than you and Lester, that ever stood up for me. And he did not have to. He had no reason to."

Elsie did not need a reminder of those days. She had also paid a price for being the mother of Brandon Smallwood. However, it was a price she lovingly paid. And she would walk through the fire again. "Grant was a good boy. I remember him from the cafeteria at school. Even when he was at the elementary school, he was always so respectful to the workers. He always said 'thank you' and 'yes or no, ma'am.'"

Elsie was giving Brandon a drink of apple juice from a straw when the front door opened. It was Brother Clark dropping by to check on them. Pastor Lollis Clark had served as a bi-vocational minister for fifty-five years. He was Elsie's preacher at Cedar Grove Full Gospel when he first entered the ministry. He worked at the shipyard, a garment factory, the local Piggly Wiggly, and as a carpenter throughout his ministry. He had served at seventeen different churches, and none were able to pay him enough to preach full-time. Nonetheless, he never complained. He truly was an humble servant. He always wore a big smile and volunteered at almost every benefit the community held for a needy person or family. He was loved by many.

"Good morning, Elsie. Well, hey Brandon!" Brother Clark had become Brandon's crutch. When Elsie would run her errands, Brother Clark would prepare Brandon for death. They had had many conversations about death. Brandon was not religious, but he and Brother Clark prayed together often. Brandon made things right with God while Brother Clark held his hand. It was a special moment on a cold, wet February morning that Brother Clark cherished.

"Elsie, I forgot to tell you yesterday that Grant Hicks called."

Elsie and Brandon both focused completely on Brother Clark in anticipation of the answer. "What did he say?" Elsie could not wait for the pause in Brother Clark's usually deliberate conversational style.

"He said he would not be able to come...." Before he could finish his sentence, Brandon turned his head to face the wall to hide his disappointment from his mother. Brother Clark walked around the bed to look into Brandon's eyes. "Brandon, I gave him my cell number. I have been praying for him to come. Remember our conversations about faith?" Brother Clark looked at Elsie, who was about to cry, and then back at Brandon. "Brandon, keep the faith, son. He has my number should he change his mind. He already has this number."

Brother Clark then asked Elsie if she needed anything from Lucedale while he was down there running his errands. She did ask if he could get a few things from Wayne Lee's grocery for her. He took her list and refused her money. Brother Clark, a widower, at seventy-five years old cut grass to earn extra money. Most local people felt sorry for him. They thought he had to cut grass to support himself. What they did not know was that he used every penny of that money to take care of the needy he discovered in his path. The Smallwoods were at the top of his list for benevolence.

As Brother Clark walked to his old Chevrolet pickup, he muttered to God, "Please, Lord, see fit for that Hicks boy to come."

chapter eight

SUBCONSCIOUSLY DELAYING HIS ARRIVAL in Mississippi for as long as possible, Grant arrived in Mobile just before noon. He decided that he would eat lunch there and then drive past his grandparents' old store on Old Shell Road before driving to Lucedale where he would stay at the Rocky Creek Inn. Grant's mother, Sylvia Turner Hicks, was from Mobile, and when he was young, he enjoyed spending a few weeks in the summer helping his grandparents in their store. He often helped his Grandpa Turner count the money at the end of the day. Grant's grandparents on both sides of his family had children at a late age, and all had passed away before he graduated high school. He especially missed his Grandpa Turner.

Grant was pleasantly surprised to find that Wintzell's Oyster House was still in business. He suddenly craved some good southern oysters. And Wintzell's had the best when Grant last ate there while he was in high school. After Grant finished lunch, he made his way to Old Shell Road. As he approached the location of the old store, he noticed that the area had changed drastically. The neighborhood had seen better days. Grant pulled into the vacant lot that once contained a vibrant, colorful convenience store. The store had been taken by eminent domain in anticipation of the widening of Old Shell Road. The home was still there on the backside of the lot. The shingles were swollen and folded. It clearly had not been roofed in many years. The house was slowly decaying.

A sadness enveloped Grant as he walked over the deserted, unkept property. The memories were pouring out from behind each tree. He sat on an old stump and spent the next hour recalling events of happier times–a time before he was introduced to pain, bitterness, bigotry, hatred, courtrooms, and death. Oh, how he longed to return to that time of innocence.

Grant pulled his cell phone from his pocket to check the time. He never wore a watch. He also despised anything in his pockets. He carried a money clip instead of a wallet, and he always emptied his pockets when he sat down. It was 3:00 p.m., and he had four text messages and three missed calls from Samantha asking how he was doing. Grant usually left his cell on silent because he hated the noise and preferred all calls go to voice mail so that he could set the terms of when the caller was fortunate enough to talk to him. He tried to call Samantha, but she did not answer. Grant remembered she was at the wedding, so he left her a voice mail saying that he was fine and would call her before bedtime.

He then set out for the Rocky Creek Inn in George County. He would delay his entrance into Greene County for as long as possible. As he entered Mississippi, he was welcomed by a large blue sign: *"Mississippi: It's Like Coming Home."* For Grant, it was indeed. He pulled into the hotel parking lot and checked in. He had saved the preacher's number in his cell, so he scrolled down to the Ps and found the number. He wanted to limit his contact with the Smallwoods, so he decided he would let the preacher set up his visit.

"Hello? Brother Clark speaking."

Grant could hear a television blaring in the background. Obviously, the old preacher was hard of hearing. "Reverend, this is Grant Hicks. I'm in Lucedale, and I wanted to visit with Brandon tomorrow."

Brother Clark could not hide his excitement. "Praise the Good Lord! I've been praying you would come! You have no idea how much this will mean to Elsie and Brandon!"

Grant really had not been thinking of them, and he wondered if this self-revelation should make him feel bad. He decided it did not. "Reverend, if you don't mind setting up my visit, I would appreciate it. Do they live in the same place?"

The preacher had turned the television off, and Grant had his full attention. "Yes, they do. It's best to visit Brandon early. He stays knocked out with morphine most of the time to deal with the pain. He usually wakes up around eight each morning. Do you remember how to get there, son?"

It was then that Grant realized that the place had never left him. "Yes, sir, I do."

Reverend Clark agreed to call Elsie as soon as he hung up the phone. Finally, he would be able to deliver some good news to her. Before Grant could get off the phone, Reverend Clark asked, "By the way, son, where are you staying?"

Grant thought for a few seconds and wondered if it were a good idea to let anyone know where he was, but he trusted this man. "I'm at the Rocky Creek Inn."

The preacher's voice simply could not hide his enthusiasm. "What are you doing for supper tonight, son?" Ugh! The last thing Grant wanted to do was hang out with an old preacher. Before Grant could think of an excuse, the preacher continued, "I'll pick you up at 5:30. I'm going to take you to eat the best catfish your mouth has ever tasted. A place called Rocky Creek Catfish."

Grant wondered if everything around here was named after Rocky Creek. "Then, I want you to go somewhere with me for a little while. There is no use in you sitting in a hotel all night."

Grant was searching for an excuse. "Reverend, I've traveled a lot today, and I kind of wanted to rest tonight."

The preacher would not take no for an answer. "You'll be my guest tonight, son. I'll be there at 5:30."

Grant hung up the phone and wondered how in the hell he had let that just happen: his first night in Mississippi and he is hanging out with a preacher. This trip spiraled downward faster than Grant had anticipated. Samantha would be amused. Grant was not.

Grant walked to the lobby of the Rocky Creek Inn to wait on Reverend Clark. He dreaded the evening. Dreaded it. This was not the way Grant envisioned his first night back in Mississippi. He much preferred picking up something to eat, bringing it back to the room, and preparing for his upcoming trial. But, his inability to control the conversation with the preacher had him waiting in the lobby to go who knew where.

Grant watched a green Chevrolet pickup pulling into the parking lot and an aging figure behind the wheel. For the first time, he wondered what the old man looked like. The preacher stepped out of the truck wearing a brand new pair of work khakis, a pressed green work shirt with two front pockets, and a freshly polished pair of black cowboy boots. Reverend Clark's skin was weathered and wrinkled from countless hours spent outside working in the sun to supplement his pastor's pay. His hairline had receded from the sides, and he had one very thin strip of hair retreating toward the back of his balding head. The smell of Old Spice arrived through the door before the preacher did.

Grant walked toward the entrance, and when the preacher stepped inside, he asked, "Grant?" He stuck his hand out to Grant.

"Yes, sir, Grant Hicks, nice to meet you." The preacher's hand felt like sandpaper. It was coarse, certainly not the grip of a preacher. But this preacher was different.

"Good to finally meet you, son." Then, the preacher looked up and down at the younger man's outfit which caused Grant to do the same. "You didn't have to dress up tonight, son. I'm sorry. I should've told you."

"Actually, Reverend or Preacher–by the way, what should I call you?"

The preacher grinned and said, "My name is Lollis Clark. People call me Brother Clark. But that's up to you. You can call me whatever feels comfortable to you."

Grant then looked back at his own clothing and said, "Reverend, this is the most casual outfit I brought. I did not expect to go out."

Brother Clark then patted him on the shoulder, and they walked to his pickup. "Son, I'm going to drive tonight if you don't mind riding in my old truck."

Grant opened the door to the pickup truck which was at least twenty years old, but it was as clean as it was when the reverend drove it off the dealership's parking lot. "Oh, I don't mind. Wow, you sure keep it clean!"

The preacher, with a smile of humble pride, winked at Grant and said, "Cleanliness is the sign of being a good steward, son." They drove out of the parking lot and onto the road. Grant smiled as he noticed the road sign, *Rocky Creek Road*. When Grant had left this area in 1990, there were few roads that were named, and none had road signs. The emergency 911 system demanded road names and signs. For a moment Grant viewed that sign of progress as sadness. No more explaining directions by using fence posts and barns and churches and power lines. Grant wondered what else had changed.

Grant had decided that he would just be along for the ride. He would ask no questions, listen to the preacher, and get the night behind him. They pulled into Rocky Creek Catfish, and the parking lot was already filling. Reverend Clark was obviously a regular because each time he passed a staff member, he was greeted with, "Well, hey, Brother Clark." The other patrons knew him, too, and Grant began to wonder if they would ever sit down. The host was waiting at their designated table in the corner of the restaurant, so to avoid being introduced to everyone the preacher spoke to, Grant quickly sat down. The preacher finally joined him and then gave Grant a detailed history of the restaurant.

Not long after their food arrived, a man approached their table. "Hey, Brother Clark, you going to the auction tonight?"

Reverend Clark got up and shook the man's hand. "Why sure I'm going. They auctioning off some power tools tonight, and I hoped to pick up a drill and maybe a skillsaw. By the way, Oscar, I want you to meet this young man." Grant reluctantly stood and shook hands with the man. "This is Grant Hicks. Grant, this is Oscar Jones."

As Oscar was sizing him up, he asked, "What you do for a living?"

Grant looked at the preacher, then back at Oscar. "I'm an attorney."

Oscar grinned. "I knew you must be a lawyer. I could just tell. Your hands are soft, and you got on that fancy coat. Look. Let me ask you a question. I stopped by this fella's machine shop and backed into some hot metal. It burnt the farr out of my leg. I had to go to the doctor and everthang. The owner at that shop didn't even offer to pay my doctor bills or for my medicine." Grant could not believe this conversation was taking place. Oscar continued, "What did you say your name was?"

Ready to end the obvious effort for free legal advice, Grant responded, "My name is Grant and...."

Before Grant could get any further, Oscar pulled up his pants leg. "Look at this. That sore ain't gettin no better, and it keeps runnin with puss and junk. I took the patch off and tryin to air it out a little."

Grant almost vomited at the sight of the man's leg; two things were going through his mind at that moment. First, he no longer had an appetite. Second, he had a bad feeling he was about to go to an auction.

Oscar left after Grant encouraged him to make an appointment with a local attorney. Oscar told him that the local lawyers were either crooked or lazy, and the judges were paid off anyway. Grant was simply glad he left. As they were finishing their meal and preparing to leave, Grant could not help but notice the table next to them. There were four elderly ladies and three elderly men sitting at the table. The men did not get to say much. How could they? The ladies were talking loudly in efforts to be heard over one another. At one point in the meal, the women were staring in his direction and did not attempt to disguise the obvious fact that they were discussing him. Grant thought to himself that the lucky one in that crowd was the man that was apparently already dead.

chapter nine

JADE HAD BEEN BACK IN GREENE COUNTY for five years. She had spent twelve years in California as she pursued her dreams. She was able to land some minor roles on daytime television programs and a couple of commercials, but she was never able to get the big break she so desperately desired. She attended night school and became a registered nurse, so her time in California was not a complete loss. While growing up in Greene County, Jade lived with her grandmother, Lillie Lott, whom she affectionately called Nana. Nana had fallen six years ago and broken her hip. She has been using a walker to get around ever since. Jade decided it was her time to take care of Nana, so she moved back home.

Jade was able to secure a nursing position at Forrest General Hospital in Hattiesburg and worked there for three years. However, the one-hour drive wore out its welcome, so Jade accepted a position at Greene Rural. Jade truly had a heart for the elderly, and even though she had been away for twelve years, she still knew most of the residents there. Jade had had two serious relationships in California. She had lived with both of them, and each promised he would marry her. They never did. One left her with a simple note. The other she discovered exiting a Hollywood hotel with one of her friends. It turned out that her friend was much closer to her boyfriend than to Jade.

"Nana?" Jade had been to Lucedale to pick up some things from Walmart.

"Hey, Precious, I'm in here." Nana was watching *Matlock* reruns, her favorite pastime.

"Hey, Nana, how are you? I brought us something to eat from Hokie's!"

Nana loved Hokie's Barbecue, and Jade brought her some treat each time she went to Lucedale. "Thank you, Precious. Don't you have a date tonight?"

Jade sighed, "I guess you can call it a date. Jamie Walley asked me to go with him to the auction in Rocky Creek. He does not get off work in time for us to eat first, so I told him I would eat here. He should be here at 6:30."

Nana looked at the clock. "Jade, you better get a move on. He'll be here in thirty minutes."

"I know. It's an auction. I'm just going to throw on something comfortable." The advantage to being naturally pretty with a beautiful complexion was that Jade did not require makeup. Plus, she did not like wearing it anyway. But when she did, she could stop a clock.

"Jade, I pray that you'll find a good man someday. You are beautiful and have such a kind heart. Any man would be lucky to have you."

Jade got up from the table and kissed Nana on the cheek. "Nana, you're so sweet. I love you. Who knows? Maybe one day. But I don't care if it ever happens. I love living with you, Nana.

And if any man wants me, he has to accept us both." Jade then went to her room to get dressed.

Twenty minutes later Jade walked out of her bedroom wearing jeans, ballet flats, and a crisp white shirt, buttoned up just enough to distract any man in her path. She had a long silver necklace with a silver ring on her right ring finger. Jade was 5'4" tall and weighed 115 pounds. At thirty-five, She looked as stunning as ever.

Jade was peering out the window as her date pulled into the driveway. "Nana, do you think he will come in?"

Before Nana could answer, the horn blew. "I don't think he will, Precious."

Jade walked to her purse, stuck twenty dollars into her back pocket, grabbed her Blackberry, and kissed her grandmother on the cheek. "Nana, call me crazy, but I don't think my knight in shining armor will blow the horn for me to come out to his pickup truck. So, it's just a hunch. But I'm pretty sure this one is not the guy. I won't be out late."

chapter ten

THE PREACHER AND GRANT FINALLY escaped the fish house and were on their way to the auction. "I hope you enjoyed the fish, Grant."

Grant was just happy he was able to get away from there. He did not want to be noticed by anyone that would have remembered him. He had recognized a few people from the time he lived in Greene County. "It was good, Reverend. Thank you for buying my dinner. I wish you would have let me pay."

The preacher was turning left onto Highway 98 heading toward the auction. "Nonsense, son, you are my guest tonight. Ever been to a good, old-fashioned country auction?"

Grant had not. "No sir."

Brother Clark looked at him with excitement. "You're in for a treat."

Passing an open field, Grant was staring out of the passenger window and thinking. What was he doing here? He was hoping that the auction would be over quickly. Brother Clark glanced at him. The reverend had been around the block many times. He knew the young man was troubled, but he did not pry. He had learned many years ago that some people have to come to that realization within themselves. Grant was one of those people.

The truck turned left off Highway 98 and onto a gravel lane. The sign, in big red letters painted on a white sheet of plywood, at the entrance simply read *Auction*. They pulled into a field that doubled as a parking lot the first and third Saturday nights. The crowd was making its way into an old metal barn that had been converted into an auction house. Kids were playing baseball out in the field as their parents entered the building. It reminded Grant of the times he played baseball in the fields of Greene County, a time he had forgotten until that moment. His spirit smiled at simpler times.

A line had formed just inside the door. Brother Clark signed them in and handed Grant a paddle with a number on it. "What's this for?"

Brother Clark recognized that Grant needed an education in auction participation, so he gave him one. "It's easy, son. When you see something you like and want to bid, just hold up this paddle with your number on it, and they will record your purchase if you are the highest bidder."

Grant had no intention of purchasing anything, but he said okay as they began looking for a seat. The auctioneer was perched on a table at the rear of the converted barn, and there were benches along the sides and fold-out chairs in the middle.

The shoes were the first thing Jade noticed. Soft, slip-on, brown, calfskin, Italian Prada loafers. What were they doing here? Her eyes climbed up the tailored, dark-wash designer jeans. Then to the white shirt with thin blue stripes covered by a blue tailored blazer. Brown hair, dark brown eyes, olive skin. She was mesmerized.

Jade did not notice Jamie handing her the bottle of water he had just bought for her. "You sure you don't want anything to eat?"

Jade almost did not hear him. "Uhh, oh, no thanks. Nana and I ate before you picked me up." She then realized she had lost sight of the intriguing mystery man. Her eyes frantically combed the crowd trying to find him. She did.

Brother Clark and Grant sat two rows in front of them and at an angle to their right. Unfortunately, two ladies with really, really big hair partially obstructed her view. She maneuvered her chair in order to peer around the ladies. She could not help but think that the auction had just become interesting. Jamie was engaged in a conversation about turkey hunting with the men sitting to his left, but Jade did not mind. She was captivated by her discovery sitting two rows in front of her.

The auction began with prayer, the Pledge of Allegiance, and the National Anthem sung by a local girl. Even during the prayer, Jade sneaked a peak. She noticed his eyes were not closed. She felt that odd and a bit disrespectful but then chuckled to herself because her eyes were open, too. The auction was well underway when she noticed him moving his Blackberry in an obvious effort to get a signal. She wanted to tell him that he would have to go outside. She resisted and kept her place.

The hand tool part of the auction was winding down. Brother Clark had promised Grant that they would leave when it was over and not stay for the antique auction. Grant held a bottle of water in his left hand, and he was holding the paddle he had been given in his right hand along with his cell phone. As the auctioneer was calling for bids on a one-hundred-foot extension cord, Grant was even more aggressively trying to get reception on his phone. His hand went too high, and the auctioneer shouted, "Sold, number forty-four!" Grant noticed everyone looking at him. Then, he turned the paddle around to discover that he was number forty-four. He had just bought an extension cord. Jade laughed.

When Brother Clark and Grant got up to leave, Jade realized who the man was she had been watching for the last hour. It was Grant Hicks. She had not seen him since high school. Jade was two grades behind him. She turned to look over her left shoulder as they were retrieving their items from the cashier. She desperately wanted to go speak to him. After a few seconds, she decided she needed to visit the ladies' room. By the time she walked outside, Grant and Brother Clark were already in the truck, and she watched them drive out of sight down the two-path gravel road. Disappointment dripped off her.

Jamie had walked outside looking for Jade. "There you are. I thought something had happened to you." Something had happened to Jade. Before Jade reentered the auction, she peered again down the gravel road. The auction would not be the same.

Brother Clark dropped Grant off at the Rocky Creek Inn, and Grant thanked him for his hospitality. The pastor even paid for the extension cord. As Grant was walking away from the truck, Brother Clark yelled at him, "Hey! Grant! Son, you are forgetting your extension cord."

Grant started to tell him he bought it by accident and really didn't need it. On second thought, Grant knew the joy the old preacher had received by hosting him. "Thanks, Reverend. And thanks again for dinner." Reverend Clark handed Grant the extension cord and slowly pulled away.

Grant, exhausted, walked to his room, opened the door, and dialed Samantha's number. She answered on the first ring. "Hey, Grant. I was wondering when you were going to call."

Grant tossed the extension cord in the direction of his suitcase. "It's been a long day, Sam. How was your day?"

"It was decent. I worked this morning and attended Margo's wedding this afternoon. Tell me about your trip."

"The drive wasn't too bad. I stopped in Mobile for lunch, then dropped by where my grandparents used to live. It was kinda sad. It doesn't look anything like it did when I was a kid."

Samantha's call-waiting feature indicated she was getting another call. "Hold on a minute, Grant. Let me see who this is."

"Okay." Grant waited for what seemed like an eternity. He detested call-waiting. He felt it was rude to put someone on hold in order to take another call. The interruption stymied his desire to talk. When Sam finally returned, he decided to omit many of the details of his trip. He would tell her when he got home on Monday.

As Grant lay in the bed that night, he realized that tomorrow morning he would be entering Greene County for the first time since August of 1990. He fell asleep buried beneath memories. Like death, sometimes sleep is a welcome visitor to end the pain. So, he slept.

chapter eleven

GRANT DECIDED TO SKIP HIS MORNING run. Accustomed to getting up at 6:00 a.m. Atlanta time, Grant was wide awake at 5:00 a.m. He turned on the television and began flipping through the channels. Unable to find anything remotely entertaining, he decided to take a shower and get ready. The Smallwoods were expecting him to arrive at 8:00 a.m. It was only a thirty-minute drive to Brandon's, but the hotel room was quickly closing in on Grant, so he decided to ride around a while before his visit. He was anxious to see the changes to his old hometown.

Grant pulled out of the hotel's parking lot at 6:30 a.m. He traveled down Rocky Creek Road and turned right onto Highway 63 heading North. There was a green sign which read, *Leakesville, 15 miles*. Grant slowed as he approached the sign which announced he was entering Greene County. He was now there–to a place he once knew as home. Almost twenty years had passed since that sign disappeared in his rearview mirror. Grant soaked in every house and road he passed on the ride into his small hometown.

He crossed the Chickasawhay River and slowed as he looked at the tributary that contained so many of his childhood memories. He had spent many days and nights fishing and camping on that beautiful river which was still yet to be corrupted by industrial waste, a gem only found by those fortunate enough to have met the Chickasawhay. The end of the bridge marked the beginning of Main Street. He passed the courthouse to his right and the drug store to his left, and for a moment he was sad at the state of things. Buildings that once contained businesses he would visit with his mom on Saturday mornings were now empty. Streets were in dire need of resurfacing. The old Western Auto was closed. No more buying a Western Flyer there. Leakesville's small businesses, like many in other small towns, had suffered from the Walmart syndrome. Local folks wanted to shop here, but they simply could not resist the lower prices offered by the retail giant that was just a short drive to Lucedale. And like a frog slowly boiled to death in warming water, the businesses died.

Grant then passed the junior high school that he had attended. Not much had changed. He did notice there were air conditioners now in every classroom. When he was there, the only classrooms with air conditioners were the ones in which the teacher could afford to buy his or her own. The factory that had closed many years ago, when the garment industry disappeared, was still closed. Grant thought of Springsteen's lyrics, "These jobs are going, boys, and they ain't coming back to your hometown."

He then passed Ward's, one of the two fast-food restaurants in town, and realized he was hungry. He continued down Main Street, passed Piggly Wiggly, then turned in the direction from whence he came using the loop he had made hundreds of times riding around town during his high school days. Grant was in a somber mood as he entered the Ward's parking lot. His hometown was dying, too.

He walked into Ward's, and the entire left side of the eating area was completely filled with approximately twenty locals talking, drinking coffee, and passing around the Sunday paper. All were men with the exception of four older women sitting in a corner booth. Again feeling well overdressed in a pair of chinos, pullover Polo, and sportscoat, Grant approached the counter. He ordered his breakfast and noticed that the waitress instinctively began pouring coffee. "Ma'am, excuse me. I would like orange juice, please."

"You don't want any coffee?" She looked at Grant with one raised eyebrow and much distrust.

"Actually, I don't drink it. But thanks anyway."

She looked him up and down as if to let him know that he obviously was yet to be labeled a man. "Okay, suit yourself."

Grant sat on the opposite side of the restaurant from the local crowd and began to eat his breakfast. He purposely did not make eye contact with anyone there, but he could feel twenty pairs of eyes drilling a hole through him. Grant looked out the window to his right and up Main Street. He then saw an old familiar figure. It was twenty years older, but the stagger was unmistakable. Johnny Ray Barfield. Grant wondered how his liver was still functioning. But there he was, growing larger as he approached the restaurant. Grant noticed a Leakesville patrol car passing Johnny Ray going in the opposite direction. The policeman's tail lights did not even flicker. Johnny Ray staggered to the middle of the road and turned toward the passing officer while holding his hands up, presenting both middle fingers to the officer. Grant chuckled.

The entire staff walked to the window in the collective hope that Johnny Ray would not enter. To their disappointment, he was in the parking lot and walking toward the door. They scattered. Grant recalled hearing Johnny Ray explain to his dad many years ago how he survived the sinking houseboat on which he lived when it was hit by a storm and sank. Johnny Ray said, "It was so bad that

I'll have to explain it in Spanish; it was *el rougho*!"

Johnny Ray entered the restaurant and bellowed, "I can run the fastest, jump the highest, and whip any man's ass that'll step outside! I'm part cheetah, part deer, and part alligator!" Johnny Ray staggered backwards as he waited to see who would accept his challenge.

A man in a tie was sitting at a table with his wife. They were obviously dressed for church. He did not appreciate Johnny Ray's intoxication nor his language. He approached Johnny Ray. "Johnny Ray, let me take you home."

Johnny Ray squinted as he looked at the man. "You that preacher?" Grant thought there must be a preacher on every corner down here.

"Yes, I am. I visited you last week."

The manager eased up to Johnny Ray and quietly asked him to leave. She was flanked by another employee, and both ladies were rather heavy. Johnny Ray looked at them, then back at the preacher, then back at them, then back again at the preacher. "They healthy, ain't they!" The preacher then grabbed his arm. Johnny Ray pulled away from him. "Preacher, you told me Gawd could do anything. Well, that's a damn lie. He can't straddle a mudhole with a wheelbarrow!"

The preacher was finally able to get Johnny Ray headed toward his car as he informed his wife that he would return shortly.

As Grant was looking out the window at Johnny Ray and the preacher getting in the car, he heard a voice. "Grant?"

Grant turned to look. It was Terry Lowery. Other than the lines surrounding his eyes, Mr. Lowery had not changed. "Mr. Lowery. Hello."

Terry Lowery was Grant's high school math teacher. "You are looking good, Grant. Gosh, I haven't seen you since you graduated. What are you doing now?" Grant glanced at the crowd, who was still quiet from the Johnny Ray episode, and noticed many people he knew from his days there. They were all staring at him. "Hey, everybody. Do y'all remember Grant Hicks?" Grant was forced to shake the hand of everyone there. They knew who he was. Grant, Michael Hicks, Brandon Smallwood, Sheriff McInnis, and the entire tragic episode would be discussed after Grant left the restaurant.

Grant informed Mr. Lowery that he was an attorney but that he had undergraduate and graduate degrees in math. "You were a great teacher, Mr. Lowery. Are you still teaching?" They exited Ward's and stopped outside to finish the conversation.

"No, Grant, I'm the superintendent now. I'm completing my second term. I have more than enough years to retire, Grant, but I love the kids here. Wow! An attorney. Your dad would be so proud of you." Mr. Lowery and Grant's dad graduated high school together. Grant's demeanor shrunk at the mention of his dad. He hated that man. But no use in dwelling.

It was 7:30 a.m., and Grant needed to leave for Brandon's. "It was so good to see you, Mr. Lowery."

The superintendent pulled a business card from his pocket and gave it to Grant. "If you're in town long, come by the office."

Grant took the card. "Okay, thanks, but I'm leaving in the morning. Maybe next time." He did not plan on there being a next time.

Terry Lowery watched as Grant drove his Porsche out of the parking lot and onto Main Street. It brought deep sadness to see him drive away. Yet, he did not know why. The spirit carries in it a compass; it points in the direction of so many emotions. And when a person is in the presence of deep sadness and loneliness, the needle of his or her own inner compass is affected. So discovered Mr. Lowery.

chapter twelve

SHERIFF MCINNIS WAS EATING BREAKFAST with his adoptive family at Greene Rural when Jade sat down next to him. He had never seen Jade there on a Sunday morning. "Well, good morning, lady." He was glad to see her. "What brings you here on a Sunday morning?"

Jade hugged him, placed her phone on the table, and retrieved herself a tray of breakfast. "I thought I would come check on you. I enjoyed our date Friday night."

Sheriff McInnis sensed there was another purpose for Jade's visit. There was. "I enjoyed it, too. That band is always good."

As the sheriff responded, Jade looked around the room, then at the other two residents sitting at the table with him. She decided that she had enough privacy to ask the question: "Mr. Lauvon, do you remember Grant Hicks?"

The sheriff stopped chewing for a moment. He swallowed

and sipped his coffee. "Yes, I do."

When Jade realized he was not going to say anything further, she continued. "What happened to his daddy?"

The sheriff was obviously unprepared for the question. "Why...why do you ask, Sweetie?" The sheriff had completely stopped eating his breakfast.

"I saw Grant Hicks at the auction last night. I haven't seen him since high school." The sheriff's heart skipped. Where had Grant been? What brings him home? The questions were racing through his mind. "I asked Nana this morning what happened to Grant's dad, and she said that he committed suicide. I was in California then and too caught up in my own life, so I didn't keep up with the happenings around here. Nana said you were the best person to ask. I was just curious."

Jade began eating her breakfast, and the sheriff spoke to the cafeteria worker as she picked up his tray. "Jade, that is a long, tragic story. In fact, I was sheriff for twenty years, and I'm now sixty-seven years old. This county, to my recollection, has never experienced such sadness as the events which led to Michael Hicks' death. And I hope and pray this place never experiences such sadness again."

Jade had stopped eating by now and was intently looking at the sheriff. She could tell he was uncomfortable with the conversation. "Well, I was just curious. It's no big deal. Do you want some more coffee, Mr. Lauvon?" He said yes, secretly hoping Jade's going to get him some coffee would end the conversation. She stood at the coffee pot and looked back at the sheriff as he stared blankly out of the window of the nursing home. The question had caused her friend to become sad, and she regretted asking it.

Jade placed Sheriff McInnis' coffee on the table in front of him. "Mr. Lauvon, I guess I'll go home and get ready for church."

Jade attended Mt. Pisgah Pentecostal Church. Though she occasionally wore makeup and cut her hair, which was frowned upon in the Pentecostal church, she was a favorite at the church.

The younger children loved her. She always starred in the church's dramas and could actually carry a pretty good tune. Jade loved the music at her church, and she understood that there was no perfect person or perfect church. She was comfortable with herself and never felt the need to change who she was just to fit in, especially at church.

After she left, the sheriff slowly limped back to his room. He opened the door to his closet and retrieved an old Red Wing boot box containing papers he had saved. There were many old newspaper articles about the tragic story. He slowly read a few of them, though it was not necessary. He remembered every detail. Near the bottom of the box he found it–an old white, unopened envelope from the Law Firm of Michael Hicks. Written in Michael Hicks' handwriting across the front of the envelope were these words: *To Grant.*

chapter thirteen

GRANT TURNED ONTO JONATHAN ROAD and found it just as he had left it twenty years ago, only worse. It was like driving an obstacle course full of potholes. The road had been patched and repatched so many times that it looked like a gray plaid blanket of asphalt. Certainly it was not a road friendly to Grant's Porsche. He meticulously serpentined down the treacherous road until he finally turned onto the two-path dirt road that would lead him to Brandon's home on the banks of Mason Creek.

Elsie Smallwood had been up since 5:30 a.m. She had made some blueberry muffins, and the smell was intoxicating. Elsie could cook. Her poverty taught her to make everything from scratch. Cooking had become a lost art in modern society where most things were pre-cooked and the microwave was no longer considered a luxury but a necessity. The Smallwoods had no microwave. In her loose-fitting gray dress profusely spattered with white flowers on her robust frame, Elsie kept her eyes on the road leading to her home. As she watched Grant's car enter her yard, she was overcome by nervousness. She had never seen a car like that before.

Elsie wiped her hands on a dish towel and walked into Brandon's room. "He's here, son."

Grant stepped onto the ground which was a mixture of barren sand and patches of bahia grass. He noticed a redbone hound dog tied by an old truck camper that had been converted into a home for the old mutt. Chickens ran freely in the yard, and several kittens scurried off the porch and under the house as Grant approached. The house had not changed. He walked up the weathered steps and onto the wooden porch which announced his coming with every step. The faded front door was open, and the insects were held at bay by a screen door. He gently knocked.

Grant could feel Elsie's steps as she approached. She unlatched the screen door. Elsie, with her broad, powdery pink face and a long wisp of gray hair falling near the center of her nose, greeted him. "Come on in, Grant. I'm so happy to see you again."

Grant had not shared emotion for so long that it was an awkward moment as he wondered if he should hug her. "Hello, Ms. Smallwood." He shook her hand.

"Come on back. Brandon is awake. He's anxious to see you."

Grant followed Elsie down a small, dark hallway and into Brandon's room. His throat suddenly was filled with a lump that prevented words. As he looked at Brandon for the first time in years, a tear slowly ran down his cheek. Brandon reached for his hand, and Grant held it and felt the tears streaming from his eyes. Elsie, too, was overcome by that special moment. Grant thought his heart could not have hurt more, but it did. With a broken voice he greeted Brandon, "Hey."

Grant attempted to push back the tears and restore the dam that had held them back for all these years. He reached down and hugged Brandon. He could feel Brandon's bones sticking through his shoulders. Cancer is such a savage beast.

Brandon's eyes were dark and planted deep within his face. "I'm glad you could come, Grant."

Grant was not prepared for this moment. "I'm sorry." He left the room and walked outside and onto the porch to regain his composure. After a few moments, Elsie joined him. She placed her hand on his shoulder. Grant turned, embraced Elsie, and wept, his body convulsing with every tear.

Brandon could hear him, and he silently prayed. "Lord, if you are there, comfort my friend." Brandon, too, cried, but not for himself. He had always been an emotional person. And, oh, how he hated to see someone hurting! Grant was hurting. It tugged at Brandon's fragile heart.

"It's okay, Grant. It's okay." Elsie attempted to comfort him, but her words did not register with Grant.

"I'm sorry, Ms. Smallwood. I'm so sorry."

Elsie continued to embrace him. And for the first time in years, Grant was held by another human being while his emotions were allowed to run freely. At that precise moment, his spirit was finally allowing itself to be cleansed by his very own tears. Elsie held him as if she were holding one of her sons. The boney redbone hound was watching, and he began to wimper. The kittens slowly made their way back onto the porch. Sadness enveloped the Smallwoods' battered home place on the banks of Mason Creek. Grant was finally home. And he, or it, would never be the same.

Grant let go of Ms. Smallwood, and he sat on a worn school bus seat used as porch furniture. "I'll be back inside in a minute."

Elsie perceived he needed a few minutes alone, so she walked back into the house and joined Brandon. Brandon whispered to her, "Is he okay, Momma?"

Still overcome by the moment herself, Elsie simply bit her bottom lip and shook her head yes.

Grant would spend the next hour sitting on that old school bus seat with his head low and staring at the porch trying to muster the strength to reenter the house. His life, his past, his dreams, his future, his nightmares, the whole foundation of his being swarmed around him on that porch like bees rustled from the protection of their hive. And he silently admitted to himself that he was hurting. He wondered how to fix it. No answer came.

When Grant finally reentered the home, Elsie was in the kitchen. "I am so sorry about that, Ms. Smallwood."

She looked at Grant and smiled, "It's okay, son. It does us good to cry sometimes." He wanted to debate that point, but he let it pass. He began to walk toward Brandon's room. "He's asleep now, Grant. He probably won't wake up until late this evening." Grant looked at the aged kitchen clock shaped as a rooster. It was 9:30 a.m. "Why don't you sit down? I made some blueberry muffins." Grant was still full from his visit to Ward's, but out of politeness he sat down at the kitchen table which was pushed against the wall and was fitted with only three chairs.

Elsie placed a muffin on a saucer in front of him and asked, "What would you like in your coffee?"

She was pouring already, and Grant recalled the look of confusion from the waitress at Ward's when he told her he did not drink coffee. "Just black, please." Elsie then joined him at the table. She quietly said her blessing, which caused Grant to stop chewing and awkwardly wait until she finished. "Ms. Smallwood, what type of cancer does Brandon have?"

Elsie placed her fork down by her saucer. "Pancreatic cancer. He kept being tired every day, and I finally got him to go to the doctor. He had no medical insurance, and we had to get him on Medicaid which took a little while." A buzzer was sounding on the stove. Elsie got up to turn it off.

"And he was diagnosed just three months ago?"

Elsie rejoined him at the table. "Yes. Brandon has had a tough life. He had things finally going in the right direction. Then this happened. But we can't question God's way."

Grant thought, "To hell we can't!"

Ms. Smallwood reached over and placed her hand on Grant's. "You being here means so much to Brandon. You stood by him when nobody else did." She removed her hand and asked if he would like another muffin. He politely declined.

So many questions were going through Grant's mind, but he knew the more he asked, the more he had to remember. He decided to stop the inquisition. "I would like to come back and see Brandon later today, if I can."

Elsie smiled; she was pleased with the suggestion. "He'd like that, Grant. He'll probably sleep until around 3:30 or 4:00 this afternoon."

Grant looked back at the rooster. He wondered what he would do for the next six hours. He got up from the table and placed his saucer and cup in the sink. He then noticed an old, fading hand-held fan that politicians would hand out at election time or the funeral home would place in churches to keep people cool during summer. There he was, the handsome face of Sheriff Lauvon McInnis. It was a fan from his 1991 campaign. It read, "Experience you can count on! Re-elect Lauvon McInnis, Sheriff."

Grant pulled the fan from the shelf. "Ms. Smallwood, whatever happened to Sheriff McInnis?"

Ms. Smallwood assumed Grant was informed as to the state of politics in Greene County. He was not. "Well, after he lost the election–in fact, he lost that year if I remember it right. It was close though. After that, he worked at the prison, I think. He was the best sheriff this county has seen in my lifetime." If there were one man that Grant left this place with any respect for, it was Sheriff McInnis. Elsie continued, "He had a stroke a few years ago. He's in the nursing home out at Leakesville. He lives at Greene Rural."

Grant told Ms. Smallwood that he would return at 3:00 p.m.

in the hopes of being there when Brandon woke up. She again thanked him, and they walked out onto the porch together. He retraced his trek down the little dirt road and the asphalt war zone until he reached Highway 63. He sat there idling for a moment. He was not quite sure where to go. He turned left and drove in the direction of Leakesville. The story kept coming back to him. Only for him, it was so much more than a story. It was who he had become. So he drove.

Part Three:

The Sheriff

chapter fourteen

GRANT WOULD SPEND THE NEXT TWO hours riding the back roads of Greene County. He drove past his former high school and Big Creek Fellowship Church where he attended growing up. Grant grew up in the Big Creek Community, and as badly as he wanted to drive down that dead-end dirt road to the only house he had known for the first eighteen years of his life, he was too afraid of what he might find. He wondered if the home was still there and, if so, who owned it. He wondered what shape it was in and if it looked the same. He decided his memory of the "old place" was enough. While driving, he noticed the community store he visited as a child was gone. A vacant lot had taken its place. So much had changed. Yet, so much more remained the same.

Grant pulled into the parking lot of Greene Rural at precisely noon. Three nurses' aides were eating lunch at a circular concrete picnic table under a large magnolia tree near the entrance. He sat in his car for a moment, trying to think through what to say to Sheriff McInnis. Perhaps he had family there with him. Grant certainly did not want to impose. He looked at the ladies sitting at the table as they continued to stare in his direction as if at a spacecraft upon which they awaited the exit of the visiting aliens. He opened the door, stepped out of the Porsche, and with his hands in his pockets walked toward the ladies.

"Mmm, mmm, mmm, girls, look at that!" The voice belonged to Edwina McSwain. She was not shy and never afraid to say what was on her mind. She received her name by a function of simple math. Her dad's name was Edward, and her mom's name was Tina. Hence, Edwina. The other ladies giggled at Edwina's assessment.

Grant made it to the table. "Hi. Excuse me. I hate to disturb your lunch, but may I ask you a question?"

Edwina took charge of the conversation. She had a large personality, and it matched her physical appearance. Edwina was African American, but she did not hide her taste for good-looking men of any color. She appreciated all of God's creation, especially a handsome man. "Are them Costa Del Mar shades?"

Grant took them off and looked at them. "Yes, actually, they are." He put the sunglasses inside his coat pocket.

"What kind of car is that? A Porsche or what?"

Grant turned to look at his car. "Yes, it's a Porsche."

Edwina got up from the table and walked to the car. Grant did not know whether to follow her or ask the silent ladies his question. "Hey, Mister, uhh, what's your name?" Grant realized there was no escaping this lady, so he walked over to his car to join her. "Can I sit in it?" The other ladies had joined them at the car.

"Sure, I guess so. Go ahead." Edwina sat in his car, and one of the other ladies got in on the passenger's side. Other visitors were coming in and out of the nursing home as Grant tried to figure out how he could extract himself from these ladies and, more importantly, get them out of his car.

"You married?"

First his glasses, then his car, now his personal life. This lady knew no boundaries. Grant ignored her question. "I just need to ask you a question. I figured since you worked here, one of you could help me." Grant looked at each of the silent ladies in the hope that one would finally speak.

"You ain't got no ring on that finger, unless you trying to pull a fast one." She grabbed Grant's left finger and looked at it closely. "No, you ain't married. No suntan circle on that finger. Unless you lost your ring."

A siren began to sound. It was incredibly loud. Edwina jumped out of the driver's seat of the car and ran to the passenger's side. "Get out, girl! We gots to go!" She pulled the other lady from the seat. Grant bent over and looked through the car as Edwina was backing her rather large hips into the passenger seat of the Porsche. "Get in Mister. Let's go! We gonna miss the fire truck!"

Extremely confused at this point, Grant responded, "What fire truck?"

Edwina, who was excited beyond containment, tumbled the words out, "Come on, come on! We gots to go!"

One of the silent ladies finally spoke, "She's on the volunteer fire department, and she don't have a car. So when the siren blows, someone has to drive her."

Grant jumped in and started the Porsche. They fled toward the fire department. He would never tell Samantha this story. She would not believe him. Edwina shouted directions to him, and within two minutes, they were at the fire station.

A large crowd had gathered at the base of one of the town's large water towers located behind Piggly Wiggly and within walking distance of the fire department. Grant's passenger fled in that direction. Grant slowly walked over and stood at the rear of the crowd. Everyone was looking up. A local character named Elvis Fillingim had climbed the tower and was threatening to jump.

Grant walked over to the soft drink machine located in front of Piggly Wiggly and purchased a Coke. He pulled the Costas from his pocket, put them on, and rejoined the crowd. Wondering how long this would take, he was looking for his flamboyant rider. He did not even know her name.

The police chief was trying to talk Elvis down using a bullhorn. "Elvis! You climb on down from there!"

Elvis, safely behind the railing and appearing as if he enjoyed the attention, yelled back at the police chief. "I aint gonna do it! I'm a jumpin unless un I can talk to the mayor!"

The mayor finally arrived and took the bullhorn from the chief. "Elvis! This is Mayor Davis. Come on down here so we can talk." The crowd had gotten larger from church folks driving through town who had stopped to see the commotion. Ironically, Grant noticed no one praying for the haggard soul who was threatening to jump.

"I demand two hundred dollars, or I'm a jumpin!" Elvis was pacing back and forth along the walkway of the rusting water tower as if the King of Rock-n-Roll himself had been resurrected. A large duel-wheel diesel truck pulled up, and a man stepped out who could be best described as a ruffian. He had a distinct beer gut, and his face was round, red, and unshaven. It was Elvis's Uncle Glen.

Uncle Glen explained to the mayor and police chief that Elvis would not jump. Apparently, Elvis had started to hitchhike out West a few years ago and made it as far as a small town in east Texas. Hungry, homesick, and out of money, he had climbed the town's water tower and threatened to jump. Fearing negative press from a suicide in his fair city, the mayor of the east Texas town offered Elvis a one hundred dollar bill if he would not jump. Elvis accepted the offer, climbed down the tower, took the money, and returned to Greene County. Elvis was broke again.

Uncle Glen seized the bullhorn from the Mayor. "Elvis, get yore ass down from that tirre!" Mothers began covering the ears of their children who were fresh off a sermon as Uncle Glen bellowed.

"I'm a jumpin unless un I get my money! And this ain't none of yore bitness, Uncle Glen!" Grant was amused at this strange fellow holding himself hostage seeking a ransom.

All eyes then turned back to Uncle Glen. "Well, Elvis, you ain't gettin no damn money. Come down from there!" Uncle Glen then looked at the ground near the base of the old water tower and then back up at Elvis. "Elvis! When you jump, jump off over on that side and onto that patch of grass!"

Everyone's eyes then volleyed back up in Elvis's direction. Elvis walked to the side of the tower where Uncle Glen had pointed. As Elvis looked down the two hundred feet below to the grass patch, he screamed back in reply to his Uncle Glen. "You think I'm crazy!" Grant thought to himself that Elvis's sanity, or lack thereof, was not up for debate at this point.

Edwina found Grant, "Let's go. That crazy-assed white boy ain't gonna jump. And he done messed my lunch hour up, too. I hate false alarms. When I respond, there betta be a house on fire or someone in a bad wreck or something. This ain't no good for nobody. This is messed up!"

Grant and Edwina walked to the Porsche and returned to Greene Rural. As they were approaching the front door of the nursing home, Edwina stopped, "What's that question you want to ask me?"

Grant, with a look of relief, finally asked, "How can I find Sheriff Lauvon McInnis?"

chapter fifteen

LAUVON MCINNIS INDEED HAD LOVED being sheriff of Greene County more than he loved life itself. Elected in 1971 at the age of twenty-eight after the retirement of long-time Sheriff Roy Stringfellow, he would serve twenty years before being defeated. Sheriff McInnis was known for his work ethic and movie-star good looks. Many of the county's female residents would place a distress call to the sheriff's office and request that he personally come and tend to whatever crisis threatened their well-being. He was in demand!

"Follow me." Grant walked a half step behind Edwina. They passed through a secure set of wooden doors and down a long hallway where office staff were housed during the week. They continued through another set of doors which opened out into the common area of the nursing home. The visiting public entered through a glass door from the side of the building. Grant noticed a large clock on the wall. It was 1:30 p.m. "What you say your name was?" Edwina stopped at the entrance to a long hallway with the residents' rooms on each side.

"I don't believe I had the chance. My name is Grant Hicks."

Edwina frowned. "Grant? Huh. That's a Yankee name."

Grant caught the irony. "And your name?"

Edwina pointed her right finger within inches of his nose and placed her left hand on her hip. "It's Edwina, and you better not laugh." Grant had no intention of laughing. She then pointed Grant in the direction of the sheriff's room. "The sheriff stay down yonder. Room sixteen."

Grant slowly walked down the hall nodding hello to the residents that sat at the doors of their rooms in the hopes a family member, or perhaps anyone, would stop for a visit. In the eyes into which Grant peered, he saw the loneliness contained in each aging body. He connected, and he sensed they knew it, too. He was there. Room sixteen. He took a deep breath and gently knocked.

"Come in." It was the recognizable voice of the sheriff. Grant paused for a moment before opening the door.

As Grant entered the room, he was met by Jade who was there visiting the sheriff. She could not get him off her mind during church. She regretted her questions about Grant's dad during breakfast. She felt she had caused her friend to be sad. So after church and lunch with Nana, she had brought the sheriff his favorite dessert, chocolate delight. They were enjoying it when Grant arrived.

"Hello. Grant Hicks."

She knew who he was. Grant, with a soft firmness, shook her small, tender hand. She stepped to the side to let him come further into the room. "Come in. My name is Jade."

Grant did not recognize her. But he did the sheriff. "Hello, Sheriff McInnis."

The sheriff looked at Grant as if he had discovered the bottle containing a note he had set adrift as a child. "Hello, Grant. It's been a long time. You've turned into a fine-looking young man." The sheriff was standing and moving toward Grant. The two men hugged. "Have a seat, Grant."

Jade suddenly did not know what to do or where to go. She just stood against the wall. For the first time since her auditions in Hollywood, she was exceedingly nervous. She had forgotten what she was wearing. So she slowly looked down. She had a bright electric blue dress covered by a simple white sweater paired with wedge heels. She glanced at the mirror through the open door to the bathroom. She wore her blonde hair straight with just a wisp of bangs.

"Jade, sit back down, doll." The sheriff directed Jade back to her chair.

The room was small. It contained a single bed which was made up very crisply. Directly in front of the bed and against the wall was a chest of drawers doubling as a television stand. By the window was a small table with two chairs. Sheriff McInnis and Jade had been sitting in those chairs eating their dessert. The sheriff directed Grant to his chair, then he sat on his bed.

"I did not mean to interrupt your family time, Sheriff." Grant looked at Jade, then back at the sheriff. He obviously thought she was one of the sheriff's daughters.

The sheriff chuckled. "Grant, you don't remember Jade?"

Grant looked back at Jade. He was struck by her simple yet elegant beauty. "I don't know. Last name?"

Jade looked at the sheriff. The sheriff noticed his little friend was speechless. "Grant, this is Jade Lott. She works here. I also consider her my adopted daughter."

Jade finally spoke, "I was two grades behind you in school."

Grant's faced relaxed. "Oh, yeah, I remember you now. Didn't you have long hair then?"

She did. Long hair was a necessity while she lived under the authority of Nana and the Mt. Pisgah Pentecostal Church. After she left Greene County, her first act of independence was cutting her hair. Nana and the church had since forgiven her. "Yes, I did."

Jade was speechless again. The sheriff came to her rescue. "Grant, how about some chocolate delight? Jade made it."

Grant had not eaten since the blueberry muffin at the Smallwoods that morning, and the whole ordeal with Edwina had made him hungry. He would not have time to eat before going back out to see Brandon, so he accepted the offer. "Sure."

Jade got up and retrieved another bowl and filled it. For some unexplained reason, she was nervous about his eating it. It was then that she remembered that it was Sunday, church day. She had on no makeup and no jewelry. Her first impression would not be a good one. So she thought.

Jade handed Grant the dessert. "Mr. Lauvon, I'll let you men visit. I need to run by the store for Nana. I'll see you tomorrow." She began gathering her things.

"Sweetie, you don't have to leave." The sheriff might have been sixty-seven and partially paralyzed, but he had noticed the change in Jade when Grant entered the room.

Jade hugged the beloved man and kissed him on the cheek. She then looked at Grant. "It was nice to see you again, Grant."

Grant stood as she was leaving the room. "You too, Jade."

Jade closed the door and slowly walked down the long hallway leading to the exit. She did not look at the residents as she passed, but they looked at her. For before them walked sadness. She came to give the sheriff some level of happiness. She left retaining none for herself.

"Grant, what brings you home?" The sheriff's question acknowledged what Grant had been longing to forget. He was home.

"I came to see Brandon Smallwood."

"I see. How is Brandon?"

Grant was surprised that the sheriff did not know Brandon's fate. After all, this was Leakesville. There were no secrets here.

"He's dying." Grant looked out the window and watched Jade get into her car and drive away.

"Dying? How?"

Grant turned back to the sheriff. "Cancer, Sheriff. When did Brandon get out of prison?"

The sheriff wondered if Grant were completely ignorant of recent Greene County history. "Grant, where do you live?"

Grant was always uncomfortable revealing himself to anyone, but Sheriff McInnis would be the exception. "I've been in Atlanta for the last twelve years. I work at a law firm there."

Sheriff McInnis was slightly shocked that Grant had become a lawyer, especially since that meant Grant had followed in his daddy's footsteps. "Grant, have you been keeping up with things around here since you left?" Most people who left did. However, the circumstances surrounding Grant's exodus were different.

"No, sir. I have purposely avoided it."

The sheriff suspected as much. The sheriff knew Grant did not return for his father's funeral. "Brandon was released from prison two years ago." Grant remembered that Brandon had been prosecuted as an adult and was sentenced to life without parole. How could he have gotten out? Grant began to regret not returning to visit Brandon. "It's a long story if you are up for it." The sheriff waited for Grant's permission to continue.

Grant pulled his cell phone from his pocket to check the time. It was already 2:10 p.m. "I have to be back at Brandon's house at three. He sleeps most of the time. I only was able to see him a few minutes this morning while he was awake, so I told Ms. Elsie I would be back at three."

The sheriff looked at his watch. "How long will you be in town, son?"

Monday was almost here. "I'm leaving tomorrow morning. I need to be back at work on Tuesday."

The sheriff was reluctant to begin Grant's historical education at that moment. He also sensed Grant's urgency to return to

Brandon's. "What are you doing after you leave Brandon's?"

Grant had not planned that far ahead. "I have no plans, actually. I'm staying at the Rocky Creek Inn. I brought some work with me. So, I guess I'll work some when I get back to my room."

"Why don't you come back by here? I usually don't go to bed until around 9:30."

Grant pondered the offer. The work could wait. "I can do that, Sheriff. When I leave Brandon's, I'll probably grab something to eat. Would you like me to bring you anything?" The sheriff thanked Grant for the offer but declined. Grant then stood to leave. "I guess I'll head out to Brandon's. I want to be there when he wakes up."

The sheriff stood, too. "It's so good to see you, Grant. I'll see you after while."

Grant left the nursing home and stopped by a local convenience store that doubled as a Subway. He purchased a Coke and a bag of peanuts to quiet the roar of his stomach. There was a group of black men sitting in a booth near the window. Grant nodded in their direction as he entered the store.

As Grant was leaving, he was stopped by the voice of one of the men sitting in the booth. "Hey. Ain't you Michael Hicks' son?"

Grant turned in the direction of the voice. "Uhh. Yes, sir. I am." Grant did not need a reminder of whose son he was. The mirror admonished him daily.

"Yo daddy was a good man." Grant thought to himself that this fellow obviously did not know his daddy very well. Grant looked at him in silence. "My name's Henry. Henry Malone. Whatever happened to your momma?"

Grant looked at the store's clock. It was 2:30. He did not want to be rude, but he had to go. "I'm sorry, Mr. Malone, but I'm late for an appointment. My mom's in North Carolina and doing fine."

Grant left the store before Henry could delve any further into the Hicks' family tree. Henry watched Grant get into his car.

"That fella must be doing good." Everyone in the store walked to the window and watched the Porsche drive away.

chapter sixteen

GRANT PULLED INTO THE SMALLWOODS' driveway and parked. Reverend Clark's truck was in the yard. Grant noticed for the first time the beautiful dogwood trees that were in full bloom. He was so nervous earlier that he had failed to see them. Spring had come early to the banks of Mason Creek.

As Grant walked toward the porch, Reverend Clark appeared from behind the house holding a large coffee can. "Hello there, young man."

Grant waited as the preacher joined him at the steps. "Hey, Reverend."

The preacher sat down on the top step leading to the porch. "Brandon's still asleep. Sit down."

Elsie walked out and took the coffee can from the preacher. He had gathered her eggs. "Would you like something to drink, Grant?"

Grant looked at Ms. Smallwood. "No thanks. I just finished a Coke." She walked back inside the house.

"How has your day been? Elsie told me you were able to see Brandon for a few minutes this morning."

The preacher began wiping the dust off his shoes. He was still dressed in his church clothes. Grant wondered how much she had told him. "I did. I was shocked at how small he is. Cancer is a terrible disease."

The preacher agreed. "Indeed it is. Were you able to go visit any of your family here?"

Grant paused to wonder if he had any family still here. His mom was in North Carolina. The last he heard his sister was on the coast. He never was close to his extended family. "No, sir. I did ride around a little. And I involuntarily responded to a fire call in town." Reverend Clark looked confused, so Grant explained. "Ms. Elsie told me that Sheriff McInnis was at the nursing home, so I went to see him and ended up giving a volunteer fireman, or firewoman rather, a ride to the fire department."

Reverend Clark laughed. "Met Edwina, did ya?"

"Yes sir, I did. She is quite the character." Grant wondered if Brandon were awake. He walked to the door and peeked inside. Elsie told him she would come get him when he woke up. Grant then rejoined the preacher.

"We appreciate our volunteer fire departments around here. Other than the fire department at the prison, all are voluntary. These men and women give of their time to help their neighbors. Edwina has a big heart." The preacher chuckled. "The only shame on our fire departments happened about ten years ago."

Grant decided to move the conversation further along to kill some time. "What happened?"

"There was a house fire, and the Neely and McLain fire departments responded. They both arrived about the same time. The fire chief from Neely began shouting instructions. He took charge. The chief from McLain thought the house was in his department's area, so he wanted to be in charge. He was a hot-tempered fella. An argument erupted. Then a fight broke out. Before it was over, they were both arrested. Needless to say, the house was a total loss."

Intrigued, Grant wanted more. "Who was right?"

The preacher grinned. "Neither one. It was in the Pleasant Hill department's district. They responded, but earlier in the day it had come a flood. Their truck got stuck on the way to the fire. The house was deep in the woods at the end of a slick, red clay road." Grant and the preacher looked at the old redbone as he was stretching after a long nap. The preacher continued, "About a year or two after that incident, the McLain department received a brand new fire truck with some federal money. They had a huge fire truck dedication. The governor, our congressman, and many other important folks came. Before turning the program over to the emcee, the McLain fire chief, fresh from a revival at his church, confessed all his sins including, among many others, starting the fight. I was there to give the opening prayer. Up to that point, it had remained our county's secret."

"Interesting story, Reverend."

Reverend Clark decided to steer to the conversation toward church. "Where do you go to church in Atlanta, Grant?"

Grant did not mind him changing the subject, but he did not want to be preached to. "Various churches. It depends on where the wedding is." Not wanting to pry any further on the subject, the preacher invited him to go with him that night to his church. Grant politely declined. "Reverend, no offense, but this place turned me against religion. I have not been to a church service since before I left here."

Recognizing the door to this part of Grant's life had been slightly opened, Reverend Clark thought he would peek inside. "Want to talk about it?"

Grant pondered for a moment as he recalled the treatment Brandon received when they were in high school. Brother Clark could tell Grant was retreating quickly. He regretted asking the last question. He should have waited until their next visit. "Not really, Reverend. Growing up here, I found religion to be more form than substance. I would go with Dad to work around the church some Saturdays, church work day. There would be deacons who referred to black people as 'Niggers.' And when I asked to put Brandon on the prayer list one Wednesday night at so-called prayer meeting, somehow his name never appeared in the bulletin." It broke the preacher's heart to watch Grant walk away from the porch and out into the yard. "Reverend, I'm going to check my messages if I can get reception."

As Grant moved about the yard, the preacher walked inside to sit with Elsie and Brandon. He wondered how he could teach Grant to forgive. He hoped he would have the chance.

chapter seventeen

JADE TURNED INTO NANA'S DRIVEWAY OFF Brown Town Road and remembered she had forgotten to stop by the Dollar Store. She also realized that she had driven home from Greene Rural on auto-pilot because she did not remember any part of her drive. Nana lived in the house her parents built, a wood-framed house that had been bricked twenty years ago, a standard red brick. Before Nana's health prevented her from tending to her various flower gardens, she had the prettiest yard in the community. Jade tried to keep the yard up as Nana did, but a green thumb she had not.

The patrol car was parked in the front yard. Jade's demeanor changed from melancholy to anxiety within seconds. Was Nana okay? She stepped out of her black Honda Accord without shutting the door. She was hurriedly walking past the patrol car when she saw Speed sitting in the back seat. She stopped. "Speed. What's going on?" Speed's real name was Theodore Rousevelt Lett, a/k/a "TeddyRo," a/k/a "RoLett."

Speed was stoned, and all he could say was, "Sup Gurl."

There was a story for each of Speed's aliases. Jade's favorite was the one behind Speed. He was running from the highway patrol after making a U-turn to avoid a road block. The chase exceeded 120 miles per hour before his car eventually ran out of gas. The officer asked him why he was driving so fast. Speed's response: "Man, I thought you was gonna run over my black ass, so I was trying to get outa yo way, man." Speed consented to the search of his car, and five years later he would get out of prison. He was on his way back.

Deputy Danny Narbo walked onto the front porch and watched every step Jade made as she approached the house. He did not hide the fact that he enjoyed each move. "What's going on, Danny?"

Danny slowly looked down Jade's body and back up it again. Try as he might, his eyes failed to undress her. "When you gonna let me take you out, Jade?"

Jade was visibly frustrated. "Just tell me what's going on?"

The deputy put on his mirrored shades. "We busted your sister and her boyfriend. Meth. Sheriff Coaker is in there with her and your grandma." As Jade began to walk past Danny, he grabbed her arm. "You didn't answer my question. When are we going out?"

Jade removed his hand from her arm. She despised Danny Narbo. When she first moved back to Greene County, he pulled her over for a "so-called" equipment violation. The real reason for the stop was he wanted to violate her equipment. "Not interested, Danny. I tell you that every time you ask." It wasn't Danny's looks that turned Jade off; it was his unadulterated arrogance. He was a player. His scheme often worked on unsuspecting women, but it did not on Jade.

"You'll come around, Jade, and when you do, you'll enjoy it. I promise."

Jade was now angry. "It will never happen." As she walked into the house, she wondered why some men thought their penises grew six inches when they put on a badge.

The tramp stamp was staring at Jade as she walked through the door. Jade's little sister, Stormy, had a collection of tattoos without any attempt at artistic arrangement. She had met Speed right after he got out of prison, and the last time Nana or Jade heard, they were living in Big Point with Jade's mom and her boyfriend. Stormy was indeed her mother's daughter. She was a wild child. It had been a few years since Stormy had been to see Nana. Jade used to be angry at her mom for passing her off on Nana while choosing to keep Stormy. She was angry no more.

Stormy was staring intently at Nana. "Grandma, it will only be until I can get Momma to come get him. I swear." Stormy was pleading with her grandmother who looked deeply into Jade's eyes. Jade had seen that look before.

The sheriff greeted Jade and then spoke to Nana. "Ms. Lott, I'll call the sheriff in Jackson County to find her. Otherwise, I have no choice but to turn him over to the Department of Human Services." The sheriff waited patiently for Nana's response. Jade then noticed the subject of the conversation.

He was asleep on the couch. He looked to be about three years old. A mixed-race, mostly black, little boy. He had on a sagging diaper with a dirty, adult sized T-shirt. No pants. Jade did not know he existed until that moment. "I'm gonna walk outside while y'all talk. Let me know when y'all are ready for me." The sheriff then joined Danny on the porch.

"Jade, your sister wants us to keep the baby until they can locate your momma to come get him. Stormy has been arrested."

Jade sat down in a chair in the corner. She placed her hands on her knees. She was thinking. Stormy awaited the decision. The baby was oblivious to the circumstances surrounding his immediate future. Jade looked at her grandmother. "Nana, you can't keep a baby. I have to work. Do they even know if Momma will take him?" Everyone knew the answer, but no one would say it. The chances of Jade's momma taking the toddler, even if they found her, were slim to none. Jade looked at Stormy. "Does he have any clothes, diapers, anything?" Stormy looked down and began to cry. Her life was a mess. She looked horrible. And she was about to go to jail. Jade looked at the toddler. "How old is he?"

Stormy wiped her tears away. "He's three. He turned three on February 14."

Jade looked back at Nana, and Nana's eyes told Jade what she already knew. The question wasn't "if *they* would take care of the toddler." It was, "Would *Jade*?"

"Nana?" Jade needed guidance.

"It's up to you, Precious. I understand if we can't." Jade looked out the window at Speed sitting in the patrol car and then at Stormy sitting on the couch. Jade was three when her Momma dropped her off at Nana's. She had no choice then; she had no choice now.

The toddler began waking up. He climbed into his momma's lap. Jade sat down next to them. "Hey, little fella, what's your name?" He had his thumb in his mouth and stared at Jade with his huge brown eyes.

"His name is Ladetrus, but we call him Lad for short." After revealing that the clothes he had on were all Stormy could provide, the sheriff took the troubled parents away. The baby did not cry. He went straight to Jade. He obviously had been left before. Jade's life had taken another turn. Fate can often be a cruel jester.

chapter eighteen

"HE'S AWAKE." ELSIE'S VOICE INTERRUPTED Grant's momentary solitude. He had made friends with the sluggish redbone hound. Grant entered the kitchen and washed his hands. "You can walk on back. Brother Clark is praying with him before he has to leave for church."

The nerves Grant thought were gone returned. Reverend Clark was holding Brandon's hand as he prayed. Grant waited at the door until he finished. After the preacher left, Grant took the seat next to the bed. "Hey, Brandon."

Brandon smiled. His eyes were beginning to retreat into his head. They seemed to want to die first. Grant was getting uncomfortable with the silence. Then, Brandon spoke. "Catch me up on what you've been doing, Grant."

Grant seemed hesitant to use Brandon's fading time discussing himself. Grant acknowledged the life lesson in that realization. Time is indeed precious. "I'm an attorney in Atlanta." Then he thought to himself, that was it. He had nothing else to tell. Just work. Another life lesson. Work is the repository of time. But it was Grant's safety net. There was nothing here to protect him. He was vulnerable.

"Are you married? Kids?"

Brandon seemed more awake now and alert. This relaxed Grant. "Not married, no kids. I do have a girlfriend. We live together. Have since college."

Brandon was listening intently to every syllable. "Do you love her?"

Now where did that come from? Brandon's question was easy enough. The answer was not so easy. "I must. Gosh, we've been together since 1994." Brandon's look told Grant he was not satisfied with his answer, so Grant continued. "Her name is Samantha. She works for CNN. She doesn't believe in marriage. Tough childhood."

Brandon adjusted in his bed. "What do you believe? About marriage?"

Grant had never been asked that question. "Hmm. I don't know. I guess it works for some. I've never thought about it." He gave Brandon a sip of juice from a cup next to the bed. Grant was a master at avoiding questions; it was a gift. He was using his natural disposition and hoped Brandon would not demand more direct answers.

"Grant, I know I'm dying. I don't know when, but it'll be soon." The lump returned to Grant's throat. Only this time he held it at bay as it burned inside him. "Would you speak at my funeral?"

Grant had hoped he would not ask. It would have been easier to decline the invitation after Brandon's death from 350 miles away. "Brandon, are you sure? I've never spoken at a funeral before. Heck, I haven't even been to one since my Grandma Turner died while I was in high school." Grant's selfishness had finally met its match. He simply could not refuse a dying man's desire. Another life lesson.

"Grant, I'm sure." Brandon began looking at the ceiling. Grant looked out the window and at the stack of Gideon Bibles sitting in the windowsill. "Grant, I want you to tell the people who come that I have forgiven them and then ask them to forgive me too." The two friends' eyes met as Grant wondered who would come. To whom was Brandon referring? After all that Brandon had endured from the people of this place, surely not them. But who? "And that I love them."

It must be the morphine, Grant thought. What's the harm in playing along? "Sure. Sure, Brandon. I'll do it. I'll be happy to." Grant's mind then returned to his office in Atlanta and to his upcoming trial. Would Brandon be so kind as to die when it was convenient for him? The selfishness would not retreat without a fight.

Brandon then looked intently into Grant's eyes. "Grant, I'm so sorry about your daddy. Please forgive me."

The plea for forgiveness from such a vulnerable man who needed no forgiveness was more than Grant could handle. The lump melted, and the tears returned. But they were quiet tears. Neither noticed the silent drops were there. "Brandon, you need no forgiveness."

Brandon never knew why Grant did not return to see him at Parchman. He learned about Michael Hicks' tragic death from Elsie during one of her monthly visits. He wanted to be there for his friend, but the chains and the guards and the barbed wire kept him from being there for Grant as Grant was for him. "Grant, you're the only friend I've ever had. I'm sorry my friendship cost you so much." Brandon's tears found their way past the holes around his eyes and rested on the pillow beneath him.

Grant wiped his own tears away with the back of his hand. "Brandon, nothing that happened was your fault. None of it." Grant could see the innocent sincerity on his friend's face. "Brandon, it's me that needs forgiveness from you. I shouldn't have stopped coming to see you. But, after dad...." The moment was too much for Grant to control any longer. The words stopped. They both sat in silence for the next several minutes.

The home health nurse, Jesse Bolton, had arrived and was in the kitchen talking to Elsie. A few moments later, Elsie came to the door. "The nurse is here, Brandon. She'll be in here in a minute to check on you."

Grant wanted so badly to continue the conversation, but he knew it was time to leave. Brandon was in obvious pain and needed her treatment. "Brandon, I'll be back to see you, okay?" The friends knew that each time Brandon went to sleep, he may not wake up again. Grant leaned toward the bed, "Brandon, if you feel you need forgiveness from me, you have had it all along." Grant simply could not utter the words "I forgive you." They were not in him.

"Grant, you don't need forgiveness from me. I never felt betrayed by you. But, if you believe you need it, then I forgive you."

Jesse Bolton entered the room, apologized for interrupting, and attentively, she began taking Brandon's vital signs. She smiled at her patient as she was doing so and wiped his bangs away from his forehead. In the short time she was there, Grant was comforted by the fact that such a sweet, gentle lady was caring for his friend.

Grant pondered his conversation with Brandon as he drove toward town. Sometimes, those who need forgiveness do not know to ask. And those who don't need forgiveness seek it. The heart is the teller of such truths. Grant's heart had been punctured by his time with Brandon. Again.

chapter nineteen

IT WAS 5:00 P.M., AND GRANT WAS HUNGRY. He stopped at a convenience store in town that also had a dining area. He ordered a hamburger and sat in a booth that gave him a full view of the loop which he and countless other teenagers, past and present, had driven around on Friday and Saturday nights. A group of kids had ridden their bicycles to the store and were admiring Grant's Porsche.

There she was. Edwina. She was wearing a white dress that was even too big for her. Edwina, though excessively overweight, carried herself well. Her hair was parted slightly on the side with unruly strands showing off orangy streaks. She began showing the Porsche to the onlookers. Then, she began to laugh. He had not noticed the gold teeth before. Edwina was indeed full of life. She entered the store and found him.

"Hey, Yankee!" She joined him at the table.

"Hey, Edwina."

Grant's burger was delivered to the table. Edwina looked at the burger and then at the waitress. "I'll take one a them."

Grant was not comfortable eating in front of his unexpected dinner company. "Why don't you take this one? I'll get the next one."

Edwina did not hesitate in accepting the offer. She grabbed the burger. "Where you stay, Yankee?" Edwina looked at Grant as she ate.

"I live in Atlanta, but I grew up here."

Edwina thought she knew everybody that passed through this place. "For real? When you stay here?"

Grant noticed two patrol cars pulling up to the store. "I lived here until I graduated from high school in 1990."

Edwina looked at the patrolman. "You see those two cops?" She pointed at them with the remaining half of the burger. Edwina was talking and chewing at the same time. Grant had never seen a lady eat so fast before. "They ain't no good. That skinny one work for the town. We call him Barney. I could pistol whip his ass with a water gun. That other one, Danny Narbo, he think he a ladies' man. He always hittin on Jade. She work at Greene Rural with me. He gonna get that sheriff beat next year. He need a good country ass-whoopin."

Both cops walked toward the entrance admiring the Porsche as they passed it. Edwina frowned at the cops as they walked by. "Did you grow up here, Edwina?" Grant decided he might as well get to know her.

"I moved here to stay with my auntie in 1993. I graduated high school in 2000. I am twenty-seven. I stay in the quarters here behind the store." Grant's burger was delivered. "You kin to that Lawyer Hicks that shot hisself?"

Grant tried to act like the question was an ordinary one. "Yes, I was kin to him."

Edwina had devoured her hamburger, and her arms were

folded on the table as she watched Grant. The shiny rainbow-colored costume rings clicked as she tapped her fingers on the table. "Where you works at, Yankee?" Edwina looked at the patrol cars pulling away from the store.

"I work at a law firm in Atlanta."

Edwina's head snapped back in Grant's direction. "You a lawyer?"

Grant peered out the window as a truck pulling a boat stopped in front of the gas pumps. "Yes, I am."

Edwina was impressed. "I ain't never talk to no lawyer before. I'll declare." Edwina's smile returned. "You sure you not married?"

Grant decided total honesty was the best policy with Edwina. "No, I'm not married. I have a life partner though."

Edwina's smile vanished. "You a queer?"

Grant chuckled. "No, I'm not gay. I have a girlfriend. She lives with me."

Edwina smirked. "That'll send you to hell around these parts. Don't advertise that shit." The man with the boat was heading toward the store. He had on black water boots, baggy shorts, a dirty T-shirt, and a John Deere cap. Edwina was shaking her head at his attire. "Umm, Umm, umm, who dresses these rednecks?"

Grant glanced at the man. Then, he thought he would tease Edwina. "Edwina, your dress is white. I don't believe you're supposed to wear white before Memorial Day or after Labor Day."

Grant watched as Edwina looked at her dress. "That's a lie. Some skinny-ass white woman probably came up with that rule. Black is beautiful, Yankee, no matter what color Edwina have on."

The poorly dressed man passed Grant and Edwina's table and nodded at Grant as he strolled to the drink cooler. Grant recognized him. A well-dressed lady had entered the store, and Edwina got up to talk to her. Grant finished eating and waited for the man to get a drink from the cooler. "Uncle Ronny?"

Ronny Hicks turned to look at Grant. "Grant? Wow! Is

that you?" They shook hands and hugged. Ronny was Michael's brother. He was eighteen months younger. "I thought I'd never see you again. Man, look at you! How are you? You look great." Grant could not say the same for Uncle Ronny. Michael and Ronny were never close. Grant did not recall them visiting each other, unless Uncle Ronny needed something. "What you doing in town, Grant?"

Grant noticed Edwina pointing at him as she said goodbye to her acquaintance. "I came to see a friend. I live in Atlanta now. I have to go back tomorrow though. Where do you live, Uncle Ronny?"

"I live at Daddy's old place in Saint Ellen. I was able to buy it about five years ago. Why don't you ride out to see me? You can meet the wife."

Grant looked at the clock on the wall. It was 6:00 p.m., and the sheriff was expecting him. Too, Grant was exhausted. It had been a long, emotional day. "I'm coming back in a few days. I'll ride out when I do."

Ronny grinned. "That'll be great! I can't wait. Do you still remember how to get to your grandpa's old place?"

"Yes, sir."

Ronny slapped Grant on the shoulder. "Good deal. I'll see you in a few days."

When Grant rejoined Edwina at the table, she handed him the tab. "That's my Uncle Ronny, Edwina."

Edwina watched Ronny lumber toward his pickup. "You better count your blessings that you didn't get that DNA." Grant laughed. "And, oh, Yankee, you got to take me to church. It's across the river." There was no need in debating Edwina. They got in the Porsche, and five minutes later Grant pulled into the parking lot of Edwina's church. Several parishioners were looking on. "Yankee, I want a picture with you and this car. Get out."

Grant stepped out of the car, and Edwina found someone to take the photograph. She put Grant's arm around her and smiled.

The picture would be on Edwina's Facebook page before Grant would make it back to town.

chapter twenty

WAITING FOR GRANT AT A TABLE in the corner, sat the sheriff. "Hey, Sheriff."

Sheriff Mcinnis pointed to a chair. "Have a seat, Grant. How was your visit with Brandon?"

Grant pulled off his coat and laid it across an empty chair. "We had a nice visit. It's so tough knowing he's dying and seeing him in pain."

The sheriff shook his head. "I understand, Grant, especially when he's so young. If I remember correctly, he's your age?"

Grant's and Brandon's birthdays were one month apart. "He is. He's lost so much weight. He's in a hospital bed and will never leave it alive."

"So, you going back to Atlanta tomorrow?"

Grant watched a family leaving after visiting a loved one. "Yes, sir."

"Are you coming back?"

Grant turned his attention back to the sheriff. "Yes, sir. Brandon asked me to speak at his funeral."

The conversation then turned to Brandon's freedom. "Grant, you were right all along. He was innocent." Grant stared at the sheriff, waiting on more. "About three years ago, one of our board of supervisors, Orville Taylor, was arrested in a kickback scheme related to a gravel company. As it turned out, that little scheme was the tip of the iceberg." Sheriff McInnis could see and feel the intentness as Grant listened. "Mr. Taylor was the son-in-law of Frank Jenkins who had been supervisor before him for thirty-two years." Grant remembered Frank Jenkins. No one died without Frank Jenkins visiting the funeral home. "Orville was in his second term. Frank still called the shots though." The sheriff adjusted his sitting position. "Orville and his wife were going through a nasty divorce when he got arrested, so when it came time to plea for his freedom, he sang like a canary."

The lines in Grant's furrowed brow communicated to the sheriff his need for the rest of the story. The sheriff continued, "Frank Jenkins was then arrested for a laundry list of federal and state crimes. At the time of his arrest, Frank was battling lung cancer and was near death. In an effort to cleanse his soul, he confessed his sins to God and to the FBI. But not necessarily in that order." Grant was trying to digest the information. He now regretted not keeping up with Brandon more. "Before Frank quit confessing, he revealed the largest crime syndicate these parts had ever seen. Twenty people were arrested before it was over."

Grant was speechless. "Grant, did you not hear about this? It was all over TV and in the newspapers."

Grant was so busy practicing law that he rarely watched television or read the newspaper. He thought about the irony of his apathy for the news since Samantha's life was the news. "No, sir. I had no idea."

The sheriff thought to himself that Grant had totally shut

this place out of his mind. "Darwin Gordon, the editor for the *Herald*, wrote a detailed history of the entire episode. In fact, he was named Mississippi's Journalist of the Year for his stories about it."

Grant stood to pace as he listened. "But how did it relate to Brandon?"

Sheriff McInnis could sense Grant's curiosity turning to anger. "Grant, would you like to read all those articles Darwin wrote?"

Grant sat back down. He became suddenly eager to know the entire story surrounding Brandon's release. "Yes, sir, I would. Do you have them?"

The sheriff thought about the old boot box in his room. If he opened it, he knew he would give the envelope to Grant. His gut told him Grant was not yet ready. "Grant, there's a Greene County Historical museum here now. It's on the fourth floor of the courthouse. The old jail was converted a few years ago to house it. They have every *Greene County Herald* since the paper was first published. I'll be happy to go with you over there."

Grant began to think about his unquenchable thirst for the information. It forced him to ponder his return. "Sheriff, I have to go back to Atlanta tomorrow and sort out some things at the office. I'll be speaking at Brandon's funeral, whenever that is." Grant was pacing again. "Sheriff, who killed Tony Sylvestor?" Tony Sylvestor was a thirty-year-old former narcotics agent who had been working for Sheriff Mcinnis for three years when he was murdered. Sylvestor had been an excellent deputy. He could literally smell crime. His keen sense of smell cost him his life.

"A man named James Thomas. He was not from here. He was hired to do it. He'll spend the rest of his life in prison."

Grant's thoughts returned to Brandon in 1989. Brandon was seventeen years old when he stood before the judge to hear the verdict read. Grant sat behind him in the courtroom. Brandon shed no tears, nor did he look at the jury. He simply stared at the judge. Grant recalled Elsie bellowing out with uncontrollable anguish. He recalled looking at the jury and then at the locals who witnessed the trial. He remembered Tony Sylvestor's thirty-year-old widow, who seemed old at the time, just staring at the ceiling. Grant recalled the defeated look on Sheriff McInnis' face as he came to take Brandon away. The bitterness resurfaced in Grant's soul for what had been taken from Brandon. And though Grant's thoughts were on Brandon's tragic life, his spirit whispered to his own soul that he, too, was bitter for what had been taken from him.

Grant told the sheriff he would come by when he came back to see Brandon and then shook his hand and told him good-bye. Grant looked forward to reading the articles describing the events which led to Brandon's short-lived freedom.

Grant was exhausted. It had been a long day. As he neared the George County line, he decided that he would drive into Lucedale for gas and something to eat. While sitting in the line at McDonald's drive-thru, he noticed Jade walking to her car holding a little boy, a mixed-race boy. He pondered the ridicule that poor child would have to endure in this place, a place where if one is different, opportunities evade and judgment is often quick and harsh.

Grant watched the Honda Accord's taillights fade out of sight while he mourned the future of the little boy. The Grim Reaper of sadness, bitterness, and unforgiveness enveloped him once more.

Part Four:

A Fork in the Road

chapter twenty-one

IT WAS MONDAY MORNING, AND JADE BEGAN calling daycares to see if there were an opening for Lad. She located one on Vernal Road which was not very far out of her way en route to work. The owner suggested she come in at 2:00 p.m. to complete the paperwork since the kids would be having nap time then.

Jade and Nana spent Sunday afternoon and night adjusting to the presence of a three-year-old. A neighbor had some of the basic necessities that her child had outgrown, and she had an extra highchair and car seat for them to borrow. Jade made a trip to Walmart to buy some diapers and a few clothes for Lad. She then stopped by McDonald's to get her nephew some ice cream. They had made it through the first night. Many more would follow.

"Nana, I'm going to take Lad to work and let them know I have to take off today to get him situated at the daycare."

Nana was feeding Lad some grits. They were all over his little brown face. "Precious, do you want me to watch him while you run to the nursing home?"

Jade began wiping Lad's face and hands. "No, that's okay, Nana. We'll be back in a couple of hours." Jade lifted Lad from the borrowed highchair. She then dressed him in the clothes she had bought at Walmart, pulling the price tags off as she went.

As Jade was driving to town, she began to think about the sudden change her life had experienced. Psychologically, she was preparing for a long stay by Lad. Jade knew her mom would not take him, and who knew how long Stormy would be in jail? She had a daycare secured, so work would not be affected, unless he became sick. She would stop by the jail after she left the nursing home to see Stormy. She needed to discuss Lad's healthcare needs and obtain any other relevant information.

Jade looked in the rearview mirror at Lad. He appeared content sitting in his car seat. Jade's mind turned to her social life. Her first thought was that it would not be affected. Then she thought about Grant. She quickly dismissed the thought as wishful thinking, but for a moment, she looked at Lad and wondered if his presence would matter to Grant. She smiled at herself for pondering the prospect. She knew Grant's name, that he was good-looking, and that he was a distinct dresser. She knew nothing else. Was he married? Did he have children? Was he a jerk? So many questions were pouring through her mind as she pulled into Greene Rural's parking lot.

Jade and Lad entered the nursing home and stopped by the work station where the nurses and aides gathered to complete paperwork and receive orders. Several employees were gathered around a computer.

"Hey, guys, what's up?" Her co-workers said hello to Jade without removing their eyes from the computer. Jade wondered what had captured their attention. "What are you guys looking at?"

"We's looking at one hot white man." Edwina had captured everyone's attention with her Facebook profile picture. The crowd parted as Jade eased through the onlookers to see. One by one the employees took their eyes off the computer screen and settled on Lad. "And look at that car." Edwina was admiring the picture. Jade noticed Grant's picture with his arm around Edwina. She smiled and wondered, how in the world? "Daammn! Somebody shit!"

"Edwina! Watch your language, girl. I have a baby with me."

Edwina looked at the baby, then back at Jade. Her eyes were big as saucers. "Where you get that black baby?" Edwina and the group were waiting for Jade to answer.

"He's my sister's baby. His name is Lad, and I need to change his diaper."

Edwina looked suspiciously at Jade. "I see how it is. She gave that baby a white man name."

Jade retrieved a diaper and some wipes from the borrowed diaper bag. "His full name, Edwina, is Ladetrus. He's called Lad for short." Jade walked to the bathroom and changed the diaper. She then rejoined Edwina and one of the nurses' aides at the work station. "Edwina, how'd you meet, Grant?"

A slow smile began with Edwina's eyes and erupted into a full-blown grin that covered her entire face. "You like him, don't ya?"

Jade blushed and began to busy herself to avoid Edwina's stare. "No, I barely know him. I remember him from high school. I was with Mr. Lauvon when he stopped by to see him yesterday."

Jade hoped that Edwina would move on to another subject. She didn't. "He ain't married, Jade. Got some life partner shit with some woman though." Inside Jade was pondering the classic good news, bad news. Not married. But involved. Jade's demeanor changed. Edwina's did, too. Edwina loved Jade as everyone did. Jade's heart harbored a triple dose of love and compassion. The nurses' aide left the work station, and Edwina looked around to make sure she could not be overheard. "Jade?" Edwina grabbed

Lad from Jade. Jade was recovering from lost hope. Edwina gave her a few seconds, and then she continued. "Jade, you gonna find a good man one day. You the nicest person I ever knowed." Edwina then looked at Lad. "How long you gonna have this baby?"

"Thanks, Edwina, I love you." She hugged Edwina. Edwina hoped nobody saw her softer side. "My sister is in jail. I don't know how long I'll have him."

"Look on the bright side, Jade. This little fella will keep them rednecks away." They both laughed.

Jade left the nursing home and went by the jail. The dispatcher told her that Speed was still there, but Stormy's bond was set low by the judge so that she could get out and tend to her baby. A lady named Vicky Lusk picked her up. Jade walked out of the jail holding Lad on her left hip. Her fear was being realized faster than she had anticipated. Her mom had picked up Stormy, and they were gone. She strapped Lad in his seat and headed home. A tear rolled down her cheek. Her childhood dreams had faded, and circumstances had dealt her a life that she would not have chosen for herself. But for whatever reason, it was hers to live, and live it she must. Nana, and now Lad, depended on her, too.

chapter twenty-two

GRANT ARRIVED AT HIS OFFICE AT 2:00 P.M. On his drive back to Atlanta, he called Elsie to check on Brandon. She said that Brandon was doing about the same as he was on Sunday.

Linda greeted Grant as he walked into the office. "Hello, Grant. Welcome back. Here are your phone messages, and Mr. Rimes wants to see you." Emmitte Rimes was the polished managing partner of Rimes and Yancey. He was the picture of a distinguished gentleman with gray hair, and he was still in great physical shape at sixty-two years old. When Grant first arrived at the firm, the other associates resented the apparent favoritism Grant received from Mr. Rimes.

"Okay. Thanks. I'll stick my head into his office." Linda wanted to ask about his trip, but she contained her curiosity for the moment. Grant walked through the office on his way to see Mr. Rimes to the delight of the legal secretaries and the paralegals.

"Mr. Rimes, you wanted to see me?"

The managing partner got up to greet him. "Yes, Grant, close the door." Grant and Mr. Rimes sat down in the client chairs across from his desk. Emmitte Rimes never separated himself from his guests. He thought this strategy made them feel equal. It did not. "I understand you went to Mississippi this weekend. That was a quick trip." Emmitte Rimes always made eye contact. There was no escaping his inquisitive green eyes.

"I did. I needed to go see an old friend."

Mr. Rimes' billing rate was $800 per hour, so he got to the point. "Grant, I'm concerned about you." Grant was surprised at the personal tone of this conversation. Combined, their billing rate was $1,300 per hour. Personal conversations were not the norm. "I ran into Judge Rayborn at the bar association's social Friday night. She said the Summary Judgment hearing did not go well and that you seemed off your game."

Grant's mind rewound to the hearing. "We had a weak argument." Grant could sense his boss was about to give one of his patented directives. It was not an option to refuse such instructions.

"Grant, I had Human Resources pull your personnel file. You've been here twelve years and have only taken six weeks of vacation. Since you arrived at this firm, you have billed more hours yearly than any partner or associate. Grant, you are the star of this firm. You will eventually take my place as managing partner. But, I need you healthy for that to happen." Grant concentrated on Mr. Rimes' words and remained silent. "I also pulled Linda's file. She has not taken a vacation in three years, and her dedication to you and this firm is unmatched by any other para-professional."

Grant's mind turned to Linda. He had not even noticed. He was often so busy that he forgot when it was Administrative Assistant's day. He would have to call for some last-minute, thoughtless gift. "Linda is an amazing employee, Mr. Rimes. I've taken her for granted."

Mr. Rimes walked behind his desk and opened his desk drawer. "Grant, I'm giving you and Linda a bonus. I know we give bonuses at Christmastime, and we will again this year if we continue to be successful. However, there is one contingency in order to receive this bonus. You have to take a paid leave of absence."

Grant's mind immediately turned to next week's trial. "I can't, Mr. Rimes. I have a trial next week."

The managing partner sat back down next to Grant. "I have agreed to a continuance in that matter. Judge Rayborn signed an order this morning. I'm reassigning that case to Jason Burgess." Grant got up and walked to the window overlooking the Atlanta skyline. Mr. Rimes joined him. "Grant, I'm sixty-two years old. I'm on my third marriage. My kids are spread out all over the place, and I barely know them. I made the mistake of marrying this firm twenty-five years ago. I was your age then." The two men stood at the window gazing across the Atlanta sky.

"Can I decline the bonus and leave?" Grant's life was tied to his work. It scared him not to be here.

"Yes, you can, Grant. However, if you do, Linda will not get hers." Mr. Rimes knew Grant would not forfeit Linda's.

"Okay, then when can I come back?"

The two litigators faced each other. Mr. Rimes smiled. "I'll see you on the first of May."

Grant left and returned to his office. It was March 22. The realization that he had thirty-eight days off depressed him. Linda cried when she opened the envelope. Enclosed was a check for five thousand dollars and instructions to take three weeks paid vacation starting today. She hugged Grant. After she left, Grant opened his envelope. A check for twenty-five thousand dollars was enclosed. He felt dirty for receiving it. He called Samantha, and they agreed to meet for dinner at their favorite restaurant. She, too, had some news for him.

chapter twenty-three

THE CROWD GATHERED AT THE Leakesville Community Center to devise a plan. Word had spread quickly that Grant Hicks was in town to see Brandon Smallwood who had returned home to die. Though the source of Grant's reason for returning home could not be traced, it was clear now that he was home to tell his friend good-bye. Scharlotte Bounds, the county's tax assessor, arranged the meeting. She called the group to order. "I would like to thank everyone for coming. As y'all know, Brandon Smallwood has a terminal illness and is at home with Ms. Elsie. I need not tell y'all that Ms. Smallwood has extremely limited means. I've asked Brother Clark to bring you up to date. Brother Clark?"

Reverend Clark walked up to address the crowd. As he looked at his neighbors, he saw black and white folk, religious and nonreligious folk, affluent and poor folk. He saw young, middle-aged, and elderly. He had participated in hundreds of these benefit-planning meetings for local people. He had never seen this large and diverse a turnout before. "Thank you, Ms. Scharlotte, and thank each of you for being here. Elsie nor Brandon is aware of this meeting. We would need to get their permission to hold this benefit. I'll be happy to discuss it with her and, if possible, with Brandon." The people in the crowd listened intently. Many were shaking their heads in agreement.

"Most of you know Brandon was released two years ago as a free and innocent boy." Brother Clark felt moisture glazing over his eyes. But as a preacher, he needed to be strong. "He moved away to get a fresh start. Unfortunately, his future included this terrible disease. Cancer. And it's terminal as Ms. Scharlotte just told you. I've been visiting him daily. He's on hospice now. He sleeps most of the time due to the medicine." Reverend Clark paused. No one moved.

"There's no doubt that this benefit will help Elsie. She's doing the best she can. Brandon has been amazing. *Courage* is an understatement. He wanted to come home to die by his momma's side. He requested that, and he requested to see Grant Hicks before he died. Both of those requests have been fulfilled." The door opened, and a few more people entered the community center. There were no chairs remaining. "I'll help all I can."

Scharlotte resumed control of the meeting. The mood in the room was solemn. "Since most people get paid on the first, we thought we would try to have the benefit on April 3. I know that this is incredibly short notice."

Hands began to rise. Terry Lowery spoke first. "On behalf of the school board, we will make available the cafeteria and any school facilities that may be needed. I'll be there and volunteer in any manner helpful." The crowd continued to discuss the benefit, and before they knew it, a plan began to develop to hold the benefit on April 3.

Darwin Gordon spoke next. "The *Herald* will publicize it, but we need the approval of the Smallwoods before noon tomorrow." The *Herald* went to press at noon on Tuesdays for distribution on Thursdays. It was agreed that Reverend Clark, Scharlotte, and Terry Lowery would go and see Elsie. Time being of the essence, they immediately left for the Smallwoods while the crowd continued making preparations and giving assignments.

Elsie heard the car and walked outside. "Y'all get out and come in." Scharlotte and Terry hugged Elsie while expressing their sorrow. Reverend Clark explained to Elsie what the community wanted to do. She was grateful but not quite sure how Brandon would feel. The reverend asked to speak to Elsie alone, so Scharlotte and Terry retreated to the car.

Elsie and Reverend Clark sat on the old bus seat. "Elsie, these people want to help, and this is the only way they know how. Now, you know as well as I do that they are doing this for you and Brandon. But, Elsie, they also need to do it for themselves." Elsie and the preacher looked at Scharlotte and Terry who were standing by the car.

"I imagine that Brandon would be honored for them to do this." Elsie wiped a tear away. "Brother Clark, he's always blamed himself for all this."

Reverend Clark placed his hand on Elsie's. "I know he has, Elsie. He blamed himself for Michael Hicks' death and for the severed relationship between Grant and his daddy. Grant's coming has helped him deal with that pain. I believe this benefit will help him and this community heal." Brother Clark let the words sink in and paused to let Elsie think.

"Okay. They can do it. Tell them we appreciate it so much."

After they left, Elsie walked back to check on Brandon. He was sleeping, and she began to caress him on the forehead as she cried. He had experienced so much pain, both emotionally and physically, yet he so easily forgave. She leaned over, kissed him, and whispered, "I love you, son. So, so much."

chapter twenty-four

SAMANTHA WAS ALREADY SEATED AT THEIR table when Grant arrived at Alfredo's Italian Restaurant—their favorite. She stood to hug him as he approached. "Hey, Grant, good trip?" They sat down, and the waiter took their drink orders.

"Tiring, but good." Grant indeed looked tired. His hair was slightly disheveled, which indicated to Samantha that he was either feeling bad or tired. Otherwise, each strand of hair would be in its proper place.

"How did your visit go with Brandon?"

Grant looked up from the menu as his mind returned to Brandon. He was lying there waiting to die while Grant waited for his drink. "Sam, it's so incredibly sad. I did get to talk with him though." The waiter returned with their drinks, and as he walked away, Grant wondered how death would find Brandon.

"Are you going back?"

Grant wanted to leave at that very moment. With every mile he had driven back to Atlanta and further away from Brandon, his emotions tugged at his heart. He wanted to be there when Brandon died. "Yes. Yes, I am. I'm leaving in the morning. He doesn't have much time left. He may actually die before I get back down there." The waiter came to take their dinner order, but both Sam and Grant had ignored the menu. The waiter would return later.

Samantha wondered when the best time would be to break the news to Grant. She decided there was no time better than the present. "Grant, I've been offered the international correspondent position in East Africa."

Grant's eyes again left the menu and met Sam's. They had known this day would come, but as time passed, the thought of Sam going overseas quietly had left their mental processes and conversation. "Congratulations, Sam. Wow! When do you start?" The waiter returned, and they paused their conversation long enough to give him their orders.

"I leave Thursday."

Grant's mind began to race. Should he stay with Sam until Thursday? What if Brandon died before he got back? "Is this a permanent assignment? When will you return?" Grant stopped at two questions.

"Yes, it's permanent, and I don't know when I'm returning."

Grant stared at the salt and pepper shakers on the table. "What does this mean, Sam? For us?"

Samantha placed her precisely manicured hand on Grant's forearm as it rested on the table. "Grant, we knew this would happen one day. You can always come with me." Sam and Grant knew that was impossible, but the offer needed to be made.

"I know. I know. I'm happy for you, Sam. This has been your dream since I met you. Although it's been a long time coming, it seems so sudden now that it's here." Their salads were delivered.

"I'll wait until you leave to go back to Mississippi."

"No, Grant. You need to be there. If it makes you feel better, I'm flying to Memphis in the morning and driving over to Hickory Flat to tell my grandma good-bye. I'll fly back here Wednesday to pack."

So this was their last dinner together. Although many would define this as a breakup between two lovers, it was more like two old friends parting ways with a simple "See you later."

"What about the house? Furniture? Your things?" It was obvious that Sam had been planning this day for a while. She meticulously suggested a plan for them to divide their toys. The division was made much easier by the fact that neither really cared about material things, which was ironic considering how much they owned.

"I'm more concerned about my babies: Max, Ringo, and Muffy." Max was Sam's aging Golden Lab, Ringo was Sam's three-year-old Jack Russell, and Muffy was her mixed-breed cat. "Can you take Max with you?"

Although Max was Sam's, Max always preferred Grant. He would sit at the base of Grant's chair at night, and Grant would rest his feet on Max's side, rubbing him occasionally with his bare feet. "I guess I can. But I would need to take the Range Rover." Grant actually had planned to ask Sam to swap vehicles with him when he returned to Greene County. He wanted to visit some places the Porsche was not welcomed.

"Good. Angela from work is taking Ringo, and Mrs. Hawthorne next door is taking Muffy." Their food was delivered, and for the next several minutes, they ate in silence.

After dinner, Grant followed Sam home to spend their last night together. They would share a bottle of wine and make love for the last time. Their relationship was an oddity. Just enough feelings to stay together, but not enough to forego their independence. The next morning, before daylight, Grant loaded the Range Rover. He ordered Max to jump into the front seat.

He then returned to the kitchen, unplugged the microwave, and placed it in the SUV. Elsie was soon to receive her first microwave oven. Grant walked back into the bedroom, sat on the edge of the bed, and rubbed Sam's cheek. He gently kissed her, walked to the bedroom door, and paused to look at her one last time before he left.

The fork in the road that had been a distant vision on the horizon was now at their threshold. At times, Samantha's dream was like trying to catch the setting sun. Samantha and Grant had become so busy that they did not realize the vision had grown larger until they were staring in its eyes. Today, they would walk separately. Alone. Sometimes, forks just work that way.

chapter twenty-five

JADE STOPPED BY SHERIFF MCINNIS' ROOM during her morning break. He was sitting and looking out the window. "Well, good morning, handsome."

The sheriff smiled. "Good morning, Jade. I missed you yesterday."

Jade sat down. She informed him of the dramatic change which had taken place in her life on Sunday. She discovered that she was an aunt and assumed custody of a three-year-old all in less than thirty minutes. Jade noticed the sheriff continuing to peer out of his window toward the parking lot. She then asked, "You expecting company?"

The sheriff glanced at Jade. "I was just wondering when Grant may stop back by. He's going to drop by when he comes back to see Brandon."

Jade looked out the window then, too. "Brandon who?" Jade

had been so busy adjusting to Lad's presence that she had not heard the reason for Grant's returning home.

"Brandon Smallwood."

Jade looked back at the sheriff. "Is Brandon living here now?" She did not remember his trial, but she was familiar with Brandon's release two years ago after he had spent eighteen years in prison for a crime he did not commit. Jade had attended high school in George County her ninth grade year and was not around during Brandon's trial.

"Yes. He's with his momma, Elsie. He's dying with cancer."

Jade's eyes did not leave the sheriff as his left hers to gaze at the parking lot. "Oh, that's terrible. I guess he and Grant are close friends?"

The sheriff never broke his stare. "Until Sunday, Grant had not seen him in years. He didn't even know Brandon had been released until last week. I brought him up to speed as to how Brandon came to be released. When he comes back, he wants me to ride with him over to the history museum so he can read the *Herald* articles detailing the events which led to Brandon's release."

Jade's curiosity about Grant's role in Brandon's past, Michael Hicks' death, and Grant's long absence from Brandon became insatiable. She wanted more. "Sheriff, my break's over, but can I come back and eat my lunch with you?" The sheriff gladly agreed.

Jade returned to work. A few minutes later, a knock sounded at Sheriff McInnis' door. "Come in."

Reverend Clark walked in holding his old tattered Bible. "Hello, Lauvon." They shook hands, and the preacher sat down.

"Hey, Brother Clark. Finished your devotion?" Brother Clark led a devotion every Tuesday morning at ten.

"Yes, and I missed seeing you there. Thought I would check on you."

The sheriff's eyes volleyed between the parking lot and Reverend Clark. "I'm doing fine. It slipped my mind this morning.

I'm sorry I missed it." The two men sat in brief silence.

"Lauvon, I understand the Hicks boy has been by to see you."

The sheriff turned to look at the preacher. "Yeah, he has. He's come by twice. I'm waiting on him to stop by when he comes back to see Brandon. How is Brandon?"

"He's getting weaker. Sleeping more. It won't be long." Both men turned their attention to the parking lot. "Lauvon, the community is giving a benefit for Brandon. The Smallwoods have accepted their lot in life. Brandon's ready." He paused for a moment. "But I'm worried about Grant. He's a troubled young man. And with how his daddy died, it has me concerned."

The sheriff turned to look at the preacher. The possibility of Grant's following so closely in his dad's footsteps had never crossed the sheriff's mind. "Grant was a special kid. He endured a lot of ridicule when he stood by Brandon, and the adults were the worst. I'll talk to him, Preacher."

The preacher got up to leave. "Thanks, Lauvon. I'll see you next Tuesday." Reverend Clark left Sheriff McInnis staring out the window. He hoped the watched pot would soon boil for the sheriff.

chapter twenty-six

GRANT AND MAX WERE GETTING CLOSE to Leakesville when Grant noticed a stranded motorist flagging him down. He slowed as he approached the man standing alongside his stalled pickup. It was Pete Ball. Grant remembered Pete from his days growing up in Greene County. Pete was always a mystery. He never worked, but always appeared to have enough money to get by. Pete's eyes were off-center, and they pointed in two directions. It was always a challenge to figure out which eye Pete was using. In his mid-fifties now, Pete was still thin as a rail. It was 11:30 a.m. and Grant was in a hurry to make it to the nursing home, get the sheriff, and go to the museum before driving out to Brandon's at 3:00 p.m.

"Feller, I shore am glad you stopped. She run out of gase on me. Can you drop me off in town?" Before Grant could answer, Pete opened the door, and Max retreated to the back seat. Pete did not recognize Grant who was relieved. “I was in town earlier, and this womern asked me for a ride. She said she was from Louisiana, but Johnny Newbill told me years back that if someone is from Louisiana, they say they from Louisian. Without the *a* at the end.”

Now where did this conversation come from? It did not matter to Grant. He just wanted to drop Pete off at the nearest gas station. At every awkward interval in the conversation, Grant simply said, “Uh, huh.”

“I figure she’s from Mobile. She asked me to drop her off at a trailer on Dickerson Sawmill Road. She had me so messed up when she lied about where she was from that I plum forgot to get my gase.”

Grant looked at Max. Max looked confused, too. “Uh, huh.”

“When I got to where she told me to go, it wouldn’t no trailer. It was a beat-up ole house. But I didn’t say nothin. I was just tryin to get shed of her. She then asked me for a few dollars, so I gave her what was in my pocket.”

Grant still had no words. “Uh, huh.”

“They ain’t no telling what she gonna do with that money. Maybe she will hightail it back to Mobile.”

Grant was amused that Pete had her so figured out. Grant added a different word to the conversation. “Probably.”

“I will say this here for her though. She’s an honest crook.”

Grant simply could not leave the question unasked. “An honest crook?”

“Yes sir. She asked me for the money. So that makes her an honest crook. A shore nuf crook will take it without askin.” Finally, they had made it to the BP station in town. Grant pulled over to let his rider out. Before he closed the door, Pete had one final question. “Hey, feller, can you loan me a few dollars since that womern stole my gase money?”

Grant noticed the word *loan*. So what did this make Pete? “Sure.” Grant handed him a twenty dollar bill and left him standing at the gas pumps. As Grant drove away, he laughed. The conversation was worth the twenty dollars.

Grant arrived at Greene Rural at noon. He let Max stretch his legs and use the bathroom before he put him back in the Range Rover with the windows down for Max to enjoy the pleasant weather. He then entered the nursing home. Everyone there knew who Grant was by now. Edwina's Facebook photo and the small-town communication network assured that fact. One of the silent ladies Grant had met on Sunday approached him as he walked through the door. "Are you looking for Edwina?"

"What? Edwina? No, I'm here to see Sheriff McInnis."

She looked around the common area. "He must be in his room." Grant made his way to the sheriff's room. He opened the door as he knocked.

"Hey, Grant. Come on in."

Jade and the sheriff were finishing their lunch. He greeted Jade, then spoke to the sheriff. "You feel like going to the museum, Sheriff?"

The sheriff had a thought. It was worth a try. "Jade, come go with us?"

Jade was startled by the suggestion. "I can't, Sheriff. I have to work." But, oh she wanted to go!

"Now, I can't leave the nursing home without a nurse. Come on. I'll ask Becky." The sheriff, Grant, and Jade made their way to the exit. Becky allowed Jade to go with the sheriff. He was one of the few residents that was healthy enough to leave. It was great therapy for him, and he was Becky's favorite, too. So her telling him no was not likely to happen.

"Grant, what are you doing with a dog?"

Grant explained the circumstances surrounding Max's trip to Mississippi. He left out the part about Samantha's move. He just said she was out of town on business. "I need to find a place where I can keep him. Any ideas?"

Jade spoke up. "He can stay at my house. I live out in the

country." Jade was sitting in the back and petting the lab. "What's his name?"

"His name is Max. And I can't impose on you, Jade. But thanks."

Jade thought about Lad. "It would be no imposition. My nephew would love him."

Grant's mind rewound to McDonald's. "Oh, I saw you with him at McDonald's Sunday night. I guess that was him."

"He's my sister's baby. I'm keeping him for a while. I have no children of my own." Jade wondered why she threw that in. Maybe he did not notice her obvious effort at self-marketing. Grant did not seem like the type of guy that was interested in a pre-existing family.

"Well, Max has been an inside dog, but not by his choice. He loves the outdoors. Do you have a fenced yard?"

Jade did not, but she quickly recovered. "No fence, but he can stay in my room at night." The sheriff smiled at Jade's eagerness.

They pulled into the courthouse parking lot and made their way to the elevator which took them to the fourth floor where the museum was located. A volunteer greeted them as they stepped off the elevator. She called each of them by name. Grant did not notice that she called his name, too. Another indication that he was home.

While Grant and the sheriff read the papers detailing the criminal conspiracy that unraveled and eventually freed Brandon, Jade found the papers from the fall of 1994. There he was, Michael Hicks. A front-page story was titled: "Former State Senator Takes Own Life." Jade peeked over the top of the paper to make sure that Grant was occupied as she read the article.

The article detailed the contributions Senator Hicks made during his brief stay in the Senate. There were quotes from local people expressing shock and grief and listing the many ways the senator and attorney had helped them or helped someone they knew. Senator Hicks had been defeated in the 1991 election and had been sued by a disgruntled client over a land matter. On the morning of the trial, he did not show up for court. He was found in his office by his secretary, Suzanne Pattie. One single shot to the temple, and Michael Hicks was dead at only forty-six years of age.

Jade felt herself tearing up when she heard Grant. "What has you so occupied, Jade? We are finished."

Startled, she quickly folded the paper before Grant could see what she was reading. "Oh, I'm sorry. Just reading these old papers. I was gone from here twelve years and did not keep up with things around here when I was gone." She hoped her answer was acceptable.

"Where did you move to?" Grant and Jade had something in common. They both had moved away. Grant's dad used to say that people needed to move away for a while to gain a broader perspective on life.

"Oh, it's silly, but I went to Hollywood trying to hit the big screen."

Grant respected that. She had courage. "Sounds adventurous. By yourself?"

"Yep, eighteen and ignorant. I moved back here five years ago." Jade felt she was admitting failure to Grant.

"That's cool."

They had made their way back to the SUV and had begun heading toward the nursing home when the sheriff spoke. "Grant, dial the nursing home for me, 555-2371." Grant dialed the number and handed the phone to the sheriff. "I need to speak to Becky, please." Jade and Grant both looked at the sheriff. "Becky, Grant Hicks and I are going to see Brandon Smallwood in a bit, and I need Jade to go with me. We'll be back before 5:00." The sheriff thanked Becky and handed the phone to Grant. "Turn around. We're going to take Max to Jade's. Then we're going to see Brandon."

Grant turned the SUV around, and they headed toward Jade's. As they crossed the Chickasawhay River bridge, Grant saw

Pete Ball walking with a gas can in his hand. Pete waved him down once more. When Grant rolled the passenger window down, Pete spoke. "Hey, Sheriff. What happened to yore car?"

The sheriff ignored the question. "Get in, Pete."

Pete opened the back door and got in. "Hey, feller, my truck should be in the same place you picked me up." Pete looked at Max and Jade, then back at the men. "Sheriff, I need to find a notorious republican."

The sheriff did not act like the question was out of the ordinary. "What you need one of them for, Pete?"

Pete pulled a sheet of paper out of his shirt pocket. "I need to sign this for my Social Security." He handed the paper to the sheriff.

"Pete, you mean a notary public." The sheriff grinned at Grant.

"Yea, that's what I said."

The sheriff handed the paper back to Pete. "Stop by the Circuit Clerk's office on your way back through town. She'll notarize it for you."

Pete put the paper back in his pocket. "Hey, Sheriff, you member when Robert Coxwell pissed on Johnny Newbill's leg?"

The sheriff tried to cut him off before he explained further. "Pete, there is a lady present."

Jade sat in silence as Pete looked at her. "I'm sorry, lady. Sheriff, that night was so dark that Robert didn't see Johnny. You member what Robert said to Johnny when Johnny jumped on him?" The sheriff did not respond. It was obvious Pete was going to finish the story. "He said, 'But we buddies, ain't we?'" Pete laughed hysterically, then looked at Jade. "Robert had a clopper, too."

Jade took the bait and hesitantly asked. "A clopper?" Biting her bottom lip in anticipation, she nervously awaited his answer. Grant was amused as he watched Jade in the rearview mirror.

"Yeah, Robert never were circumcised. Has a clopper."

Fortunately, they had made it to Pete's truck and dropped him off. They all laughed as they pulled away.

chapter twenty-seven

THE SHERIFF WAITED IN THE RANGE Rover while Jade ran inside to change clothes, and Grant fixed Max a temporary place to stay. Grant brought along a portable chain to secure Max should it be necessary. He hated to tie his pet, but it was a must until Max adjusted to being in the country.

"Max, buddy, I'll be back to check on you later." Grant rubbed his head and filled his bowl with water and food. Max seemed content in Nana's plush St. Augustine grass. He looked at Grant as if to say, "Take your time. I'll be just fine."

The screen door slammed. Jade was ready. She was excited for the first time in a while. She sat in the back seat and listened to Grant and the sheriff discuss the incredible turn of events that led to Brandon's freedom. The conversation then turned back to 1989.

"Grant, how did you know Brandon was innocent? Was it a hunch?" The sheriff looked at Grant as he awaited his response.

"Sheriff, it's really hard to explain. I was in the same grade as Brandon from kindergarten through the eleventh grade when he was convicted. Brandon would get picked on a lot, especially in junior high. He never fought back. Never. Sheriff, Brandon does not have a mean bone in his body."

The two stared at the road as Grant drove. Sheriff McInnis broke the silence. "I know y'all visited a lot when he was in jail awaiting trial."

Grant then looked at the sheriff. "When I heard Tony Sylvestor was shot and that Brandon was arrested and charged with the crime, I knew in my gut that the wrong person had been arrested. It made no sense. Brandon was trying to make it through high school and go to a place where he could be himself. He almost made it."

"Grant, I know you underwent a lot of criticism for being his friend. I know it affected your life, too." Grant focused on the road even more intently. He was pondering the sheriff's statement. He did pay a price, but not anything close to the price Brandon paid. Jade was assimilating the information. She now had bits and pieces of this very complicated puzzle and would wait with patience a time until all the parts were in their proper places. She had several questions but felt it was perhaps not her place to ask.

"Sheriff, when did you believe Brandon was innocent?"

The sheriff looked at Grant. "To be honest, Grant, I did not believe in Brandon until right at the very end. But my curiosity was piqued, so I thought I'd investigate on my own a little. You see, the Mississippi Bureau of Investigations took the case over from the beginning. Since it was one of my officers, my deputies and I were understandably angry. At the time, I agreed. Tony was my best deputy. It made sense for an independent agency to take over the investigation. Boy, was I wrong." The sheriff's voice trailed off at the end.

"Sheriff, what caused you to be curious?" Grant took his eyes off the road to look at the sheriff.

"It was a sixteen-year-old kid who had nothing to gain and everything to lose who believed Brandon." The sheriff turned to look at Grant. "It was you, son."

They turned onto Jonathan Road and made it to Brandon's drive. Grant stopped the vehicle and looked at the sheriff. "Sheriff McInnis, thanks for believing in Brandon...and in me." Jade did not move a muscle. She barely breathed. She did not want to interrupt them with the slightest movement or noise.

"Grant, I watched and listened to you visit with Brandon one night. It was a Sunday night. I usually did not monitor visits, but I had to come by the jail to assist in a child custody exchange that night. I saw you walk in, so I followed and stood behind the one-way mirror and observed." The sheriff had Grant's unwavering attention. "Brandon told you his side of the story. I watched as you believed him. You promised to do what it took to help him prove his innocence. You told him you were going to talk to your dad about helping him." Grant's eyes left the sheriff and looked out his window and into the woods. Grant was closing up again. The mention of his dad did that to Grant. "Grant, you and I and the rest of this county know why Brandon was convicted. The evidence was scant. Brandon just happened to walk out of those woods up at Piave at the wrong time. People were angry. And that anger found a place to rest. It rested on Brandon Smallwood."

Jade wanted the conversation to continue. She hoped it would. Grant put the vehicle in drive, and they eased down the narrow road that opened into the Smallwoods' yard. Nothing further was said. Jade would have to wait.

Elsie, looking more frail herself, walked out on the porch to greet them. "Y'all come on in. Hey, Sheriff McInnis, Grant...." She then looked at Jade.

"Hey, Ms. Elsie, I'm Jade Lott."

Elsie finally smiled. "I remember you, Jade. You cut your

hair." Jade smiled and hugged Elsie. They then walked into the kitchen.

"Oh, Ms. Smallwood, I brought you something." Grant walked back to the Range Rover while the others sat down at the kitchen table. A few minutes later, Grant walked into the kitchen holding a microwave oven. "Where can I plug this in for you?"

Ms. Elsie got up to clear a spot on the counter. "Grant, you didn't have to do this." Grant placed the microwave on the counter and realized he would need to buy an adapter to plug it in. Elsie's house was so old that the outlets were not equipped for the microwave's three-prong plug.

Jade had gotten up to help. "They have those at the Dollar Store, Ms. Elsie. I can pick up one after work and run it out here to you." Grant looked at Jade and noted the ease by which the kind gesture left her lips.

"Grant, this will be a big help. Thank you." Elsie hugged Grant. She then looked at Jade, "I can give you the money for the adapter, Jade." Jade assured her that it would not be necessary.

The sheriff then spoke. "Ms. Elsie, how's Brandon today?"

Elsie sat back down. Jade and Grant stood and leaned against the counter. "He had a pretty good morning. Reverend Clark and Terry Lowery visited him this morning. They told him about the benefit the county was giving for him." Grant's heart hardened. Hypocrites! He wondered why the Smallwoods did not tell them to take their benefit and stuff it.

"Momma." Brandon's dim voice found its way to the kitchen.

Elsie got up. "Let me see if he's feeling like company." She walked down the hall to Brandon's room. Grant, Jade, and Sheriff McInnis waited in the kitchen without conversation. "Y'all come on back." Jade refused the customary ladies-first and followed behind Grant who followed the sheriff.

"Brandon, look who came to see you. You remember Sheriff McInnis?"

Brandon looked smaller to Grant than when he had seen him on Sunday. Death could not be far away. Brandon's eyes could only focus on one object at a time, and at the moment, his attention was on Lauvon McInnis. Brandon painfully swallowed. "Hey, Sheriff." He swallowed again. "Kind of you to come."

"Brandon, I'm honored. I'm happy to see you again."

Brandon cracked a slight smile. His head slowly moved and found Grant. "Grant." Brandon's smile grew slightly brighter.

Grant walked over and placed his hand on top of Brandon's. "Hey, Buddy. I told you I'd be back. I missed you." A tear welled up in Brandon's eye and slowly puddled on the lid before spilling over. Time and space had kept the friends apart, but their hearts had never separated. Jade felt honored to witness this special bond. "Brandon, do you remember Jade Lott?"

Jade was caught off guard by the sudden introduction. She was on the opposite side of the room from the sheriff and Grant. She quickly wiped the tears from her eyes and brushed them on her pants leg. She then joined Grant so that Brandon would not have to turn his head. "Hey, Brandon."

The sheriff stood so that Jade could sit in the chair next to Brandon's bed. Jade sat down and held Brandon's left hand with both of hers. Brandon's eyes combed Jade's face and hair as Jade silently let him familiarize himself with her. She hoped he would remember her, but would not have been surprised if he didn't. Brandon attempted to swallow, but his mouth was too dry. Jade gave him a sip of the juice by the bed.

"Hair?"

Though her eyes were glossy from the tears, Jade laughed. "You remember! Yes, I cut my hair." Grant watched Brandon as he looked at Jade with the movement only a snail could imitate. The cancer was feverishly working on every aspect of Brandon's body.

"Thanks for coming."

The sheriff walked over and touched Brandon's shoulder. "Brandon, we're going to let you sleep."

Brandon's eyes moved toward the sheriff. "Sheriff?"

"Yes, Brandon." The sheriff waited on Brandon to speak.

"They...giving...a benefit." The visitors could see this pleased Brandon. The people most deserving of Brandon's justifiable wrath extended their collective hands, offering repentance toward Brandon in the only way they knew how. And the community's gesture touched Brandon deeply.

As the old sheriff, battered by a stroke and time, looked down at Brandon, he, too, felt that familiar feeling that a man feels when the tears are pounding against a dam of manhood. "Brandon, these people love you. This county loves you. I know I can speak on behalf of them when I say that they, we, are so very sorry."

Brandon used every bit of the strength in his body to smile through the unbearable pain that only morphine could hold at bay. "I love them, too. They've forgiven me, Sheriff." Brandon closed his eyes and fell asleep. Everyone slowly left the room. They each hugged Elsie and told her good-bye. Grant informed Elsie he would be back in the morning. The ride back to the nursing home would be a quiet one.

chapter twenty-eight

GRANT AND HIS PASSENGERS PULLED INTO the parking lot of the nursing home at 4:00 p.m. They each had left a part of themselves at Brandon's.

"Grant, where will you stay?" The sheriff looked at Grant before he exited the Range Rover.

"I have a room reserved at The Grand Avenue Inn here in town. I'm about to go check in." Grant walked to the passenger's side to assist Jade in making sure the sheriff got out of the SUV safely.

"Jade, I'll come by later to check on Max if that's okay?"

Jade's stomach became queasy. Here was her chance. "Sure. Uhh, do you have supper plans?"

Grant knew he was back home as *dinner* became *supper*. Grant did not want to impose on Jade's kindness. She already was housing Max. "Oh, that's okay. I can pick up something in town."

The sheriff squinted his eye at Grant. "Boy, don't ever turn down a home-cooked meal."

Grant looked at the sheriff, then back at Jade. "Are you sure?"

Jade smiled. "Of course, I'm sure. You can meet Nana. She is my grandmother. You can also meet Lad." A hint of gloom fell on Jade as she realized that she was now officially tied down in the evenings.

"Okay. I'm going to see my Uncle Ronny after I check in. I'll head your way after that. Need me to bring anything? Perhaps some wine?"

The sheriff and Jade laughed. Greene County was still dry, except for a couple of local bootleggers, and all they sold was beer. The sheriff patted Grant on the shoulder. "Grant, son, this place is still dry."

Jade responded, "Just bring yourself. See you in a couple of hours." The sheriff and Jade walked arm in arm into the nursing home.

Grant checked in at the Grand Avenue Inn, but he soon left town heading toward Saint Ellen. He then dialed Samantha's number.

"Hello, Grant."

"Hey, Sam."

"I assume you made it safely back to Mississippi?"

Grant pulled his cell phone from his ear to see if he had adequate cell reception. He had two bars. "Yes. I'm here. I'm driving out to my uncle's house, and I don't have very good reception. I wanted to make sure you made it to your grandma's okay."

Sam could hear Grant's phone breaking up from the obviously poor reception. "Yes, I'm here. I'm about to tell her my news. I'll call you tonight."

As Grant responded, his cell phone dropped Sam's call. Cell reception was horrible in the woods of Greene County. The county was one of Mississippi's most rural. There was not a traffic light in the entire county, and the people counted that as a blessing.

Grant remembered exactly how to get to his grandparents' old place. It was a shotgun, A-framed house with two bedrooms and porches that extended across the front and back. It rested on forty acres just off Saint Ellen Road. When Grant pulled up to the house, he noticed a lady sitting on the front steps.

Grant walked to the steps. "Hello. Is Ronny here?"

She was smoking a Virginia Slim. She blew the smoke straight up as if she were blowing it up her nose. "He's in there sleeping on the couch."

Grant pondered his next step. She seemed bothered by his presence. She was skinny and had long, stringy hair which was peppered with gray and black. "My name is Grant Hicks." He extended his hand in a weak attempt to shake her hand. She was looking down the road and either did not see his attempt at courtesy or did not care for it.

"I'm leaving his ass as soon as I finish this pack of cigarettes."

Grant looked at the cigarettes resting on the steps beside her. The pack was almost full. She would be here a while. The door opened. It was Uncle Ronny. "Hey, Grant. I see you and Dana have met." Grant did not feel it necessary to explain that he really had not met her. He was glad Ronny had come to his rescue. "Come on up and have a seat." They sat down on the porch as Dana began to get off the steps to walk inside. "Hey, Grant. Want a beer?" Although the county was dry, that did not prevent those who preferred adult beverages from indulging.

"Sure."

Dana stopped at the door and looked at her husband. Ronny held his hand up in Dana's direction as if he were a crossing guard at a busy intersection. "What kind you want?"

Grant looked at Dana who appeared extremely annoyed. It was obvious Grant had interrupted an argument. "Do you have a Heineken?"

Ronny looked at Dana. "Old Lady, bring the boy a Heineken

and me a Bud Light." Without a word she walked into the house.

"I hear you in town to see Brandon Smallwood, Grant. He still a queer?" His words scraped across Grant's ears like fingernails across a chalkboard. Dana walked back onto the porch with two Bud Lights. Grant was afraid not to take it. "Sorry, Grant, but our neighborhood bootlegger only carries Bud Light." Uncle Ronny popped the top and devoured at least half the can before catching his breath.

"No problem. This is fine." He looked at Dana. "Thank you, ma'am." She walked back into the house without uttering a word.

"When was the last time you been to this place, Grant?"

Grant looked around at the rundown place. "I really don't know. Maybe when I was ten or eleven." Grant took a swallow of his beer.

"Me and yo daddy growed up here. We had some crazy times out here. I remember one Saturday mornin me and Mike was in the den playin when some Jehovah's Witnesses pulled up. Momma came runnin in there screamin, 'Hide, hide!' Me, Mike and Momma jumped behind the couch. Mike got to cryin, and Momma held his mouth. Me and Mike didn't know what the hell was goin on. I remember thinkin them Jehovah Witnesses must be some bad-ass people." Grant cracked a smile at the thought of them hiding. He was also thinking this little visit was a mistake. "You look just like yore daddy, boy." Ronny was grinning from ear to ear. "I miss him. I know we weren't close, but I still miss him."

As Ronny spoke of his brother, Grant's mind drifted to his sister, Lauren. He wondered how she was doing. "Uncle Ronny, what do you do for a living?"

Ronny belched, catching it in his mouth before blowing the gas into the atmosphere. "I do a little plumbing here and there. Daddy did teach me a trade. I stay as busy as I want to be." Grant noticed the yard full of fishing gear. Drying out from Ronny's latest fishing expedition, trotlines stretched from the trees. "But yo daddy was different. Daddy used to get so mad at Mike. No matter how hard Daddy tried to teach him, he just didn't get it. It used to piss Daddy off. So he gave up on teachin him and taught me I guess."

Grant's interest in his dad's childhood had ignited without his realizing it. "Is that why Dad ended up going to college, Uncle Ronny?" Grant took another swallow of his beer.

"I reckon. Once yore daddy started college, it changed him. We kinda drifted apart." The phone rang, and Grant could hear Dana speaking to an obvious bill collector.

"How so?"

Ronny had finished his beer and belted out orders for another one. "He started makin good grades, getting awards, and shit. He got his picture in the paper. Started usin long words and braggin a lot. No offense, but we all felt like he got above his raisin."

Dana brought two more beers. Grant set his down beside him. His first beer had barely been touched. "I see. I wondered why y'all were not close."

Ronny popped the top of his second beer. "But we had some good times growin up. I wished things would have turned out different." Grant could sense another childhood story coming. "Daddy used to play poker here on Saturday nights with our Uncle Cletus and their buddies. Me and Mike liked to watch 'em play. One night a car pulled up, and Mike went to look out the winder at who it was. When he said it was Brother Deweese, the preacher, you should have seen them men scatter. They went out the back door and to the barn. Me and Mike run with 'em. We didn't know what the hell was happenin. Uncle Cletus was chain-smokin Pall Mall cigarettes and justa cussin that preacher for messin up their card game. We later learned it was a sin to play poker." Ronny laughed at himself.

"Did the preacher ever find out?"

"I don't know, but I remember thinkin Uncle Cletus was shore nuf pissed." They sat in silence a few seconds. "Grant, I wish I woulda knowed yo daddy was depressed. I coulda saved him."

Grant stared at the ground not knowing what to say. "I believe it was all that success. Deep down he was still ole country Mike. He started gettin all those awards in college. Then he made a lawyer and become a senator. But when he lost, he never got over that. He was what they call a perfectionist." Grant did not come for this, but he was seeing a part of his daddy he never knew existed. "You know I almost kept yo daddy out of law school, Grant."

Grant looked at him with curiosity. "How?"

"When we was teenagers, we picked up two gals over in Hattiesburg and brought them back to Greene County. We was takin 'em to Uncle Cletus' camp. The road had washed out so we was walkin down that old road, and it was nighttime. One of them gals said, 'Where y'all takin us?' I looked at them and shined the flashlight on 'em and said, 'We aim to kill you ole gals.' They run like hell. They was screamin like they was mad. We like to never caught 'em and convinced 'em it was a joke. We had to take 'em home. Turns out one was a lawyer's daughter, and he wanted to press charges. But Sheriff Stringfellow talked him out of it and made us apologize. If we'd been charged, yo daddy never woulda made a lawyer."

Ronny finished his second beer. Grant stood. "I need to run, Uncle Ronny. I just wanted to come say hello."

Ronny walked Grant to the Range Rover. "Grant, yo daddy couldn't stand not bein perfect. Don't you get caught up in that shit like he did. You see, I turned out just like your Grandpa Hicks. I wished I could change who I am sometimes, but I can't." He reached in and patted Grant on the shoulder. "You come on back, Grant."

Ronny backed away from the SUV, and Grant turned around and made his way toward town. He thought of his dad's childhood and how his dad must have felt when he disappointed his own father. And for the first time in his life, Grant felt a hint of pity for Michael Hicks.

chapter twenty-nine

JADE LEFT THE NURSING HOME AND stopped by the Dollar Store to pick up an adapter for Elsie. While there, she picked up some basic kitchen and bathroom necessities for her. Helping people came naturally for Jade. She was just born that way. When she walked out to her car, Danny Narbo was leaning against the driver's side door. He was off duty and in street clothes. Jade sighed with frustration as she approached her car.

Danny smiled as Jade walked up. "What you doin Friday night, beautiful?"

Jade opened the trunk to put in the items she had purchased for Elsie. Danny did not offer to help. She added that to the many reasons not to like him. "I have a date." She lied, but, darn, it felt good!

"Who with? Jamie Walley?"

It was none of his business, but Jade continued. "He's not from here. You don't know him. I have to go, so if you will excuse me?"

Jade pushed her way past Danny to her car door. Danny then grabbed her arm a little too firmly. "Jade, I'm going to keep asking until you say yes. So why not get it over with. I'm no dummy, Jade. You're single and in your thirties. I know you have needs, too." Jade jerked her arm away from Danny, got in her car, slammed the door, and left. Danny was getting more and more aggressive with her. She knew she had to find a way to keep him from harassing her. However, she did not want to say anything to worry Nana or overreact to the situation. Maybe he would finally get the message.

Jade and Elsie had a delightful visit while Jade taught Elsie how to use the microwave. Elsie was grateful for the supplies, too. They hugged good-bye. Then Jade left to pick up Lad from the daycare and head home to prepare supper for Grant. She suddenly became nervous again as she wondered if Grant would enjoy her cooking.

Grant left his Uncle Ronny's and drove to the road which led to the Hicks Family Cemetery. The two-path road turned off a dirt road and was lined with huge water oaks with woods reaching for miles on each side. The old cemetery housed three family trees that began with Theobald Hicks in 1855. The road sign simply read *Cemetery Road*. Grant pulled into the road and stopped. His daddy was down there. A part of him wanted to go see him. Grant's hands were slightly shaking. He looked in his rearview mirror as if traffic were backed up for miles. His right foot was on the brake as the SUV idled. A rabbit eased into the road and slowly crossed. Grant sat there a few minutes before putting the Range Rover in reverse and slowly backing out. His nerves prevented him from going any further.

Grant arrived at Jade's and noticed Max was no longer tied in the yard. He wondered where the lab was. He hoped Max had not broken loose and run away. Jade met him at the door. "Come in, Grant."

Grant stepped inside and saw Max lying on the floor as if he had always lived there. Lad was sitting as close to Max as he could without being on top of the dog. It was obvious the child and the dog had become friends. Grant kneeled down beside them. "I bet your name is Lad. I see you and Max have met." The boy stared at Grant without expression while Max wagged his tail.

"Lad loves Max. This is the most I've seen him smile since I got him on Sunday. Come into the kitchen. I want to introduce you to Nana." Grant stood and followed Jade toward the kitchen. The smell was intoxicating. Grant and Sam rarely had cooked, and when they did, it did not ignite his senses as he was experiencing now.

"Nana, Grant Hicks. Grant, this is my Nana, Lillie Lott."

Grant shook Nana's hand. "Nice to meet you, Ms. Lott. I hope Max is not an imposition."

Nana was seventy-nine years old, and she had never allowed a pet of any kind in her house. Nevertheless, she simply could not refuse Jade's request. "Oh, he's no problem. He's entertaining Lad. Have a seat." Grant joined Nana at the table while Jade finished serving the food. Jade then left to get Lad who was not happy that he had to leave his new friend. Jade put him in his highchair and wiped his hands.

"Jade, thanks for inviting me to dinner."

Jade smiled at Grant. "Nana and I enjoy company for supper."

Nana looked at Jade as if to remind her that it had been months or even years since anyone joined them for supper. Jade gave her a look of acknowledgment but hoped she would play along. "We sure do, Grant." With a guilty look, Nana peered at Jade as if she had just committed the unpardonable sin with her exaggeration.

"Wow, Jade, this is amazing." Grant looked at the

baked pork chops, butter beans, broiled new potatoes, salad, homemade biscuits, and, of course, sweet tea. "Did you cook all of this, Jade?"

"Oh, it was nothing. Nana made the biscuits. Mine would have been a disaster." Jade then looked at Nana. She meant to tell Nana before Grant arrived that they would not say the blessing tonight. Jade remembered Grant not closing his eyes during prayer at the auction. Jade was afraid that saying grace may make their guest feel uncomfortable.

As Jade was thinking, Nana spoke. "Grant, would you like to return thanks?" It was obvious that Nana's question caught Grant off guard. Jade's heart fell to the floor. Oh, how embarrassed she was for Grant, and for herself. Jade gave Nana a stern look.

"Well, I guess I can give it a try." Grant had not said a blessing before a meal since he lived at home with his mom and dad. Jade's nerves were beating at the wall of her stomach. "Momma taught me one when I was a kid. Let's see if I can remember it." Nana grabbed Jade's hand and then Grant's. Grant figured the system out, and he grabbed Jade's. The touch of her hand instantly gave him confidence. "Okay, here goes." They bowed their heads. "God is great, God is good. Let us thank Him for our food. Amen." He remembered! Grant, and Jade, were relieved. Nana became worried about the boy.

After the meal, Jade prepared Lad for bed, and he fell asleep in his great grandmother's lap. Grant took Max for a walk. A little later, he saw Jade walk out onto the porch and figured it was time to go. He and Max joined her there. "Thanks for everything, Jade. Keeping Max, getting the adapter for Elsie, cooking dinner. I owe you dinner now."

Jade barely could control her eagerness. "Oh, that's okay, Grant. It was nice having company. You going to see Brandon tomorrow?"

Grant reached down to pet Max. "Yes, I am. I will go out there around eight in the morning. You working?"

Jade sat down on the steps to pet Max. "Yes, same routine for me. Or new routine for me rather. I drop Lad off around 7:30 at the daycare and start work at 8:00."

Grant bent down to pet Max one last time. "I may stop by and see the sheriff tomorrow. If I do, I'll look you up and tell you how Brandon is doing."

Jade was pleased that Grant seemed to want to include her in Brandon's life. "I'll be looking for you." They said good-bye, and Grant began his drive back to town.

It had been another long, emotional day. Grant was once again exhausted. He wondered what tomorrow would bring. It had been one week since Elsie located him in Atlanta. Life can change on a dime when it is least expected. Grant had said good-bye to Sam and returned to the place he had hated for almost twenty years. Two unlikely scenarios combined as ingredients in the healing of Grant Hicks. But more ingredients were needed.

Part Five:

The Past

chapter thirty

GRANT CUT SHORT HIS MORNING RUN. Each time he would get into a rhythm, someone would stop and ask him if he needed a ride. Grant surmised the sight of someone running down Main Street must have been an oddity. He went back to the Grand Avenue Inn and selected one of Sam's books which he had brought with him to pass the time. Grant rarely read for entertainment. His job required constant reading, and the last thing he wanted to do with his leisure time was read. He had brought a couple Grisham books, but decided he needed a break from the law. He selected *A Confederacy of Dunces* by John Kennedy Toole. Grant had always wanted to meet Ignatius J. Reilly anyway.

Grant read for an hour and decided he would go out for breakfast before going to Brandon's. He showered and drove to the White Oak Restaurant. The parking lot was full. He opened the door, and every eye in the place landed on him. The lady behind the register instructed him to sit anywhere he liked. He walked to a table in the rear and sat with his back to the crowd.

A group of men entered and sat at the table behind him. Grant did not turn around to see who they were. He was reading the *Atlanta Journal Constitution* on his Blackberry when the waitress came to take his order. After she left him, she stopped at the table of men behind him. He could not help but overhear one man at the table going overboard in flirting with the waitress. Grant could tell she was uncomfortable with the overbearing man, but he decided to stay out of it. She finally managed to take their orders and retreat to the safety of the kitchen.

Their conversation suddenly interested Grant. Jade's name was mentioned. He adjusted his seat in order to catch a glimpse of who was discussing her. He recognized Danny Narbo from the convenience store on Sunday when Edwina mentioned that he harassed Jade. One of the other men was in work clothes for a local utility company, and the third man was in a prison guard uniform.

Danny was responding to a question from the guard when Grant picked up the conversation. "...not yet, but she'll come around. She's just playing hard to get."

"Danny, if you don't get her to go out with you soon, I'm going to ask her." The prison guard waited for Danny's approval.

"Jade is off limits to anyone in this town. If I can't have her, none of you pecker heads will."

Grant noticed the name on the shirt of the utility worker. His name was James. James chimed in. "You two boys can have her. I saw her with a nigger baby yesterday morning." Grant instinctively looked at the table in anger. He was glaring at a table full of ignorance. The guard glanced in Grant's direction, but he escaped eye contact.

"That's her slutty sister's baby. He ain't Jade's. When I marry her, we'll send that nigger baby to an orphanage or something."

The waitress returned with Grant's order and she once again had to endure the collective stupidity that sat ten feet away.

The door to the restaurant opened, and Edwina walked in. She had the eyes of a hawk and came straight to Grant's table. "Hey, Yankee."

Grant, for the first time, was glad to see her. "Sit down, Edwina." Grant stood to pull out a chair for her.

"Can't stay. I called in a to-go order. Got to be at work in a few minutes." She looked at Danny's table and frowned. Grant noticed they were quiet all of a sudden. "Yankee, what you doin tonight?"

Grant had no plans. But he was reluctant to admit it for fear of Edwina's proposal. "I'm not sure yet." The lady at the front called out to Edwina that her order was ready.

"We's have a fellowship supper at church tonight. I want you to come. Meet my Pastor. Willie Mimbes. Jade gonna come. She says she know you."

All three men looked at Grant awaiting his response. Grant could feel their stares. It thrilled him. "Sure, what time?" Edwina told him to be there at 6:00 p.m.; then she left. Grant sat back down to finish his breakfast. He could hear their whispers. Some people just do not know how to whisper. They wondered who the damn Yankee was.

Grant arrived at the Smallwoods a little after 8:00 a.m. They were expecting him. Elsie had her own doctor's appointment at 9:00 a.m., and she was awaiting Reverend Clark's arrival so that he could sit with Brandon while she was away.

"Hey, Ms. Elsie. How are you today?"

She gave her usual response. "Just fine. Come on back. Brandon's awake." They entered the room as Brandon opened his eyes.

"Good morning, Brandon." Grant sat in the chair beside the bed. The phone rang in the kitchen, and Elsie left to answer it.

"Hey. Good to see you."

Grant looked at the Foley bag that was fastened to the bed railing. It contained less fluid than usual at this time of day. "You, too, buddy. I hear this town is going to have the biggest community benefit in the history of Greene County." Grant had seen how encouraged Brandon looked yesterday when his dying friend mentioned the benefit to Sheriff McInnis. He sensed Brandon was down, and he thought the mention of it would help.

"Grant, I'm scared."

Grant did not know how to respond. He wondered what words to muster to allay his friend's fear. He leaned toward the bed. "Brandon, you are the bravest person I have ever met." Grant hoped that would do it. It did not.

"Do brave people get scared?" Brandon's eyes would not leave Grant's.

"I guess they do, Brandon. We all get scared." Grant was losing this battle. Where the hell was Reverend Clark when he needed him most?

"What scares you?"

Grant was forced to answer a question. He wanted to say something admirable. He could not. "To be honest, Brandon, lots of things."

"What scares you the most?"

Grant thought for a few seconds more. He knew the answer. There was nobody in the room, and Brandon was dying, so he thought he could admit it. "Failure, Brandon. Failure scares me the most."

Brandon's weakening mind tried to comprehend Grant's answer. "How do you keep from being scared?"

Grant looked at Brandon, and without a hint of hesitation he answered. "I outwork everybody, Brandon. I accomplish my goal. And when I do, I accomplish another one and then another one and just keep doing it."

Brandon squinted his eyes at Grant. "Well, I shall accomplish death." Oh my God! Grant did not expect that response. Grant utterly failed in his efforts to defeat Brandon's fear. He looked at the door for Reverend Clark, but no one came. He looked back at Brandon. He was speechless and nervous. "Grant, don't be afraid."

Grant's efforts to cheer up Brandon now had the dying friend trying to encourage him. Grant felt dirty, selfish, and ashamed. "Okay, Brandon. How about let's both be afraid together. That way we got each other's back." Grant thought Zig Ziglar would not be proud of his effort at being positive.

"Okay, Grant...." Brandon closed his eyes and fell back to sleep. Grant looked around the room. He was glad the conversation had no witnesses. The superstar of Rimes and Yancey had crashed and burned. But at least there was no court reporter transcribing the conversation and no jury sitting in the box. He left the bedroom and joined Elsie in the kitchen.

"Reverend Clark called. He thinks he has a touch of a virus, and he's afraid to be around Brandon." Elsie was looking through the phone book for her doctor's number. "I need to cancel my appointment."

"I can sit with Brandon, Ms. Elsie."

It took some encouragement, but Elsie eventually agreed. Grant gave her his cell phone in case he needed her. A house phone was all Elsie could afford. He showed her how to answer the Blackberry and sent her on her way. Grant sat by Brandon's bed for the next two hours pondering his fear. He thought of his Uncle Ronny's description of his dad. The hint of pity he had felt the day before when he learned of his dad's failing his grandpa had grown into empathy. For the first time, he had begun to wonder how his dad had felt before he pulled the trigger. Grant still wanted to hate his dad, but his heart encouraged him to dig deeper. Grant decided that he would learn more about the man that he had hated for over twenty years. Grant would soon discover that by doing so, he was about to meet himself.

chapter thirty-one

GRANT STAYED WITH ELSIE UNTIL Brandon woke up mid-afternoon. The home health nurse was there treating him during the brief time that he was awake. He was getting weaker. His body fluids were decreasing, and his body was getting smaller. Jesse Bolton had a frank discussion with Elsie and told her it was close to the time when Brandon would not be able to talk, and when he did, it would be the morphine speaking.

Grant listened to Elsie and the nurse as he stood in the hall. The door to Elsie's bedroom was open, so he leaned against the facing and peered inside. The door was always closed before. Elsie's room was barren. It contained an old bed with a steel headboard, a night stand, a lamp with a tattered shade, and a dresser with an opening where a drawer once was. Her closet was open, and it was essentially empty. There were four or five dresses hanging neatly in the closet along with an old winter coat. Three pairs of worn dress shoes were lying on the floor. Grant thought of his house full of toys in Atlanta. He wondered why he had not heard Elsie complain. She truly was a remarkable lady.

Grant left the Smallwoods and stopped by the nursing home to see the sheriff. Jade, Edwina, and some other employees were visiting at the work station.

"Hey, you." Jade saw him first.

"Hey, Jade. Hey, Edwina. Ladies." Grant looked out at the common area and noticed a small group of residents playing bingo as an aide yelled out the letters and numbers.

"Yankee, don't forget about church tonight."

Grant remembered back to the White Oak. He only accepted to piss off the rednecks at the table next to him, but he could not back out now. "I haven't. I'd like to bring something. Any ideas?"

Edwina jumped at the offer. "No. But you can run me to Lucedale when I get off work at 4:30. I need to pick up a fruit tray from the deli at Walmarts."

Grant noticed Edwina did not ask. It was more of an order. "Okay. I can do that."

Edwina looked at Jade. "You comin, too." The thought of Jade going comforted Grant.

"Edwina, I have to pick up Lad." Grant peered back at Edwina. Surely she would not let that weak excuse be acceptable.

"Jade Lott! You got to go. I don't want to be seen alone with no Yankee."

Jade and Grant smiled and looked at each other. Grant assisted Edwina in encouraging Jade. "I have plenty of room, so I'll drive. Lad can come with us."

Grant then left to visit the sheriff. It was 3:00 p.m. Grant and the sheriff spent the next hour and a half discussing the events of the past. Tony Sylvestor was shot by a hit man hired by the Russian Mafia. The gravel pit in the Rounsaville community was owned by a company which was owned by a company which was owned by the Russian Mafia. Almost three decades ago, they had infiltrated county government in Greene County through Frank Jenkins. Five current and former supervisors were arrested, a former chancery clerk, the former county board attorney, a former justice court judge, and several other current and former employees. A few of those implicated had already died. The syndicate involved everything from old-fashioned kickbacks to transfer and sale of drugs along with money-laundering. Tony had become suspicious when he was doing undercover narcotics work and had witnessed Frank Jenkins' former road foreman accepting a package from a suspected drug dealer. Tony was beginning to connect the dots. Thus, his elimination became a necessity.

"Sheriff, tell me about the morning Tony got shot." Like a child listening to his wise grandfather, Grant tuned in.

"Tony loved to hunt. It was January 1, 1989. He had planted a ryegrass patch on a neighbor's land which abutted the national forest in Piave. He climbed into his treestand right before daylight. Just when it got light enough to see a little, a single shot was heard by some area hunters and, as you know, by Brandon. The bullet entered the back of Tony's neck and exited the front as quickly as it arrived. Tony probably never heard the shot or felt the pain. It was instant death."

Grant remembered most of these details. "Where were you that morning, Sheriff?"

"I was at July Barkley's house. July had been drinking all night, and his wife could not take his abuse any longer, so she called the house. As I was walking to my patrol car after settling the Barkleys down, I heard my radio dispatcher frantically trying to get in contact with me. It was awful. Just awful."

"Sheriff, do you remember when you first saw Brandon that morning?"

The sheriff had his fingertip touching his lip as he thought about the question. "By the time I got there, Brandon was sitting in the back of a patrol car. He had no idea why. As you know, he and the Johnson boy had camped out. The Johnson boy had left a good bit before Brandon. When Brandon walked out of those woods, he walked right into police cars from eight counties and numerous highway patrol. Wrong place, wrong time." Both the sheriff and Grant had the look of two men struggling to turn back the clock to correct all the wrongs that had occurred that long-ago morning. They could not.

"Sheriff, Brandon went to trial in July that year. I know enough about criminal law to realize that his prosecution was on the fast track."

Grant waited on the sheriff to respond. "People were angry. Law enforcement wanted closure, too. We had a new district attorney who was a camera hound, and he saw fit to keep the story in the news and in the courtroom. He had the resources of the state of Mississippi behind him. Brandon was defended by Ray Boutwell, the laziest public defender in the state, and had no resources."

"Sheriff, what evidence did the jury have before it that came close to convicting Brandon beyond a reasonable doubt?"

The sheriff appeared to be getting angry. "Not much. He was in those woods that morning, and the shooter used a .30-06 high-powered rifle. The shooter apparently dropped a sleeve of cartridges either going in or coming out of those woods. Brandon had the misfortune of finding it. The cartridges were in his pocket when he was searched. No gun was ever found." Grant and the sheriff sat in silence for a few moments.

"Grant, would you have put Brandon on the stand?"

The sheriff looked at Grant as he pondered the question. "I'm not a criminal attorney, so I really can't say. Brandon had an alibi. Unfortunately, Tommy Johnson was going to deny his presence with Brandon. By the way, whatever happened to Tommy?"

The sheriff's eyes turned to look out the window. "The last I heard he was in Atlanta, too."

Grant pondered how small the world was. The sheriff seemed

tired, so Grant decided to continue their discussion another day. As hard as we try sometimes, discussing events of the past simply cannot change them. But it helps us just the same.

chapter thirty-two

EDWINA, JADE, LAD, AND GRANT ARRIVED at Walmart in Lucedale just before 5:00 p.m. They split up to go purchase the items they each needed and agreed to meet by the entrance when done. Grant finished first and was sitting on the bench near the door when he heard a familiar voice.

"Hey, feller." It was the ever-present Pete Ball.

"Hey, Pete."

Pete sat down next to Grant. "I saw yore van outside and thought I would catch a ride back to Leakesville."

Grant was amused that Pete could confuse an $80,000 Range Rover for a van. "Uhh. Well, I have some people with me, but I guess you can." Grant wondered how his riders would react to their new passenger.

"Much obliged. My truck's in the shop. I'll be right back."

Pete disappeared into the store. After a few minutes, Edwina, Jade, and Lad appeared with their items and ready to go.

"Uhh, we can't leave just yet. We have company riding back with us to Leakesville."

Before they could inquire, Pete walked up. "I'm ready."

The crew headed to the Range Rover. Pete got in front with Grant, and the ladies sat in back with Lad. It did not take long for Pete to start talking. "Robert Coxwell has got the pneumonia. Johnny Newbill says he might not make it."

Grant decided he was going to take the offensive with Pete today. "That's terrible, Pete. By the way, who's Johnny Newbill?" This was the third time Pete had been in Grant's vehicle and the third time Johnny Newbill's name had been mentioned.

"You ain't never heard of Johnny Newbill? Feller, where you been?" Grant decided not to explain. "Johnny Newbill is the baddest man around."

Edwina thought she would chime in. "I know him. He's a scrawny fella."

Pete's head shot back toward Edwina. "Ooh wee, you better not let Johnny Newbill hear you say that. He'll whoop yore ass." Edwina rolled her eyes.

Grant responded to Pete's obvious worship of Johnny Newbill. "I bet Johnny Ray Barfield can whip him." After all, Johnny Ray was part cheetah, part deer, and part alligator.

Pete looked at Grant with total shock that anyone would suggest that Johnny Newbill could be whipped. "Shoot, Johnny Newbill can whip him with one hand and make a sandwich with the other. Johnny may be a little piece of leather, but he's well put together."

Edwina smirked. "You think you a Longfella or somebody?" Jade was taking it all in. Lad had dozed off in his car seat.

Pete ignored Edwina's remark. "You know what makes Robert's pneumonia so bad?" Grant was afraid to ask. But he did not need to. Pete kept talking. "He caught it from a dog, and the dog caught it from a nigger man." Grant was taking a drink from his water bottle and almost spit it all over the dash.

Edwina was about to explode. "Don't tell me you just went there. I oughta whoop your skinny white ass!"

Pete looked at Edwina as she awaited an apology. He then looked back at Grant. "I said nigger man not a nigger womern. I don't know why she so upset."

Jade tried to change the subject by discussing the weather. Edwina would have none of it as she glared at Pete. "You betta take that back!"

Grant looked at Pete. Grant was trying to figure out how to diffuse the situation when Pete spoke. "Feller, pull over. If she gonna talk to me that a way, I'll walk to Leakesville." Grant thought that was the best thing to do for Pete's safety. So they dropped him off at AJ's Quick Stop.

After they pulled back onto the highway, Edwina was still fuming. "Them rednecks are so ignorant! Make you want to slap the hell out of 'em."

Jade placed her hand on Edwina's knee. "Shug, I thought you were going to sock him."

Grant looked in the rearview mirror at Edwina. "Edwina, I do believe Mr. Pete Ball is afraid of you."

Edwina snorted, "He damn well better be! I'll whip his skinny ass next time, along with that squirrelly-lookin Johnny Newbill."

Jade changed the subject. "Edwina, I'm hungry. I hope there's plenty to eat at the church."

Edwina finally grinned, "You won't go home with no empty stomach. I promise you that."

The church fellowship hall was bustling with activity. Children were running in and out of the building. Three large tables were filled with food of every variety. No one would leave hungry tonight. Reverend Mimbes, with one word, quieted the crowd. He had the deep, soothing voice of Barry White.

"Brothers and sisters, it is time to do what we do best. Eat!" The crowd laughed. Grant surveyed the flock, recognizing some folks from his days growing up here. Edwina had located a highchair and was helping Jade get Lad situated. Reverend Mimbes continued. "As is custom here at Temple Harvest, we invite our guests to be first in line. If you have a guest or guests, please introduce them so we can give them a hardy Temple Harvest welcome."

Individuals began introducing their guests. Edwina waited with pride to introduce her friends. She decided to go last. Her turn had come. "Brothas and Sistas," she said, hands behind her as she turned her body in rhythm with her words, "I brought with me tonight, Jade Lott. She work with me at the nursing home." The members of Temple Harvest clapped and welcomed Jade. "This little fella is her nephew, Ladetrus. We's call him Lad. He her sister baby, but she ran into a problem, and Jade takes him in." The crowd welcomed Lad who was oblivious to the attention. He was eating some mashed potatoes. "And, last but no ways least is my new friend, Grant Hicks. He a lawyer. He stay in Atlanta, Georgia." Edwina's eyes met Grant's, and they shared a look of compassion. "He in town to tell his friend Brandon Smallwood bye."

The people there knew all about the Brandon Smallwood story. As Grant was welcomed, Tyrone Burley watched him from the corner of the fellowship hall. He had not seen Grant since Brandon's trial.

Reverend Mimbes then spoke again. "To all our guests, you're always welcome here at Temple Harvest. We hope you enjoy our fellowship tonight." The reverend then blessed the food, and two lines formed in buffet style to begin the feast.

Edwina sat with Lad as Jade and Grant filled their plates. Edwina laughed at Jade having to help Grant manage the buffet. He was evidently a picky eater. Grant did not know how to tell the difference between white and dark meat fried chicken. The novice eventually held both plates while Jade filled them. They then joined Lad while Edwina got in line.

"How long have you known Edwina?"

Jade looked at Edwina. "Since I started working at the nursing home. She was working there when I arrived. She puts on a front, but she is a softy. I love her to death."

Grant looked at Edwina. "She is unique, but you can't help but like her."

Jade turned to Grant. "She wants a car. But she does not have a driver's license. Nor does she know how to drive."

Grant laughed. "Well, how in the world did she get on the fire department?"

Jade turned her attention back to Edwina as she progressed in the line. "She lives a block behind the fire station. She would always attend their monthly meetings. One night one of the men asked her if she would like to join the force." Jade then looked at Grant. "I've never seen her more excited. You would have thought she had won a million dollars." Jade's attention went back to Edwina as the happy hostess finished preparing her plate. "It was so sweet of them to ask her."

Edwina finally joined them at the table, and they ate and laughed at their previous conversation with Pete Ball. After they finished eating, Edwina took the empty plates to the kitchen and headed for the bread pudding. Tyrone finally got up the nerve to sit down next to Grant.

"Mr. Hicks? I'm Tyrone Burley."

Grant wiped the chicken grease from his fingertips and shook Tyrone's hand. "Hello, Mr. Burley. Good to meet you." Grant did not recognize him.

"I remember you, Mr. Hicks. I was on the town police force when you were in high school."

Grant still could not place him. "I'm sorry, Mr. Burley, for not remembering. I left right after high school, and I didn't get out much my senior year."

Tyrone looked as if he had the weight of the world on his shoulders. "Oh, that's okay. I would not expect you to remember.

You never got into any trouble, so we did not have a chance to meet."

Grant smiled. "I was kind of boring in high school. I used to ride around town a little, but that's about it." Jade and Edwina took Lad to the nursery to play and left Grant and Tyrone alone.

"Mr. Hicks...."

Grant interrupted. "Please call me Grant, Mr. Burley." Tyrone Burley was in his sixties, and Grant knew the protocol of respect.

"I was the last person to talk to your daddy, Grant." Grant's stomach suddenly ached. The only thing he could do was stare at Tyrone. "He was representing me in a case I had. I'd bought a car. It was a lemon, and he was handling my case for me." Grant did not know what to say, so he remained silent. "I went by his office the morning he died. I saw him pull into his office, so I followed him in to get an update on my case." Tyrone looked at the crowd as most were finishing up their meals. Grant was still speechless. Grant noticed Jade walk back into the room and begin talking with a group of ladies. She instantly knew something was wrong with Grant. The sparkle had left his eyes.

"We talked about the case and our children. He was sure proud of you. He had framed all those clips from the paper where you made honor roll at Ole Miss." Grant felt the knot growing in his throat. All he could do was stare into the crowd blankly. Jade was staring at him. "He was a good man. This town sure misses him. Glad you could be with us tonight." Tyrone got up from the table, patted Grant on the shoulder, and walked away.

Grant waited a few seconds and then walked out the side door of the fellowship hall. He found an old picnic table under some pine trees and sat down with his back to the building. Jade followed to see where he went, but she remained at a distance. He seemed okay, so she turned to go back inside.

Reverend Mimbes was standing behind her. "That young man needs a friend. I'm glad you and Edwina brought him tonight, Jade."

The concern was evident in Jade's eyes. "Reverend Mimbes,

he's so sad. I wish I knew how to help him."

The pastor looked at Jade. "Just keep being his friend. That's all you can do at this point." Jade thanked the reverend and left to check on Lad. Reverend Mimbes stared at Grant a few seconds more and reentered the fellowship hall to find Tyrone.

Grant silently cried at the thought of his daddy sharing his pride of his son's accomplishments just moments from ending his life. Grant wanted to talk to him. He wanted to ask him to forgive him, but he could not. Michael Hicks was Grant's hero as a child. He was perfect in Grant's eyes. But his dad made a mistake, and Grant never forgave him for it. He wanted to now, but he simply did not know how.

The crowd was thinning, so Grant prepared himself to reenter the fellowship hall and locate Edwina, Jade, and Lad. Reality hit him hard. His friend was dying. He was in the place he vowed never to return, and he was hurting. Samantha was about to be gone, and he could not run to the office to escape into his safe haven. His momma was in North Carolina, and he was estranged from his sister. He had no one to turn to, except for his daddy.

chapter thirty-three

IT WAS THURSDAY, MARCH 25. IT HAD BEEN nine days since Elsie first called Grant's office. He was supposed to be preparing for an upcoming trial. Instead, he was on his way to work in Elsie Smallwood's yard. In addition to helping Elsie, he thought it would keep him busy and occupy his mind. On his way to Hattiesburg to visit a neighbor in the hospital, Reverend Clark had dropped off his lawn equipment for Grant to use.

Grant had just finished the yard when Jade pulled into the driveway. It was a little after noon. She stepped out of her car and began to unload what was obviously food. She had called Elsie and insisted on bringing lunch. Grant once again was struck by her simple beauty. She wore khaki shorts that were a little short, but not too short. She had on a green pullover T-shirt with flip-flops and a small diamond necklace.

"Hey, you."

Grant looked a mess. There had not been an abundance of rain lately, and the mixture of sand and grass had left him dirty and sweaty. He did not wear a cap, so his normally ordered hair looked, well, disorderly. For the first time, he thought of his appearance and how he looked to Jade. "Hey, Jade, what are you doing here? I thought you had to work today?" Grant had a hand towel Elsie had given him, and he wiped his face.

"When you told me last night you were going to work in the yard, I thought I would take off this afternoon and clean and dust for Elsie. I brought everybody lunch. Come on."

They walked inside, and Elsie joined them at the table. "Grant, Reverend Clark called and will be here around 3:00. He asked if you wanted to fish with him at the creek when he got here." Grant had not been fishing since he used to go with his Uncle Cletus on the Chickasawhay as a child. He wondered if he still knew how.

Jade could not contain her enthusiasm. "I want to go. That'll be fun. I love to fish."

Grant suddenly had the craving to fish. "Sounds good. After I eat, and while y'all clean the house, I'm going to run to the Grand Avenue and take a shower." They finished their meal, and Jade and Elsie started cleaning the kitchen. Grant left to go clean up and change clothes. He was going fishing.

Brandon was mostly sleeping now. His body fluids were continuing to decrease, and the oxygen machine was helping him breathe. The hospice staff was taking good care of him, and Elsie sat beside his bed most of the day. She had to take a leave of absence from the cafeteria, but Terry Lowery had been collecting donated leave from school employees to keep Elsie on the payroll.

Before Grant left the Grand Avenue to drive back to the Smallwoods, he called Samantha. She was excited about her new adventure, and Grant was happy for her. Grant brought her up to speed on Brandon, and Sam told him she would email him when she arrived at her assignment location. Grant and Sam spent half an hour on the phone before awkwardly saying their good-byes. Their relationship was ending as quickly as it had begun. Neither felt compelled to explain the time in between.

When Grant arrived at the Smallwoods, Reverend Clark, who was rigging up three fishing poles, was sitting on the tailgate of his truck. "Hey, Grant, ready to catch some red bellies?"

"Yes, sir."

Elsie walked out on the porch followed by Jade. "Grant, come see what Jade has done to my house."

Grant walked inside. It looked like a new place. In two hours, Jade had worked a miracle. "Wow, Jade."

Elsie was smiling. "Kids, thank y'all. It looks so nice, both inside and out. Y'all are so sweet." Grant and Jade hugged Elsie and then rejoined Reverend Clark. They walked down a path to a small, dark fishing hole. The creek flowed so slowly it was like fishing in a miniature lake. Jade grabbed a cricket and put it on her hook. Reverend Clark and Grant followed her lead.

"Thanks for suggesting this, Brother Clark. I haven't been fishing in years."

"Glad you could join us, Jade." Grant's cork went under immediately, and he pulled a large red belly from Mason Creek. It was exhilarating.

"Way to go, Grant!" Jade was acting like a kid. Her cork disappeared, and she responded by pulling a bream from the creek.

"Good job, Jade! Do you want me to take it off the hook?" She declined Brother Clark's offer. Jade removed the bream and was placing her catch on the fish stringer. She noticed Grant struggling to figure out how to hold his fish without it finning him. She chuckled to herself.

"Damn it!" Grant had been finned.

Jade cut her eyes at him and then pointed with her eyes to

the preacher. Grant had forgotten that around here a person can do pretty much anything he or she wants, as long it was not in front of the preacher. “Sorry, Reverend.”

Reverend Clark grinned. “That’s okay, Grant. Those fins can sting.”

Jade walked over to Grant. “Let me see your hand.”

Grant shook her off. “I got it. I got it. I’m okay.” To keep from laughing, Jade bit her bottom lip. Grant finally got the hook out and resumed fishing. After about an hour, they had caught around twenty large bream.

“Will you kids eat some fish if I go on up and clean these and cook ’em?”

Jade looked at her watch. “Brother Clark, I have to pick Lad up by 6:00, so I’ll need to take a raincheck.”

The reverend looked at his watch. “Well, y’all keep fishing, and I’ll clean these and send some with you to cook for Lillie.” Reverend Clark left them and returned to Elsie’s. They sat in silence for a moment. The fish seemed to have stopped biting.

“Grant, I’ve been talking to Mr. Lauvon about what happened to Brandon. He said you endured a lot of criticism for standing up for Brandon. I respect that. It had to be hard on you.”

Grant did not turn to look at her. “Thanks, but Brandon was crucified. It was horrible.” They both pulled their lines in to check their bait. Although both hooks needed to be rebaited, they chose to put their hooks back into the water.

“I was attending school at George County during that time. I don’t remember all of that going on. I mean, I knew vaguely, but I did not know details. I looked at my high school annuals last night. I noticed every year you were class favorite and most popular, among other honors. But nothing your senior year.”

Grant looked down the creek, then glanced at Jade. “I guess I was blackballed. The faculty committee that selected the students to be on the ballot for Mr. GCHS refused to include me, but that's okay. By that time, I hated it here." Grant kept watching the lifeless cork floating in the creek.

"Well, it's just sad when people are so judgmental. Small towns can be tough places to live sometimes."

Grant pulled his line in and laid his pole on the ground. "Right, you are. Brandon was convicted of capital murder because he was poor and gay. The evidence was not there. Every preacher in this county preached on the abomination of homosexuality the Sunday before the jury venire was called in on Monday. The jury pool was so poisoned that there was no way he could get a fair trial. Plus, Tommy Johnson would not back up Brandon's alibi, so he stood alone."

Jade pulled in her pole and laid it beside Grant's. "Tell me about Tommy Johnson. I noticed in the annuals he was Mr. Football, a real jock. I just don't remember much about him. Sports were not my thing." Jade looked at Grant as he continued to stare at the creek.

"He was the star. He just happened to be gay, too. But, nobody knew it. He was from a prominent family. His dad was on the town board of alderman. I used to blame him, but I realized that he was in a prison here already. He could not admit who he really was; Brandon did. So, ironically, they both were sentenced to prison. Brandon to Parchman. Tommy to his conscience." Jade so admired Grant. He was so handsome. The things about him that he considered flaws, Jade considered strengths. He just needed to smile more. She sensed he was getting there, but he still had a way to go.

"Grant, can I ask you a more personal question?" Jade nervously waited for his permission.

"Sure. Go for it." Grant turned to look into Jade's blue eyes.

"Did people say you were gay, too? Is that why they ostracized you?"

Grant's eyes returned to the lazy creek. "Of course. Around here, people love to gossip. Several people believed I was gay. Even if they didn't believe it, they still liked to discuss the possibility. But I didn't care. I was so tired of dealing with the unmitigated ignorance of some people, I just wanted out of here."

Jade and Grant sat silently for a few moments. "What happened between you and your daddy?" Grant stared at her with no answer. Jade regretted the question as soon as it left her lips. "Grant, I'm sorry for prying. You don't have to answer."

Grant threw a stick into the creek, then looked at Jade. "Daddy was my hero up to that point. He came from a poor background and accomplished so much. He finished number two in his law school class at Ole Miss, but he chose to come back here to practice law and get into politics. He wanted to be governor. He was well on his way, too." Grant paused as he dwelled on the successes of his daddy. "I tried to get him to represent Brandon. He wouldn't do it. He said he would help where he could, but he couldn't be associated with a 'gay boy' accused of killing a cop. He said it would be political suicide for him. He asked me to stay away from Brandon because people were beginning to talk about me, and it was hurting him politically. He even interrogated me to be sure I wasn't gay. I started to tell him I was just to piss him off." Grant stood first then helped Jade. "After Brandon was convicted, I refused to speak to him unless I had to. I lost respect for him. The tragic irony for him was that he lost his election anyway." They gathered their poles and began walking toward Elsie's.

"You probably don't want to hear this, Grant, but Nana remembers your daddy being a kind man. She says you look a lot like him and are as polite as he was." Grant did not acknowledge the comparison. Jade reached for his arm to get him to stop walking. "This may not be my place to say anything, but I hope you can come to terms with your daddy." Grant looked into Jade's kind eyes without saying a word. "Grant, he's still your daddy. My momma left me when I was three, and I've never met my daddy. Heck, I don't even know who my daddy is. But I still love them. And maybe, just maybe, one day I can have a normal relationship with my momma. And if I am really fortunate, I'll meet my daddy." She released his arm, and the rest of their walk to Elsie's would be in silence.

Reverend Clark gave Jade a mess of fish, and she left to pick up Lad and then head home to cook them for supper. Grant stayed and ate dinner with Reverend Clark and Elsie. On his way back to town, his mind was racing. He could not stop thinking about his dad. He thought of the words of Tyrone Burley again and of Jade's situation. There was one question to which he did not know the answer: How did his dad lose his reelection campaign? He was popular and actually doing a good job. And he lost Greene County. It made no sense. It was time for another visit with the sheriff.

chapter thirty-four

GRANT SLEPT IN FRIDAY MORNING FOR THE first time since his arrival in Mississippi. He woke up at 9:00 a.m. which meant he had missed breakfast which was normally served at the Inn from 6:00 to 8:00 each morning. He felt lazy for sleeping that late. He lay in bed trying to remember when he had actually slept past 8:00 a.m. He could not remember that long ago. He decided to shower, throw on some jeans and a T-shirt, and head to Ward's for something to eat. As he showered, he thought of Elsie's barren closet and Brandon's clothes for his burial. After Grant finished his shower, he dialed Elsie's number.

"Good morning, Ms. Elsie."

Elsie seemed to be getting more weary as each day passed. "Hello, Grant. How are you this morning?"

Grant bent over to tie his tennis shoes. "I'm well. How's

Brandon doing this morning?"

Grant could hear Elsie turn off a water faucet. She was at the kitchen sink washing dishes when he called. "He's about the same as yesterday. He only woke up a minute or two this morning. He asked for his brother Lester." Lester was Brandon's older brother. He worked for a house-moving company on the coast and was six years older than Brandon. Grant wondered where Brandon's other brothers were. Elsie had not mentioned them, and Grant had not asked.

"Where is Lester?"

"He lives in Pass Christian. I just got off the phone with him. He's going to try to locate Ernie. We have not heard from him lately. He lives in Taylorsville." Elsie failed to mention Brandon's little brother, Larry.

"Where's Larry?" The thought instantly crossed Grant's mind that if she wanted him to know, she would have told him.

"Oh, Grant, I thought you knew. He got killed in a car accident six years ago."

Grant grieved for Elsie who was about to bury her second child. He felt terrible for bringing up the subject. He had asked one question too many, a fatal error careless lawyers often made. "I'm so sorry, Ms. Elsie." Elsie assured him that his question was perfectly okay. Grant then moved on to the purpose of his call. "Ms. Elsie, I want to buy Brandon a suit for the funeral. Unless, of course, you already have something in mind."

After a brief silence, Elsie responded. "Grant, Brandon will be pleased that you picked out his outfit. I haven't thought about that yet."

Grant was happy that Elsie seemed so willing to accept his offer. "Does he have a preference?"

Elsie sat down at the kitchen table. "Grant, why don't you pick him out something. Something you would wear will be fine." Elsie provided him Brandon's sizes, and Grant headed for Ward's.

When Grant arrived at the small fast-food eatery, it was

10:00 a.m. There were three high school kids eating at one table in the back. The place was otherwise empty. He ordered a sausage biscuit and a box of milk. Afterwards, Grant called Jade's cell.

"Hello." Grant loved her voice which was a little on the low side with a slight raspy sound to it.

"Hey, Jade. Grant." He watched a truck stop in the street and the passenger door open. Two men stepped out before the truck continued down Main Street. Oh, Lord, Grant thought, it was Pete Ball.

"I recognize the number and the voice, Mr. Hicks. How are you today?"

"I was doing well until I just saw Pete Ball step out of a truck. He's about to walk in Ward's where I'm eating breakfast." Pete pointed at the Range Rover as he and his friend approached the door.

"Ha, ha, ha! That serves you right for eating breakfast so late! Did you oversleep?" Pete walked in, and he and his friend sat down at the table with Grant. Pete was telling his buddy that Grant Hicks was a lawyer just like his daddy, Michael Hicks. Grant did not hear Jade's question.

"Jade, I have a proposition for you and Lad."

Jade suddenly became serious. "Okay?" Jade could hear Pete in the background.

"I'm going to drive down to Biloxi this afternoon and buy Brandon a suit for the funeral." Pete and his friend were getting louder, so Grant walked away from the table for privacy. "I thought if you were not busy, perhaps you and Lad could go with me. I also want you to help me pick out a couple dresses and some shoes for Elsie."

Jade continued to be amazed at the heart of Grant Hicks. "I would love that. Are you sure you're okay with Lad coming?"

"Sure, I want to buy him something, too, for being so kind to Max. How is Max by the way?"

"Max is great. He's been so good for Lad. Lad was riding

him like a horse in the den last night while I cooked supper. Even Nana likes Max." Like a new day's dawning, Jade's smile spread all over the nursing home. Edwina walked up and gave her a suspicious look.

Jade told Grant that she would work through lunch and take off early. Grant agreed to pick her up at her house at 4:00 so they could make the ninety-minute drive to Biloxi and not be rushed to shop. When Jade hung up the phone, she recalled the lie she told Danny Narbo on Tuesday about her having a date on Friday night. She decided that even though Grant did not couch it as such, she felt better about her little fib.

"Hey, Feller." Darn, Grant thought, Pete was still there.

"Morning, Pete." Grant sat down.

"This is Johnny Newbill."

Grant looked at Johnny. He looked like a squirrel. If this was the "baddest" man in Greene County, then this place was in need of a gym. "Good to meet you, Mr. Newbill." Johnny nodded at Grant.

Pete did the talking. "Johnny has court at eleven and needs a lawyer. I been checking up on you and found out you a lawyer like yo daddy was. I knew I knowed you when I first laid eyes on you." Pete was clearly lying. He had no clue who Grant was the first three times they were together. Grant looked at Johnny. Damn, he looked like a squirrel! Pete kept talking. "They trying to frame Johnny. Some ole gal from Jackson County has charged him with all kind a shit. It's all lies."

Grant was licensed in Mississippi, but the last thing he wanted to do was use his license in Greene County Justice Court defending Johnny Newbill. "I don't practice here, Pete. I practice in Atlanta." He looked at the two men who were looking at each other.

Pete then looked at Grant. "Can you at least give us a ride, feller?"

Grant figured that was the quickest way to hurry them along.

"Sure. Let's go." They loaded up in the Range Rover, and Grant dropped them off at the Justice Court building which was housed in a double-wide trailer. Grant thought it might be entertaining to watch, so he made the block and parked behind the building. He slipped into the crowded courtroom and sat on the back pew. A few years ago, a church donated some pews to be used by the court when the church bought new ones. Justice Court Judge Walter Eaton was an elderly man with a long, white beard. He would have looked like Santa Claus if he had not been so skinny. He called court to order and began working his docket. He finally called Johnny's case.

"Are you ready to proceed, Mr. Prosecutor?"

The prosecutor was a tired-looking gentleman named Felix Bufkin. He had been county prosecutor since he was twenty-seven. He had not been opposed in eight elections. His lack of opposition was not because he was good at what he did, but because he was there. There were only three lawyers in the county. The other two did not want the job. "Yes, Judge. This won't take long."

The judge then looked at Johnny and spoke. "Mr. Newbill, are you ready to proceed? Johnny did not utter a word. He turned to look at Pete. A deputy walked into the courtroom and stood close to the judge. It was Danny Narbo. Grant figured he must be serving as the bailiff. Then, Grant saw the accuser sitting at the table next to Mr. Bufkin. She was beautiful. Grant noticed Danny staring at her with no attempt to disguise his admiration. "I said, Mr. Newbill, are you ready to proceed?"

Johnny finally spoke. "Yeah, I reckon so, Judge." Grant had never heard such a nasally voice before. He felt sorry for him.

Judge Eaton then turned to Mr. Bufkin. "State your case, Mr. Prosecutor." The judge conducted court as if he had his own television show. There was no attempt at following the rules of criminal procedure. Judge Eaton believed in fast trials and quick decisions. Poor Johnny did not have a chance.

"We will prove, Judge, that on the morning of February 2,

2010, the defendant, Johnny Newbill, attempted to assault this poor lady by use of his pickup truck. Her name is Kati Lechler, and she was en route from Pascagoula to Hattiesburg to a deposition. She is a court reporter, Judge." Grant noticed no official court reporter present. Apparently, Justice Court was still the same as when Grant first knew it. If a person were not satisfied with the ruling, he or she could appeal to Circuit Court de novo, which meant a do-over before a state court judge.

"I object!" The loud voice startled the courtroom. Pete Ball was making an objection. One eye looking at the judge, one eye looking at the prosecutor.

"Pete, you ain't no lawyer. Sit down!" Judge Eaton was visibly agitated. The onlookers were trying to hide their laughter.

Pete held his ground. "But, Walter, it's an El Camino. It ain't no pickup truck."

Judge Eaton was now angry. "Pete, if you don't sit down and be quiet, I'm going to lock you up! And you refer to me as Judge in this courtroom!" Pete meekly sat down.

"You may proceed, Mr. Bufkin."

The county prosecutor pointed at Ms. Lechler. "Your Honor, Mr. Newbill noticed this young lady as she passed him on Highway 98. He would pass her, then slow down and let her pass. He would pass her again. Then he would slow down again to let her pass. He would ride her bumper whether she sped up or slowed down. He placed this woman in fear for her life, Judge. He would pull up beside her and stare at her. He almost side-swiped her a couple of times, causing her to run off the road. Your Honor, that's what we aim to prove." The prosecutor sat down.

The judge turned his attention to Johnny. "Okay, Mr. Newbill, how do you plea? But before you plea, I must warn you that you're still on probation. And if I find you violated that probation by committing a crime, you're going to jail today. You understand me?" Johnny turned to look at Pete. Pete looked away. Pete was not about to go to jail for Johnny. "I'm not going to ask you again,

Mr. Newbill." Judge Eaton was now past angry. His boat was in the back of his pickup truck. The white perch were biting, and he was planning to go fishing after court.

"Judge, I didn't mean no harm to the lady. I thought she was purty. I was tryin to be nice to the lady." Grant could not help but think that Johnny Newbill was about to go to jail.

"So you plead guilty then?"

Johnny looked at the lady and back at the judge. Before he could seal his fate, Grant stood. "Your Honor?"

Judge Eaton found the man to whom the voice belonged. "State your business."

Grant slowly walked to the front of the small courtroom. "My name is Grant Hicks, and I'm an attorney. I apologize for my attire, Your Honor, but I hadn't planned on being in Your Honor's court this morning. May I address the Court regarding Mr. Newbill, Your Honor?"

Judge Eaton squinted his eyes in Grant's direction. "Go ahead, Mr. Hicks."

"I would like to enter my appearance on behalf of the defendant, Mr. Newbill." Pete was smiling from ear to ear, now sitting erect in his pew. He reached up and slapped Johnny on his shoulder.

Judge Eaton began to relax. "You may. Go ahead." Felix Bufkin stared at Grant.

"Your Honor, I move for a continuance in order that I may have the time to adequately defend my client." Grant's first Mississippi client was Johnny Newbill! "I need the opportunity to propound discovery, take depositions, review the file, and locate and prepare witnesses."

Judge Eaton then turned to Felix Bufkin. "Mr. Prosecutor?" Grant looked at Mr. Bufkin, hoping he would cooperate.

"Judge, we object to a continuance. The defendant has had nearly two months to get a lawyer, and this lady took off work to be here today."

Judge Eaton then looked back at Grant. "Son, where do you practice law?"

"Atlanta, Your Honor."

The inquisition continued. "Where did you go to law school?"

"University of Virginia, Your Honor." Grant wondered the relevance of his legal pedigree.

"How well did you do in law school, Mr. Hicks?"

Grant never bragged about his successes. He was too afraid failure would overtake him if he did. "Your Honor, I finished number one in my class."

Judge Eaton had heard enough. He spit in a styrofoam cup which had been fitted inside with a paper towel to absorb the tobacco juice. "Well, you sound well-prepared to me. Your motion to continue is denied."

Grant quickly moved to plan B. "Your Honor, may I have a recess to return to my room at the Grand Avenue to properly dress for Your Honor's esteemed courtroom?"

Judge Eaton looked at Grant standing there in tennis shoes, blue jeans, and a red T-shirt. "You look good to me, counselor." The judge then looked at the prosecutor. "Call your first witness, Mr. Bufkin."

The prosecutor called Ms. Lechler to the stand. As she approached the stand, Grant asked one more question. "Your Honor, may I see the court file to review what exactly my client is being charged with?" Judge Eaton closed the file and handed it to Grant. Grant returned to the table and quickly reviewed the file.

After Ms. Lechler was sworn in, Grant had another motion. "Your Honor, I have a motion."

Felix Bufkin was now aggravated. "Judge, Mr. Hicks is wasting our time."

Judge Eaton thought of the white perch. "This is your last interruption, Mr. Hicks. State your motion."

"Your Honor, I move to quash this charging affidavit. There is no reference to any crime being committed in Greene County first of all. Secondly, it doesn't identify a specific statute. Thirdly, it is impermissibly vague and violates several of my client's constitutional rights. I can detail those violations if you'd like, Your Honor."

Judge Eaton instructed Grant to hand him the file while the prosecutor responded. "Judge, the affidavit is no different than the ones we see every day." Judge Eaton was reading the affidavit. Everyone was sitting in silence.

"Young lady, step down from the witness stand and sit back at the prosecutor's table, please. Counselors, y'all approach." Grant and Felix approached the bench. Judge Eaton looked at Felix. "Felix, what do you think?"

Felix shook Grant's hand. "He's probably right, Walter. I don't care if you dismiss it." Felix looked at Ms. Lechler and then back at Judge Eaton. "Plus, she's from Jackson County. There ain't no Lechler's that vote in Greene County that I know of. And you know there are Newbills under every log." Judge Eaton was shaking his head in agreement. Grant was shocked at the discussion. Judge Eaton directed the attorneys back to their tables.

"I grant the defendant's motion and dismiss the case." Judge Eaton then banged his gavel and left the bench. Grant noticed the boots and blue jeans beneath the robe as the judge walked out of the courtroom. Pete acted as if he had won the lottery. Grant looked at Ms. Lechler. She appeared to be stunned.

The prosecutor gathered his files and left the courtroom. He was headed to eat lunch with Judge Eaton before they went fishing. Danny Narbo was trying to get Ms. Lechler's phone number while she sheepishly walked out the door and to her car.

Grant decided to approach her. "Ms. Lechler, I'm so sorry." Danny was irritated by Grant's interruption. He was not making any progress with her anyway, so he left to walk to the sheriff's office.

"Hey. I'm a court reporter. I understand what just happened

in there. You were doing your job. I just need to get out of this place and never come back."

Pete and Johnny were standing at a distance waiting on Grant as he and Ms. Lechler glanced in their direction. Grant then looked at her, "Damn, he looks like a squirrel, doesn't he?" They both laughed. She then got in her car and drove away.

Pete ran up to Grant. "Feller, we taking you to the fish house! But you gotta drive."

Grant politely declined Pete's offer. As Pete and Johnny walked away, Grant silently wished Emmitte Rimes could have witnessed the trial of Johnny Newbill. Grant smiled as he pulled out of the parking lot to drive toward the nursing home.

chapter thirty-five

AS GRANT REACHED THE GREENE RURAL parking lot, Sheriff McInnis was getting into a car with his son, Paul. Paul and the sheriff were going to eat at Rocky Creek Catfish and then spend the afternoon together. The sheriff was excited. Grant was happy for him, and they agreed to visit Saturday morning. Grant decided to return to his room and relax until time to pick up Jade and Lad at 4:00. He needed the rest.

Grant's phone woke him at 2:00 p.m. It was Jade. "Hey, Grant. What's up?"

Grant sat up in the bed. "Not much. I was reading and fell asleep." Grant was ashamed and guilty for taking a nap in the middle of what would normally be a workday for him, especially after sleeping so late.

"The rest is good for you. Hey, I need to tell you something, and I hope it does not upset you."

Jade waited for the go-ahead from Grant. Grant hoped she had not called to cancel. "Okay." Grant was now fully awake.

"I kind of mentioned to Edwina that we were going to Biloxi. She wants us to drop her off at the Beau Rivage while we shop. Edwina likes to gamble on occasion."

Grant was relieved that Jade had not cancelled. It put him in an agreeable mood. "Oh, that's fine. I was afraid you were cancelling on me."

Jade was pleased that he would have been disappointed had she done so. "I told her we would pick her up after we left my house since she won't get off until 4:00. I hope you're not upset."

"Not upset at all. Look, I may be at your place around 3:30 so I can spend a little time with Max, if that's okay." Jade agreed, and they hung up. Grant sat on the foot of his bed and looked in the mirror. He wondered if Jade found him attractive. He was rather confident she did. When it came to his looks, he was a bit cocky. He decided it was okay to be a little vain since people made him that way. He thought of Sam and wondered if his time with her had been wasted. He and Sam had some great times together, and both had fulfilled their career goals. Thus, he rationalized that their relationship had been a success.

Grant was crossing the Chickasawhay River bridge when he noticed the flashing blue lights ahead. He slowed as he approached and noticed that Danny Narbo had pulled Jade over. Grant parked in front of her car and got out. Danny was so busy harassing Jade that he did not notice Grant approaching.

"Hey, Jade. Officer, what seems to be the problem?" Jade looked at Grant as if her hero had arrived. Danny looked at Grant with obvious impatience. This was the second time in just a few hours that Grant had interrupted his pursuit. First, he had spoiled his effort to obtain Kati Lechler's phone number. Now, he had ruined his efforts with Jade.

Jade, seeming bolder with Grant's arrival, responded for

Danny. "Mr. Narbo has pulled me over to ask me who my date is tonight." Danny, though clearly the bigger of the two men, was speechless.

"Officer, is there a problem with Ms. Lott? Did you observe her breaking any laws?" Danny knew Grant was a lawyer, and it paralyzed him. "Because, if you did not and you are simply pulling her over to harass her, there are several federal and state laws that prohibit that type of behavior."

Danny began to get angry. "I'm checking her license and seeing if her tag is expired. I'll check yours while I'm at it." Danny walked over to the Range Rover. "Are you a liberal, Mr. Hicks?"

Grant joined Danny at the back of the SUV. Danny was reading Sam's bumper stickers. "Excuse me, officer?" Jade could not hear the discussion, so she got out of her vehicle and joined the men.

"These bumper stickers. Peace, gun control, pro-choice, animal rights. Are you one of them left-wing people? I bet you voted for Obama, too, didn't you?"

Grant looked at the deputy. "Well, I didn't vote in the Presidential election." Grant then pointed at the bumper stickers. "Hmm, peace is a good thing, I believe in the Second Amendment for most people, the choice issue I will leave to the ladies, and I enjoy a good steak; therefore, I guess I'm selective about the animal rights I support. How about you, Mr. Narbo? Are you a liberal?" Jade admired the apparent confidence Grant displayed as he intellectually toyed with the deputy.

Danny raised his voice and removed all doubt as to his ignorance. "Hell no! I ain't no liberal, and I ain't for none of this shit on these bumper stickers. Obama needs to carry his liberal ass back to Africa along with every other African in this country." Danny put his finger in Grant's face. "Let me tell you something, Mr. Hicks. If you get in my fucking way again, you are going to wish you had never stepped foot in Greene County."

Grant smiled with amusement. "I'm way ahead of you,

Mr.Narbo. I've wished that I had not stepped foot in Greene County for twenty years. Now, if you will excuse us, Jade and I have a date tonight." Jade had become so nervous and afraid at what Danny might do to Grant that she did not hear the word *date* come out of his mouth.

Danny was fuming. He walked past Grant, intentionally bumping his shoulder. "I'm not through with you, Mr. Hicks. You either, Jade. Y'all better watch your steps."

As Danny was walking to his patrol car, Grant called out to him. "Officer?" The deputy turned to look as Grant pulled his cell phone from the front pocket of his coat. "Just so you know, I've recorded this entire episode. Unless you want to find yourself in a courtroom, I suggest this be the last time you harass Ms. Lott." Danny slammed the car door and sped away.

"Wow, Grant! What can I say? Thank you so much. But I must tell you, I was afraid Danny was going to jump on you."

Grant finally exhaled and relaxed. "Me, too, Jade. Me, too. I'll meet you at your house."

Grant spent half an hour with Lad and Max as Jade prepared for their outing. They then picked up Edwina and headed toward Biloxi. Jade told Edwina every detail about Grant's confrontation with Danny Narbo. Grant listened as Jade described the many times Danny had harassed her. She hoped this would be the last time. Grant merged onto Interstate 10 as Edwina was giving him the quickest directions to the casino.

"Edwina, what will Reverend Mimbes do if he finds out you are at the casino tonight?" Grant thought he would have a little fun with Edwina.

"He know I come down here. Edwina don't hide nuttin."

Grant looked at Edwina in the rearview mirror. "But isn't it a sin to gamble, Edwina?"

Edwina, with a stern look on her face, responded. "Looka here, Yankee. Edwina love the Lord, and the Lord love Edwina, but ever now and then, Edwina love to sin. This happen to be one of those times." Grant and Jade smiled at each other.

After they dropped Edwina off at the casino, Jade, Lad, and Grant drove along Highway 90 toward the Edgewater Mall discussing the rebuilding efforts after Hurricane Katrina. Grant was pleased to see several of the old live oak trees still standing. Sadly, however, there was no escaping the fact that Hurricane Katrina had changed the coast forever.

The first order of business was to locate the food court. Jade needed to change and feed Lad if they expected him to cooperate with them as they shopped. While Jade was tending to Lad, Grant ordered their food from Chick-Fil-A. They met at a table in the corner of the eating area.

"What's the plan, Grant?" Jade was feeding Lad some fruit and vegetables she had brought him from home.

"I don't really have one. First, I guess we can find Brandon a suit along with a tie, shirt, socks and...hey, do they wear shoes in a casket?"

Jade gave Grant an inquisitive look. "You know, I don't know. I've never thought about that before."

"Well, Elsie did not give me a shoe size. I'll buy a pair my size, and if he doesn't need them, I guess I can keep them." Grant could not help noticing the occasional glances in their direction. He mused that it must not be every day that a white couple is feeding a black baby. Well, mostly black. Grant looked at Lad. "Let's take Lad to pick out a toy first. Then we will buy Brandon a suit. After that, I will take over Lad patrol, and we will follow you as you shop for Elsie."

Jade finished feeding Lad and turned to her food. "Thanks for dinner, Grant."

"Oh, I owe you dinner after Tuesday night, but this isn't it. I'm amazed at how good you can cook. And you are a natural with Lad. Have you heard from your sister?"

Jade's smile turned into a sad, serious look. "Thanks. No. Not a word from Stormy. She is scheduled for a court appearance on

April 20, so I'll be there waiting on her."

Grant again looked at Lad. "He really is a well-behaved kid. Has he adjusted well being with you and Nana?"

Jade smiled at Lad. "He's done remarkably well. He's developmentally delayed in almost every area. He should've been potty trained already. But we're working on that. He rarely makes a sound. He says *Max* though. Calls me *JaJa* and Nana, *NaNa*. But, he won't make a sound if anyone else is around." They finished eating their meal and spent the next two hours shopping.

Lad picked out a Batman suit with a Batman cape and mask. He would not let them take it off, so a miniature batman accompanied them. They then picked out Brandon a dark blue suit with a small white pinstripe. To complete Brandon's outfit, Grant purchased a white shirt, red tie, belt, a pair of socks, and shoes. Jade picked out the tie color. She said red was the color of love, and it suited Brandon. Jade could not decide which two dresses to select out of the three she picked out for Elsie. Grant bought all three. Jade gave Grant a lesson in women's apparel, and he bought shoes, purses, and matching costume jewelry. Before the night was over, Grant spent a little over fifteen hundred dollars.

They picked Edwina up from the casino around 10:00 p.m. She had won twenty dollars for her night's gambling efforts. Edwina had a blast, and she talked constantly until they dropped her off at her house. Lad fell asleep, and when they arrived at Jade's, Grant carried him to his bed. Max was on the floor next to Lad's bed waiting on him. Jade watched through the door as Grant leaned over, kissed Lad on the forehead, and bent down to tell Max goodbye. Jade silently admitted to herself that she was falling in love with Grant Hicks, and it scared her.

chapter thirty-six

GRANT WALKED INTO THE DINING AREA of the Grand Avenue Inn at 7:00 a.m. The Inn only had five rooms to rent, and usually there were vacancies. A man, woman, and two teenage girls were eating breakfast when Grant arrived. Grant fixed his plate and sat down at the table next to them.

"Grant Hicks?" Grant looked up to see his former high school classmate, Travis Crocker.

"Travis?" Travis and Grant were not close friends in high school, but they did occasionally hang out.

"Man, Grant, how have you been?" Both men stood to greet each other.

"I'm well. How are you?"

Travis looked at his wife. "Honey, this is Grant Hicks, a high school classmate of mine."

Grant shook her hand, and he met their two daughters. "It's nice to meet y'all. Travis, you're looking good. Time has been kind to you."

Travis was always smiling in high school. He still was. "Thanks, Grant. But you're the one time has been kind to." Travis joined Grant at his table.

"What have you been up to, Travis? Where do you live?"

Travis reached to grab the coffee he was drinking from the table where he had been sitting. "We live in Pensacola. I own a landscape architect business down there. When I graduated from Mississippi State, I took a job down there and loved it so much that I never left. My wife is from there. It's home now." Grant wondered if Atlanta were his home. "What about you, Grant?"

Grant was tired of answering that question but realized it was necessary. "I live in Atlanta. I'm a partner in a law firm up there. Not married. No kids." Grant figured he would get those answers out of the way, too.

"Last I heard, you were majoring in math. I thought you were going to get your Ph.D. in math and teach at a college. What changed your mind?"

Grant had decided he would go to law school in the fall of 1994. His trip to Greene County was beginning to reveal why he made that decision. "I enjoyed studying math, but I woke up one morning with the urge to go to law school. After a couple weeks, the urge was still there. And, as they say, the rest is history. What are you guys doing in town?" Grant resumed eating as he listened to Travis.

"Nothing in particular. I just wanted to bring the family over to visit my relatives and show them around a little. Even though Pensacola is not that far away, we rarely come here, and when we do, it's usually to visit Mom and Dad for Christmas or Thanksgiving. Mom and Dad don't know we are here. We'll surprise them later today." Travis stood to refill his coffee cup. "What are you doing in town, Grant?"

Grant had answered this question multiple times too. "Do you remember Brandon Smallwood?"

Travis sat back down. "How could I forget Brandon? I subscribe to the *Greene County Herald*, so I keep up with what happens around here. What a tragic story! I saw in Thursday's paper that the community is giving him a benefit. I guess that proves that people can let go of the past."

Grant wondered if he could. "I guess so. I'm here to see him. He has terminal cancer."

Travis gave the room key to his wife, and she and the kids left the dining area. "I wondered what was wrong with him. To be honest, I assumed it was AIDS."

Another stereotypical assumption, thought Grant. The ridiculous belief that every gay person who is sick has AIDS. Grant let it go. "No. He has pancreatic cancer." Grant poured his second cup of coffee since his arrival in Greene County. The first was at Elsie's. He figured he might as well acquire a taste for it.

Travis' smile gave way to a more serious look. "That's too bad. Grant, I want to apologize to you." Grant curiously looked at Travis. "When we were in high school, I never could get why you stood up for Brandon. I was one of those people who thought Brandon was a freak and needed to be put away. Heck, everybody pretty much did but you. I said some hateful things about you, and you never even knew it." Grant continued to listen. "I've thought about my actions a lot over the years, but it wasn't until Brandon was declared an innocent man that it became evident just how despicable my actions were."

Grant appreciated Travis' honesty. "Travis, that's all in the past now. I'm over all that." Grant lied, but saying it was a sign of progress.

"Grant, did you notice my sixteen-year-old daughter, Emily?"

Grant tried to remember her. It had only been ten minutes ago, and he had already forgotten what she looked like. "Yes." Grant hoped he would not be asked to describe her.

"Her momma caught her kissing another girl about year ago. I'm having a hell of a time with her. We rarely speak, and I often wonder if she is my penance."

Grant noted the disappointment in Travis' eyes. "Travis, I'm no parent, so I don't have any parental words of wisdom. But I can tell you what Brandon longed for. He just wanted to be accepted and loved for who he was." The two men stood as they were preparing to leave.

"It was good to see you again, Grant." Travis shook his hand and walked toward the door.

"It was good to see you, too, Travis." Before Travis exited the dining area, Grant spoke. "Travis, I'm far from a relationship expert, but I believe the ones who are a bit different need to be shown the most that we care about them. Take care." Grant's statement caused Travis to pause for a moment before he left the dining area.

When Travis got back to his room, he slowly, and a bit awkwardly, walked over to Emily and hugged her. This was the first time they had embraced in over a year. Travis' wife wept as she finally witnessed Travis embracing Emily with a hug only a daddy can give a daughter. A chance encounter with Grant Hicks had led to reconciliation.

As Grant drove toward the Smallwoods, his mind returned to Travis and his family. He thought of his own momma and his sister, Lauren. He thought of his dad. Grant recalled some of the good times they had shared when he was a child. He remembered the days his dad would play catcher as he learned to pitch. Why was it so hard to forgive those who are often the closest? As Grant passed each house, he wondered what battles were being fought behind each front door. And why, oh why, couldn't the King's men put Humpty Dumpty back together again?

Grant pulled into the Smallwoods yard as Reverend Clark was getting out of his pickup. The preacher welcomed Grant with a smile. "Good morning, Grant." Reverend Clark then pulled a legal pad from his truck.

"Hey, Reverend. Thanks again for taking Jade and me fishing Thursday. We enjoyed it."

"I had fun, too, Grant. That Jade sure enjoyed herself. She is one sweet young lady." Grant's thoughts agreed with the reverend. They walked into the house to find Elsie sitting by Brandon's bed. He was awake but was not talking.

"Hello there, Brandon!" Reverend Clark was always excited to see him. Brandon stared at him, his only movement an occasional blinking of his eyes.

Grant stepped into his line of sight. "Hey, friend. Good to see you, Brandon."

Grant placed his hand on top of Brandon's, while Reverend Clark put on his glasses to read from the legal pad. "Brandon, this is the sign-up sheet from the organizational meeting we had on Monday night for your benefit. There were eighty-three people who signed in. I have participated in more benefit organizational meetings than I can count, and never have there been more than twenty-five people at one. These people love you, Brandon."

Grant backed away from Brandon's range of vision and listened to Reverend Clark read each name and explain who each person was. Although Brandon's voice was silent, it seemed his eyes understood every word Reverend Clark spoke. After the last name was read, as if on cue, Brandon fell asleep. Elsie, Reverend Clark, and Grant retreated to the kitchen for some coffee. Grant was now on cup number three. It was tasting better.

"Lester and Ernie are coming after while. Lester has to drive from Pass Christian to Taylorsville to pick up Ernie. Ernie don't have a car. Brother Clark, I haven't made any funeral plans for Brandon. Will you help me? When am I supposed to do that?" Elsie pulled a piece of rolled-up toilet paper from the pocket of her long nightgown to wipe her nose.

"Of course, I'll help you, Elsie." The preacher lowered his voice. "Grant and I will handle the service, so don't worry about that." Grant thought the mention of Brandon's funeral was premature. He felt cold discussing it. He walked to Brandon's room to make sure he was still asleep. He did not want Brandon to hear his own funeral being planned.

"Where will we have it, Brother Clark?" Elsie was not on the roll of a local church although she was considered religious. She had not attended church regularly since Reverend Clark left Cedar Grove Full Gospel over forty years ago. The truth was she always felt a little intimidated at church. She simply could not dress herself or her boys well enough. Too, she could not stand to see the regular church kids pick on her boys. Therefore, she stayed home. The preacher at Cedar Grove Full Gospel delivered a tape of his weekly sermons to her every Monday. Elsie appreciated his kindness and listened faithfully to each week's message.

"Elsie, we can have it in the chapel of the funeral home if you like." Elsie just stared at the kitchen table.

Grant had rejoined them in the kitchen. He hated funeral homes. The look in Elsie's eyes told him she did, too. "Ms. Elsie, would you prefer a church?" Grant could read her thoughts.

Elsie looked at Grant and then at Reverend Clark. "Brother Clark, do you think a church would let us?" Grant recalled a time at his former church where a controversy was created because a black couple wanted to get married there. It almost split the church. Grant could not imagine any of the churches he remembered lining up to volunteer hosting a funeral for a gay person.

"I'll ask around, Elsie. Any preferences?"

"No. I have no preference. I trust your judgment." Grant once again walked to Brandon's room to make sure he was still asleep and then returned to the kitchen.

"Brother Clark, I don't want him buried where Luther is." Luther was buried in the cemetery behind the funeral home in

Leakesville where the county buried paupers. The local officials had purchased a section of plots from the cemetery for that purpose. Larry was buried in Cedar Grove Full Gospel's cemetery in a plot donated by a church member. There was no vacancy next to Larry.

"Let me think about that, too, Elsie. Give me a day or two to work on some ideas."

Grant excused himself, told them good-bye, and drove toward the nursing home. It was time for another visit with Sheriff McInnis. Before he went there, he stopped by Edwina's house to ask her a favor. She gladly agreed to his request. Grant then dialed Jade's number.

"Hey, you." Jade was happy to see his number appear on her caller ID.

"Hey, Jade. How are you today?" Grant could hear Lad in the background. The little boy was slowly beginning to open up.

"I'm well. I had fun last night. You're quite the shopper, Mr. Hicks."

Grant laughed. He did not shop. He bought. "Thanks for your help last night. I couldn't have done it without you. Anyway, I called to ask you a question."

Jade blew her bangs from her eyes and sat down at the kitchen table tucking her left leg under her right thigh. "Ask away."

"Can I take you to dinner tonight?"

Her heart fluttered. Jade could barely contain her excitement, and then Lad walked into the kitchen. "Grant, I would love nothing more than to go to dinner with you, but I have nowhere to leave Lad." She instantly became depressed at the thought of declining his invitation.

"I have that covered. I hired Edwina. We are to drop Lad off at her house at six o'clock. Now, I'll ask again. Can I take you to dinner tonight?"

The smile slowly spread across Jade's face. "Mr. Hicks, I gladly accept your offer. What should I wear?"

"I'm wearing khakis, a polo, and sports jacket, so you take it from there." Jade hung up the phone and began to sing as she finished cleaning. Whatever would she wear?

chapter thirty-seven

GRANT WALKED INTO THE NURSING HOME and spoke to the staff as if he had been coming there for years. He had become a regular. The truth was he had visited there more in less than one week than some people visited their loved ones in six months. He found the sheriff in his room listening to *The Best of Waylon Jennings* and reading a Louis L'Amour western.

"Good afternoon, Sheriff."

The sheriff laid his open book on the table that separated the chairs. "Hello, Grant. I'm sorry I couldn't visit yesterday."

Grant sat down. "Oh, that's no problem. Did you and your son have a good time?"

The sheriff smiled. "We did. It was good to see Paul. He works construction and is gone most of the time. By the way, Pete Ball and Johnny Newbill were at Rocky Creek Catfish, and Pete was singing your praises. How in the world did you end up representing Johnny Newbill?" They both laughed as Grant told him the story. They spent the next thirty minutes discussing the sheriff's visit with his son and Grant, Jade, Lad and Edwina's trip to the coast.

"Sheriff, I don't know a whole lot about politics. In fact, I don't keep up with the political world too much. My dad loved it, and I used to love it, too, when I was little and he first ran for office. But I can't figure out how he lost in 1991."

The sheriff turned his music off. "Grant, politics can be confusing, and as they say, 'Politics can make strange bedfellows.'"

Grant began to fidget in his chair. "He seemed to be doing a good job. He was progressing in Jackson at an almost meteoric pace. Yet, he lost. Why?"

The sheriff knew Greene County politics better than anyone. Even at his age and at his stage in life, politicians still coveted his support and advice. "Grant, your daddy represented Senate District 43 which includes Wayne, Greene, George, and part of Stone County. Your dad was the first senator to be from our county since Greene became part of this district in the 1960s. As you know, Greene is the least populated of the four counties. It was a shocker that your dad won in 1983 in the first place." Grant listened as the sheriff continued. "The man your daddy defeated in the '83 election, Herb Gadd, had been there twelve years and lived in Wayne County. Senator Gadd also grew up in Stone County. People usually vote for their own in these legislative races. Your dad won Greene County by 1500 votes and practically split the George and Stone vote. The people in Wayne were getting tired of Senator Gadd, and he only carried his home county, Wayne, by around 1000 votes. Your dad upset him by 500 votes."

Grant stood to pace in front of the sheriff's bed. "Sheriff, I remember the 1987 election. The man who ran against Daddy was from George County. Wasn't he?"

"Yes, he was. His name was Darryl Maples. He was not a

serious contender though. Your dad was doing a good job, he was well liked, and he was one hell of a speaker."

Grant realized that he was pacing, so he sat back down. "But what happened in 1991? I mean, Dad would not represent Brandon solely for his political career. However, he still got beat." Grant crossed his legs in an effort to keep them still.

Sheriff McInnis adjusted in his chair. "Senator Gadd decided to run again. He had switched to the Republican Party, and the district–and state for that matter–had gone Republican. Kirk Fordice came out of nowhere and was elected governor that year. There has been a Republican senator in District 43 ever since. Your dad was a Democrat and a trial lawyer, and one of the hot issues in 1990 leading up to the election was Tort Reform. Your dad voted against most of it, which assured him a well-financed opponent by the business and medical community."

"By how much did my Dad get beaten?"

"He lost by around 650 votes. Senator Gadd beat him by 800 votes in Wayne, and your dad won George and Stone by 200 votes. Your dad lost the election right here at home. He lost Greene by forty-eight votes."

Grant looked out the window trying to digest the information. "It just doesn't add up, Sheriff. Am I missing something?" Grant looked at the sheriff.

"Grant, I lost that year, too, by twenty-four votes. The same reason I lost is the reason your dad lost." The look on Grant's face told the sheriff that Grant was more confused than ever. "Son, Greene County politics are unlike any in this state, probably unlike any in this country."

Grant stood and walked toward the door. He stopped and turned to look at the sheriff. "But, Sheriff, you believed Brandon. Dad did not, or he didn't care about Brandon anyway. He was all about saving his own political skin." A nurse's aide stopped in to empty the sheriff's wastebaskets and make sure the bathroom was properly supplied. After she left, the conversation continued.

"Grant, the political clique in Greene County was run by Frank Jenkins and the Board attorney at that time, Walter Sellers. In order for them to keep their political dynasty and their criminal activities hidden, they used money and old-fashioned political back-scratching to control the politics here. When I no longer believed that Brandon was guilty, it made them nervous. They made sure I understood that if I did not abide by their wishes, then as Walter Sellers put it, 'There would be hell to pay at election time.'"

Grant put his hands in his pockets as he processed the information. The math would not add up. "But Brandon was found guilty in 1989. The election was in 1991."

The sheriff retrieved a Sprite from his miniature refrigerator. "Sprite?"

"No, thank you. I mean, Sheriff, why were they after you in '91?"

"I just did not believe Brandon was guilty, so I continued researching and investigating. Apparently, they did not agree with my approach. And we now know why that made them nervous."

Grant still looked puzzled. "I see. And how did all this tie to Dad?" Grant was nervous as he waited for the answer. He was hoping that his dad was not involved in any criminal activity. He had finally begun to garner some measure of respect for him. He wondered if his relationship with his dad was about to be destroyed forever.

"Walter and Frank went to your dad and asked him to support my opponent, Van Carlson. Van was not qualified to be sheriff nor did he have the temperament for it. Your dad refused to support him, so they turned on him. I could see the writing on the wall and felt like I was going to get defeated anyway. So I went by to see your dad." Grant was hanging onto every word the sheriff spoke. "Grant, I told your dad that he was going to get beaten if he didn't support Van. I will never forget what your daddy told me." The sheriff looked deeply into Grant's eyes. "Grant, are you sure you want to hear this?"

As nervous as a child on the first day of school, Grant responded, "Yes sir." Grant swallowed.

"Your dad told me that he had already lost the respect of his son for making selfish political decisions. He said that he was tired of being ashamed when he looked into the mirror every morning. He said that he was going to support me if it cost him his seat in the Senate. Well, Grant, it did."

Grant looked out the window and felt ashamed. He thought of his dad and how he must have felt during that difficult time. For the first time since he could remember, he was proud of his daddy. He wanted to tell him. But he was gone. Grant thanked the sheriff for sharing the information with him and left. After he was gone, the sheriff pulled the letter from the old boot box and placed it in the top drawer of his chest of drawers. Grant was almost prepared to receive it.

Grant pulled into Jade's driveway as she peered out the window of the den. Lad was ready, and Nana was sitting in her favorite recliner.

"Do you think Grant will blow his horn, Nana?" Jade watched Grant exit the vehicle and walk toward the house. She scurried to sit down to avoid looking anxious.

Nana looked at Jade and then stared at the front door. Grant knocked. Nana then looked at Jade and grinned from ear to ear. She whispered. "Well, let him in, Jade."

Jade snapped back to reality and answered the door. "Come in, Grant."

Max ran to meet Grant. He bent over to pet the dog as he spoke to Jade. "Hey, Jade. You look nice." Jade wore a floral dress, denim jacket and pair of flats, with her outfit accented by gold bangle bracelets.

"Thank you, Grant."

Jade turned to Lad. "You ready to go play with Edwina, Lad?"

As Jade was gathering the boy's things, Grant spoke to Nana. "Hey, Ms. Lott. How are you tonight?"

Nana was still smiling. "I'm doing well. *Matlock* comes on in a few minutes. Max and I plan to watch it." They told Nana good-bye and left for Edwina's.

"Grant, can you stop by Piggly Wiggly so I can run in and get Lad some juice and cookies to take to Edwina's?"

"Sure." Grant dropped Jade off at the door and parked. Just before Jade walked out of the store, Grant noticed a man and woman walking out of Piggly Wiggly pushing two carts full of groceries. The couple appeared to be in their late thirties, and they were followed by five children that looked like steps as they walked toward their vehicle, a duel-wheeled truck that had been converted into a homemade dump truck. The man was skinny, but the woman was well over three hundred pounds.

Grant was so busy staring at the family that he did not see Jade as she opened the door to the Range Rover. "Who are they?"

Jade looked at the family. "That's the Spell family, Arthur and Mary Spell. She sure has lost a lot of weight." Grant jerked his head toward Jade, then back at the Spells. He could not imagine her weighing more. Mary opened the passenger door and pulled out a small stool that had a rope tied to it. The kids piled into the back of the homemade dump truck and sat with the groceries. Mary adjusted her stool, placed her right foot on it and her left foot on the running board of the truck. When she put her weight on the runner, the truck sank low toward the ground under the stress of Mary Spell. She finally got into the truck and pulled in the stool by the rope as if it were a fish being pulled from the Chickasawhay. Jade spoke. "Bless her heart."

Grant could see the genuine concern and pity being displayed by Jade so he chose not to comment. But he secretly wondered if "Bless her heart" really meant "Damn!"

They dropped Lad off at Edwina's and headed west on

Highway 57 toward McLain en route to Hattiesburg.

"This is the deal, Jade. I need a break from reality tonight. I don't want to discuss anything depressing like death or funeral arrangements. I want tonight to be two friends enjoying a nice dinner. Nothing depressing will be on the discussion table, agree?"

Jade focused on the phrase "Two friends enjoying dinner." Reality. Ugh. Jade, still focusing on the words two friends, responded. "Sure. Of course, we don't have to pretend we just met; we practically have just met. I barely knew you in high school, and I don't believe we ever held a conversation then. So this is like a first date, only between friends, and we will treat it as such." Grant's iPod was playing songs from the '70s and '80s. "I have an idea, Grant. Let's play the question game. We take turns asking a question, and both of us have to answer it. Okay?"

Grant smiled at Jade. "Sure, you ask first."

Jade twisted her legs in the direction of Grant in order to attempt eye contact. "Okay, Grant, favorite movie?"

Grant did not hesitate. "*A Few Good Men*. 'You can't handle the truth!' Yours?"

Jade was a little more deliberate in considering the question. "*The Notebook*. It's so sweet."

Grant had not seen it. It was Grant's turn. "Okay, Ms. Lott, favorite band or singer?"

Jade was concentrating. "There are so many. I think I will go with Journey. I love them. Steve Perry is the best ever."

Grant gave her a look of approval. "They are good. Mine is Pink Floyd." Jade was thinking of her next question as Grant gave her the history of Pink Floyd and the phenomenal success of *Dark Side of the Moon*.

"Okay, I'm ready, Grant. Best-looking actress?" Jade was enjoying this game. She was beginning to learn a little more about Grant Hicks.

"Gosh, there are so many beautiful ladies to chose from. Hmm. I'm going with Nicole Kidman. She is one sexy lady."

Jade looked slightly surprised. "She is pretty. Do I pick the best-looking actor or actress, Grant?"

Grant glanced at Jade, then focused on the road. "Pick both. I say the best-looking actor is Robert Redford, when he was in his prime."

Jade was still thinking. "Okay, for me the man is Harrison Ford, also when he was in his prime, although he is still handsome. And I think the actress is Jennifer Aniston. She is so cute." They played the question game all the way to Hattiesburg and drove downtown to find a restaurant that was not a chain. They parked along the street in front of Brownstone's.

Before they got out of the car, Jade asked one final question. "What are you most afraid of, Grant?"

Grant thought of his conversation with Brandon. It was easy to be honest with him. He was dying. But Jade was young, vibrant, and cute, too. He was hesitant about answering. "You go first, Jade. Then I'll answer."

Jade did not hesitate. "My greatest fear is turning out to be like my momma." Grant looked at Jade as she peered out the front window of the Range Rover. She was wondering where her momma was and if Stormy were with her. So many thoughts were pouring through her mind.

"Well, Jade, I don't know your momma. But from what I know about you, you need not fear that happening. Let's go in the restaurant."

Jade grabbed his arm. "Wait a minute, Pal. You have to answer." Jade gave him a fake mean, but sweet, look.

Grant's mind began to race, too. He figured he might as well answer the question. "It's failure, Jade. I feel like I am in a constant battle against failure."

Jade's smile slowly faded as she pondered Grant's answer. "Well, Grant, you have succeeded, so you don't have to fear that happening either." They walked into the restaurant, both pondering their fears. Over dinner they reminisced about their high school days and past relationships. They laughed at, and with, each other.

An older lady approached their table as her husband was heading toward the door. She had been watching Jade and Grant since they first sat down. "I want y'all to know that you make the cutest couple." They blushed and thanked her without explaining their status. When Grant and Jade were preparing to leave, the waitress informed Grant that the woman had paid for their dinner and handed him the ticket. On the back of the ticket, she had written, "Don't ever stop laughing." Jade stuck the note into her pocket.

Lad was asleep when they picked him up at Edwina's. Grant would once again carry him inside and put him into his bed. Jade then walked Grant out onto the front porch. She thanked him for a wonderful evening, and before he walked off the porch, they shared a few seconds of awkward silence. Then Grant left. As he was walking to his car, he wanted to stay, but he was having trouble compartmentalizing his relationship with Jade. He also thought of Samantha.

Jade stepped inside and watched from behind the screen door as Grant's taillights disappeared. She pulled the restaurant ticket from her pocket and read the scribbled message on the back. Jade smiled as she walked to her bedroom and placed it on her mirror.

Part Six:

Forgiveness

chapter thirty-eight

IT WAS SUNDAY MORNING, MARCH 28. IT HAD been twelve days since Elsie located Grant in Atlanta. Grant lay in his bed digesting the circumstances and events that had transpired since then. He had returned home, back to Atlanta, and home again. He and Sam had parted ways after sixteen years of living together. He wondered for a moment why it was so easy for both of them to do so. There were no tears shed. He thought of Brandon, Elsie, Reverend Clark, Sheriff McInnis, and Edwina. He thought of Nana and Lad, and he smiled as he thought of Jade. Jade had invited him to church today, but he had declined. He thought of his dad, mom, and sister, Lauren. He thought of Uncle Ronny and grinned as he wondered if Dana left him after she had finished that pack of cigarettes. He thought of Elvis Fillingim, Uncle Glen, Pete Ball, and Johnny Newbill. Grant sat up on the side of his bed pondering the uniqueness of this place and its people. His phone rang.

"Hello." Grant looked at the clock. It was 7:30 a.m.

"Hey, son, how are you?" It was his mom, Sylvia. She usually called once a month. After Michael's death, she married a former high school classmate, David Peabody, whose wife had died in a car accident. David was an executive with Hendrick Motorsports, and since their kids were grown, they spent most weekends following the NASCAR circuit. Grant knew his mom had to be in love because she was far from a racing fan.

"Well, hey, Mom. How are you?" Grant lay back down for their conversation.

"I'm well. We're in Martinsville for the race. I thought I would check on you." Much had changed since they had last spoken sometime in February.

"I'm fine, Mom." He was not in the mood for an extended conversation about the last twelve days of his life. He hoped she would not ask specific questions.

She moved on to Samantha. "How is Samantha?"

Grant passed on another potentially long conversation. "She's fine. How's David?" Grant had only been around his stepfather a few times, but he liked him. He took great care of his mom, and he seemed genuinely nice.

"Oh, he's doing well. It looks like the race may get rained out, so he's watching The Weather Channel."

They small-talked a few minutes more. Then Grant asked a question he had not asked in years. "Mom, how is Lauren?" Grant knew the question surprised his mom because she became uncharacteristically quiet.

"Your sister? Oh, uhh, she is doing well. I just got off the phone with her."

Grant nor his mom could remember the last time Grant and Lauren had spoken. Lauren was furious that Grant did not attend their dad's funeral, and though she never said it, she had partly blamed Grant for his death. "Where does she live now?"

Sylvia wondered if she should tell him without Lauren's

permission. She used to attempt to broker reconciliation between them, but eventually had stopped. It was an exercise in futility. She decided to slowly reveal specifics. "She's still on the coast."

That was it? Grant would be forced to ask a follow-up question. "I thought so. Where on the coast?"

One more answer surely would be fine, Sylvia thought. "Ocean Springs."

Grant decided that he might as well ask what he wanted to know. It was obvious his mom was being guarded with her answers. "I was just curious. She and Jonathon still married?" Lauren was three years older than Grant. She had met Jonathon Pickering at Jones County Junior College, and they were married within a year. They had two children, both boys. They had married in June of 1989 one month before Brandon's trial. Their first son, Brent, was born in 1991, and their second, Tallon, was born in 1995. She was pregnant with Tallon when Michael Hicks shot himself.

"Yes, they're doing fine. Jonathon works at Northrop Grumman in the engineering department, and Lauren works part-time at a clothing store in Biloxi." Lauren graduated in fashion design but never had worked outside the home when the kids were young. Now that Brent was in college and Tallon was in high school, she had decided to work occasionally to fight the boredom.

"Do you know her street address?" David called out to Sylvia to let her know it was time to leave for the track.

"I have to run, Grant." She paused and wondered again if she should give it to him. She did not have time to inquire as to why he wanted it, but she hoped it was a good sign that he asked. "It's 1500 Mattina Drive."

"Thanks, Mom. Y'all enjoy the race." After Grant hung up the phone, he picked up the book he was reading, but could not concentrate. He decided to clear his mind by hitting the pavement. He would run ten miles before he was done. He simply did not have the stamina to run far enough to take his mind off the dramatic turn his life had made.

Grant walked into Molten's restaurant at noon, and it was already packed with local people dressed in their Sunday best. As usual on Sundays, it was a race between the methodists, baptists, presbyterians, and pentecostals to get to the buffet first. Grant sat down and asked for a menu. He despised buffets. First, buffets were lethal. He believed society's obesity problem was directly linked to "All-you-can-eat for $9.95." As he was looking at the buffet line, he observed a little boy who picked up a roll and put it right back where it came from. That was his second reason for his aversion to buffets. After he finished eating, he called Jade to see if she and Lad wanted to ride to Elsie's to deliver the clothes which they purchased Friday night.

"Sure, Grant, we'd love to go with you." Grant managed to escape Molten's without anyone asking him who he was and what he was doing in town. They did not need to ask. They already knew. Every pastor in Greene County had announced from the pulpit that morning that Brandon's benefit would be next Saturday, and in its own special way, each church had prayer for Brandon and Elsie.

"Hey, Jade? Ask Nana if she wants to come to."

Jade smiled. "Grant, that is so nice of you to ask. She never gets out. I'll ask her."

When Grant arrived at Jade's, she and Nana were sitting on the porch waiting for him. Lad and Max were playing in the yard. Before he turned off the Range Rover, Nana was up, and Jade was helping her down the steps.

"Hello, Ms. Lott. I'm happy you're going with us." Grant opened the front passenger door and directed Nana to the front seat.

"Thanks for asking, Grant. I haven't seen Elsie in years. I can sit in the back. Jade, you get up here."

Jade was buckling Lad's seat in the back. "No, Nana, I'll sit back here with Lad." Darn. Jade realized she had put Lad behind Nana which meant she would be sitting behind Grant. She would not be able to see him. She thought about moving the car seat, but she did not want her motive to be obvious. After everyone was in the vehicle, Grant decided to tie Max, but Nana insisted on Grant letting Max stay inside.

Elsie walked onto the porch as the SUV pulled into her yard. Grant helped Nana out of the vehicle while Jade unbuckled Lad. "Y'all come in. Well, hello, Lillie." Elsie seemed so tired. Other than an occasional trip to the drug store or doctor, she never left Brandon's side.

"Hello, Elsie." Nana hugged Elsie. Grant and Jade looked on in admiration of two angelic warriors. Neither obtained fame, but neither desired it. They never questioned their lot in life. They just lived.

"Lillie, it's so good to see you." Grant assisted Nana as she entered the house and sat at the kitchen table. Elsie joined her. Grant then walked to Brandon's room.

"Who is this little fella, Jade?" Elsie was holding her hands toward Lad as he bent to get into her lap.

Jade handed Lad to Elsie. "This is Ladetrus, Ms. Elsie. We call him Lad. He's my nephew."

"You are so cute." Elsie was touching Lad's nose as she spoke.

Elsie continued baby-talking to Lad while Nana looked on. "Elsie, I've been praying for you and Brandon. Can I help you with anything?"

Elsie looked at Nana as Lad got down to walk toward Jade. "No, thank you, Lillie, but, you are sweet to ask. The ladies at Cedar Grove Full Gospel are bringing lunch and dinner every day. People have been good to us. Brother Clark runs my errands. I don't know what I would do without him."

Jade put Lad in Nana's lap and walked down the hall to check on Brandon and Grant. When she walked into the room, Grant was sitting beside the bed rubbing Brandon's arm which was covered by the sheet. The oxygen machine was in full rhythm assisting Brandon's weakening lungs. Jade rubbed Brandon's head and felt his hair which was oily and in need of washing. She checked the Foley bag to make sure it did not need emptying. Jade then whispered to Grant. "I'll be back in a minute." Grant nodded his head as Jade left the bedroom and then turned his eyes back toward Brandon.

Jade walked into the kitchen and interrupted the conversation between Elsie and Nana. "Ms. Elsie, when was the last time Brandon was bathed?"

Elsie looked at Jade. "They did Friday, but the lady that bathes him is out sick. A different person came Friday to clean him, but she was new. She did the best she could. The lady that normally bathes him will be here tomorrow afternoon." Nana knew the look on Jade's face. That was not acceptable to Jade.

"Ms. Elsie, can I bathe him? Grant can help me turn him." Grant walked into the kitchen just in time to hear Jade's statement. Grant did not like touching people. Period. Surely Elsie would say no!

"You don't mind, Jade? His hair needs washing, but I'm scared to do it." Grant was wondering if he would have any input. He would not.

"I'll be happy to do it, Ms. Elsie." Elsie got up, and she and Jade went to the bathroom to get the soap, shampoo, bath cloths, and two pans the home health agency used to bathe him. They walked past Grant and did not ask him for his input. In fact, he wondered if they noticed him standing there.

"Grant? Can you come here?" He did not want to go, but how could he resist Jade's request?

"Sure." His response lacked confidence.

"Grant, we're going to bathe Brandon. I need you to help me turn him. Ms. Elsie, you can go visit Nana. We can handle this." Jade had taken charge, and Grant had no choice but to participate.

Jade began by washing Brandon's face, ears, and neck. Grant watched her as she gently cared for Brandon. Jade pulled back the covers to his waist. She then carefully washed his arms, shoulders, and chest. Grant was looking just above Jade's eyes. He wanted to be able to adjust his vision in the event Jade made eye contact with him, but he did not want to see Brandon's body. "He is such a sweet person. I will never understand why bad things happen to such kind people. Grant, pull back the sheet to just below his feet." Grant was forced to look down. He was not prepared for what he saw. Brandon's body was nothing but skin and bones. Grant felt sick. He pulled the sheet back without saying a word.

As Jade gingerly bathed every inch of Brandon's body, Grant's phobia of touching another slowly slipped away. He was amazed at this lady named Jade. She caught him staring at her. She smiled and returned to the task at hand. Grant would help her gently move Brandon as she made certain every part of his body was clean. She then shaved Brandon with precision and patience. After she had washed her hands, she obtained fresh water and positioned a shampoo board under Brandon's head and methodically washed his hair.

"We need to change his bed, Grant." Grant was wordless. He did what Jade instructed him to do. Jade pulled the sheets from Brandon's closet and briefed Grant on how to roll Brandon in order to remove the dirty sheets and replace them with new ones. Afterwards, Jade changed Brandon's hospital gown. When Jade was done, she bent over and kissed Brandon on the forehead and walked to the bathroom. Grant covered Brandon with the clean sheet and sat back down in the chair beside his bed. Brandon was now sleeping all the time. Death could not be far.

When Grant returned to the kitchen, Reverend Clark had arrived and had joined Elsie and Nana who were drinking coffee and eating vanilla wafers. Elsie was enjoying the visit. Lad was sitting with Reverend Clark and had vanilla wafers daubed over his hands and face. Soon, Jade entered the kitchen. "He's clean, Ms.

Elsie. Hey, Brother Clark." Brother Clark stood as Jade entered the room. Grant took note. The good reverend knew how to respect a lady.

Elsie looked at Jade and Grant. "Thanks, kids." Elsie then looked at Brother Clark. "Jade and Grant bathed Brandon."

Reverend Clark sat back down. "I know Brandon feels better now. He may not can say it, but he does. Lillie, has Jade cooked those fish for you we caught yet?"

Nana laughed. "She cooked them that night. She couldn't stop talking about that fishing trip." Nana looked at Grant. "She said you got finned, Grant?"

Grant meekly smiled. "Yes, ma'am. I think Jade enjoyed that part the most."

Jade flirtatiously hit Grant with the hand towel with which she was drying her hands. "I did not, Grant! It was kinda cute watching you try to get that fish off your hook though."

Grant suddenly remembered why they came and said, "Reverend Clark, Jade, can y'all come help me for a second?" They walked outside while Elsie continued her conversation with Nana. Brandon's brothers had visited Saturday. Ernie went home with Lester to help him move houses until they were needed. Ernie had no car or phone, and he agreed to go with Lester so he would be accessible. Also, he needed a payday.

Jade stuck her head in the door. "Ms. Elsie, close your eyes for a second. We have a little surprise for you." Elsie played along and closed her eyes. "Okay, Ms. Elsie, you can open your eyes." When Elsie looked up, Brother Clark and Grant were holding three dresses as if they were human clothes hangers. Elsie's left hand covered her mouth, and she began to cry. Nana reached over and gently placed her hand on Elsie's free hand which rested on the table.

Jade walked over and knelt down beside Elsie and put both her hands on the hurting mother's knees. "Ms. Elsie, these are from Grant. He asked me to go with him to help pick them out.

If they are not the right size, we can take them back and exchange them."

Elsie hugged Jade. "They are beautiful, Jade."

Elsie stood and walked over to Grant. The tears were still flowing. They embraced as a tear ran down Grant's cheek. He had accomplished much academically and professionally, but at that moment, he had never felt better in his life. He thought of the Grinch whose heart grew three sizes. So this is how the old Grinch felt?

Elsie looked at Grant, "Thank you, Grant. You are such a good boy. Thank you so much." They hugged again. It had been since before Lester died, over thirty years ago, that Elsie owned a brand new dress. Now, she had three.

"Elsie, I think Jade and Grant have something else for you, too." The reverend was soaking in the display of love that was unfolding before his eyes. Jade and Grant retrieved some bags from the porch.

Grant set some of the packages on the floor and looked at Elsie. "Ms. Elsie, Jade will have to explain how this all goes together." Jade laughed at Grant's assignment. She then pulled shoes and purses and jewelry out that matched each dress. Jade handed Elsie yet another bag with ladies undergarments and some new makeup and toiletries. Grant did not remember buying those. That Jade was sneaky!

Elsie sat back down at the kitchen table and wiped her eyes with the tear-soaked tissue. "I don't know what to say."

Grant walked over to his astounded friend and knelt beside her. "Ms. Elsie, you honor Jade and me by accepting these gifts. We both respect you so much. You have been through so much and still have a tough path to walk. We didn't want you worried about clothes. Jade is modest. She bought quite a few of these items, too." Elsie wiped the tears away and looked into Grant's eyes as he spoke. "Ms. Elsie, I know I speak for every person in this room when I say that we love you."

Elsie lovingly looked at Grant. "Grant, I was so worried you would not be able to come. Your being here is the greatest gift I have ever received. The day you told Brandon you were going to speak at his funeral, after you left, he told me his last wishes had come true. He was at home with me, and the only friend he ever had was going to speak at his funeral. He told me he was ready to go." Elsie paused as she cried all over again. Everyone in the room was wiping tears, except Lad. Reverend Clark had pulled his handkerchief from his pocket and was drying his eyes. As Elsie cried, Lad walked over and climbed into her lap. Lad just sat in her lap and looked at her as if he had come to dry her tears.

Grant stood and grabbed a hanging bag that he had put on the knob to the kitchen door. "Ms. Elsie, we have Brandon's suit, too. I want to see if you like what we picked out." Elsie looked at Brother Clark in disbelief. The reverend looked at her, and his eyes communicated to her the sincerity of the moment. Grant showed her the suit, shirt, tie and shoes. "Jade picked out the tie."

Elsie held the silk tie in her hands. "Kids, this is perfect. He will be so handsome in this suit." Elsie looked at Grant and Jade. "Thanks for everything. I love y'all."

Grant took Nana, Jade, and Lad home, and then he drove in the direction of the Grand Avenue Inn. When he arrived at his room, there was an envelope taped on the door. He opened it to find a note and a check. The note read:

Grant:

It was so good to see you. Thanks for our little talk at breakfast yesterday. It meant a lot to me and to my family. I have enclosed a check for one thousand dollars payable to the Brandon Smallwood benefit. I hope it helps in some small way.

Your friend,
Travis Crocker

Grant turned on his laptop and checked his email. Sam had emailed him once to let him know that she had safely arrived at her assignment location and another to give him her mailing address. It was evident from her email that she was happy. Grant emailed her and provided her a brief update on Brandon. He detested email, so he kept his reply brief. He also had an email from Mr. Rimes and Linda checking on him. After he finished responding to his mail, he turned off the computer, walked out on the porch of the Grand Avenue Inn, and sat in the swing watching the occasional car or passerby. He spent the next two hours dissecting all that had happened to him since Elsie had called him on March 16. For some unexplained reason, he felt better about his life. He just could not put his finger on why.

chapter thirty-nine

GRANT WOKE UP MONDAY MORNING WITH no definite plans for the day. He ran five miles, showered, and was eating breakfast in the dining area of the Grand Avenue Inn when his phone rang. He recognized the number of the nursing home.

"Hello."

It was Edwina. "Oh Lord, I shore am glad you answered your phone, Yankee!" Edwina was hysterical.

"Good morning, Edwina. What's the matter?" Grant put his fork down to give her his undivided attention.

"I got a problem. A big problem and need a lawyer in the worst kinda way!" Edwina was pacing back and forth as she spoke to Grant on the phone.

"Calm down, Edwina. What seems to be the problem?"

"You know Edwina likes to gamble. Oh Lord, I can't believe

I done gone on and done this!"

Grant was nervous now. Had she been caught stealing? "Well, Edwina, before I can help you, I need you to calm down and tell me what's happened." Grant, too, was up pacing at this point. He had a nervous habit when he talked on the phone with clients. He paced.

"Yankee, can you help me? Please?"

"I don't know, Edwina. I have no idea what the problem is. Just calm down, take a deep breath, and explain your situation." Grant decided that if she did not get to the point soon, he would drive over to the nursing home.

"Jade gave me your cell number!" Edwina began to breathe heavily.

Grant was beyond concerned at this point. "Edwina, do you want me to ride over to the nursing home and talk to you?"

Edwina blurted. "I don't got time for that, Yankee! That casino has done me wrong. I got to have some help!"

"Is Jade near you, Edwina?" Grant thought perhaps Jade could explain the legal dilemma facing Edwina.

"She makin her rounds! Oh, Lord have mercy on me!"

"Okay, Edwina, I'm on my way. Meet me out front at the picnic table." Grant was in his car and backing out of the drive.

"Don't hang up on me, Yankee!"

"I'm almost there. Hang up and walk outside, Edwina." The nursing home was only three blocks from the Grand Avenue Inn.

"I comin."

Grant pulled into the parking lot as Edwina walked outside. "Now, Edwina, what has happened?"

"Yankee, you know I gamble, and I don't got no car. Edwina been saving her money for a car." Grant was thinking ahead and now assumed she had lost her savings.

"I'm listening." Grant stared at Edwina.

"Well, I were down there a few weeks back and won ten thousand dollars at the slot machine. I told nobody. I signed some papers, and now I am in one hell of a mess, Yankee!" Edwina was on the verge of tears.

"What papers?" Edwina threw a page from Sunday's *Sun Herald* newspaper down on the table in front of Grant. There she was! Edwina holding one of those big checks golfers get when they win a tournament. With her gold teeth sparkling, she was broadly smiling from ear to ear.

"Well, congratulations, Edwina!" Grant was excited.

"Yankee, this ain't good. You ain't heard the worst part. They's got Edwina on one a them billboards on I-10. Oh Lord, what will I do when Reverend Mimbes find this out. I need them to take that billboard down, Yankee! Can you help me?"

"Well, Edwina. Did the papers you sign authorize them to use your picture in this manner?"

Edwina sat at the table and put her head down for a second. Then, she looked back at Grant. "I didn't read them papers. I was so happy I won that I would've signed anythang."

"Edwina, two things. First, if you gave them permission, then there is nothing that can be done." Grant looked again at the picture. "Second, I don't understand the problem. The picture is a nice one. It looks just like you. So, Edwina, I would not worry about this. Someone else will win soon, and your picture will be replaced by another happy patron."

Edwina shook her head. "Sista Bernadean from the church brought me this paper, and she saw the billboard. She probably already told Reverend Mimbes. What am I gonna do, Yankee?"

"I thought Reverend Mimbes knew. Let's see, how did you put it? 'Edwina loves to sin every now and then!'"

Edwina gave Grant a stern look. "Yankee, Reverend Mimbes gonna say this is the devil money, and I got to give it all to the church."

Grant folded his arms. "Edwina, just give the church ten percent of it. Isn't that how it works?"

With her eyes like saucers, Edwina glared at Grant. "I don't want to taint the Lord's house with no devil money!"

Grant explained that she had no legal basis to order the casino to remove the ad or billboard since she obviously gave them permission. He also agreed to go with her Wednesday night to meet with Reverend Mimbes and negotiate a settlement with the church. Edwina became his second Mississippi client.

Grant left the nursing home and drove the back streets of Leakesville. The town was undergoing extensive water and sewer repairs, and the streets were in bad shape. He drove past the old tennis court where he used to play. Having been replaced with yet another church, the court was no longer there. Before he knew it, he was riding past the feed store and staring at his dad's old law office. Until now, he had purposely avoided that part of town.

Grant slowed as he looked at the abandoned office. It apparently had been vacant for some time. He stopped on the opposite side of the street and looked at the building. It sat next to the old theatre which had stopped showing movies well-before Grant was old enough to remember. The feed store used the old theatre building for storage. Grant pulled the Range Rover into the parking lot of the abandoned law office. A limb from a large pecan tree had pierced the roof from a storm long ago. No one had cared to repair it. He wondered who owned it. He was deliberating his next move when someone tapped on his window. It startled him, but immediately he relaxed to see a meek, older man, stooped beside the vehicle.

"I'm sorry, I didn't mean to scare you. Can I help you?"

Grant opened the door of the Range Rover and got out. "No thanks. I was just looking at this old building."

The man looked at the deserted office. "You looking to buy it?"

"Oh, no sir. Just checking it out."

The man walked toward the office. Grant followed him. "This building has been abandoned since that lawyer shot himself." He twisted the handle of the door and pushed it open.

"Do you know who owns it?"

The man took a pack of cigarettes from his pocket and shook one out, grabbing it with his teeth. "I believe some fella from Laurel bought it at a tax sale, but I ain't totally sure. He comes and cleans it up about once a year. He puts a *For Sale* sign up every now and then. Nobody wants it since that Hicks fella shot himself in there." The man stuck his hand out to shake Grant's hand. "My name's Harlan."

Grant shook his hand. "Grant. Nice to meet you."

"I own the feed store over there. I don't live here, so you may need to ask some local folks. Anyway, I have to go. Good to meet you." Harlan walked back toward the feed store as Grant stepped inside the office. He paused as he stood in the lobby where clients used to wait for his dad to see them. The furniture was gone; the building was empty. He remembered where every piece of furniture was located and where every picture hung. The memories were crystal clear.

Grant noticed a stack of old books in the corner where Mrs. Pattie's desk once sat. Suzanne Pattie had been Michael's legal secretary his entire career. She was around Michael's age and loyal to a fault. No one got to Michael Hicks without going through Suzanne. She was a lovely but stern lady. She was married to Ryan Pattie, who was a poultry and cattle farmer near State Line. Grant noticed an old Greene County phone directory in the stack of books and picked it up. It was from 1993. He thumbed through it and found the phone number for Michael and Sylvia Hicks. He decided to keep the local directory as a memorial.

Grant looked at the closed door to his dad's office. He pictured his dad sitting behind that door meeting with clients and looking over files. He pictured him on the phone or preparing for a trial. Grant remembered stopping by after school to get a dollar for a snow cone or just dropping by to chat. Grant remembered the pictures of his mom, Lauren, and him that sat on his dad's desk. But the picture in Grant's mind that kept him from opening that door was of his dad lying in a pool of blood after the trigger had been pulled. It was a mistake coming here. Grant hurriedly walked from the office and got back into the Range Rover. He backed out of the parking lot and drove to the inn. Before he exited the vehicle, he looked at the old phone book lying in the passenger seat. He picked it up, turned to the Ps, and found the number for Ryan Pattie.

"Hello, Pattie residence." Their number had not changed. Grant searched for words. "Hello?" Mrs. Pattie still awaited the caller's response.

"Uhh, Mrs. Pattie?" Grant could hear country music playing in the background.

"Yes, this is Suzanne Pattie. Who's calling please?" The music got louder, then quiet. She had walked to the stereo and turned it off.

"Mrs. Pattie, this is Grant Hicks."

"Why hello, Grant. How are you?" She had not seen Grant since his high school graduation in May 1990. It had come a terrible storm that night, and the graduation was delayed for two hours. She did not stay until the end to congratulate him. She had often regretted that decision.

"I'm pretty good. How are you and your family, Mrs. Pattie?"

"We are fine. I'm retired now, Grant. Ryan is working the chicken houses this morning as usual. Our kids are grown and married. I have five grandchildren now. What about you, Grant?"

"I live in Atlanta. I'm still single." There was a moment of awkward silence before Grant continued. "Mrs. Pattie, do you mind if I come see you today?" She knew Grant was in town to see Brandon, and she also knew he had followed in his daddy's footsteps and had become a lawyer. She was a master at the computer and followed Grant electronically. Google is a powerful tool. In addition, she knew a little about *Martindale-Hubbell's* listing of attorneys.

"I would like that, Grant. Why don't you come at noon, and you can eat lunch with Ryan and me. He has to haul some cattle to the Hattiesburg stockyard afterwards. We can visit then. I can't wait to see you, Grant. We still live in the same place."

Grant could sense the smile on her face. "Great. I'll see you then." Grant hung up the phone, exited his vehicle, and spent the next two hours finishing the novel he had started a few days before.

Grant slowly made his way up to State Line, traveling Old Avera Road which connected Leakesville to State Line. He passed Lake Luther where he had swam as a teenager and was impressed by the addition of Lake Gary and the housing development that surrounded the moderate-sized lake. He passed through Knobtown where a large number of Greene County's African Americans lived. Michael Hicks always carried the Knobtown vote with at least ninety percent. He then turned on to Pattie Farm Road and found the Pattie residence sitting in the middle of their four-hundred-acre farm.

The property was beautiful and well kept. Grant entered it from the south. Six large poultry houses sat to the west of the house. On the east side of the house were two huge red barns. One housed the farm equipment, and the other was used for hay storage during the winter months. To the north of the house were two hundred acres of pastureland that contained at least 150 head of Black Angus cattle. A blue healer met Grant at his vehicle.

Ryan Pattie was approaching the house as Grant arrived. "Get out and come on in." Mr. Pattie was a short, balding man. He wore a big sun hat to shield himself from the sun. He wore long-sleaved work shirts to protect his arms. His work pants were high-waters, exposing the top of his ankle-high work boots.

"Hello, Mr. Pattie."

The farmer took his hat off and slapped it against his leg to loosen the dust. He then stomped his feet on the steps to prepare to enter the house. "I hope you're hungry." Grant was hungry before he left the Grand Avenue but now not so much. He found himself nervous again. They entered the house, and the smell of home cooking woke up Grant's stomach once more.

"Grant!" Smiling from ear to ear, Mrs. Pattie walked up to Grant and hugged him. "You look so good." She wanted to say that he looked just like his dad but decided that she would not mention his dad unless he brought it up.

"You do, too, Mrs. Pattie. The food smells great." Grant followed the Patties into the kitchen and sat at a breakfast table which gave them a view of the farm through a bay window.

"Have a seat. Everything is ready. I'll fix you a plate." Mr. Pattie was piling his food high from the pots that were still on the stove. Mrs. Pattie then fixed Grant's in the same manner. Mr. Pattie sat down, and Suzanne placed Grant's food in front of him, stood behind her chair, and closed her eyes. Without prompting, Mr. Pattie then mumbled a prayer that Grant could not hear or understand. Mrs. Pattie then prepared her plate and joined them. They spent the next twenty minutes eating as the old friends caught Grant up on their kids and grandchildren.

"I gotta run." Mr. Pattie got up, placed his dishes in the sink, and walked over and kissed his wife on top of her head. "Good to see you, Mr. Hicks." Grant stood and shook Mr. Pattie's hand. "I'll be back in a few hours, Suze." Mr. Pattie then left for the stockyard as he had done many times before.

"Would you like some more tea, Grant?" Sweet tea to the South is like apple pie to America. Suzanne Pattie's was the best around.

"Sure. Thanks for lunch. It was delicious."

She filled Grant's glass with fresh ice and tea and rejoined him at the table. "I'm glad you enjoyed it. It's so good to see you. How long are you in town?"

Grant sipped from his tea glass. "I'm not quite sure. I'm here to see Brandon Smallwood. I'll leave after his funeral." Grant looked out the bay window at a black cat slowly walking through the Pattie's yard.

"I know this is tough on Elsie, too. How is she?"

Grant brought her up to date on Brandon, Elsie, and the Smallwood brothers. They chatted for a few minutes before Grant broached the subject he had come to discuss.

"Mrs. Pattie, do you miss my dad?"

She looked into Grant's eyes with affection. "Every day, Grant. I do miss him." Her eyes then found the cat that was walking through the yard.

"I know you found him that morning."

Grant stared at her as her eyes slowly left the cat and returned to his. "I did." She had not discussed that morning in years. Hundreds of times she had replayed in her mind the days leading up to Michael Hicks' suicide. She blamed herself for not noticing the little hints that Michael unintentionally left.

"I stopped by his old law office this morning."

Suzanne Pattie rarely went to Leakesville anymore. Her shopping trips took her to neighboring Waynesboro or to Hattiesburg. "I assume it's still vacant?"

"It is. I just walked into the lobby and your office. I did not enter his." She knew everything about Grant and Michael's tumultuous relationship. She had lived through the Brandon Smallwood trial and the rise and fall of Senator Michael Hicks. Also, Michael shared everything with her. He trusted her more than he trusted his wife Sylvia.

"Grant, I haven't seen you since you left here after high school. I'm so sorry everything happened the way it did."

Grant's eyes left hers and stared blankly out the window. "That's okay. That was a long time ago. I'm glad that I have been able to spend some time with Brandon, however. I also have spent a lot of time with Sheriff McInnis since I've been back here. He's a good man."

"Yes, he is. Our church choir visits Greene Rural occasionally. I always enjoy seeing him when we sing there."

Grant looked at Mrs. Pattie. "I have learned a lot from him

about Dad's senate loss. He also educated me on the circumstances that led to Brandon's release from prison." Staring out the window, Grant paused. "I was surprised to learn that he respected my dad so much."

Mrs. Pattie was pleased that Grant had been learning about his dad. She also knew how heart-broken Michael was over the schism with his son. "Grant, I know you and your dad had some rough spots. However, he loved you more than life itself." Mrs. Pattie regretted her poor choice of words but noticed that Grant did not appear to be offended. "Grant, you look just like him." She placed her hand on his.

Grant stared at her for a moment. "I know you can't answer this question, but I'm going to ask it anyway. Why do you think Dad shot himself? He was only forty-six. He was successful. I just don't understand it. It was such a selfish act." Grant's demeanor slowly changed from curiosity to anger.

"You're right, Grant. I don't know why. However, I'll tell you what I do know. Your dad was one of the most unselfish people I've ever known." Grant looked at her with disbelieving eyes. "No person in need of an attorney who walked through his door was ever turned away for lack of money. Your dad could have made a fortune elsewhere. He was bright, articulate, and a very good lawyer. But he chose to come home to practice and represent the people with whom he grew up."

"But he shot himself, the ultimate selfish act. And not only would he not represent Brandon, he would not even go visit him at the county jail. He didn't want to hurt his precious political career. I'm sorry, Mrs. Pattie. I don't want to be disrespectful, but those actions seem to me to be indicative of a pretty selfish person."

Mrs. Pattie pondered his words. She decided she would not retreat from the truth. "Grant, you were so young then. I don't expect what I'm about to say to matter too much to you, but I'm going to say it anyway. Your dad came from a very poor background where the idea of becoming a lawyer was foreign. Yet, your dad did it. He finished number two in his class. Did you know his dad, your Grandpa Hicks, refused to go to his law school graduation?"

Grant did not. "No, ma'am."

"Your dad was President of the Law School Student Body at Ole Miss. He spoke at his graduation, yet his dad would not come, and he never congratulated him." Grant's eyes began to feel the tears seeping into them. "Grant, your dad never gained the approval of his own daddy. He would have traded his law degree and his senate seat for one 'good job' or one 'I am proud of you, son' from your grandpa. But it never came. So your daddy compensated by setting new goals and working." Grant felt so ashamed of himself as he listened to Mrs. Pattie. He could not speak. He was transfixed.

"Grant, I don't intend this to be mean, but I have always been direct with people. You have no right to hold on to this hatred you have for your daddy. Son, he worshiped you. He was so proud of you. Every time your name was in the paper for making the Chancellor's list at Ole Miss, he bragged for days. I know he was not a perfect dad. I know that he let you down when he did not get involved in Brandon's situation. But, Grant, he was scared. The only validation your daddy ever received was from his own accomplishments. When he ultimately lost the senate seat, the people he thought were his friends were no longer around. Then, he got sued over some legal work by a former client. In his mind his legal reputation was ruined. So on the day of your daddy's trial, alone in his office, for whatever reason, he ran from his fears and his perceived failures." They sat in silence for a couple minutes staring out of the window. Grant was processing the very direct words of Suzanne Pattie.

Grant looked at Mrs. Pattie. "Did you go to his funeral?"

She looked at Grant. "Yes. There was no wake the night before. It was a simple graveside service at the Hicks' Cemetery. But it was a sweet service."

Grant again stared out of the window. His pride had prevented him from attending the funeral. His pride was finally retreating enough to at least discuss it. "Who conducted the funeral? The preacher at Big Creek?"

"I knew you didn't attend the funeral, Grant, but did your mom ever discuss it with you?"

The look on Grant's face gave her the answer to her question. This was the first time Grant had ever discussed his dad's funeral. "No, ma'am. I didn't want to talk about it."

"Grant, we all just gathered around the grave. Nina Taylor sang "Beulah Land" at the beginning and "Amazing Grace" at the end. Reverend Mimbes brought a beautiful message."

Her words startled him. Reverend Mimbes? Why him? Grant wondered why Reverend Mimbes did not mention this to him the night he was at the fellowship hall at Temple Harvest. "Reverend Mimbes? That's surprising. Why him? What was their connection?"

She patted Grant on the hand. "You will have to ask Reverend Mimbes that question, but they were friends." Mrs. Pattie got up and cut them a piece of the chocolate pie that had finally cooled. They ate their pie without discussion.

"Grant, I have a few things I want to give you. Follow me." They got up from the table, and Grant followed her to a bedroom that had been converted to an office for the farm. Mrs. Pattie opened a fire-proof gun safe in the corner of the room. She handed him a frame that contained his dad's law license. She also gave him a frame that contained Michael's group picture from his first term in the Senate.

"Thank you. I figured Mom or Lauren had all this stuff." Grant sat in the desk chair and read every word of his dad's law license. He looked at the thirty-five-year-old face of freshman State Senator Michael Hicks. For the first time, Grant realized that his dad was two years younger than he when he was first elected to the Senate.

"I have two other items here for you." She fumbled around

in the safe and pulled out a group picture of Grant's Little League baseball team. Michael Hicks was the coach, and he was standing next to Grant with his arm around his precious son. As Grant looked at the picture, tears began to stream down his face. Mrs. Pattie looked on in silence. No words were necessary.

After Grant was able to contain the pain, Mrs. Pattie continued. "Grant, each month your dad had me anonymously deposit three hundred dollars into Elsie Smallwood's account to cover expenses for her monthly trips to see Brandon at Parchman. A week before he died, he had me deposit five thousand dollars into her account." Grant looked at her with compassion and utter sorrow as she continued talking. "This was in the mail the day your dad died." She handed Grant an unopened letter addressed to Mr. Michael Hicks from Brandon Smallwood. Grant stared at the letter as he held it in his hand. Mrs. Pattie got up and walked to the door. "Stay in here as long as you like." She then left the room and shut the door.

Grant never knew his dad was the man he was. Grant felt so selfish for having held his grudge for so long. He regretted the words he had said to his daddy when he refused to represent Brandon. He regretted not shaking his daddy's hand as he left home, never to return. The tears appeared once more. After a few moments, Grant's vision was still blurred by the tears floating in his eyes. When he finally could see clearly, he opened the letter and began to read. It was dated one week before his dad's death. These are the words Grant saw.

Dear Mr. Hicks,

Thank you so much for coming to see me today. Words cannot express to you how your visit made me feel. Other than Mom, you and Grant are the only two people that have ever visited me here. I know that it is a long drive from Leakesville, and as busy as you are, it was a great sacrifice for you to come see me. Again, it meant a lot.

I just wanted to let you know again that you did not need to ask me to forgive you. Rather, I was the one that needed forgiveness. I have not seen Grant in a little over a year, but I think of him daily. I hope that you and he can restore the relationship that I feel so responsible for hurting. He is a great guy, and I will never forget his willingness to be my friend when I needed one so badly.

I hope to see you again soon. When you see Grant, please tell him hello.

With many thanks,

Brandon

P.S. Grant looks just like you!

As she stood outside the closed door, Mrs. Pattie could hear Grant sniffing. She thought of the pain that had been bottled up inside of him for so long. She often wondered if he blamed himself for his daddy's death. She quietly walked back down the hall, onto the porch, and sat in the swing.

A half hour later, Grant walked out with the items she had given him. "Mrs. Pattie, thanks so much. Thanks for everything."

She walked Grant to his vehicle. "Grant, I have waited since 1994 to give you these things. You come back anytime. You're always welcome here. You're family to me."

Grant spent the rest of the day thinking of his visit with Suzanne Pattie. The sheriff helped him understand his daddy's political demise. Suzanne helped him understand his physical and mental demise. Grant was slowly letting go of the past. Like a found treasure that had been corroded by the elements of time and now scrubbed with gentle care, Grant's heart was slowly beginning to sparkle again. Another ingredient had been added to the healing process of Grant Hicks. His soul was finally surfacing to breathe again.

chapter forty

IT WAS TUESDAY, MARCH 30. IT HAD BEEN nine days since Lad came to live with Nana and Jade. They had not heard from Stormy or Jade's mother. Lad had adjusted amazingly well. His potty training was progressing, and he was talking more. Max helped with the verbal part. Lad could say Max better than any other word. The child would not go to sleep unless Max was beside his bed. Boy and dog had become inseparable.

Jade was getting ready for work when the phone rang. "Hello."

"Jade?" It was Jade's mother.

"Hey, Mom." Jade always kept her responses short when talking to her mother. She had almost given up hope that she would have a normal relationship with her mom. Long conversations always confirmed that reality, so she avoided them.

"How's Momma?"

"Nana is doing okay. She asks me daily if I hear from you." Jade could hear her mom blowing the cigarette smoke from her lungs.

"I can't talk long. Stormy was arrested again last night. I thought you should know."

Jade's mother waited for her reaction. Gathering her thoughts, Jade sat on the edge of the bathtub. "Where?"

"Pascagoula. She was with some guys with a mobile meth lab, and they got caught." Jade was silent as she thought of Lad. "Anyway, I thought you should know."

"Mom, what about Ladetrus?" Jade walked into the bedroom to make sure Lad was still asleep. Max slowly wagged his tail as he looked up at Jade.

"You should just turn him over to the Department of Human Services. I told Stormy to stay away from that nigger."

Jade's demeanor changed to anger as she walked to the kitchen. "Mom, please don't say that word."

"Well, Afro-American, black, whatever Speed is. That baby ain't your problem either way. Stormy won't be coming to get him. Thought you should know."

Jade sat down at the kitchen table and stared at the borrowed highchair. "I'm not turning Lad over to anyone, especially DHS. Lad is precious. Where is Stormy?"

"She's in the Jackson County jail. There won't be anybody bailing her out this time. She can sit there and rot as far as I'm concerned." Jade wondered how her mom could be so callous. "Got to go. Tell Momma hello." Before Jade could respond, her mom hung up the phone. The conversation confirmed what Jade already knew. Lad was now her child to raise.

Grant walked into the Smallwoods' at 8:00 a.m. The hospice

nurse, Jesse Bolton, was already there when he arrived. Nurse Bolton, Elsie, and Brother Clark were talking when Grant stepped into the kitchen.

"Ms. Elsie, at this point it's a matter of keeping him comfortable." The nurse looked with compassion at Elsie.

Elsie was concentrating. "How much longer?" No one felt it necessary to acknowledge Grant's presence. He had become a regular at these meetings.

"It's hard to tell. Based on his urine flow, it probably will be no more than two or three days. He's starting to gain more fluid in his lungs, too, so it will be very difficult to turn him much anymore." They sat in silence for a few minutes.

"Thank you for all you have done, Jesse. You've taken good care of my baby." Nurse Bolton explained the protocol for the next few days, which included a health care worker's presence most of the time, unless Elsie requested otherwise. She explained that an aide would be there later in the day to bathe and change his sheets. Tomorrow, there would be someone there at all times until the end. Jesse Bolton left with a heavy heart. Her job ended with each patient dying. Like everyone that was privileged to meet Brandon Smallwood, Jesse's life had been forever altered by her time with Brandon.

"Good morning, Grant." Brother Clark was the first to acknowledge his presence.

"Hey." Grant poured himself a cup of coffee, his acquired taste now entrenched.

"Let's walk outside." The two men walked out onto the porch and sat down. Reverend Clark went over the order of service for the funeral. It included an opening song, Reverend Clark's welcome and scripture reading, another song, Grant's eulogy, yet another song, then the reverend's message.

"Where will the funeral be held, Reverend?"

"That is still not settled. Several churches have volunteered to host it. Based upon the interest in the benefit Saturday, I fully expect a large crowd. So, I'm leaning toward First Baptist. It has the largest sanctuary in the county."

Grant continued to look at Reverend Clark. He was so relieved that the experienced minister was in charge of the details. "Where will he be buried?"

Reverend Clark had the look of intense concentration. "Elsie wants him buried in a place with some shade trees. She doesn't want his grave in the open sun all the time. She described what she wants the site to look like, but I haven't located one yet. If we can't find one, then I expect him to be buried behind the funeral home in their cemetery."

"But isn't that the place where Luther is buried?"

"It is, but the paupers are buried in a separate section the county purchased. Brandon would be on the other end."

The phone rang inside. Elsie answered it and walked out onto the porch. "It's for you, Grant."

Grant wondered who knew he was there. He walked inside and took the phone from Elsie. "Hello."

"Good morning, Grant." It was Linda.

"Well, hey, Linda. How are you?"

"I'm doing well. I'm enjoying my time off. My husband and I are in Gulf Shores, Alabama. We arrived yesterday and will be here a week. Does your cell phone not work where you are?"

Grant pulled his cell from his pocket. There were no missed calls. "Hmm. It usually does. I have no missed calls." He put the phone back in his pocket.

"I may have dialed the wrong number. Anyway, I was just thinking about you. Since I was this close, I thought I would call and see how you are doing. I kept Ms. Smallwood's number in case I needed it. I'm lucky to have caught you there. How are you, Grant?"

"I'm okay, actually. I'm glad I came."

Linda could sense the change in Grant's voice. He seemed more relaxed. "That's good, Grant. How long will you be there? I thought you could join us a day or two if you like. We have a three-bedroom condo, and two of those rooms aren't being used."

"That's sweet of you to ask. I'm not sure when I'll leave. I agreed to speak at Brandon's funeral. I'm not sure when that will be." Grant briefed Linda on Brandon's situation. He told her he missed her, and if it worked out, he would drive over. She reminded him of her cell number and gave him the name and address of the condo.

"Grant, would you let me know when the funeral will be?" Grant agreed to do so, hung up the phone, and walked back into Brandon's bedroom. He sat by Brandon's bed for a while before joining Elsie and Reverend Clark in the kitchen. Reverend Clark was about to leave, so he and Grant told Elsie good-bye and walked toward their vehicles.

"Grant, there is a benefit planning meeting tonight. Come go with me?"

Grant stopped to ponder the offer. He was not quite sure he was up for a meeting with that many local people. He still remembered the viciousness of the rumors and the treatment Brandon received when he was charged with Tony Sylvestor's murder. "I don't know about that, Reverend. I've tried to stay as low-key as possible since I've been here."

Reverend Clark looked at Grant, and as Grant was becoming accustomed with him, no was not an option. "The meeting is at 7:00. I'll pick you up at the Inn at 6:45."

Grant arrived at the Inn to find the sheriff's cruiser backing out of the parking lot. When he saw Grant drive up, he pulled back into the parking lot and got out of his car.

"Grant Hicks?"

Grant had the look of nervous curiosity. "Yes sir. I'm Grant Hicks."

The sheriff shook Grant's hand. "My name is Wilson Coaker. I'm the sheriff here." Sheriff Coaker was about six feet tall, around sixty years old, and walked slowly. He talked slower. "Judge Eaton wanted me to come find you. He needs you at the Justice Court building."

Grant looked confused. "Me? What for?"

The sheriff was getting back into his car. He shut the door, cranked the car, and rolled his window down. "He has appointed you to represent somebody."

Grant was furious. The judge had no right to appoint him. He did not practice here. He and Jade were planning to leave at 2:00 p.m. to ride to Lucedale to pick up something Grant bought for Sheriff McInnis. He got in his Range Rover and left for the double-wide trailer which housed the Justice Court.

There were cars parked all over the place. Grant had to park a block away and walk to the building. When he stepped inside, people were standing in the hallway leading to the courtroom. He made his way into the legal arena and stood in the corner. Judge Eaton was sitting on the bench, leaning back in his chair, and watching the witness answer a question. Grant noticed a six-person jury sitting in cowhide-bottomed straight chairs.

Interrupting the witness, Judge Eaton recognized Grant standing in the corner. "Excuse me, sir, but we need to take a five minute recess. Mr. Hicks? Come on back with me." The judge left the bench, and Grant followed him to his office.

"Hello, Mr. Hicks. I'm glad the sheriff found you." Grant was not. "I've appointed you to represent Roscoe Gipson. He and the Gipson clan have been charged with moonshining."

Grant felt as if he were in the twilight zone. "What? Moonshining? I thought that went away with prohibition." The office was too small for Grant to pace, so he shook his knees incessantly.

"It pretty much has, except for the Gipson clan. They're good boys and mind their own business, but they like to drink, and they're poor. Hence, they make their own. It's election year next year, so the sheriff usually busts them every four years around this time. I call a jury in because the Gipson clan will vote in a block, at least the ones that don't have felonies. That way I'm not the one who finds them guilty." The judge smiled, winked, and got up. "Come on. I'll introduce you to Roscoe."

"Judge, I'm not a criminal lawyer. I really don't want to commit legal malpractice. Do I have to accept the appointment?"

The judge pulled some Red Man chewing tobacco from his pocket and placed a handful in his mouth. He then looked at Grant with strands of tobacco hanging between his lips. "No, you don't. But, son, I really need you to do this. There are three lawyers in this town. Two of them are in there. Felix is the County Prosecutor, Joe Barker is the public defender, and we can't find George Brewer. Trust me when I say this, Grant; George has earned the nickname 'No-Show George.'"

"Why can't the public defender represent him? Isn't he representing the others?"

"The last time Joe represented Roscoe, they got in a fight afterwards. Rosco beat the shit out of him. Obviously, there is a conflict there. It won't take long. After we finish with Bubba's trial, we only have Willie's and Roscoe's left." The judge then introduced Grant to Roscoe and resumed Bubba's trial. Grant called Jade and asked if she could come to the Justice Court building to meet him. He told her he would explain his dilemma when she arrived.

After Roscoe and Grant visited outside, they reentered the courtroom just as Judge Eaton announced the jury's verdict. Bubba Gipson was guilty. The county prosecutor had three Gipson convictions, with two more to go. The public defender, Joe Barker, was a freckled-faced man in his mid forties. His hair was a mixture of red and gray. He had fat cheeks but a slender body. He was not having a good day. The look on his face did not hide his frustration with the jurors.

"Okay, let's seat another jury. We have two more trials left.

Mr. Bailiff, get all the remaining jurors in here." The judge was ready for trial number four. After all the potential jury members were seated, he began going over the basic instructions given to a jury venire. Grant noticed all the jurors knew the defendant, the judge, the attorneys, and the witnesses. Apparently this did not matter because nobody was disqualified. The prosecutor then began voir diring the prospective jurors. Lawyers use the voir dire process to ensure that qualified, unbiased people sit on juries.

Joe Barker had all he could take. He stood. "Judge?"

"What, Joe? You can't interrupt the prosecutor when he's questioning the jury venire."

Mr. Barker looked at the remaining panel members and then at the judge. "I can save us all some time, Judge." Jade entered the courtroom and sat down next to Grant. He and Roscoe looked at her. She crinkled her nose as she smiled at Grant. Grant smirked.

"Well, if you can save us some time, go ahead. Any objection, Felix?"

Felix sat back down at the prosecutor's table. "No objection."

Joe Barker looked at the prospective jurors and practically yelled at the group. "Six of you son-of-a-bitches get up there. I don't care which ones!" Jade laughed out loud. Grant looked at the ceiling. Felix looked at the judge.

His Honor spit and slowly spoke. "Okay, I need six of y'all up here." The jurors looked at each other, and eventually six took their places in the jury box. Grant had one thought: unbelievable.

It took about thirty minutes for the trial of Willie Gipson to be completed and a guilty verdict returned. It was now time for trial number five of the Gipson clan. Jade was excited to get to see Grant in action.

"Okay, Roscoe. You and Mr. Hicks come on up and have a seat."

Grant addressed the court. "Your Honor, I would request a

continuance to properly prepare my case, but I'm afraid it would be denied. Or, Your Honor, I would ask for a continuance to properly dress for Your Honor's esteemed court, but I also fear it would be denied. Unless I'm wrong, we're ready."

The judge smiled. He had taken a liking to this Hicks boy. "You're right, counselor." The judge then looked at the remaining prospective jurors. "Since there are only six members of the jury panel remaining, you six come on up." Grant thought about objecting there, too, but figured he was wasting his breath. He would just take his whipping and head to Lucedale with Jade.

The prosecutor gave his opening statement. Grant elected to defer his opening statement until after the prosecutor rested his case. Felix's star and only witness was the sheriff. After the sheriff detailed how he had saved the county from the scourge of corn whiskey, the prosecutor tendered the witness.

Grant chose not to ask the sheriff any questions. The prosecutor then rested. Grant waived his opening statement. "Judge, I have a motion, but I would like to call the sheriff to the stand to answer a couple of questions before I make it. I can make my motion now, but I believe the sheriff answering a few questions will assist the court and make my point. Would that be permissible, Your Honor?"

Judge Eaton adjusted in his chair. "Certainly, Counselor. Felix, that okay with you?"

The prosecutor looked at Grant as if Grant were trying to perform a magic trick and Felix was trying to figure out the slight-of-hand. "Uhh. I reckon so, Judge. It might be interesting to see."

Grant called the sheriff back to the stand. Sheriff Coaker had been looking back and forth at the lawyers and Judge Eaton, wondering if he would have any input. They ignored the sheriff's inquisitive looks. Judge Eaton leaned back in his chair. "Go ahead, Mr. Hicks."

"Thank you, Your Honor. Sheriff, I won't ask you but a few questions. First, how are you today?"

The sheriff looked at Grant with one raised eyebrow. "I'm good. Thank you."

"Sheriff, have you ever tasted homemade whiskey?"

The sheriff was a deacon in the church he attended. He sat up erect in the witness stand before he answered. "Well, of course not, Mr. Hicks. I'm a God-fearing Christian." The sheriff looked at the jury to make sure they heard the God-fearing part.

"Well, how do you know that you confiscated corn whiskey from my client?" Grant noticed the prosecutor had not introduced any physical evidence of the crime. After four identical trials, Felix had simply forgotten.

The sheriff began to relax. "Well, you can tell by looking at it, and you can smell it." The sheriff's eyes were following Grant. Grant was walking around the courtroom, looking under chairs and tables.

Finally, the judge spoke. "Mr. Hicks, what in the world are you a doin? Did you drop something?"

Grant then looked at the judge. "Your Honor, I'm ready to state my motion."

Felix jumped from his chair. "Here we go again with his motions, Judge. I object!"

The judge sternly looked at the prosecutor. "Felix, you approved of this method. Sit down. State your motion, Mr. Hicks."

"Your Honor, the prosecutor rested his case and did not introduce any physical evidence against my client. I have looked all over this courtroom and find not one ounce of corn whiskey. I move for a dismissal."

Felix responded. "Judge, I introduced the moonshine in the four other cases. Let me reopen my case, call the sheriff back as a witness, then introduce the whiskey." Felix began hurriedly searching for the evidence.

Judge Eaton actually liked Roscoe. He was secretly delighted Roscoe whipped Joe Barker's ass the last time he was in court.

"I deny your request, Mr. Prosecutor. I grant Mr. Hicks' motion and dismiss the charges. Jurors, you are free to go. Thank you for your service." The judge quickly left the bench. Jade was lightly clapping for Grant's victory. Roscoe was looking at Jade's legs that were exposed several inches above her knees and was oblivious to his own victory. Felix began gathering his files to leave. Grant was looking down shaking his head. The winning attorney then explained to Roscoe that he was not guilty. Roscoe tried to convince Grant that he was. So goes Justice Court.

chapter forty-one

YOU WERE SO CUTE IN THAT COURTROOM. That was fun!" Jade smiled as she looked at Grant.

He took his eyes off the road briefly to look at Jade. "Thanks, but I would not classify that as fun. I need to get out of this place before my law practice grows any more. I now represent Johnny Newbill and Roscoe Gipson, and I have to negotiate a settlement with Reverend Mimbes on behalf of Edwina tomorrow night regarding her gambling winnings." Jade and Grant both laughed. "Jade, thanks for coming with me. I hope it was not a problem for you to take off a little early."

"Oh, thanks for asking. I have several weeks of vacation saved up, so Becky gives me some liberties as long as my rounds are completed. Besides, what you're doing for Mr. Lauvon is very sweet. He's such a good man. He's like a daddy to me. How did you come up with the idea to do this?"

Grant looked at Jade, then back at the road. "I noticed that there was nothing in his room commemorating his days as Sheriff of Greene County. So, I called his son, Paul, who said that to his knowledge his dad was never recognized for his service. Paul seemed to remember Sheriff McInnis' staff having a going-away luncheon or something, but since they were all losing their jobs, too, it was kind of a sad gathering."

Jade looked at Grant's profile as he watched the road. She had already admitted to herself that she had fallen for him. She planned to keep that her secret. She could not stand public rejection again. "Well, Mr. Lauvon will appreciate it. Who all will be there?"

"Paul told me his brother and two sisters will be there with their families. He also said a few of Sheriff McInnis' former staff members will come. Since dinner is at 5:30, I told them to be there at 6:00. Ms. Berry said she and the staff would have everything ready but would keep it a surprise. She said they would make sure the sheriff was in his room, and that the curtains would be closed so that he couldn't see people arriving from his window."

Jade and Grant pulled into the trophy shop and inspected the plaque Grant had ordered for Sheriff McInnis. The inscription read: "To Greene County's Most Trusted Sheriff, Lauvon McInnis. For Twenty Years of Devoted Service to the Citizens of Greene County and for Your Tireless Commitment to Protect Its Citizenry. Your Service Will Never Be Forgotten." At the bottom was written, "Lauvon H. McInnis, Sheriff, County of Greene, January 2, 1972, through January 1, 1992."

"Grant, it's perfect."

"I hope he likes it. It's not much, but it's something." Grant paid for the plaque, and he and Jade drove through the Gatlin Creek Hills to the home of Charlotte Turner to pick up the cake for the ceremony, which was decorated with a miniature patrol car and an officer standing beside it. The words on the cake were perfect: "Greene County's Most Trusted Sheriff." Grant and Jade then left for the nursing home. When they arrived, they met with Becky Berry to go over the final details for the ceremony.

"Grant, thank you for coming up with this idea." Becky looked at Grant with appreciation.

"It's my pleasure, Ms. Berry, and thank you for the job you do here. As an attorney, I have defended nursing homes when family members sue on behalf of an injured or neglected loved one. I wish all nursing homes were like this one. You and your staff are special."

Grant left the care facility and spent the rest of the afternoon at the Inn. He called Reverend Clark and invited him to the celebration and told him he would meet him at the benefit meeting after the ceremony was over. Grant was enjoying the inner peace he was discovering by helping others. What Grant did not realize was that his heart's desire to help others had been imprisoned by bitterness and unforgiveness for all these years. As he slowly let go of the past, his heart began to escape the cage that had trapped it for so long. Grant sat on the swing on the front porch of the Inn and found himself waving at the random cars that passed. If his heart had a face, it would be looking up at him and smiling at that very moment.

Jade kept the sheriff engaged in a game of Scrabble. He enjoyed working crossword puzzles and playing Scrabble with Jade. They played at least twice per week during Jade's lunch hour. He was delighted she wanted to play tonight. They were in the middle of a game when a knock sounded.

"Come in." The sheriff and Jade looked at the door as it opened.

It was Becky Berry. "Hey, Sheriff. We need you and Jade in the dining area. We are having Edwina a cake recognizing her work anniversary. She has been with us five years today. I know she would want both of you there." The little fib rolled off Becky's tongue with conviction.

Jade got up first. "We'll finish our game after while, Mr. Lauvon." Jade grabbed his arm, and he picked up his cane. Becky walked ahead of them. When the sheriff and Jade rounded the corner, the dining area was packed with people. The sheriff noticed his children and grandchildren were there. They all walked over and affectionately hugged him as Jade stepped aside and joined Becky and Grant near the front of the room. The sheriff was silent. He wondered why they were all here. It was not his birthday nor any other special occasion that he could recall.

Each holding an arm, his daughters led him to an executive chair at the front of the room. He still had not spoken. He saw his former dispatcher standing alongside three of his former deputies. He saw former Justice Court Judges and one retired Circuit judge who had made the trip up from Pascagoula. The room was filled with his family, friends, residents and staff members.

Becky grabbed the microphone which was connected to the portable speaker system. "Sheriff McInnis, I can tell you are surprised." Everyone laughed. The sheriff looked at Becky with a stoic, yet humble, gaze. "You have been with your extended family here at Greene Rural for a little over two years, and we each love you. A few days ago, Grant came to my office with an idea. As evident from the attendance today, it was obviously a great idea. I'm going to ask Grant to come say a few words."

Grant looked at Jade and motioned for her to walk up to the microphone with him. "Thanks, Becky. Once again, you and your staff have outdone yourselves. Thanks everybody for coming to honor this special man. On Sunday, March 21, I walked into this nursing home to visit an old friend. Over the last several days, I have enjoyed my visits with you, Sheriff McInnis." The sheriff nodded his head at Grant as the tears began to fill his eyes. The sheriff's three-year-old granddaughter climbed into his lap. "Sheriff, I have respected you all of my life. And I want to personally thank you for helping me understand some things that, until recently, I had no knowledge of. I'm a better man today because of you. As we visited, Sheriff, I noticed that there wasn't anything displayed in your room commemorating your devoted service to this county. Well, Sheriff, that is about to change." Grant whispered in Jade's ear to retrieve the plaque. "I'm going to ask Jade to make a presentation to you as a token of not only our appreciation but this county's appreciation."

Darwin Gordon had arrived and was taking pictures of the ceremony for the *Greene County Herald*. Reverend Clark stood in the corner noting the change he had seen in Grant. He was impressed by Grant's display of natural leadership. Edwina's normally huge smile was replaced with sniffles and dripping mascara as she watched the sheriff begin to wipe the tears streaming down his face.

Jade held the microphone and walked over to the sheriff. "Mr. Lauvon, I'm going to read you this plaque, and I look forward to seeing it hanging in your room each time I visit." The sheriff could not stop the emotion trickling from his eyes. "'To Greene County's Most Trusted Sheriff, Lauvon McInnis. For Twenty Years of Devoted Service to the Citizens of Greene County and for Your Tireless Commitment to Protect Its Citizenry. Your Service Will Never Be Forgotten. Lauvon H. McInnis, Sheriff, County of Greene, January 2, 1972, through January 1, 1992.'" Jade handed the plaque to the sheriff and kissed him on the cheek as the crowd erupted in applause.

When the applause receded, Jade handed the microphone to the sheriff. He wiped his eyes with his handkerchief. Wondering what to say, he looked at the crowd. He looked into the eyes of each one of his family members present. Even his sons' eyes were misting. He then looked at Grant and pointed at him. "Thanks." He choked up and could not continue. His granddaughter held on tightly to his free hand. He finally was able to gain his composure and then he looked at his friends and neighbors. "This means so much to me. I enjoyed every minute being your sheriff. I will never forget this day. Thank you so very much." Those were the only words his emotions would permit. The applause erupted once more.

People lined up to speak to the sheriff while Becky and her staff began serving refreshments. Grant watched Sheriff McInnis being loved by his family and friends. Reverend Clark patted Grant on the shoulder and reminded him it was time for the benefit meeting. Grant asked Jade to tell the sheriff that he would be back in a day or two and for him to enjoy his family and friends. Before Grant left, Jade hugged him and told him she had never seen the sheriff consumed with so much gratitude.

Jade later informed the sheriff that Grant had to leave to attend the meeting. The sheriff asked Jade to tell him to stop by when he had the chance because he needed to give him something. Grant, the sheriff thought to himself, was finally ready to receive the letter.

As Grant neared the Leakesville Community Center, he noticed the parking lot was full. Cars and pickups were in every available spot, and the street was lined with automobiles. Observing people walking toward the door, Grant slowly drove past the community center. He saw Reverend Mimbes and Tyrone Burley among the crowd approaching the door. Grant drove around the block and chose a parking spot near the tennis court located behind the community center. A large group of kids were playing basketball and kicking a soccer ball as they waited for their parents.

Grant slowly approached the entrance. He was ten minutes late. He hoped the meeting had already begun. He cracked the door, and the preacher whom Grant had seen take Johnny Ray Barfield home from Ward's was in the middle of a prayer. Through the narrow opening, Grant listened for the preacher to conclude. Several other people had walked up and were waiting to enter. After the prayer ended, Grant opened the door for the others. He followed behind them and stood in the back against the bar separating the kitchen from the meeting area.

"Thanks, Reverend Hillman. Wow! What can I say? The attendance tonight is outstanding. I've been the tax assessor here for sixteen years, and I've never seen the community this involved in a benefit." Scharlotte Bounds was the picture of humility. She appeared to be in her early fifties. She had a dimple on her left cheek. Her hair was black, and she wore it shoulder length. Grant liked her instantly.

"Before we start talking about the mechanics of Saturday's benefit, I want to tell you about our trip to visit Elsie last week. For those of you that were not here last Monday night, Terry Lowery, Brother Clark, and I rode out to the Smallwoods' place to get Elsie's permission to hold the benefit. Folks, she was so sweet." Scharlotte's voice cracked with emotion as she continued, "Elsie said that Brandon would be honored for us to do this for them." She looked down and shook her head fighting back the tears. "I know y'all will agree with me that it's our honor to do this for them. I've asked Brother Clark to give us an update on Brandon."

Scharlotte stepped aside as Brother Clark approached the microphone. "Good evening, neighbors." Grant's eyes slowly moved across the crowd. He saw many people he did not recognize. Yet, there were more familiar faces than those he did not know. He noticed some people there that he recalled not being so kind to Brandon and his family in 1989. He wondered why they came. "I met with Elsie and Jesse Bolton, his hospice nurse, this morning. Elsie gave me permission to share this information with you. Brandon is gathering fluid in his lungs, and his urine flow is continuing to decrease. The nurse figures two or three days, tops. Of course, only the Lord knows when. Hospice will have someone there around the clock starting in the morning." Grant noticed the stillness of the crowd. He could sense the sadness in the group.

Reverend Clark continued, "The folks at Cedar Grove Full Gospel are still bringing Elsie food each day. They have been very good to her." Reverend Clark was about to tell them about Grant buying Elsie some clothes and Brandon's suit for the funeral when his eyes met Grant's. The two communicated from across the room without words. Reverend Clark understood that Grant wanted no public recognition for what he had done in private. "Elsie sends her gratitude on behalf of Brandon and herself. God bless y'all."

The reverend sat back down, and Scharlotte resumed control of the meeting. "Thank you, Brother Clark. Ladies and gentlemen, I have an incredible challenge to us all in a minute. But before I get to that, let's get an update from our committee chairs." One by one, individuals walked to the microphone to update the group on their committee's efforts. Ms. Bobbie Brown gave an update on the ticket sales for the quilt the Greene County Quilting Club had made for the event. It was on display and beautiful. The crowd oohed and awwed when she announced that they had sold over two thousand tickets to date. She turned in $2,154 to Carey Byrd, the town's only CPA, who was the treasurer for the benefit.

Mitchell Ham updated the crowd on the barbecue plate sales. Mr. Ham worked at the shipyard as a welder. He had built the large barbecue grill used by every benefit organizer in the county. His committee had pre-sold five hundred tickets at seven dollars per ticket so far. He turned in $3,500 and sat down. Next came Ralph Everette, in charge of the silent auction which would be held. He reported on the generosity of the local merchants who willingly contributed items for the auction. He turned in $825 in cash donations received from local businesses. He then handed the microphone back to Scharlotte.

"I have received a $1,000 check from Brother Clark that was donated by Travis Crocker, a former classmate of Brandon's. Carey, so far, how much have we raised?"

Carey walked to the microphone. "Tonight I have received

$7,479. Usually, we would have to deduct the cost of the chickens, but individuals have agreed to purchase and donate those so every dollar we receive will benefit the Smallwoods. Prior to tonight, I had deposited $950, so our total to date is $8,429." Grant was shocked. These people were economically hurting just like everyone in America. Yet their generosity was astonishing.

"Thanks, Carey. I'm co-chairing the boxing of the barbecue plates with Bonita Sowell. We have had several ladies volunteer. To keep everyone from getting too tired, we will need several others willing to fix the plates. I placed a sign-up sheet back there on the bar. Also, Jeff Vanderford is heading up a motorcycle ride for Brandon. He could not be here with us tonight, but he wanted you to know he is here with us in spirit." Scharlotte finally completed all the details except for one last item.

Scharlotte paused, then addressed the attendees. "Folks, before we conclude, I have an incredible announcement to make." The crowd quieted. "We have received an anonymous gift in memory of Michael Hicks." People began to mumble and then became quiet once more. Scharlotte looked about the crowd with grace and sincerity. Without being noticed, Grant slowly slipped out the door. Scharlotte finally continued. Reverend Clark turned to look at Grant and discovered he was gone. "We have received a check in the amount of $25,000." The crowd collectively sighed. They had just broken the record for the largest amount ever raised at a benefit, and they were four days away from the actual event. After the crowd quieted, Scharlotte continued. "There's a stipulation on the donation. As some of you know, Elsie's house is in bad shape. For years, it has been deteriorating. She doesn't have a utility room. She has an old washer that sits in her kitchen. She has no dryer. The stipulation for receipt of the money is that it has to be used for materials for the house. It needs rewiring, roofing, painting, and several other things. The benefactor has agreed to have delivered a brand new washer and dryer if we donate the labor to build Elsie a utility room."

Shaun Burnett, a local contractor, along with Travis Morris, a local roofer, agreed to co-chair a committee to organize the work. Scharlotte Bounds concluded the meeting, and the various committees huddled in preparation for Saturday's event. Greene County, like all other places, was not perfect. But shining through the imperfections were a people who would bind together and help one another, even those who were different. Grant had hated this place for over twenty years. As he aimlessly drove toward Sand Hill, he digested what he had just witnessed. The love he saw directed toward the Smallwoods tonight was genuine. Home, he thought. Home. This place was indeed his home.

chapter forty-two

AS GRANT WAS SHAVING, HE NOTICED THAT he needed a haircut. Growing up, his dad took him to the barber shop on Main Street. It was still there with its distinct barber's pole–red, white and blue light. With Brandon's death imminent, Grant thought this might be the last time he would have a chance to get a trim before the funeral. He walked in the barber shop at 9:00 a.m. The barber, Tim Lewis, had been cutting hair for almost forty years. He was a one-man show.

"Good morning, Mr. Lewis." The patrons had paused in mid-conversation as Grant entered the shop.

"Hello, Grant. I'll be with you in a few minutes." Grant was pleased that Mr. Lewis remembered his name.

"Okay. No hurry." Grant nodded at the men waiting their turns. He then sat down on one of the green padded chairs and picked up a copy of *Newsweek*. Fox News was on the television hanging from the ceiling in the corner of the room. The door opened, and a man walked in with a little boy.

"Mr. Lewis, we have an emergency!" It was Dennis Mason, the local bank president, and his five-year-old son, Colby.

Mr. Lewis tried not to laugh. But he couldn't help himself. "Ha, ha, ha, ha! Dennis, who got ahold of your head?" The other patrons joined in the laughter. Grant looked up from the magazine he was reading and saw the object of everyone's amusement. The man looked like a dog with the mange. His son was in even worse shape.

"Mr. Lewis, I'm in a bind. Men, I'm sorry to ask y'all to do this, but I need to get Colby in that chair now. Grace will be home in an hour. " The man sitting in the chair got up mid-haircut to make way for the emergency. "We're supposed to take family pictures at the church Saturday morning."

"Well, Dennis, I don't grow hair. I cut hair. How in the world did this happen?" Mr. Lewis was grinning while trying to contain his laughter.

"Well, you know how I like to save a dollar." Dennis was famous for pinching pennies. Rumor had it that he even made his own soap.

"I believe the whole town knows that, Dennis."

"Well, I was in the pharmacy the other day, waiting on a prescription to be filled for Grace. I spotted some hair clippers, the electric kind, like you have there. They were only nineteen dollars, so I figured I would save a little money and cut mine and Colby's hair. Well, I misread the instructions and set it too low, thinking I was setting it high."

Mr. Lewis laughed again and shook his head. The other patrons were doing all they could to contain their laughter directed at the pitiful pair. "Colby, come on up here and sit down. Dennis, I'll do the best I can." Mr. Lewis stopped and looked at Dennis. "But, if you tell one living soul that I was responsible for these haircuts, I'll change banks." Dennis and Colby agreed not to breathe a word that would implicate Tim Lewis in the mess Dennis had created.

The conversation in the barber shop turned back to the place it was just before Grant and the Masons disrupted it: politics.

Dennis sat down in the chair next to Grant. "Dennis Mason, good to meet you." Dennis and Grant shook hands. They were the same age. Dennis was from Richton, but he married a Leakesville girl and settled down here.

"Grant Hicks. Tough morning, huh?" Grant had an up-close view of Dennis' disastrous haircut.

"You can say that again. My wife is going to be pissed."

Grant could not disagree. "Maybe Mr. Lewis can shape it up for y'all."

"I hope so. Anyway, I saw you last night at the meeting. I wanted to meet you, but I couldn't find you after it was over." Dennis and Grant glanced at Colby sitting in the chair as Mr. Lewis attempted reconstructive surgery.

Grant looked at Dennis. "Sorry I missed you. I left before the meeting concluded. I was impressed by the genuineness of everyone there. To be honest, I didn't think the people here cared what happened to Brandon."

Dennis looked at Grant. "I grew up in Richton. I didn't know about the Brandon Smallwood story until two years ago when he got out of prison. I can't imagine spending the best years of my life in prison for a crime I didn't commit. That was terrible." One by one, the other patrons began listening to the conversation about Brandon Smallwood.

Mr. Lewis chimed in. "Brandon Smallwood is the poster child for an imperfect judicial system. Unfortunately, he's not the first and won't be the last innocent man that goes to prison. But it hits home when you know someone that it happens to."

An older gentleman named Elmo Easterling spoke next. "I remember his trial well. Old Roland Nelson was the jury foreman. That boy didn't have a chance. I remember him talking about it.

The thing I remember him saying the most was that the Smallwood boy was a queer. I just wish Roland Nelson would've lived long enough to see that the Smallwood boy was innocent. Roland was a mean old fart."

Mr. Lewis stopped shaping Colby's hair to talk. "Well, most of the jurors from that trial are still alive. Ray Brashier was on the jury. I used to cut his hair. They say he's had a tough time with all of this. He's depressed and is in and out of a clinic in Hattiesburg. He never gets out in public any more. His wife runs all their errands. I don't think he goes to church either." The place was quiet for a while as Mr. Lewis finished Colby's hair and Dennis replaced him in the barber's chair. Grant had not thought of the fact that the jury members who convicted Brandon were still around. He was surprised that he felt sorry for them.

Mr. Lewis looked at Grant. "Grant, you're a lawyer. How does that work? If a jury wrongfully convicts someone, can they be sued?"

Grant refocused on the conversation. "Anybody can be sued, but jury members will not be liable. They have protections like judges do. The system must be that way for it to work. Unfortunately, our jury system is not perfect. For example, there have been African Americans convicted because of skin color, and the judicial system for the wealthy is far better than the judicial system for the poor. In Brandon's case, he had a double disadvantage. He was extremely poor, and he was the victim of bias and prejudice." The barber shop had never been this quiet. Each man was silently contemplating Grant's words.

Elmo Easterling finally broke the silence. "Well, I ain't no queer lover, but you're right, Mr. Hicks. To be honest, I was glad they convicted him then. I think most people were." The other patrons were uncomfortable at the honest words spoken by Elmo. But his words summed up their feelings back then as well. "Those jury members for a time were put on a pedestal. They did exactly what the community wanted done. Now, twenty-one years later, the ones still living are in hiding. But the truth is, they have every right to come to town or go to a ballgame as any one of us. We, this entire community practically, bear responsibility for that boy's conviction."

Grant looked at Elmo Easterling with astonishment. Grant now understood why the community needed to hold the benefit for Brandon. Guilt will gnaw at a person. In this case, it was a community. Grant recalled Brandon's words a few days before when he had agreed to speak at his funeral: "Tell the people that come that I have forgiven them...." Grant did not hear the words spoken as the barber shop conversation continued. He was thinking of Brandon's words. Brandon was such a kind person. He was dying, yet he knew the community needed to have those words spoken. For the first time, the importance of Grant's role in Brandon's funeral came into focus. Brandon wanted Grant to be his voice, his advocate. Brandon's words returned to Grant, "...and tell them that I love them."

The Masons left the barbershop looking like two Marine recruits. They decided they would try to convince Grace that they wanted matching crewcuts for the family photo. Grant left with his hair trimmed and a new understanding of his role in Brandon's funeral. He recalled how nervous he typically was as he stood before a jury and delivered a closing argument when millions of dollars were on the line. The nerves in his gut at the moment were double those as he thought of the significance of the words he would need to deliver at Brandon's funeral. He thought of Elmo Easterling's frank comments. He thought of those jury members and wondered who they were. Somewhere out there was a handful of people that wrongfully convicted Brandon. Two weeks ago, Grant would have hated them. Today, he felt sorry for them. What a difference a few days can make!

The fire alarm sounded as Grant stepped out of his vehicle at the Inn. Before he could think about his next move, he was backing out of the parking lot and heading for the nursing home. When he pulled up, Edwina and a co-worker were running toward the lady's vehicle. Grant rolled the window down. "Get in, Edwina!"

She jumped in, and they sped toward the fire station. As Grant and Edwina were pulling up, the fire truck was pulling onto Main Street. "Foller 'em, Yankee!"

Without hesitation, Grant followed the fire truck through town en route to the emergency. Grant looked in the rearview mirror, and a convoy of cars was following him. "Dang, Edwina, how did they get the fire truck out so quickly? I got to the nursing home before the whistle stopped blowing."

Edwina was not taking her eyes off the fire truck which slowed to pass through a four-way stop on Main Street. A chubby man wearing a Stetson hat and an old seersucker suit jumped on the rear of the truck as it slowed. "Yankee, we's got these pagers." Edwina pulled a pager from her pocket and showed Grant.

"Well, why do they blow the whistle?"

Edwina finally cut her eyes to look at Grant. "The whistle blows to let the town folk know there be a fire."

Grant was perplexed. "Why?"

Edwina shook her head. She and Grant began to worry about the man in the suit on the rear of the fire truck. He was trying desperately to hang on. "Because, Yankee, people want to know when there is an emergency in case they want to come watch!"

Grant was now more worried about the man hanging on for his dear life as the truck bounced across the Chickasawhay River bridge. His hat blew off which exposed his balding head. "Edwina, who's that man on the back? I'm afraid he's going to get thrown off the truck!"

"That's George Brewer. He's a lawyer, too. He's one of us volunteers. He usually don't show up though."

Grant remembered the words of Judge Eaton, "No-Show

George." The fire truck sharply turned left onto Annex Road. When it did, George flew off the fire truck, tumbling down the embankment. He looked like a roly poly. "Oh, my God! Edwina!" Grant pulled over to check on the injured volunteer. The fire truck, along with the string of vehicles following behind, kept going. Grant and Edwina jumped from the vehicle and ran to George.

"Ugh, ugh, ugh." Grant and Edwina were standing over George as he grunted in pain. The first thing that hit them was the smell. He was drunk.

"You okay? Mr. Brewer, you okay?" Edwina was shaking the injured volunteer.

George opened his eyes to see Grant and Edwina looking down at him. "Did y'all find my hat?" George's arms were scraped badly, and the knees were torn out of his pants legs. The right side of his face was scraped, too. Both knees were bleeding.

"We need to get you to a doctor, sir." Grant helped him to his feet.

"I'll be fine. Just take me back to my office." Edwina and Grant helped him to the Range Rover.

Edwina opened the door. "You're going with us to the nursing home. We's get a nurse to look at you."

As George was getting into the vehicle, he suddenly became angry. "The whole town was following that fire truck, and y'all the only ones that stopped. That kind of pisses me off."

George's feelings were hurt, so Grant thought he would try to encourage him. "Mr. Brewer, we are the only ones that saw what happened." Grant looked at Edwina. She was shaking her head no. Grant held his index finger to his lips to indicate for Edwina to keep quiet.

Grant's sympathy seemed to be working. George was buying his explanation. "You think so?"

"Mr. George, Lawyer Hicks be tellin you the truth." Grant looked at Edwina with approval and then called Jade to meet them outside the nursing home to take a look at their patient. Jade cleaned and patched his wounds while Edwina called to find out about the fire. It turned out to be a small grass fire. A man was burning his garbage in a fifty-five gallon drum when the wind blew some burning paper onto the ground. Edwina was happy she did not miss the excitement of a house fire.

Grant looked at Jade. "Jade, do you think you can take off a little early? I want to ride out to the house where I grew up. I thought you may want to go with me." Edwina grinned and looked at Jade.

Jade looked at Edwina, then at Grant, as she placed the last bandage on George Brewer's knee. "I'm a step ahead of you, Grant. Becky just gave me the rest of the week off. I wanted to spend some time with Elsie and Brandon tomorrow, and I'll be helping with the benefit Friday. I can't leave until 3:00 today though."

Grant smiled. "I'll pick you up at 3:00." He then returned George to his office. With all the excitement and pain, the injured man seemed to have sobered up. After George thanked him, Grant returned to the Inn. He smiled as he walked into his room. There was never a dull moment in his hometown.

At promptly 3:00 p.m., Grant picked up Jade from Greene Rural. After he had asked her to go with him earlier, she ran home and brought back a change of clothes for the trip to Grant's "old place." It was the last day of the month, and March was going out like a lamb. The day was beautiful with a crystal-blue sky. They both wore blue jeans with T-shirts. Grant had on an aging T-shirt from a U-2 concert he had attended years ago, and Jade's T-shirt had the word "Hollywood" written across the front. Although neither discussed wardrobe, they almost matched perfectly.

"When was the last time that you saw your old house, Grant?"

"August 1990. Almost twenty years ago." They turned onto Highway 57 and drove the seven miles to R.D. Herndon Road which then took them to a dirt road named Lewis Road. Grant became more tense as he got closer to the old home place. He had slowed to almost a crawl. Jade looked at him and wondered what was going through his mind. After following Lewis Road about a half mile, they turned onto Hicks Road, a dead-end dirt road.

"Wow! They named the road *Hicks Road*!" Grant said, impressed by the little green sign on top of the metal pole. Grant stopped the Range Rover as he looked down the dirt road which was a mixture of sand, clay, and gravel. For a moment, he pictured Lauren and himself riding their bicycles home after a trip to the store. He recalled the Sunday mornings when his Grandma and Grandpa Turner would visit from Mobile, and he and Lauren would meet them on this spot and ride their bicycles in front of Grandpa Turner's green Plymouth back to the house. Grandpa Turner never failed to bring Grant his favorite treat–Krispy Kreme doughnuts.

Grant turned to Jade. "We are sitting on top of what we called 'the big hill.' You see those next two hills?" Grant pointed as Jade looked down the dirt road. "We called the middle one 'the second hill' and the last one 'the first hill.'" Jade looked at Grant and slightly smiled. He put the vehicle in drive, and they slowly made their way down the road. As they crested the "first hill," the house appeared. It was a conventional ranch-style house, nothing fancy at all. It certainly did not look like the home of a state senator and lawyer.

"Dad bought this house and forty acres from Marion Ball. Mr. Ball built it himself. Mom never liked it much, but Dad loved this place." They got out of the Range Rover and walked up the cracking sidewalk to the steps leading onto the front porch. Grant looked at the large red oak trees that were the same size when he was a child. A gentle breeze blew as if to welcome him home. Grant noticed that the old red swing on which they used to sit and shell peas and butter beans was gone. He looked at the ceiling and saw two anchor bolts still there as if they waited to swing again.

"I like it, Grant." Jade was taking everything in. Her gut told her not to say much. Rather, she would keep Grant company as he shared his memories. She felt honored to be there. As Grant knocked on the door, they could hear what seemed to be an argument going on inside. "Do you know who lives here, Grant?"

Grant was combing every inch of the porch with his eyes. "No. I have no idea." Grant knocked louder. A few seconds later the door opened.

"Can I help y'all?" The old man was at least eighty years old. He was wiry with high cheek bones. He looked as if he had a touch of Indian blood in him.

"Sir, my name is Grant Hicks."

The man shook his hand. Grant noticed the old man's hands were curled from arthritis. He could not straighten his fingers. "Lewis Seals." Jade stood behind Grant.

A voice yelled from inside the home. "Lewis, you gotta get me to a hospital. You have blinded me!" Jade and Grant looked at each other as Mr. Seals went back inside. He left the door open. Grant shrugged his shoulders, and they stepped into the house. Mrs. Seals, dressed in a nightgown, was lying on the couch with one leg on the floor and one leg propped up on two pillows on the couch, a wet rag lying across her forehead.

"Damn it, Ethel. You ain't blind!"

Grant was looking at the living room as he recalled watching *The Andy Griffith Show* with his dad almost every day while they ate supper. Jade bent down next to the couch. "Can I help? I'm a nurse."

Ethel opened her bloodshot eyes. "Lewis is trying to kill me. My eyes were hurting, and I asked him to put some eye water in 'em. Now I can't hardly see." Lewis shook his head.

"Let me take a look, ma'am." Jade peered into Ethel's eyes and then looked at the bottle Mr. Seals used to medicate her. Ear wax removal. "You're going to be fine, Mrs. Seals. I need to flush your eyes. Let me get some water and a towel." After opening a couple of doors, she found the bathroom and returned with some water and a couple of hand towels.

"Oh, Lord, have mercy. First my head's a swimmin this mornin and now this." Mrs. Seals was in a panic. Jade slowly flushed her eyes and gently wiped the water away. After a few minutes, Ethel calmed down and sat up on the couch. Jade sat next to her.

Grant felt it now safe to speak. "How are you, Mr. Seals?"

"I'm fine and dandy."

Ethel spoke up. "You ain't fine either! He has arthritis and heart problems. He has the gout in his feet, too. Lewis, why do you always tell people you are fine when you ain't? Beats all I've ever seen."

Agitated, Lewis had not yet remotely looked as if he might crack a smile. "Because, Ethel, people don't give a damn how you feel. They just making conversation. They damn sure don't want to hear all your problems."

Grant was back in charge. "Mr. Seals. I hope we didn't disturb y'all, but I was wondering if I could look around the place. I lived here from the time I was born until I graduated high school."

"You Michael Hicks' boy?"

"Yes, sir."

Mr. Seals, now somewhat relaxed, continued, "I used to work with your Grandpa Hicks. He was a hell of a hard worker. They called him Pharaoh when he became a foreman. "

Grant was pleased that they had made a connection. "Yes, sir, Grandpa believed in a hard day's work." Grant used to despise having to do chores for his Grandpa Hicks.

Mr. Seals then waved his bent hand toward the rear of the house. "Go ahead. Look around. Make yourself at home."

Grant stood first, and Jade joined him. "Do you mind if I look at my old bedroom first?"

Ethel had calmed down and spoke. "It's probably a mess. I stay too sick to clean up around here."

"That's okay, Mrs. Seals. We won't be inside long."

Grant led Jade through the kitchen and into a long hallway. He pointed to their right toward a closed door. "That was Mom and Dad's room." He then looked down the long hallway. "The last door on the right was Lauren's room. The middle door is the bathroom. This was my room." They stepped across the hall and opened the door. The room was almost empty. It had one single bed, one dresser, and an ironing board standing in the corner. Grant soaked it all in. They sat on the edge of the bed.

Grant then pulled the curtains back to look out the window. "I used to spend nights lying awake in here dreaming about the future. In the spring and fall, I would sleep in here with the windows open to hear the crickets, or frogs if it had rained." Grant pointed toward the corner of the room. "That's where my stereo was located."Grant laughed. "I used to listen to whatever my favorite bands were at the time and imagine I was the lead singer."

Jade laughed. "Can you sing, Grant?"

Grant looked at Jade. "Oh, yeah, in my imagination, I rocked! The girls went wild. But in reality, I can't carry a tune in a bucket." They sat in his bedroom for about half an hour as Grant reminisced. He did not want to leave, but the afternoon was getting away from them. He and Jade got up and walked back into the living room.

"Mr. Seals, Jade and I are going to look around outside, and then we will leave. I appreciate your letting us do this." Mr. Seals had turned on the television. He and Mrs. Seals were watching a rerun of *Little House on the Prairie*.

Mr. Seals stood and walked them to the door. "No problem, Mr. Hicks. Good to meet you. You, too, ma'am." Grant and Jade shook his hand, said good-bye to the Seals, and walked onto the porch. They sat down on the top of the cement steps.

"Jade, I spent hours pitching a tennis ball from the end of the sidewalk to these steps. I started out with a regular baseball, but it deflected off the edge of this step and went through the window of the front door. Dad made me use a tennis ball after that." Grant stood and grabbed Jade's hand to help her. Without even noticing, he held her hand as he walked through the front yard and to the side of the house, the memories thick and loud.

Grant's eyes brightened with enthusiasm. "Wow! It's still here! Grant pointed at a grass-covered mound. My dad made me a pitcher's mound, and we would practice out here all the time. Dad would come in from work, and while Mom cooked dinner, Dad would catch for me as I pitched." They walked over and stood on the mound. Grant still held her hand. Jade was trying to concentrate on his words, but the fact that he was still holding her hand dominated her thoughts. Grant noticed the movement of a curtain in Lauren's old bedroom window. He caught a glimpse of Mrs. Seals.

"Jade, I think Mrs. Seals is watching us."

Jade smiled. "She's been watching us all along. She watched us from the front door when we were on the steps."

Grant looked at Jade with a mischievous grin. "Let's mess with her a little."

Jade squinted her eyes at Grant. "Okay, how?"

Grant let go of her hand and looked into Jade's eyes. He then put his hands around her waist just above her hips and pulled her close. "Do you mind?" Jade's body was light. Standing atop the grass-covered remains of the pitching mound, she simply shook her head no. Grant's lips slowly met hers. As he kissed her, her eyes closed, and her hands became two fists as her body reacted to the electricity traveling through it. She gradually relaxed, and her hands opened as she began to kiss Grant in return. After the kiss, Grant slowly backed his face from hers. She then instinctively moved her hands behind his head and into his brown hair. They met again for a second kiss.

They had forgotten Mrs. Seals was watching. "Lewis, get in here! They out there kissing!"

"Ethel, leave them be! If they want to swap spit, it ain't our business. I can't get up anyway, I'm as stiff as a wedding-peter today. This arthritis has whipped me." Ethel's eyes continued to watch Grant and Jade.

After the kiss that began as a joke, Grant and Jade held each other and stared into the other's eyes. "Jade, that was amazing."

She smiled at him. "Grant, I believe you just threw another strike."

They left the mound and spent the next half hour looking around the "old place." Grant shared with Jade his childhood memories. She noticed that most centered around the time he had spent with his dad. Less than two weeks ago, Grant's words indicated that he hated Michael Hicks. Today, Jade watched Grant smile as he discussed childhood memories of his daddy.

Grant had a sad look on his face. He was reluctant to leave. Staring at the old pitcher's mound, he spoke. "I miss my daddy so much." He then looked at Jade.

Jade grabbed his hand. "Grant, I know. I know you do. Y'all loved each other very much."

Grant then looked at the yard and house one more time. "Yeah, we did."

Grant and Jade drove to the nursing home to get Jade's car. They agreed to meet at Edwina's church at 6:00 p.m. Before she got out of the vehicle, she leaned toward Grant, and they kissed for the third time. The sheriff smiled as he watched through the window to his room.

Grant pulled into the parking lot of Temple Harvest at 5:00 p.m. He hoped to find Reverend Mimbes there in order to discuss his dad's funeral. There were no other cars in the parking lot. Grant got out of the vehicle and walked to the picnic table at which he had sat a week ago after his conversation with Tyrone Burley. He sat down and watched the cars passing along the highway.

"Hello, Grant."

The booming voice startled him. "Oh, hey, Reverend."

Reverend Mimbes sat down at the table across from Grant.

The weather was changing. What had been a picture-perfect day was now turning to cloudy. "Looks like we may finally get some rain. We need it though."

Grant looked toward the clouds. "Come to think of it, Reverend, it has not rained since I've been back here." Grant struggled for the best way to approach the subject he wanted to discuss with Reverend Mimbes. Reverend Mimbes was a gentle giant. He appeared to be in his mid-fifties, but his frame still appeared athletic. A pillar in the black community, whatever direction he turned, his community followed. Not because he demanded them to. They followed out of deep respect.

"The Lord sends the rain to us when we need it. How is the Smallwood kid?"

"It's getting close. I plan to start spending most of my time out there tomorrow. The nurse said yesterday he had two or three days, tops."

Grant was about to broach the subject of Michael Hicks when Reverend Mimbes spoke.

"Grant, how has your return home been?" Reverend Mimbes looked into Grant's eyes.

"Honestly, it's been better than I expected. I had planned never to come back here, but it's hard to deny a dying man his last wishes. So I came."

Reverend Mimbes knew Grant's story. "Good. I'm glad you came back home."

"Reverend?" Grant focused on the dark black eyes of the respected reverend. "How did you end up preaching my daddy's funeral?"

"Your daddy came to see me about a week before he...his death. He asked me to preach his funeral if I was alive when he died. Grant, that was a great compliment to me."

Grant squinted. His furrowed brow told Reverend Mimbes that he was in deep thought. "Were y'all close?" Grant knew the black community always supported his dad politically, but he did not recall his dad and Reverend Mimbes being close friends.

"We had a mutual respect for one another. Your dad was a good man."

Grant's furrowed brow would not recede. "Reverend, I've spent the last twenty years hating this place." Grant paused. "And hating my daddy." The first car pulled onto the church grounds and parked in front of the fellowship hall.

"Grant, why hate it here?"

Grant looked toward the road and then back at Reverend Mimbes. "The short version is that this place represented everything I despised: judgmental attitudes, hypocrisy, bigotry, racism." Grant looked at Reverend Mimbes expecting him to agree.

"Well, son, you've just described every place under the sun, including Atlanta, Georgia." Grant was digesting the reverend's statement. Reverend Mimbes continued, "Grant, let me ask you a question."

Grant thought there was no "let" to it; Reverend Mimbes was too intimidating a figure to say no to. "Okay."

"Do you believe that some white folk have treated black folk wrongly?"

"Of course, I do." Grant was now engaged one-on-one with the reverend, and though more cars were pulling into the parking lot, Grant did not notice.

"Well, Counselor, should I hate all white people?"

Grant felt as if he were on the witness stand in a trial. He surmised it was much better to ask the questions, rather than answer them. "No sir."

"Grant, you are an educated man, a bright man. So I will not insult your intelligence, but you get my point." Reverend Mimbes looked at Grant as the younger man pondered his words. Grant was speechless. "Grant, this is not a perfect place. No place is. But the overwhelming majority of people here are good people. Does that mean mistakes are not made? Of course not. Look up there,

Grant." Reverend Mimbes pointed at the people walking from their cars toward the fellowship hall. "Those are salt-of-the-earth folk. Far from perfect. But as good as they get, Grant."

Grant looked back at the reverend. "Reverend, I'm beginning to understand. At last night's benefit meeting, I was amazed at the sincerity of this town's effort to help the Smallwoods."

Reverend Mimbes leaned in closer to Grant, and in almost a whisper asked, "Grant, have you been to the cemetery to visit your daddy yet?"

The question punched Grant in the gut. "Uhh, no sir." Reverend Mimbes let his silence speak for him. Grant finally spoke. "It's just hard. There's been so much pain. He let me down so badly, Reverend."

Reverend Mimbes straightened up and with his soothing, deep voice said, "Son, your daddy loved you immensely." The minister's eyes would not release the grip on Grant's.

"But, how do you forgive someone that made such a critical error?" Grant retreated to his previously stated hatred of his dad and took a shot at him. "I mean, he let you down, too, Reverend. I remember when changing the state flag was up for a vote in the Senate, and despite the fact that this state's flag offends you and a majority of African Americans, he voted not to change it." Grant felt good about pointing out his daddy's shortcomings to the reverend.

"Grant, let me tell you the truth behind your daddy's vote on that flag. There was a man running against your daddy in 1987 that was a card-carrying racist. The flag vote came up in the '87 legislative session. The black community had never had a senator more concerned about our needs than your daddy. A group of black pastors and I met with him. We asked him not to vote to change it." Reverend Mimbes paused to let the words he had just spoken settle in with Grant. "We did not want to be represented by a man that would beat your daddy over that flag. That flag will change one day, Grant. The people just need more time to accept it." Grant was again left without words.

The reverend continued, "Grant, this place, this community, white or black, is not perfect. But I would rather live here than any other place in the world. Your daddy was not perfect either, Grant. But I would give anything to have him be my senator today. Son, before we get up and go to the fellowship hall, I want to leave you with this: In order to forgive someone else, you have to be able to forgive yourself. And just because you forgive someone does not mean you approve of what the person did. And remember, the things we don't like in others are often the things we don't like about ourselves."

Reverend Mimbes left him sitting at the picnic table. In his mind, Grant rewound the conversation with Reverend Mimbes. He thought about his dad. He thought about himself. He thought about this place. The bitterness and unforgiveness that had built a cocoon around Grant's heart had been pierced in many places by his return home. The butterfly that had been longing to escape from his heart finally began to prepare its wings.

chapter forty-three

WHEN GRANT ARRIVED AT THE Smallwoods on Thursday morning, several cars were scattered about the yard with no effort at organized parking. Grant noticed Jade's car and Reverend Clark's truck. He also noticed Jesse Bolton's car. There were two other cars he did not recognize.

Jade met him on the porch. "Hey, you." Jade was still glowing from their kisses the day before.

"Hey, Jade. What's up?" They sat on the old bus seat on the porch.

"I just got here. Jesse Bolton and the nurse's aide are cleaning Brandon and changing his sheets. It's so sad. His breathing is labored now. You can hear the fluid in his lungs as he breathes."

"Who else is here?"

"Ms. Willa Massey is visiting with Ms. Elsie. Ms. Massey was

Ms. Elsie's boss for a long time. She brought her a freshly baked pound cake, and I'm dying to eat a piece of it. It smells so good."

"When they finish with Brandon, I'll go in and see him. By the way, you look nice today, Jade."

Jade looked at her simple outfit. "Thanks, Grant. I'm sorry I had to leave the church so early last night, but Lad was ill. I don't think he got his nap out yesterday. But he was fine when I got him home, and he saw Max."

"How is Max? I need to go see him. I'll run out there tonight if that's okay."

"Sure. We can pick up something for supper if you like."

Grant agreed. "Sounds good. Any suggestions?"

"Well, I guess we could run to Hokie's barbecue in Lucedale. Nana loves it. She's not supposed to eat very much barbecue due to her diabetes, but she does anyway."

Grant smiled at the thought of Nana being a rebel. "Sounds like a plan, Jade." He then laughed as he thought of Edwina. "I wish you could have been with Reverend Mimbes and me last night when we met with Edwina about her gambling winnings."

"Oh! I forgot. What happened? Poor Edwina could not eat last night. She was so worried about what would happen...." Jade made a face like Edwina, then said, '...to the devil's money.'"

Grant laughed and then spoke. "It was classic. Reverend Mimbes asked me to play along, so I did. He was quoting Scripture and their church covenant like it was the alphabet. Edwina finally had enough and said, 'Reverend, just tell me how much I got to pay!'" Jade and Grant laughed. "I finally said, 'Edwina, the church has to vote on it.'"

The suspense was getting to Jade. "Ooohhh. What happened then?"

Grant laughed again. Jade was smiling as she awaited his answer. "Edwina frowned, stood up, put her hands on her hips, and said, 'Reverend, you know them heathens gonna make me give the money to the church. You can have the money!'" Grant and Jade laughed again. Grant continued, "Reverend Mimbes then stood, walked over to Edwina, put his arm around her, and said, 'Sister Edwina, Grant and I are just having a little fun with you. You can keep the money. Spend it as you see fit.'"

Jade's face became curious. "What did Edwina do then?"

"She looked at me, pointed her finger, and said, 'Yankee, you fired from being my lawyer!' Then she looked up at Reverend Mimbes and suggested that she give twenty percent to the church. He agreed, and Edwina left. Reverend Mimbes and I shared a good laugh afterwards."

"Grant, there is only one Edwina in this world. And I love her to death."

"I do, too. She has become one of my favorite people." Grant and Jade were looking into each others' eyes, and just before Grant could share how he was beginning to feel about Jade, the front door opened.

Elsie walked Jesse Bolton out onto the porch as Jesse was preparing to leave. "Thank you, Jesse." They hugged.

"Ms. Elsie, I'll be back no later than three." Jesse then looked at Jade. "Thanks, Jade. I'll be back as soon as I can." Jesse's son had an orthodontist appointment, and Jade agreed to stay with Elsie until the nurse got back in case Brandon needed help.

"No problem, Jesse. See you after while." Jesse walked to her car as Ms. Massey walked out of the house, spoke to Grant and Jade, then hugged Elsie good-bye.

After Ms. Massey left, Jade jumped to her feet. "Ms. Elsie, it's time for some coffee and pound cake!" Jade grabbed Elsie by the arm, and they entered the house. Elsie sat down at the kitchen table while Jade put on a fresh pot of coffee.

Grant noticed Reverend Clark was not around. "Where is Reverend Clark, Ms. Elsie?"

"Oh, he and Terry Lowery went to look at cemeteries for Brandon's burial."

Grant hoped they would finally find a place. "I see."

Elsie then spoke, "Grant, the funeral will be at First Baptist. Do you think that's okay?"

Grant leaned against the counter as the coffee pot was hard at work. "Sure, Ms. Elsie. The sanctuary used to be beautiful there. I'm sure it still is." He was trying to remember the last time he stepped inside First Baptist Church of Leakesville. His memory failed him.

"I've never been inside of First Baptist before. I'm so thankful y'all bought me some clothes to wear for the funeral." Grant could tell Elsie was a bit intimidated about being in First Baptist Church. Most of the educated people from the county attended there. Those that were baptist did anyway–a lawyer, a couple doctors, the town dentist, both pharmacists, plenty of school teachers, and several administrators from South Mississippi Correctional Institution.

"Ms. Elsie, I saw several people who I believe are still First Baptist church members at the benefit meeting Tuesday night. Brandon, you, and your family will be welcome there." Grant acknowledged his words and realized that times had indeed changed. Brandon would be welcomed there. Elsie stared at Grant and slowly nodded her head.

As Grant walked toward the hall leading to Brandon's room, he managed a tease, "While y'all visit, I'm going to see Brandon a few minutes. Jade, don't eat the whole cake. Save me a piece." Jade smirked at Grant in a flirting manner.

The first thing Grant noticed when he walked into Brandon's room was the smell, a smell he had never sensed before. It was the odor of death. It was a sweet, sweaty smell. Quite sickening. Grant would not be eating any cake. He noticed the IV which was now being used to deliver an increased dosage of morphine. The nurse's aide was using a cotton swab to moisten the inside of Brandon's mouth. Grant felt nauseous.

The aide looked at Grant, and after she was finished with Brandon's mouth, she began treating his eyes with an ointment.

The dying man's eyes were no longer providing the needed fluid to keep them moist. The aide then applied Vaseline to Brandon's purplish and cracked lips. Grant was near vomiting when she wiped her hands, gathered her things, and left the room.

Grant stood paralyzed just inside the door. He looked at the empty chair next to the bed. Then he looked at Brandon's skin. It had a gray cast to it. Grant stood aghast at the change in his friend's appearance since he last saw him only two days before. The oxygen machine was in a steady rhythm. Grant thought about leaving the room, but he couldn't. After a few minutes, he eased over and sat in the familiar chair next to the bed.

"Hey, friend." Grant put his hand on Brandon's arm. The only sound he could hear was the rasping sound as Brandon breathed. He wondered if Brandon could hear him. "The whole town is planning to be at the benefit Saturday. I went to the meeting Tuesday night, and they have raised enough money to fix up your momma's house." Grant's emotions were bearing down on his soul. "Thanks for asking me to come see you. It has changed my life. You are my best friend. I promise I'll look out for your mom, too." Jade had walked to the door. "Brandon, I love you, Buddy." Jade retreated to the kitchen to give the two friends their privacy. Grant leaned over and kissed the fevered forehead, straightened the sheets, and returned to the kitchen.

Jade looked at Grant before she spoke. She could tell his time with Brandon had affected him emotionally. "Would you like some cake, Grant?

"No thanks. Maybe later."

Jade remembered she was supposed to deliver a message to Grant. "Oh, Grant, I forgot to tell you. Sheriff McInnis has something he wants to give you."

Grant looked at Jade with curiosity. "Okay. I need to drop by and see him anyway. Since I had to leave early from his ceremony Tuesday night and go to the meeting, I did not get to talk to him afterwards. "

Grant looked at Elsie. "Ms. Elsie, I'm going to run to town and see Sheriff McInnis. I'll be back after while."

"Okay, Grant. Take your time."

He walked over to Jade and mischievously ate the last part of the cake which remained in her saucer. "Call me if anything changes, Jade." Grant looked out the kitchen window. It had started to drizzle outside. It was the first sight of rain since Grant had arrived in Greene County.

"I will, Grant. Be careful." Grant smiled at her, then walked to the Range Rover.

As Grant was driving past the feed store on the way back to town, he noticed Justice Court Judge Walter Eaton getting out of his pickup and walking toward the building. Grant turned around, drove back to the store, and pulled into the parking lot. When Grant walked in, there were several men drinking coffee sitting in a wide assortment of makeshift chairs.

"Hello, Counselor." Judge Eaton patted a stack of fifty-pound bags of cattle feed for Grant to sit down.

"Hey, Judge." Grant shook hands with the other men sitting around the Judge.

"So, is this the feller you been talking about, Walter? Good to meet you, Mr. Hicks. I'm Gerald Crocker."

Judge Eaton smiled. "Yeah, this is Johnny Newbill's and Roscoe Gipson's attorney." They all laughed. "Grant, these fellas and I drink coffee out here every Thursday morning at 10:30. Catch up on the gossip and talk politics. You want a cup of coffee?"

"Sure." Judge Eaton got up and poured Grant a cup of strong, black coffee. Grant looked at the group of men. Each one had his own special coffee cup.

"Say, Mr. Hicks. Where you live now?" Gerald Crocker was the talker of the group.

"I live in Atlanta." The judge handed Grant his coffee and sat down. The group discussed the Atlanta Braves a few minutes and Michael Vick's dog fighting days before the conversation returned to politics.

"Grant, you a republican or democrat?" Gerald asked the question but did not wait on Grant to answer. "We all republicans. Well, except the judge. He runs as a democrat, but he votes republican." Gerald liked or disliked a person depending on his or her political persuasion.

"I'm not much into politics. I vote for the person though. I don't vote for the party."

Gerald decided to find out Grant's political persuasion. "You believe in abortion?" The entire group was watching Grant and waiting on his answer.

"I don't take a position either way. I guess it has not affected me directly."

Gerald Crocker squinted his eyes. Grant's answer did not satisfy him. He had to dig deeper. "Would you vote for someone who believed in abortion?" Gerald figured this would smoke him out.

"I'm not a one-issue voter. I vote for the person who I believe is right for the times. Sometimes that's a democrat; sometimes that's a republican."

Judge Eaton decided to steer the conversation away from politics. He could tell Grant was not scoring any points with the coffee group. Gerald Crocker was not sure Grant answered his questions to his satisfaction. As a matter of fact, he was pretty sure Grant had not. "Grant, what's the latest on the Smallwood boy?" Grant updated the group on Brandon's health as the front door opened and Danny Narbo walked in wearing his deputy's uniform.

"Morning, Danny." Judge Eaton stood. "You boys met yet?" Grant then stood. Danny stared at him and sat on the opposite side of the group without shaking Grant's hand. Judge Eaton detected the obvious tension between the two men. Apparently, they were acquainted.

"Danny, you a republican, ain't you?" Gerald Crocker only knew one topic: politics.

"Damn right I am." Danny looked at Grant. "I don't have any use for no queers either." Grant ignored Danny, looked at the group, and wondered what had changed. When he left here twenty years ago, almost everybody was a democrat. Now, some of the poorest people in the country were calling themselves republicans. Grant reflected at how time changes so many things.

Judge Eaton looked at Grant. "Grant, what are you about to do?"

"I was on the way to see Sheriff McInnis at the nursing home."

"You got time to take a ride with me?"

Grant looked at the clock on the wall. It was almost 11:00 a.m. "Sure." Grant and the judge told everyone good-bye and walked out of the feed store.

"Do you want me to drive, Judge?"

Judge Eaton read the bumper stickers on back of the Range Rover. "Grant, let's take my truck." Grant opened the passenger door of the truck, and there was everything in there from empty Red Man tobacco pouches to a volume of the *Mississippi Code Annotated*. After a minute, Judge Eaton had cleared enough room for Grant to sit down. They pulled onto Highway 63 and then turned left onto Old Highway 24.

"Judge, why is Johnny Newbill on probation?" Grant had forgotten to ask the day he was thrust into representing Johnny.

"Now that's a crazy story. Johnny Newbill, Pete Ball, and Robert Coxwell are peas-in-a pod." The judge grinned as he turned left onto Vo-Tech Road. "Johnny was mad at his neighbor, Clyde Strahan, so he concocted this plan to shoot Clyde's prize Black Angus bull. He talked Robert and Pete into walking to the pasture with him. Of course, Johnny and Robert were drunk. Pete don't drink. Anyway, Johnny shot the bull between the eyes, and they fled back to Johnny's trailer."

Grant looked at the judge. "For some reason, Judge, that story doesn't surprise me. How did they get caught?"

"They got back to Johnny's and began to discuss the tragedy it would be if all that beef went to waste. So Robert and Johnny went back down there to clean it. Pete got scared and went home. Johnny's wife figured that that was as good a time as any to leave him. So she called the sheriff, and Johnny and Robert were arrested in the field. They had blood all over 'em." Judge Eaton glanced at Grant, then back at the road.

"Did they all go to jail?" Grant watched the judge as he drove his pickup. Walter Eaton was indeed a man's man. He looked like he had stepped out of a western movie.

"Robert and Johnny did. Clyde did not file charges against Pete. Robert got thirty days and six months probation. Johnny would have gotten ninety days and one year probation, but his mouth got him in trouble. They had to pay for the bull, too."

Grant was curious. "How did Johnny's mouth get him in trouble?"

Judge Eaton laughed. "The case was in circuit court. Judge Beard don't play. Johnny was represented by the public defender, and he waived a jury trial. On the morning of the trial, Johnny decided he might as well plead guilty. During the plea colloquy, Johnny saw his soon-to-be ex-wife standing by the prosecutor. She was there to be a witness for the state. After Judge Beard sentenced him to ninety days, one year probation, and ordered him to pay for the bull, Johnny looked at his wife and said, 'I can do ninety days standing on my head, Judge.' Judge Beard immediately replied, 'Good, do the first ninety days on your head and the next ninety days on your feet!" Grant and the judge laughed.

"Want some lunch, Grant?" Judge Eaton turned right into Wildkat Korner, a convenience store with a short-order cook.

"Sure." They got out of the truck, walked in, and ordered

hamburgers. Judge Eaton and Grant visited for the next hour, often being interrupted by the locals who entered the quick stop. Around 1:00 p.m., they pulled back into the parking lot of the feed store.

Grant was about to open the door to get out when Judge Eaton spoke. "Grant, I hear you're speaking at the Smallwood boy's funeral."

Grant concentrated as he looked at the judge. He sensed some advice was soon to follow. "Yes, sir, I am."

Judge Eaton looked at Grant in a fatherly manner. "This town, these people, feel bad about the boy spending time in prison for a crime he didn't commit. All of us agree that was wrong." The judge paused as he ordered the words that would follow. "But..." The judge paused again. "But that does not mean they approve of his lifestyle." Grant waited to see if there was more to the conversation. There was. "I don't know what you are planning to say at the funeral, but you will be in a churchhouse."

Grant slowly began to feel a hint of anger. "Judge, what are you saying exactly?" Grant's hand was still on the door handle as the truck sat idling.

"Son, let me put it this way. I don't recommend you trying to justify, you know, what Brandon is. The vast majority of the people around here are uncomfortable with the fact that he is a homosexual. You know what I'm saying, Grant?"

Grant released the door handle. "Judge Eaton, with all due respect, I will say what I feel like saying. At this point, I have no idea what that will be. But rest assured, I will not be censored by anyone. Can I be direct with you, Judge, without our leaving enemies?"

Judge Eaton looked at a truck that had pulled into the feed store, waved at the man who got out, then looked back at Grant. "Of course, Grant." Judge Eaton liked Grant, and in his own way, he thought he was protecting Grant by the advice he was giving him.

"Brandon is the kindest person I've ever met. He's my friend. When I see him, I don't see his sexual orientation. I see a person, a living, breathing human being whose momma loves him. To the very people that slammed him in the past and would slam him today, Brandon would give his last nickle. Perhaps I'm not as obsessed with others' personal lives as 'people' think I should be, but you know what, Judge?" Grant did not give him time to answer. "I have enough problems of my own to be worried about. I don't have time to worry about whether Brandon, you, or anyone else for that matter, lives his or her life the way I think is right." Grant stared intently at Judge Eaton awaiting his response.

"Grant, I didn't mean to upset you. Like I said, this town feels terrible about what happened to Brandon. But a lot of people still have a hard time understanding Brandon's lifestyle."

Grant looked toward the woods and back at the Judge. "I understand what you're saying, Judge. And I'm sorry if I got a bit defensive. But I just wish people would quit judging others based on their own life's paradigm. When I was little, I used to hear so-called Christian people say that baptists were going to Hell or pentecostals were going to Hell or so-and-so was going to Hell. The fact is, Judge, most people are baptist or pentecostal or methodist or whatever because their parents were, and their grandparents were. What if the first one who decided the family's faith was wrong? Heck, they may all be wrong. Or they may all be right." Both Grant and Judge Eaton stared toward the feed store as patrons walked in and out of the busy establishment.

"Well, Grant, as President Obama would say, 'That's above my pay grade.' But you are a fine young man. I just want you to know that some people may take offense if you say certain things. That's all."

Grant opened the door to the pickup. "Judge, I appreciate your advice. I do. When I speak at the funeral, I won't be speaking for anyone but Brandon. He is the consummate peacemaker. Do you know that he requested me to ask these very people you are talking about to forgive him? And, Judge, he doesn't have a damn thing he needs to ask them to forgive him for."

The two men shook hands and parted. Grant pointed his SUV in the direction of the Grand Avenue Inn. He needed some time to digest his conversation with Judge Eaton before he went to visit Sheriff McInnis. He lay on the bed and realized that he had no idea what he would say at Brandon's funeral. However, his gut told him that when the time came, he would be ready.

Reverend Clark and Terry Lowery arrived at Elsie's and did not have encouraging news. Jade and Elsie were sitting on the porch watching the drizzling rain and drinking glasses of tea. "Elsie, we've been to every public or church cemetery within a twenty-mile radius of your house and did not find one that fits the description you want for Brandon." Reverend Clark sat down visibly tired and perplexed.

Terry Lowery spoke next. "Elsie, I'm so sorry we didn't find a gravesite for Brandon. If I can think of any other places to look, I'll let you know." He then handed Elsie an envelope. "The ladies at the cafeteria sent this to you."

Elsie took the envelope full of one and five dollar bills. She poured two dollars worth of quarters into her hand. Her coworkers were giving money they did not have. Their sacrifice deeply touched Elsie. "Thanks, Mr. Lowery. You've been so good to me. Thanks for holding my job for me, too. Tell the ladies I appreciate this and that I love and miss them." Terry hugged Elsie and slowly walked to his car.

"Jade, how's Grant?" Reverend Clark was beginning to see a change in Grant. When he first met the young attorney, he had seemed distant and unhappy.

"Brother Clark, it has been an incredible transformation. In the time I've been around him, I've seen him change. He has opened up so much. At first, he rarely smiled. But now, he even jokes around a little."

Elsie spoke next. "He's such a generous boy. I'm so happy he came to see Brandon. And Jade...I'm also happy that I've gotten to know you, too." Elsie smiled at Jade.

"Oh, Ms. Elsie, thank you. I feel the same way. And I got to go fishing with Brother Clark!"

"Has he talked much about his daddy, Jade?" Reverend Clark steered the conversation back to Grant.

"He actually has, more so over the last couple of days. I went with him to visit his homeplace, and he talked constantly about the times he spent with his daddy. As we were about to leave, he said he missed his daddy."

A slow smile appeared on Reverend Clark's face. "That's an answered prayer, Jade." They sat in silence a few moments before Reverend Clark spoke to Elsie. "Elsie, I have a suggestion for a change in the order of service for the funeral." His look turned serious as he focused on Elsie.

"Okay, Brother Clark, whatever you think is best."

"I figured we would open the service with a song. I would then have a word of prayer and read some Scripture. Then we follow with another song. After the second song, Grant would speak."

Elsie stared at Reverend Clark as if she were waiting on him to finish. "When will you preach?" Elsie looked confused.

"Elsie, I've been thinking and praying about the service. My instinct tells me this is the way we should do it. Brandon's been challenged in more ways than anybody I've ever known. Yet, he's brought healing to Grant Hicks, and he's lifted the guilt off the conscience of this community. I'll bring a very short message at the gravesite." Reverend Clark paused as Elsie considered his suggestion. He then continued, "Elsie, there's no man alive more suited to be the central speaker at the service than Grant. Of course, Elsie, you have the final say."

Elsie looked out into the yard and stared at the chickens

scratching in the rain. Her eyes turned to Jade. "Jade, baby, what do you think?"

The look on Elsie's face bore an uncanny resemblance to the look on Nana's face just before Stormy left Lad with them. "Oh, Ms. Elsie, I think that will be a beautiful service."

Elsie turned back to Reverend Clark. "Okay, Brother Clark. We'll do it that way. Have you discussed it with Grant?"

Reverend Clark stood. "No, I haven't. I will when I see him. I have to go, Elsie. I'll be back tomorrow morning. Call me if you need me at any time." Reverend Clark left, and Jade and Elsie went inside to check on Brandon. The drizzling rain was getting harder.

Sheriff McInnis stood as Grant walked into his room at 2:30 p.m. "Hey, Grant."

The plaque hanging on the wall next to a picture of the sheriff's children and grandchildren was everything Grant had hoped. "The plaque looks great, Sheriff."

"Thanks again for what you did, son. It was one of the best days of my life. And guess what, Grant?" The sheriff had never looked so happy and excited.

"I give up, Sheriff. What?" Grant was smiling.

"Paul's going to run for sheriff next year. He said that he had been thinking about it for some time, but after the ceremony Tuesday night, he decided to do it."

Grant grinned on the outside as well as within. "That's wonderful, Sheriff. Wow! That makes me want to vote here."

The sheriff patted him on the shoulder, and they sat down. "Grant, this has been one of the best weeks of my life. I owe it all to you."

"Sheriff, actually, this has been one of the best weeks of my life, too. We can both thank Brandon Smallwood for being the common denominator for it all."

"Indeed, we can, Grant. How is he?" The sheriff's smile turned into a look of concern.

"If he makes it through tomorrow, I'll be surprised. I sat with him a little while this morning. Jade is out there now." Grant stared into the distance as he looked out the window and thought of Brandon.

"Speaking of Jade, she is a special lady isn't she, son?" The sheriff had been hoping all along that Grant and Jade would hit it off.

Grant looked at the sheriff as his thoughts turned to Jade. "She is special, Sheriff. I've never met anyone like her. For some reason, when I'm around her, I feel safe."

The sheriff was pleased with Grant's words. "Some fella will be lucky to marry her."

Grant felt a touch of jealousy as the words "some fella" sunk in. The sheriff noticed Grant was thinking, so he waited for him to focus again. Grant finally re-engaged. "You're right, Sheriff." Grant wondered if Jade would date anyone now. Of course, she had every right to. They were not dating. Or were they? Grant suddenly wanted to see her.

"Grant, when you were speaking the other night, it was like watching your daddy speak. He was the best I've ever heard, until Tuesday night. You have a gift, son." The sheriff looked at Grant with admiration.

"That's a great compliment, Sheriff. Daddy was smooth with his words." Grant began to think of his dad. He realized that he had never missed him more than he did at that moment.

Looking at Grant with sincerity, the sheriff said, "You are a lot like him, you know."

Grant responded to the sheriff with appreciation. "Sheriff, I've learned more about my dad in the time I've been back here than I had ever known before. I feel terrible for what I did. But when you're seventeen or eighteen years old, it's hard to understand things sometimes. Then, pride got involved. I just hope he forgave me before he...before he died."

The sheriff could read Grant as if he had known him since birth. Grant had somehow forgiven his daddy. He had forgiven this place. However, Grant needed two more events to happen. He needed to have some understanding that his daddy forgave him. Furthermore, he needed to forgive himself. "Son, I have something for you. I've held onto it since September 1994, almost sixteen years."

The sheriff walked over to his dresser and opened the top drawer. He pulled the envelope out and handed it to Grant. Grant looked at the unopened letter from the Law Office of Michael Hicks with the handwritten words on the front, *To Grant*. He turned the letter over and noticed that the seal had never been broken. Grant's stomach was spinning. He began to perspire with nervousness. The adrenaline in his body was racing. The energy with which Grant had entered the room had vanished.

As Grant stared at the envelope, his respected friend spoke. "Grant, two days after your daddy died, I received a brown envelope in the mail. In it was a letter to me and this envelope to you. Your daddy instructed me to give it to you when I felt like the timing was right. Judging from the letter your daddy wrote to me, the time has finally come. The only other person that knows the letter exists is Paul. I told him that if something happened to me before I could give it to you to make sure you got it."

The sheriff sat back down. The two men remained silent for a few minutes. Grant kept rubbing the letter. He had never experienced this level of anxiety. His heart was racing. His eyes finally left the letter, and he looked at the sheriff and spoke. "Thank you, Sheriff."

The sheriff watched his friend a few more minutes as Grant kept staring at the letter. His shoulders, which were normally erect, were slumped. He looked lonely. The sheriff could tell Grant did not know what to do. He walked over to him and put his hand on his shoulder. "Grant, I truly appreciate what you've done for me. I'm so glad you came home. Your daddy would be mighty proud of you."

Grant's anxiety regarding the content of the envelope paralyzed him. He finally stood. The sheriff embraced him as if he were an old warrior sending a dear son into battle. Grant walked toward the door and turned to look at the sheriff. "Thanks again, Sheriff." Grant opened the door, and before he stepped out of the room, he turned again to the sheriff. "I love ya, Sheriff."

A tear trickled down the sheriff's wrinkled face. "I love you, too, son."

So Grant left. He placed the letter on the passenger's seat of the Range Rover and drove the back streets of Leakesville until he found Jernigan Road. The road started off as pavement, but it turned into dirt as it stretched farther and farther from town and into the woods. Grant was finally going to see his daddy.

Worried about Grant, Jade had been pacing the floor. She thought he was coming back to the Smallwoods, but he had not returned. She began texting him a little after lunch and tried to call at 2:45. The time was now 3:15, and still she had no word from Grant.

Elsie noticed Jade's nervousness. "Jade, is everything okay?"

Jade looked away from the kitchen window long enough to speak to Elsie. "I'm a little worried about Grant. I thought he was coming back. I've texted and called his cell, but there's no answer." Jade walked to the front door to look outside.

"Jade, baby, you can go ahead and leave. Jesse should be back in a minute."

Jade looked at Elsie. "Oh, no, Ms. Elsie. I'll wait until she gets here. She should be here soon." Jade walked to Brandon's room to check on him. He seemed to be resting as well as could be expected. The nurse's aide was reading a Harlequin Romance book sitting in the chair next to his bed. Jade heard the sound of her phone as the text message announced its arrival. She scampered back to the kitchen.

"Is that Grant?" Elsie was now concerned, too.

Jade read the text and then responded. "No, ma'am. It's Jesse. She just turned onto Jonathan Road. She'll be here in a minute. Ms. Elsie, I'm going to go ahead and leave when she gets here. Tomorrow, I'll be helping get things organized for Saturday's benefit, but I'll ride out and check on y'all." Jade hugged Elsie, grabbed her purse, and walked out the front door as Jesse pulled into the yard. Jade updated Jesse on Brandon's day and began the drive to the nursing home. She hoped that she would find Grant visiting with Sheriff McInnis.

Grant made his way down Jernigan Road and turned right onto Roland Brewer Road. He slowly drove down the muddy dirt road a half mile before turning right onto Cemetery Road. He stopped the Range Rover in the same spot he had sat only nine days before. He looked at the letter lying in the passenger's seat. The slow rain, which had wet the parched Greene County dirt, had stopped. The clouds hung low as a reminder that the rains were soon to return. Making a loud noise as the huge raindrops hit the metal, the welcomed water was dripping off the trees and onto the SUV. Grant lifted his foot off the break pedal, and the Range Rover inched its way toward the cemetery. As the wheels oscillated, noticeably, Grant's stomach did likewise.

The road opened into about a three-acre square surrounded by a dense forest. The cemetery had not been cleaned in some time–leaves, sticks, limbs, and sagebrush dotted the burial ground. Grant instantly grew ashamed that his daddy's resting place was not meticulously groomed. Michael Hicks' yard was always the neatest in the community. Grant recalled his daddy's words, "You show me an unkept yard, and I'll show you a lazy man."

Grant parked near the entrance to the cemetery and then picked up the letter that was resting in the seat next to him. He stepped out of the Range Rover and walked to the gate that led into the graveyard which was surrounded by a rusting panel-wire fence nailed to pine lightered posts. He paused as his eyes surveyed the cemetery. He wondered which headstone was his daddy's. He felt a familiar pain as he recalled when his Grandma Hicks was buried here in 1987 and when his Grandpa Hicks was buried a few years before. He seemed to remember which graves were theirs. He looked in that direction. He stepped inside the fence and closed the gate behind him.

Grant forced himself past the tombstones until he saw from a distance the word *Hicks* written across the top of the back of a marker. Being careful not to step on a grave, he walked in that direction. He did not know why, but he surmised that there had to be something disrespectful about stepping on a grave. He stepped around the headstone to look at it. The stone was on a row of graves that bordered the east side of the cemetery and faced the woods. The marker belonged to his grandparents. He read the inscriptions and calculated their ages. He discovered his grandma was older than his grandpa.

He then moved to the next grave, his Great-Grandpa Barney and his Great-Grandma Zula. Next to them was the infamous George Washington Hicks. Grant grew up hearing the legend of his Great-Great-Grandpa George, the strongest man to ever live in Greene County. He remembered folks saying that Grandpa George could pick up an anvil and throw it like an ear of corn. His headstone stood alone. Even through the emotions that were racing, Grant slightly smiled as he remembered his Great Uncle Cletus talking about Grandpa George's many wives. Grant's favorite Grandpa George story occurred on a cold winter day as it began to rain. While Grandpa George and a passel of his kids were outside, his wife walked out on the porch and called the kids in out of the rain. She failed to call for Grandpa George. He figured a woman that did not care enough about him to call him in out of the rain was not fit to be his wife. She was gone before the rain stopped falling.

Grant stepped to his right, and his heart sank. The name seemed to be speaking to him from the place it rested. *Michael Anthony Hicks* was written across the black marble headstone. Michael Hicks was born October 10, 1947, and died September 12, 1994. On the bottom of the headstone were the words *Gone... but not forgotten*. Grant reflected on the truth of those four words. He noticed a wooden bench with a metal frame at the foot of the grave. A large dogwood tree provided a beautiful canopy from just outside the rusting wire. Overwhelmed by the emotion of the moment, he knelt down beside the headstone and rubbed the lettering of his daddy's name.

Grant noticed that the flowers in the vase at the base of the headstone had not recently been replaced. A large, weathered, plastic flower arrangement in a clay pot had fallen against the headstone. He slowly stood it back up. When he did so, he saw a picture frame. The water-proof frame had fallen over and was covered with dirt. Grant wiped the dirt away to reveal a family photo of his mom, dad, Lauren and him. The tears rushed from his eyes before he could stop them. He stood, walked over to the bench, and sat down as he cleaned the frame and stared at the picture. His tears dripped onto the frame. He wiped his eyes, looked at the headstone, and gazed across the cemetery. He missed his family.

Jade found the sheriff visiting with his daughter and grandchildren in the common eating area of the nursing home. "Hey, Mr. Lauvon. Hey y'all." Jade smiled at the sheriff's daughter and then turned her attention back to the sheriff. "Mr. Lauvon, has Grant been by here today?"

The sheriff could see Jade was nervous. "He has. He left about thirty minutes ago." Sheriff McInnis stood to talk to Jade.

"Did he say where he was going? He was supposed to come back to the Smallwoods', but he hasn't. I can't get him to answer his cell."

The sheriff instructed his daughter to meet him in his bedroom. When she and the kids left the table, the sheriff spoke to Jade. "Jade, let's sit down a second." Jade did not want to sit down. She was nervous and worried about Grant. She reluctantly sat on the edge of the chair. The sheriff told Jade the full story behind the letter. She wondered if Grant were okay. What was in the letter? Would he be okay reading it alone? Where was he? She needed to be with him.

"Mr. Lauvon, I need to find him. I need to make sure he's okay. Where do you think he is?"

The sheriff looked at Jade, placed his hand on hers, and thought for a moment. "Jade, do you know how to get to the Hicks Family Cemetery? It's just a hunch, but I'd start there."

Jade tried to recall if Grant had ever mentioned the cemetery to her. "No, sir, I don't know where it is."

The sheriff gave her detailed instructions to the cemetery. He made her write them down. "Jade, those roads will be slippery after this rain. Please be careful."

Jade stood, leaned over and hugged him. "I will, Mr. Lauvon. Thank you." Jade hurriedly left the nursing home and got into her car. She backed the Honda Accord out of the Greene Rural parking lot and sped toward Jernigan Road. She looked at the clock; it was 4:05 p.m. As Jernigan Road turned from asphalt to gravel and then to mud, she nervously wondered if she would make it to the cemetery. And if she did, would she find Grant there when she arrived?

Grant continued to stare at the letter. He turned it over and over. He looked at his dad's grave, then stared blankly into the low-hanging gray skies. He wanted to know what the letter said, but he was afraid to open it. His dad wrote these words just before his death. Grant hoped that his father had forgiven him. He was afraid the letter would indicate otherwise. He looked at the headstone and finally spoke to his daddy. He had not spoken to him in close to twenty years.

"Dad...Dad, I'm sorry I took..." Grant tried to contain the tears, but he could not. He spoke through the tears. "I'm sorry I took so long to come see you." Grant sat silently, gathering his thoughts. "I miss you so much. I'm so sorry I got so angry. I've learned a lot about you since I've been home. You're a great man." The damp breeze began getting cooler. The rain was not far away. "I'm so proud that you are my dad. I love you so much. And, I...I miss you. When you died, I decided to go to law school to honor you. I've worked so hard for you, Daddy. I finished number one in my class. I'm a partner in an Atlanta law firm, and I'll be managing partner when Mr. Rimes retires in two years. I wish you could see my office." Grant stopped talking. He looked around the cemetery to make sure he was still alone. He looked at the letter again.

"Dad, the people here still love you. They respect you so much. And, so does Brandon." Grant choked up again. "And, Dad, so do I." Grant read his name on the front of the envelope once more before turning over the envelope. He placed his right index finger under the flap of the envelope and opened it. Grant slowly removed the letter. His hands were shaking. He methodically unfolded the aged piece of paper and leaned forward with his elbows resting on his legs just above his knees. He recognized the handwriting. His dad wrote the letter longhand. Even Grant's penmanship favored his dad's.

Dear Grant:

I simply do not have words which can adequately capture what I need to say to you. First of all, I am so very proud of you. From the day I first held you at the hospital, I knew you were special. As I watched you grow up, each day I became more and more proud of you. My most cherished memories are centered around you and Lauren.

Do you remember the time you pitched the no-hitter in the All-Star game at Gulfport? I was so nervous each time you threw a pitch! After the last out and as the team stormed the mound, I was so proud of you. All those days you pitched to me on our homemade mound sure paid off. Didn't they? And what about the time you hit three homeruns at Agricola? Oh, how I enjoyed coaching your baseball teams.

Son, although those memories are special, the memories that I am the most proud of are the ones you never knew that I was aware of. I remember one time you went on a school trip when you were in the fifth grade. The school bus was full. Mrs. Woodard told me that you were the only student that offered to give up his seat for her. She declined, and you stood with her to keep her company.

Do you remember the time you won that Pluto stuffed animal at Disney World? You were seven years old. You were so proud of Pluto. You carried him with you the entire vacation and even slept with him in the hotel. On the way home, we stopped in Tallahassee for the night. The next morning, we went to a restaurant for breakfast. A husband and wife, along with their son who looked to be about five years old, were in the restaurant. I noticed you watching the little boy as his parents counted their money to see if they had enough to pay for their breakfast. When we got home, your mom asked you where Pluto was. You told her you must have lost him. Son, I saw you give Pluto to the little boy when your mom and Lauren went to the restroom and I was paying for breakfast. You have taught me so much, Grant. There are so many more memories that I could share with you.

As you read this letter, I have no idea how old you are. Son, I hope you can forgive me for letting you down. I regret daily not standing by you as you stood by Brandon. I always knew if anyone needed a friend, you would be there for him or her. And Brandon needed a friend. I know the last few years we have not seen each other or spoken. But there is not a moment that passes that you are not in my thoughts.

Son, you and I have a lot of similarities. So if you are wondering if I have forgiven you for the words that were spoken just before you left home, you were forgiven before the taillights of your car left our driveway on the day you went away. The truth is, Grant, I was so very proud of you for standing up for Brandon.

Before I go, please tell your mom and Lauren that I love them very much. I don't know much about certain things. But I know this world is better for you being in it. I have spent my whole life running from my fears and insecurities. I am tired from it all. As I close this letter, the one thing that brings me peace is the fact that I can now rest knowing that the man you have become is my greatest success.

I love you, Grant. I love you more than you can ever imagine. I am proud of you. Don't ever forget that.

Dad

Grant slumped over and wept. He held the letter in his hand and stared at the ground as he cried. After the tears retreated, he carefully observed the letter noting his dad's handwriting. His dad's last words to him. He slowly read the letter once more as the rain began to lightly fall again.

Jade made it to the entrance of Cemetery Road. As she turned in, her left front wheel slid into the ditch. The Honda Accord was stuck. And even though it was not yet 5:00 p.m., the canopy of the trees and the low-hanging clouds made it appear almost dark as she looked down the lonely road. As the rain began to fall harder, she realized that she had not put her umbrella back into her car from the last time she used it. She grabbed her purse, threw her cell phone and keys in it, and walked down the lonely, muddy road.

The road was about a quarter mile long, but under the circumstances, it seemed longer. She stepped around mudholes and attempted to walk on the grass in the center of the lane. She felt her hair beginning to flatten as the rain fell harder. She made it to the opening in the forest which contained the cemetery, and she was relieved to see the Range Rover. When she walked up to the gate, she noticed Grant sitting on the bench, bowed, holding a piece of paper in his hand. She stood there wondering if she should retreat to her car. That thought did not last long. Grant was hurting, and he needed a friend. She opened the gate and made her way past the graves.

"Grant?" Grant looked up at Jade with his blood-shot eyes. She had mud almost to her knees, her hair dripping from the rain. She sat down next to him not bothering to dry the bench. The large dogwood tree was providing a small measure of protection from the rain. Jade looked at the headstone which identified the resting place of Michael Hicks. She then turned to Grant. They embraced and held each other for the next fifteen minutes without a word being spoken as the rain continued to fall.

Grant managed to maneuver Jade's car out of the ditch. Jade and the car were a muddy mess. Grant followed her to the daycare where he went inside to get Lad. He did not want Jade seen in such a mess. The daycare worker walked to the door with him to make sure Jade was indeed there to pick the child up since Grant was not on the pick-up list. Grant strapped Lad in his car seat and shut the door. Jade rolled her window down.

"Jade, I'm going back to the Inn to shower and change clothes."

Jade looked at Grant, soaking wet. He looked innocent and vulnerable. "Okay. I'm freezing. I need to get home to do the same."

"Jade, do you still feel like going to Lucedale?" Jade's look told Grant she did not. He was relieved because he was no longer in the mood to go. "How about I bring a pizza from KD's for supper. Will Nana eat pizza?"

Grant's hands were resting inside the window of Jade's car. It was quite a natural act that she placed her hands over his. "She'll eat it, but it's not her favorite. Do you think you can bring her some chicken tenders? She likes those."

"Sure." Grant leaned in the car and kissed Jade. The ladies from the daycare watched from the window. They now had something to talk about.

Grant pulled the letter from his jacket pocket on the way back to the Inn. After getting inside his room, he read it again. He removed his wet clothes and turned on the shower. His thoughts remained with his dad. Since he had returned home, he discovered that the only person that held a grudge against his dad was he. After the shower, Grant dried his hair and sat back on the edge of the bed and read the letter for the fourth time. Grant's soul felt much lighter. The heavy cloud that had been hovering over him for almost twenty years had been lifted. His daddy loved him, and he loved his daddy. He had forgiven his daddy, and his dad had forgiven him.

Grant finished getting ready and called KD's to order the pizza and chicken. He then dialed the phone number of his mother.

"Hello." Sylvia was sitting on the couch reading a magazine while David watched television.

"Hey, Mom. How are you?" She put her magazine down and looked at David.

"Well, hello, Grant. Are you okay?" Grant rarely, if ever, called his mom. He usually just waited for her to call him.

"Yes, I'm fine. I just wanted to call and tell you that I love you." Grant's mom was worried now. David muted the television as he stared at Sylvia.

"Uhh, I love you, too, son. Are you sure you're okay?" Concerned and curious, David walked over to sit next to Sylvia.

"I went to see daddy today. He wanted me to tell you and Lauren that he loved you very much."

Sylvia stared at David, confused and worried. "Grant, I need to know what's wrong. Is this an April Fool's joke?" It was April 1 after all.

Grant chuckled. "Mom, I promise I'm fine. I don't have long to talk. I just wanted you to know that I love you, and I miss you." Sylvia wiped a tear from her face.

"I love you and miss you, too, son." She was simply stunned. Another tear rolled down her cheek.

"Tell David hello for me. I'll call you when I have more time." After saying good-bye, Grant hung up the phone and left for KD's.

Grant's mom reflected on the words her son had spoken to her. Grant had not told her that he missed her or loved her in years. She did not know what had happened to Grant. But she was glad it did. She laid her head on David's shoulder. "David, I believe my son's finally home again."

When Grant arrived at the Lotts, Jade was in her bedroom. Nana, Lad, and Max were in the den. Nana was watching a movie, while Lad played with Matchbox cars on the floor. Max met Grant as he walked in the door.

"Hey, Max! Buddy, how have you been?" Grant knelt down to pet his old friend. He then looked at Nana. "Hey, Nana."

Nana did not notice that Grant called her Nana instead of Ms. Lott. “Hello, Grant. My favorite movie is on Turner Classic Movies.”

Grant glanced at the television then looked at Lad. “Hey, big guy.” Grant sat in the floor with him to play with the cars.

Jade then entered the room. “Hey, Grant. It feels so much better to change into some dry clothes.” Nana turned and looked at Jade. Her look told Jade that they were interrupting her movie.

“The food is in the vehicle. Let me run get it. I totally forgot to bring it in.” Grant got up to walk out the door.

“Okay, just bring it in the kitchen when you come in.” Grant retrieved the pizza and chicken tenders and met Jade in the kitchen. She set Lad in his highchair and cut him a piece of pizza. Jade brought Nana’s chicken tenders to her so she could eat while she finished her movie.

“Jade, how in the world did you find me today?”

Jade poured them glasses of tea and joined Grant at the table. “Mr. Lauvon. I was worried sick about you.”

Grant smiled at Jade. “When I looked up and saw you today, I felt like everything was going to be okay. And I got to see you muddy and dripping wet. Guess what I learned about you, Jade?”

Jade stopped chewing and looked at Grant. “What did you learn, Mr. Hicks?”

“I learned that when you’re wet, your hair sticks to your head, and you somehow can get mud all over you simply by walking down a muddy road. And I also learned that you were still beautiful.”

What Jade first thought was a criticism turned out to be a great compliment. “Awww, thanks. I looked in the mirror when I got home. I did not see beautiful.” They continued to eat and visit for about half an hour. Jade let Lad down from his chair, and he ran back into the den to play with his cars while Grant and Jade cleaned the kitchen.

After the kitchen work was done, they walked into the den. Nana was watching the conclusion to *The Trip to Bountiful*. Jade and

Grant sat down to watch the ending with her. Carrie Watts had come home. Grant had never seen the movie, but he was struck by the irony of his being here, at this point in time, with a movie about coming home on the television. Carrie Watts had sat down in a field in front of her old home place. She grabbed some dirt in her hands and let it sift through her fingers. Then, she got up to walk to the car which would forever carry her away from the place she called home. She looked at the old place and said, "Bye, Bountiful," set to the old hymn, *Softly and Tenderly*. Grant noticed Nana and Jade crying. Lad stopped playing, climbed into Nana's lap, and hugged her.

"Oh, Nana's okay, baby. I cry every time I see this movie." Lad then slid out of Nana's lap, walked over to Jade, and climbed into her lap.

"I'm okay, too, Sweetie. Aunt Jade was just crying at the movie."

Grant had been keenly observing Lad. "That's interesting. Lad was playing in the floor, and as soon as he saw Nana crying, he dropped his car and went to her. Then, when he saw you crying, he went to you, Jade."

Jade hugged Lad. "Grant, Lad is the sweetest little boy. He can't stand to see someone cry. The other night we were watching TV when a lady began to cry. He stopped what he was doing, walked over to the TV, and he touched her on the screen. I had to explain to him that she was okay."

Grant stayed for another hour. Jade walked him to the front steps, and Grant kissed her good night. As she watched him walk to his SUV, she wondered about their relationship. They had not discussed it. They kissed for the first time at Grant's former home as a joke, but the second kiss immediately thereafter was for real. He kissed her at the nursing home later that day when he dropped her off to get her car. He kissed her at the daycare and now tonight. She thought about discussing it with him, but he simply had too much on his mind to bring it up right now. She wondered about

Samantha. Was he over her? As Jade watched Grant's vehicle pull away, she realized that her heart had left with him.

chapter forty-four

AS GRANT WAS EATING BREAKFAST IN THE dining area of the Grand Avenue Inn, the thought hit him. He had left his cell phone on the nightstand next to his bed, so he quickly ate his breakfast and poured a cup of coffee to take back to his room. In less than two weeks, Grant had become addicted to the taste and the caffeine. He especially loved the smell of coffee brewing in the mornings. He opened the door to his room, grabbed his phone, dialed the number, and sat down.

"Hello, Brother Clark speaking."

Grant put his cup down on the night stand. "Good morning, Reverend. I have an idea for a gravesite for Brandon. Can you come by the Inn and go with me to look at it?" Grant began to pace as usual.

"Why, sure. I just got off the phone with Elsie. The family

has been called in. I don't think Brandon will make it through the day. I was about to head out there."

Grant stared at himself in the mirror. They needed to hurry. "I'll be outside when you get here." Grant hung up the phone and walked onto the porch to sit in the swing to wait on Reverend Clark. Grant was excited about his idea. Exactly twenty minutes later, the green pickup appeared. Grant jumped into the truck before the reverend could slow to a complete stop.

"Where to Grant?"

Grant turned to Reverend Clark. "The Hicks Family Cemetery." The driver smiled. He had not looked there. It was a family cemetery and not open to the public. "Do you know the way, Reverend?"

"Yes, I do. It's been a long time since I've been there though." They made their way to the cemetery and parked just outside the gate.

"There's a perfect spot over here by the fence." Reverend Clark followed Grant as he avoided stepping on the graves of Grant's ancestors. Grant had gotten a few steps ahead of him and arrived there first. "Right here, Reverend."

The site was shaded by a huge dogwood tree in full bloom. A large live oak tree also provided shade for the gravesite. In his effort to look at the landscape surrounding the grave, Reverend Clark had not noticed the headstone immediately adjacent to where Grant suggested Brandon be buried. "Grant, this place is better than how Elsie described it." Reverend Clark noticed Grant looking at the marble headstone that would be Brandon's neighbor. His eyes left Grant, then rested on the headstone: *Michael Anthony Hicks*.

"It's perfect, Reverend. And I know my dad would be honored to have Brandon here with him."

Reverend Clark looked at Grant with astonishment. In less than two weeks, he had witnessed Grant's incredible transformation. Grant seemed like an individual from whom the weight of the world had been lifted. "Elsie will be pleased, Grant. We should go tell her. If she approves, we need to get permission from the family for Brandon to be buried here."

Grant and Reverend Clark began walking out of the cemetery. As Grant opened the gate, he spoke to the reverend. "If you'll go to Elsie's and ask her, I'll go see my Uncle Ronny to find out who makes that decision. Afterwards, I'll meet you at the Smallwoods'."

Reverend Clark paused at the gate and looked at the cemetery. "It's a mess out here. It'll need a good cleaning before the funeral. But you and I can do that. I'm sure Jade will help, too."

The two men hurriedly drove back to the Inn. Reverend Clark dropped off Grant and left for the Smallwoods'. Grant jumped into the Range Rover and headed to his Uncle Ronny's. The town was already bustling with preparation for the next day's benefit. The rain that visited the day before was long gone. A brisk wind was blowing to dry the earth. Grant was anxious to get permission for the burial to occur at the Hicks Family Cemetery, and then he aimed to drive to Brandon's. He wanted to be there when his friend finally hurt no more.

Scharlotte Bounds, Terry Lowery, Carey Byrd, Jade, and several other locals met in the cafeteria of the Leakesville Junior High School to go over the final details of tomorrow's benefit. As usual, Scharlotte ran the meeting. She had detailed notes of the various fundraising efforts that would take place throughout the benefit. The weather forecast called for a beautiful day.

"I believe we are ready, folks. Everyone has his or her assignment for today. Tomorrow morning, the men will meet here at 4:30 to start cooking the chicken. The ladies need to be here at 7:00 to get everything ready for the day. Terry, will the school be unlocked?"

"Yes, I'll be here helping cook at 4:30. I'll have the cafeteria open. Y'all can park in the back. I'll unlock the door to the kitchen so you don't have to carry the things you are bringing too far." School was in session, so Terry stood to leave in order to return to his office.

"Thanks, Terry. Let's get an update on Brandon. Jade, I believe you spent the day at the Smallwoods' yesterday. Can you give us an update?"

Jade had been in deep thought. She was thinking about Grant. She finally tuned into the conversation. "Uhh, sure, Ms. Scharlotte. Yesterday, Brandon was resting well. However, I just got off the phone with Brother Clark, and they've called the family in. It looks like he may not be with us much longer." The crowd sat in silence for a moment. Scharlotte called on Carey Byrd to pray. After the prayer, the group dispersed to gather needed materials for the benefit. Their busyness veiled their sadness. The county was about to lose Brandon Smallwood, again. Only this time, he would be gone forever.

On his way to the Smallwoods', Reverend Clark pulled his pick-up into Walco's convenience store to get gas. As he was filling his tank, an old brown and white El Camino stopped on the opposite side of the pumps.

"Hey, Robert, take this here ten dollars and go pay for our gase." Reverend Clark recognized the squeaky voice of Johnny Newbill.

Robert was obviously over the bout of pneumonia about which Pete Ball had been so worried. Robert yelled back to Johnny. "Put twenty in. I'll pay the difference!" Robert Coxwell and Johnny were buddies. They fished, hunted, loafed, smoked, chewed tobacco, got drunk, and went to jail together when necessary. Though they were the butt of a lot of jokes, beneath the surface they were good fellows. At least according to Reverend Clark, they were. Of course, Reverend Clark tended to see the good in everybody.

Reverend Clark cleared his throat and spoke. "Good morning, Johnny."

Like a box turtle peering from its shell, Johnny stuck his head between the pumps to see to whom the voice belonged. "Hey, preacher. I wouldn't cussin, was I?" Johnny had the same look he had as he stood before Judge Eaton. A nervous, guilty look.

"Oh, no, Johnny. How have you been?"

Johnny's eyes darted back and forth between the gas pump and Reverend Clark. "Purty good, I reckon. We goin fishin. The white perch are hongry, and we aim to feed 'em."

Johnny laughed as Robert walked around the El Camino to see to whom Johnny was talking. "Hey, Brother Clark!" Robert was a head taller than Johnny, but he was always afraid of him. Johnny was not afraid of anything. Once, when they were in the third grade, they were on the school bus together when Johnny purposely stuck his bare foot into an exposed heater fan to impress Regina Harvison. The spinning blade stopped from the intrusion of Johnny's wiry toes. Johnny could also ball up a piece of paper, swallow it, then somehow, after croaking like a bullfrog, make the paper come back up his throat and back into his mouth. Robert had respected and feared him ever since. Robert followed Johnny around like a little puppy.

Reverend Clark looked at Robert. "Hello, Robert."

Robert put a cigarette in his mouth and was about to light it when Johnny slapped it to the ground. "What the hell you doin, Robert? That man's a preacher!" Reverend Clark could immediately see Robert's feelings were hurt. His jaw hurt, too. Johnny's aim wasn't the most accurate in the world.

Robert looked at the reverend. "I'm sorry, preacher."

Reverend Clark decided he would invite them to church. "Oh, that's okay, Robert. Hey, fellas, why don't y'all come to church with me Sunday morning?" Johnny stared at Robert with an "I'm gonna whip your ass if you say yes" look.

"Uhh, uhh, Johnny, what are we doing Sunday morning?"

Robert passed the buck. Johnny was so nervous that he lit a cigarette. Robert promptly slapped it out of his mouth. Johnny screamed at Robert. "You son of a bitch!"

Johnny was chasing Robert around the El Camino when Pete Ball appeared. "What y'all a doin?"

Reverend Clark was preparing to get in between Johnny and Robert when they both stopped to look at Pete. Johnny looked at his watch. "Pete, you're late!"

"I know, Johnny. But I was listening in on the meetin at the schoolhouse." Johnny and Robert had settled down. "Hey, Brother Clark."

"Hey, Pete. How are you?" Johnny had finished pumping his gas, and the men stood semi-circle around Reverend Clark.

"Fine as the hair on a frog, Brother Clark. That benfit tomorrow is gonna have everthang. I volunteered to help. I goin to help unload wood tonight for the farr to grill dem hens on in the mornin. Preacher, this town is gonna be rollin tomorrow, ain't it? It's gonna be like election day!" Elections in Greene County are serious business. The whole county comes to the courthouse to listen to election returns. Although electronic voting machines had taken a lot of the anticipation and fraud out of the election, everyone still came to town on election night.

"Pete, I believe it'll be a huge success, and yes, there will be a lot of people in town."

Johnny, not to be left out, spoke next. "Preacher, can me and Robert help out you reckon? I went to school with Lester Smallwood. Well, to the ninth grade anyhow. He got sent to some reform school, and I quit that year. I told my momma that when the folks I started first grade with gradiated, I was gonna quit. I done it, too."

While Johnny was rambling, a thought crossed Reverend Clark's mind. "Boys, I believe y'all can help out. Can y'all ride out to Elsie Smallwood's when you get back from fishing?" The trio agreed to ride out later to get their assignment. Reverend Clark got in his truck and drove in the direction of the Smallwoods'. He smiled and shook his head. He realized that he never received an answer to his invitation to church on Sunday. But, he thought, they were good boys.

Grant pulled into his Uncle Ronny's driveway to find Dana hanging clothes on the line. He noticed his uncle's truck was not there. Grant wondered what he should call Dana. Technically, she was his aunt, but in reality it did not feel that way. He decided to go nameless.

"Hey." Dana turned to look at him. She then continued to hang clothes. "Is Uncle Ronny here?"

Dana finished and finally spoke. "No."

"Can you tell me where I can find him?" Grant began to lose his patience. Why couldn't she just be nice? Grant walked alongside of her until she reached the porch. "Ma'am, I'm sorry if I've interrupted you or offended you in some way. I just need to see Uncle Ronny a few minutes."

Dana lit a Virginia Slim. "He left early this morning to check his lines on the river. He was then running by the hardware store to get some plumbing supplies. After that, he is supposed to be doing some plumbing work at Wildkat Korner. Now, do you want my date and place of birth?" Grant thanked her and decided he would reverse the order of his uncle's itinerary in the hope of finding him. Grant was relieved to discover his relative's truck in front of Wildkat Korner. He was in the bathroom repairing the plumbing to a sink.

"Hey, Uncle Ronny."

"Well, hey man. Where've you been, Grant? I thought you'd have come back out to the house by now." Ronny stood and wiped his hands on his pants.

"I've been busy helping with Brandon. I just left your house. Dana told me where I could find you."

Ronny lit a cigarette. "Surprised she talked to you. She hates lawyers. She says, 'Woe to the doctors and lawyers!'" Ronny laughed. "She told me the Bible says you going to hell, boy. I hope she's wrong. Don't you?"

Grant ignored the theological discussion. "Uncle Ronny, whom do I need to see to get permission to bury someone at the Hicks Family Cemetery?"

Ronny blew cigarette smoke out of his mouth and nose. Grant wondered if any would come from his ears. "I guess you're looking at him. Nobody has been buried out there in years. Most of the Hickses are buried elsewhere. The women folk are scared of that place since it's so far back in the woods, which is crazy. They gonna be dead, so it don't make a damn where they're buried. Anyway, why you asking?" Ronny squinted at Grant as he took another draw from the cigarette.

"I would like for Brandon to be buried next to dad." Grant paused as he could tell his Uncle Ronny was thinking.

"Are you sure you want him buried next to your daddy?"

"Absolutely."

Ronny looked at Grant as he sucked on the cigarette. He then laughed. Smoke laughing with him. "I don't reckon I care. Hell, there's a lawyer out there. May as well be a queer, too."

Grant once again decided to let the offensive words of his uncle pass. Grant simply did not have the time to get into an argument with him. "Thanks, Uncle Ronny."

"No thanks necessary. But the cemetery is probably in bad shape. I'm the only one that cleans it, and I've not been down there in a year or so." Grant agreed to drop by one night for a visit and left. He was looking forward to delivering the news to Elsie. But Grant's excitement turned to sorrow. He became sad as he realized that good news for Elsie Smallwood consisted of successfully finding a burial spot for her precious child. Of course, sadness and sorrow were at that very moment circling the Smallwood home. It was adrift in the air looking for a place to land. Death was near.

As Grant slowly pulled into the yard at the Smallwoods', there were cars and pickups everywhere. Grant hurriedly got out of the Range Rover and walked toward the house. Had Brandon died? Several adults were sitting on the porch while children were playing in the yard. Grant did not recognize anyone on the porch, so he walked inside. Elsie was sitting at the table with Reverend Clark and Lester, Brandon's oldest brother.

Elsie got up and hugged Grant. "Thanks, Grant, for finding Brandon a place with a shade tree. He always loved playing under that big oak tree in the front yard."

Reverend Clark did not wait for Grant to respond. "Grant, did you find your Uncle Ronny?"

Grant shook hands with Lester, then looked at Reverend Clark. "Yes sir. He said it's okay. Brandon?" Grant did not know what to ask. He knew Brandon's time was almost up. Reverend Clark stood and motioned Grant to walk with him to Brandon's room.

When Reverend Clark and Grant walked into the bedroom, Brandon's eyes were open. He was looking around the room. They were standing on the side of the bed in the direction Brandon was looking, but it was as if he did not know who they were. "Lester? Lester? Make them stop, Lester." Grant looked at Reverend Clark. Elsie and Lester heard him and quickly walked down the hall and into the room. Jesse Bolton whispered that Brandon was hallucinating, which was normal. She encouraged whoever's name Brandon called to answer him.

"I'm here, Brandon." Lester was standing at the foot of the bed. It was obvious that he was uncomfortable with how he should respond.

"Lester, take me home. Take me home, Lester."

Lester eased around the bed and sat in the chair next to Brandon. He grabbed Brandon's hand. "Okay, little brother. I'll take you home."

"Where's momma, Lester?" Brandon's eyes were wide open, but his head was not turning. He was staring past Lester.

"I'm here, sweetie. Momma's right here." Brandon's head did not turn in Elsie's direction, so she moved to a place where she hoped Brandon could see her. "Momma's here, baby." Elsie bent over toward Brandon, hoping he would recognize her.

"Lester, I want to go home. Please take me home." Grant watched a tear roll down the cheek of Lester Smallwood. Lester did not appear to be the type to cry. He had tattoos running up both forearms. One tattoo was a snake that appeared to be coiled around his arm. His skin was red and leathery from the hard, outdoor work of moving houses. Although he was only in his forties, Lester looked much older.

"Baby, Momma's right here." Elsie desperately wanted Brandon to answer. But he would not. He fell back asleep although his eyes would not close completely. Grant had never seen someone die before. He wondered if he were prepared for it. Grant quietly left the room, walked out to Reverend Clark's truck, and sat on the tailgate.

After about ten minutes, Lester walked up. "Mind if I join you?"

Grant slid over to make room for Lester. "No. Have a seat."

Lester lit a Marlboro. "Grant, Momma told me what all you've done for her and Brandon. I want you to know I appreciate it. Cigarette?"

The coffee habit was enough. He was not about to pick up smoking, too. "No, thanks. It's a pleasure helping Brandon and your mom. They are great people." Grant looked at Lester as the brother stared at the ground.

"Brandon has had a tough go of it, and so has Momma. She

showed me the clothes you bought her. You know, I never can remember Momma owning a new dress." A little boy ran up to Lester to get him to tie his shoes.

"Is he your son?"

Lester held the cigarette with his teeth, tied the shoes, and looked at Grant. "He's my youngest. I have five, all boys. Guess it runs in the family."

Grant wondered how Lester could afford five kids. "I bet they keep you busy."

Lester pointed at two little girls. "Those are Larry's two girls. They live with us, too. When he got killed, they came to live with us instead of their momma. We don't know where she is." Lester took another long draw from the cigarette. "Yeah, I stay busy. But we make it."

Grant had a new-found respect for Lester. "Y'all live in Pass Christian?"

"Yeah, we do. My wife's family is in the shrimping business. We all work seven days a week. I never get up here to see Momma. She's too scared to drive out of Greene County, so we don't see each other a whole lot."

Grant realized how fortunate he was. He had no room to complain about his lot in life. "Wow. I'm amazed how y'all do it, Lester. Seven kids!" Lester and Grant watched the kids playing in the yard. Two of Lester's little boys had mohawks.

"It ain't easy. But I have no complaints. I don't take no gov'ment help. Guess it's my pride. And I ain't dying with cancer. At least not yet. So things could be much worse."

"Where are y'all staying tonight, Lester?"

Lester glanced at Grant then back at the children. "The nights are still cool. We brought a tent."

Grant wanted to rent them a couple of rooms at the Inn, but he was afraid it would offend Lester. But his manners made him ask. "Lester, don't take this the wrong way, but I would like to rent a couple rooms for y'all at the Grand Avenue Inn if you will permit me."

"Oh, no, Grant. The kids are excited about camping out. My wife will sleep with Momma, if there is any sleeping that takes place tonight. I'll sleep with the kids in the tent. But thanks anyway."

"If it's okay, I'd like to rent a room in your name so y'all will have access to it. It would sure be an honor for me to do it." Grant nervously waited on Lester's response.

"That'd be fine, Grant. My wife can take the kids out there to bathe at least. I appreciate everything you're doing. I know you don't have to do it."

Grant was relieved that his gesture was received. "Lester, I wonder what Brandon was thinking when he wanted you to take him home?" Grant stared at Lester awaiting his response.

Lester lit a second cigarette and paused a moment before he answered. "I don't rightly know for sure. But Brandon used to get picked on fiercely. When I was around, nobody did. I can't tell you the times that I had to take up for him. One time, Brandon had walked up to the store. The store was about a mile from the house here, up by the bridge. The store is no longer there. It closed a long time ago. Anyhow, Brandon was about twelve at the time. Some teenage boys caught him on his way back home. Brandon was different, you know, even at that age. Those boys stripped him naked and whipped him with his own belt. When Brandon did not return home when he should have, Momma sent me to look for him."

Grant could sense Lester's lingering anger. "Brandon was lucky to have you as a big brother."

Lester did not respond to Grant's compliment. He continued with the story. "When I found him, they had tied him to a tree with his belt. They had written the word *Fag* across his forehead. He kept saying, 'Lester, take me home. I want to go home, Lester.' To this day, I never knew who did it. He wouldn't tell me. He knew me and Ernie would have killed the motherfuckers."

Lester flicked his second cigarette butt toward the woods. He then stood and turned to Grant. "Grant, again, thanks for everything." Lester shook Grant's hand and returned to the house.

Grant sat on the tailgate and imagined what Brandon must have felt to have been humiliated on that day. He began to remember all the times when he was young and he saw classmates picking on Brandon. He felt a sharp pain in his gut as he realized that there were many times he did not take up for his friend. And despite all that Brandon endured, he loved others so easily. Brandon had forgiven everyone. Grant sat on the tailgate for the next several minutes and wondered how one's heart can have such a deep capacity to forgive and to love. He realized he was still learning from his dear friend.

Jade walked into the Temple Harvest Fellowship Hall and began to gather the styrofoam plates, plastic cups, spoons, knives and forks. Temple Harvest, like nearly all of the churches in Greene County, was donating the supplies needed to box the chicken plates for the benefit. It was 2:00 p.m., and the church parking lot was empty, except for Reverend Mimbes' car.

"Jade, I need to run to Lucedale. I have a dentist appointment at 2:45. Can you lock the door when you leave?"

Jade looked at the pastor who had on his gym clothes. "Sure, Reverend Mimbes. I shouldn't be here too much longer. Edwina was going to come, but she had to go in to work this afternoon."

"Well, Jade, make yourself at home. Take anything you think may be needed for the benefit. I'll see you in the morning. Our church is responsible for the car wash, so while I'm in Lucedale, I'm going to pick up some liquid detergent and a couple more buckets for tomorrow. Then, I'm going to the Wellness Center to exercise." Reverend Mimbes wrote down his cell phone number and handed it to Jade. "Call me if you need anything."

"Okay, Reverend Mimbes. Thanks. Be careful." After the

reverend left, Jade sat down and called Grant. Grant updated her on Brandon's day. Jade was happy that Brandon would be buried next to Grant's dad. She agreed to drive out to the Smallwoods' when she was finished preparing for the benefit, and they said good-bye. She was almost finished stacking the supplies by the door when she heard a car door slam. She peered out the fellowship hall window and noticed Danny Narbo's patrol car parked next to hers. She regretted parking in a place that could be seen from the road. She began to get nervous.

"Well, well, well. Hello, Jade." Jade began walking toward her cell phone. She had left it on the table after she got off the phone with Grant. Danny beat her to the phone. "Not so fast. Who you planning to call, Jade? That queer-loving lawyer?"

Jade realized she was trapped. Danny was standing between her and the door, and he now had her cell phone. "Danny, please don't start this today. I'm busy. And I need to go." Jade's eyes darted toward the door. She slowly started walking toward the wall.

"Ms. Lott, you'll leave when I let you leave." Danny began to walk closer to her. When he did, she started for the door. Danny caught her and pinned her against the wall.

"Danny, please don't. I'm late, and people will start looking for me. I need to go." Danny pushed his body against hers. Jade's mind was racing. How would she escape?

"Jade, this'll only take a few minutes. I don't like it when I get made a fool of." Danny held Jade's jaws together with his left hand. He released his grip long enough to hear her response.

"Danny, nobody has made a fool of you." Jade was on the verge of crying. She wondered if she screamed, would she be heard?

"All I want to do is make love to you one time. If you don't like it, I'll leave you alone." Danny began to move his left hand up the side of Jade's leg. He then put his right hand under her shirt and began to move it up her back. He was moving his hand toward her breast when she spit in his face. Danny's face turned red. She could see the veins in his temples moving. "Okay, we'll do this the hard fuckin way." Danny went into a fit of rage. He grabbed Jade and threw her on top of a table. He held her down with one hand and began to try to pull her jeans off with his free hand. Jade was no match for Danny. He worked out religiously, and she was so tiny. Jade was squirming, and Danny was getting frustrated because he could not get her pants unbuttoned. Jade screamed.

Danny clutched her mouth shut again. "Damn it, Jade! Be still. Don't make me hurt you." He let go of Jade's mouth in order to use both hands to get her pants off. She spit in his face again. When she did, the deputy reared back his fist and began to swing downward toward her when a right uppercut caved Danny's front teeth toward his throat. Danny staggered backwards. He was reaching for his pistol when Reverend Mimbes' left hook flattened his nose. Blood spewed across the room. Danny was not going down easily. The reverend let Danny straighten up, and he then finished him off with a thunderous right that would later require Danny's jaws to be wired. Danny was unconscious before he hit the floor.

Reverend Mimbes ran to Jade. "Sister Jade, are you okay?" Jade was crying but shook her head yes. The kind pastor then called the sheriff, asked him to come get his deputy, and to bring an ambulance. The strong minister tied Danny's hands behind his back. He then walked over to Jade.

Jade stood and hugged her rescuer. She was still crying. "Thank you so much, Reverend Mimbes. You saved my life. He would have had to kill me before I would have let him rape me."

Reverend Mimbes and Jade sat together for the next several minutes. They finally heard the sirens getting louder as the sheriff and ambulance approached. Sheriff Coaker walked into the fellowship hall and pulled the badge off Danny's shirt without unpinning it. The sheriff apologized to Jade and took her statement. He requested that Jade receive medical treatment, but she declined. Her left arm was already bruising. The sheriff took pictures of her arms where Danny had gripped them so tightly. He informed Reverend Mimbes and Jade that he had called Danny on his radio an hour before and told him to come in and bring his weapons, his badge, and a change of clothes. Danny knew he was about to be terminated. The sheriff would follow the ambulance to the hospital, and place Danny under arrest as soon as he was patched up and discharged. The bullying days of Danny Narbo were over.

After the sheriff and paramedics had left, Jade and Reverend Mimbes sat back down at one of the tables. Jade spoke first. "Reverend Mimbes, I thought you had left." Jade had stopped crying, and although she was still shaking, she slowly began to regain her composure.

"I had left, Sister Jade. But I needed gas, and I didn't think I had enough to make it to AJ's, so I went into town. I passed Danny Narbo on the river bridge heading this way. Edwina had told me how he's always messing with you. My gut told me to come back, so I did. It had to be the Lord."

Jade hugged him again. "Reverend Mimbes, please don't tell anyone right now, especially Grant. I don't want him to take his focus off Brandon."

"I won't, Sister Jade. But don't tell Sister Edwina, unless you want it known." Jade slightly smiled. Reverend Mimbes sat there with her until she finally stopped shaking. She went to the bathroom to make sure her appearance looked normal. Any lasting effects from the traumatizing event would have to wait. Jade simply had too much to do.

Jade rejoined the pastor. "Reverend, you carry a mean punch."

The kind man gave Jade one of his wide, glowing smiles. "Sister Jade, I try to apply the New Testament to most situations and turn the other cheek. But every now and again, I have to use an Old Testament eye-for-an-eye approach. For moments like this, I work out every day." He gave Jade a wide grin. She smiled and finally laughed a little. Reverend Mimbes helped Jade load her car and followed her to the school cafeteria to unload the supplies.

"Sister Jade, are you sure you're okay?" He did not want to leave Jade alone.

"Yes, sir, I'm fine. Thanks to you, I am anyway. I promise I'm okay." She looked at her watch. It was almost 4:00. "Oh, no! You've missed your dentist appointment." Jade looked at Reverend Mimbes apologetically.

"That's okay, Sister Jade. Danny Narbo needs a dentist worse than I do." They shared a brief laugh, hugged again, and went their separate ways. Jade picked Lad up early from the daycare and brought him home. She did not mention to Nana what had happened. She was too much in a hurry and she did not want Nana upset and worried. This would be the first night Nana would keep Lad by herself. Jade ensured Lad was fed, bathed, and ready for bed before she left for the Smallwoods'. She placed the phone next to Nana and set it to where all Nana had to do was hit redial to get in touch with her. Still shaken from what had happened to her, Jade cried on the way to Brandon's. She pulled over just before getting to the Smallwoods' to regain her composure. She would need it for the night ahead.

Reverend Clark had just finished discussing the final details of Brandon's funeral with Grant when the El Camino came barreling down the lane, sliding into the Smallwoods' yard. Grant laughed as he noticed the driver, Johnny Newbill, wearing a motorcycle helmet. Pete Ball was squeezed in the middle between Johnny and Robert Coxwell. The men clumsily exited the vehicle.

"Hey, Brother Clark! Come look at the fish we caught!" Pete Ball bounced to the back of the vehicle like a child showing his mom the fish he had caught with his dad.

Reverend Clark and Grant walked to the vehicle and peered at an ice chest and bucket full of fish. Reverend Clark looked at the fishermen. "Wow, fellas! How did y'all catch so many fish?" Grant could not distinguish the smell of the fish from the smell of Pete and his friends.

Pete pointed at a dirty, white five-gallon bucket filled with water, white perch, and bream. "We caught them on beetle spins." Pete then pointed to the catfish in the ice chest. "We dynamited them out of the water!"

Johnny, still wearing the motorcycle helmet, was clearly agitated at Pete for giving away their fishing secrets. "Pete! Shut up! It again the law to dynamite fish."

Pete glanced at Johnny with a look of innocence. "These fellers ain't gonna to tell nobody." Then Pete looked at the Brother Clark. "Are you, Brother Clark?"

"No, I won't tell, unless I'm asked. You boys are going to get hurt using explosives. Y'all need to be careful."

Robert finally chimed in, "Preacher, we about to clean these fish and cook 'em for everybody if that's okay? We got to talking as we was fishin and figured the folks out here needed to eat." Grant looked at Reverend Clark, hoping that he would decline their offer.

"Why, men, Elsie and the rest of the family would appreciate that. You can clean them out back."

Pete began fumbling in the back of the El Camino. "We have a cooker right here and some propane. We just need some grease."

As Reverend Clark and the men continued to discuss the impromptu fish fry, Grant could not remain silent any longer. "Johnny, why do you wear a motorcycle helmet while driving your vehicle?"

Johnny looked up to see that he still had the helmet on and took it off. "I ain't got no workin seat belt in my Camino. It's a law that you have to wear a seat belt everwhere you go." Johnny looked at Grant with skepticism. After all, Johnny thought, Grant was a lawyer. He should know such things!

Still not understanding, Grant said, "But you still don't have a seat belt. I'm not sure the helmet will suffice."

Johnny set the helmet on the driver's seat. "Sheriff Coaker told me he won't write me no ticket if I wore a helmet. Damn congressmen in Jackson are trying to make it that a feller can't take a shit without a seat belt on or somethin." Johnny then looked at Reverend Clark, "Brother Clark, how can we help tomorrow? You said for us to come by after we got done fishin."

Grant chuckled as Reverend Clark resumed control of the conversation. "Johnny, do you know where the Hicks Family Cemetery is?"

Pete and Robert had gathered around Johnny and Reverend Clark. Robert answered for Johnny, "I know where it is."

Reverend Clark looked at Robert, "Good. Brandon will be buried there, and the place needs a good cleaning. Y'all up for it?"

The three friends looked at each other, and Johnny resumed his leadership of the motley crew. "Preacher, we'll do it. We'll need some equip-ment, though." Reverend Clark agreed to meet them at the cemetery with his lawn equipment at 7:00 a.m. the next day. The friends seemed excited about the endeavor. Grant was relieved that they agreed to clean the cemetery. He had forgotten about the fact that it needed cleaning.

Reverend Clark and the crew began to get things together for the fish fry as Jade pulled into the drive. She uncharacteristically waited a few minutes before getting out of the vehicle. Concerned, Grant walked to her car and opened the door. "You planning to stay in your car all night, Jade?"

Jade meekly smiled and slowly stepped out of her Honda. She hugged Grant for a minute, but it seemed longer to him. He was puzzled at her mood and figured she was upset over Brandon. "Jade, Brandon's comfortable. Jesse increased his morphine dosage again this afternoon."

Jade released Grant, wiped a tear from her cheek, and shook her head and mumbled, "Okay." Then they walked into the house to see Brandon.

For the next several hours, Brandon's loved ones and friends stood vigil over him. The fish fry turned out well. After everyone was well fed, Johnny, Pete, and Robert left. Lester's wife loaded up the kids and headed to the Grand Avenue Inn to bathe and get them ready for bed. Earlier in the day, Grant had helped Lester put up the tent and prepare for the night. The kids were excited to be camping out.

Elsie became more and more solemn as she realized her precious son was about to be gone forever. She was no longer leaving his bedside. The funeral arrangements were made; the burial plot selected. All that was left was for Brandon to step into eternity and provide his contribution to the funeral: himself.

chapter forty-five

AS THE SKY BEGAN TO WELCOME THE SUN, Saturday morning found Elsie, Lester, Reverend Clark, and Grant waiting by Brandon's side. Neither of them had slept during the night. Jesse Bolton left around midnight the night before, and she had just arrived with sausage and biscuits. She was an incredible person and a loving nurse. Brandon's vital signs indicated that his death was now hours, perhaps minutes, from arrival. The group sat quietly by the bed. No one spoke.

At 6:30 a.m., Reverend Clark broke the silence and prayed with Brandon and the family. He whispered to Elsie that he would be back in an hour. He had to leave in order to run to his house, pick up his lawn equipment, and meet Johnny, Pete, and Robert at the cemetery. Grant walked him to his truck and encouraged him to return quickly. Grant felt safe with Reverend Clark near, and he wanted him there when Brandon died.

At 8:00 a.m., the benefit was in full swing. The men arrived at 4:30, and they had been cooking ever since. The ladies began arriving at 6:30 and now were organizing the distribution of the chicken plates. The silent auction items were set up, and the bidding had begun. The Greene County Quilting Club had Brandon's quilt on full display. The quilters had sold close to five thousand tickets. They had doubled their record. A group of motorcycle riders were filling the abandoned factory's parking lot across from Ward's for the benefit ride. The town was buzzing.

Jade drove into Greene Rural's parking lot to pick up Sheriff McInnis to take him to the benefit. He was waiting at the picnic table when she arrived. She stepped out of the car to help him get in. "Good Morning, Mr. Lauvon." She then hugged the sheriff. Her glowing smile still had not returned.

"Good morning, Jade. Any word from Brandon?"

Jade helped the sheriff get into the car before getting into the vehicle. "I left there right after Jesse did around midnight last night. Grant and Reverend Clark are still out there. Grant just texted me and said Brandon would pass soon. His breathing is more labored and sporadic now." Jade pulled out of the parking lot and drove toward the junior high school.

The sheriff looked at Jade. "Jade, are you okay?"

Jade attempted a smile, "Yes, sir. Like everyone, I'm tired and sad. I have a lot on my mind. I feel so sorry for Ms. Elsie. She loves Brandon so much."

They arrived at the benefit, and before they got out of the car, the sheriff patted Jade on the hand. "Jade, I know Elsie is hurting. But she would not swap the pain she is feeling for not having Brandon in her life. When we love someone, it hurts to see them go. But you hang on to the precious memories." Both Jade and the sheriff sat in silence as they watched the activity taking place at the benefit. They both were thinking the same thing. Elsie's and Brandon's precious memories were few. Yet, their love was unmatched and beautiful.

The mood at Ward's was a somber one. Word had spread throughout the town that Brandon would soon die. The people there did not discuss his pending death, but it was on all of their minds. Johnny Ray Barfield was in the group and sober, which indicated the significance of the morning. Someone in the crowd attempted to discuss politics, but no one seemed to have the desire. They mostly passed around the morning paper and discussed the news of the day. Although the usual morning crowd fluctuated, today's crowd was larger. No one wanted to leave. The staff at Ward's filled emptying coffee cups as the crowd waited. Though no one acknowledged it, they were waiting on word of Brandon's death.

The soccer field behind Ward's and next to the junior high building was filled with kids playing soccer. The Leakesville teams were playing the teams from Lucedale in a tournament. Although the two towns were natural rivals, Leakesville's neighbors from the south were aware of the Brandon Smallwood story and of the sadness which enveloped the community. The games were underway, but the parents from both places were not as jovial as usual. Although the young players did not have a clue what was happening, they sensed from their parents' moods that something was wrong. The games were being played, but neither team seemed eager to win.

Grant looked at the clock sitting next to Brandon's bed; it was 9:45 a.m. Elsie, Lester, Ernie, Reverend Clark, Jesse, and Grant were gathered around the bed. After each labored breath, they would look at each other and wonder if it were Brandon's last. Jesse was measuring the time between each rising and falling of the chest. Brandon's frail body would shake each time he breathed. Brandon's mouth was open, and his teeth were fully exposed. The Foley bag that used to capture the urine was empty, and it had been for hours. Elsie sat rubbing Brandon's forehead. At precisely 10:00 a.m., Brandon widely opened his eyes, slightly raised his head, looked at each person in the room, then went to sleep. A trickle of saliva seeped from the right side of his mouth as his head leaned toward Elsie. He was gone.

Elsie leaned over and lay across Brandon's chest wailing. Ernie slowly walked out of the room. Reverend Clark stood in the corner. Jesse stepped away from the bed and glanced at the reverend. Grant stood frozen staring at Elsie as she cried uncontrollably. Elsie kept calling for Brandon as if he would miraculously hear her and wake up. She lay across her precious son's dead body and wept for him. Lester patted his momma, trying to comfort her as he wiped tears from his sun-worn eyes.

So this was it? Death. As Grant stared at a mother hugging and kissing her lifeless son, he attempted to assess his own feelings. What now? What was he supposed to say? Was he to leave the room? Console Elsie? Lester? Grant could not answer his questions, so he simply stood against the wall hoping he could not be seen.

The morning had been a still one. The sun was shining, but no breeze was blowing. The flag in front of the junior high school hung limply. The benefit was already a tremendous success. Ladies were filling up plates and handing them to their rightful owners. A breeze began to blow in the tops of the tall turkey-pine trees sprinkled throughout the town. Jade looked first and then the others as the breeze began to make its way to the smaller trees and then to the ground. Napkins and styrofoam plates were being blown off tables as the ladies were attempting to grab them. The breeze made its way to the soccer fields, and the children stopped playing as the wind pushed the ball off the field. Parents were looking at their children who had stopped playing and were searching for their parents. The breeze would leave as quickly as it arrived.

Jade's phone vibrated. She picked it up and read Grant's text which said, "Brandon's gone." She looked across the crowd to find Sheriff McInnis sitting in a lawnchair staring at her. She began to cry and slowly walk in his direction. The sheriff stood and removed the handkerchief from his back pocket to wipe away the tears that began streaming down his cheeks. The crowd looked at Jade and knew what had happened. Edwina looked at the sky and wept. The activities at the benefit ceased, and people simply stared at each other. The emergency whistle bellowed from the water tower. Two short blows and one longer one announcing Brandon's departure. The crowd at Ward's quieted. Men who would not show emotion simply looked at each other, then out the window toward the blowing whistle, and finally down at their coffee cups. Cars pulled over along the road, and they parked as if some invisible funeral procession were passing through. The town was in mourning. The town was hurting.

Grant waited in the room with Brandon and Jesse until the hearse and coroner arrived. He still had not moved or said a word. Reverend Clark and Lester had managed to get Elsie to the kitchen table. The place, inside and out, was full of people, but no one spoke. Even the children were quiet. After the coroner consoled Elsie, he made his way to Brandon's room and pronounced his death. Two funeral home employees then wheeled in a gurney to remove his body. Finally able to move, Grant walked down the hall, through the kitchen, and out into the yard. He was still in shock. Although Brandon's death was expected, Grant did not know how to react. He still had not spoken. He still had not cried.

The funeral home employees placed Brandon's body on the gurney and covered him with a dark green blanket that had the funeral home's logo in full view. Grant could hear Elsie crying as she struggled with letting Brandon leave the house. Elsie fainted with shock. Lester and Ernie were able to get their hurting mother to her bedroom. Grant watched from the corner of the yard as Brandon was loaded in the hearse. The large back doors were finally slammed shut. The employees walked around the hearse and got in. The huge vehicle slowly made its way out of the yard. As the taillights vanished, Grant, overcome with grief, fell to his knees and wept.

Death can be welcomed at times. This was one of those times. However, the void death leaves can change a person. Grant Hicks was one of those people. He reluctantly had come to see his friend exactly two weeks ago. The Grant Hicks that came from Atlanta would not be the same Grant Hicks that would return there.

chapter forty-six

GRANT AWOKE SUNDAY MORNING AT 8:00 a.m. After Brandon was taken to the funeral home, he spent the remainder of Saturday and most of Saturday night at the Smallwoods'. Jade had joined him there as they assisted Elsie by welcoming the numerous visitors who came with condolences, flowers, money and food. Elsie slowly accepted Reverend Clark's words that Brandon was in a better place and that he felt no more pain. After Grant was assured that Elsie was doing better, he and Jade left. Jade had invited Grant to attend church with her on Sunday. He had reluctantly agreed to meet her there for the 10:00 a.m. service. He now regretted accepting her invitation.

Grant pulled into the parking lot of Mt. Pisgah Pentecostal Church at 9:58. He did not want to be early. Furthermore, he was nervous. The last time he had attended an actual worship service he was in high school, and that was a baptist service. Grant had never attended a pentecostal service before. He knew they would be more lively than the baptists, and he was hopeful no one pointed him out.

Jade was waiting on him as he arrived. "Grant, I was wondering if you had gotten cold feet." She hugged Grant as some small children picked on Jade, asking if Grant were her boyfriend.

"Honestly, I started to cancel. It's been a long time since I've attended church." Jade led Grant into the sanctuary as the choir was in full performance. They were singing a medley of praise hymns as Grant watched the worshipers join the energetic choir in raising their hands as they sang. The church had a band which consisted of a keyboard player, a bass player, two electric guitarists, and a drummer. The music loosened Grant a bit. He was enjoying the rhythms when the pastor tapped him on his shoulder and spoke his name into Grant's ear. They shook hands; then the pastor nodded at Jade. The minister walked up on the platform, and he joined the choir in making a joyful noise.

After thirty minutes of singing, the choir leader made some announcements, then turned the pulpit over to the pastor. "A hardy good morning, brothers and sisters!" The congregation with equal enthusiasm returned the greeting. "I hope you have come to worship the King of Kings and the Lord of Lords today!" The crowd responded with *amens*, while some were jumping up and down. The baptist in Grant was having a hard time figuring out what to do as the pastor continued. "We have some special guests with us today, and we welcome you. Church, let our visitors know that we are glad they are worshiping with us today!" The choir broke out into another song as the church erupted with noise from the worshipers, visiting each other and welcoming new faces in the audience. Grant was pasted with handshakes and hugs. He looked for Jade who had left to welcome the other visitors. Grant anxiously awaited her return.

As the choir concluded its song, the congregants returned to their pews. The pastor was a short man, about 5' 7" tall with a full head of gray hair. Grant thought he looked like Conway Twitty. There was no mistaking the fact that the pastor loved the Lord and Mt. Pisgah Pentecostal Church. He turned on his wireless microphone and spoke to the flock. "I do want to say a few words before my sermon this morning. We all know that Brandon Smallwood went to be with the Lord yesterday. Jade has brought with her this morning a very special guest. Jade bring Mr. Hicks up front."

Grant was startled and felt a rush of blood cover his face. He whispered to Jade, "I thought you said I could just sit here." Jade smiled at Grant through clinched teeth, and she nervously walked him to the front of the church. Grant was so embarrassed that he would not look at the congregation, and he was perspiring profusely.

The pastor stepped down from the platform, and he joined Jade and Grant at the front of the altar. "Brothers and sisters, this fine-looking young man is Grant Hicks. Grant, welcome to Mt. Pisgah." The worshipers shouted amens and clapped. Grant stared at Conway Twitty. The pastor then turned to the crowd. "Grant will be speaking at Brandon's funeral tomorrow, and we need to be lifting him up in prayer. In fact, let's pray with him right now." The pastor laid his hands on Grant and began to pray as the crowd prayed aloud, too. Grant was at first distracted. Then he focused on the pastor's loving words.

Shaken, but grateful, Grant with Jade returned to their pew as the pastor began his message. Grant watched Nana open her worn-out Bible and turn to Genesis chapter thirty-three as the pastor directed the congregation. "I have been preaching a series from Genesis. This morning's message is titled 'Peace in the Family.'"

As the pastor began reading the story of Jacob and Esau and their reconciliation, Grant's mind left the pastor, and his thoughts turned to Lauren. He did not hear any other words the pastor spoke as his heart and mind were focused on his sister. Jade sensed something was wrong and patted him on the hand. He leaned over and whispered to Jade. "I have to go. I'll call you later." Confused, Jade looked at Grant. He waited for the most inconspicuous time to leave the church. When the congregation began to heed Conway's altar call, Grant slipped out the back of the church. He made it to his SUV and began driving toward Highway 63 South. Grant was going to see his sister.

As Grant approached Interstate 10, he input 1500 Mattina Drive, Ocean Springs, into his GPS. He turned left onto Highway 57 South and then right onto Highway 90 heading west. Grant's last visit to Ocean Springs was for a football game in high school. He hoped this trip would have better results than the football game in which the larger Ocean Springs team trounced the Greene County Wildcats.

When Grant located the road sign which read "Mattina Drive," his nerves overcame him, so he drove past it and found a convenience store a few blocks away. Even though he was not thirsty, he went inside and bought a drink. Grant returned to his vehicle and drove back toward Mattina Drive. Only this time, he turned onto the street and began to look for the numbers on the houses. He noticed to his right the even-numbered houses that began with 1520, then 1518, then 1516. As the numbers became smaller, the tension increased. Grant looked in his rearview mirror and noticed that there was a car on his bumper, so he pulled over in front of the house located at 1510 Mattina Drive to allow the vehicle to pass. He counted the houses until he found 1500 Mattina Drive.

Grant sat there for a few minutes, wondering what he would say. Would he be turned away? Would Lauren even be home? Grant looked at the clock on his dashboard. It read 1:00

p.m. Grant looked to his left and across the street where some kids played hop-scotch in their driveway. He then looked back toward Lauren's house, slowly put the Range Rover in drive, and crept forward.

Along the curb adjacent to 1500 Mattina Drive, Grant parked and noticed a Toyota Tundra and a Nissan Maxima in the driveway. The garage door was open, and it was occupied by a boat and a jet ski. The house appeared to be relatively new, and the yard was neatly manicured. He stared at the front door, hoping that someone would see him and walk outside to invite him in. After a couple of minutes, which seemed much longer, Grant opened the door to the Range Rover, stepped onto the concrete, and slowly walked up the driveway to the sidewalk which led to the front door. He held his breath as he rang the doorbell.

The door opened quickly. Before him was the wiry frame of Tallon Pickering. Tallon was fifteen years old, and Grant had never met him. There was no mistaking the Hicks' blood in the slender frame standing at the door. Tallon had the distinct characteristics of the Hickses. He had dark brown hair, olive skin, and almost black eyes. Waiting for the stranger to announce his business there, Tallon stared at Grant. "Hello. Is your mother home?"

Tallon turned his head to the side, and yelled, "Momma! Somebody's here to see you!" Tallon turned to look at Grant who nervously smiled.

"I'll be right there!" The sound of Lauren's voice caused the butterflies in Grant's stomach to fly uncontrollably. His legs became weak.

Tallon stepped to the side, still holding the door handle. "I guess, come in." Grant stepped inside the door as Tallon left the living room where his kin was standing. Grant looked around the room and noted a large canvas painting of Brent and Tallon. Brent appeared to be around eleven or twelve while Tallon appeared to be seven or eight at the time of the painting. Brent was now nineteen. Grant was trying to recall the last time he had seen Brent. He determined it must have been when Brent was two or three years old. Grant remembered visiting with Lauren, Jonathon, and Brent when he was a student at Ole Miss and they came to Oxford for a football game.

As Grant walked to a bookshelf that contained other family pictures, he heard steps coming down the hall. He froze and peered toward the hallway. Jonathon appeared first, and he was surprised to see Grant standing there. Before his brother-in-law could mutter a sound, Lauren appeared. Grant's eyes met Lauren's. No one moved. Grant slowly turned his body to face them. Jonathon turned to look at Lauren. Lauren's chin began to wrinkle as her emotions determined their direction. After what seemed to be an eternity, Grant spoke. "I'm sorry, Lauren."

Lauren began to cry as she walked toward Grant. He, still nervous, could not move. Tallon stepped into the edge of the room to learn who the visitor was. Lauren embraced Grant and held him tightly. She continued to cry as she embraced the brother she had not seen in over seventeen years. Grant closed his eyes and held his sister. Jonathon and Tallon simply watched. Lauren finally pulled back from the embrace, but she still held onto her brother. "I have missed you so much."

Lauren embraced Grant again. After a few moments, she released him and looked at Tallon. "Tallon, this is your Uncle Grant." Tallon had heard about his uncle for all of his life. He sometimes wondered why his mom and her brother did not speak. But Grant's absence was all Tallon had ever known, so he never became curious enough to inquire.

Grant walked to Tallon and shook his hand. "Nice to meet you, Tallon." Grant then turned to Jonathon. They shook hands and briefly embraced, patting each other on the back. "Good to see you again, Jonathon."

Jonathon smiled at his brother-in-law. "You, too, Grant. It's been too long."

Grant looked at Lauren. "I hope I'm not imposing. I thought

about calling." Grant paused. "But, quite frankly, I was afraid to."

Lauren had wiped the remaining tears from her face. "You're not imposing at all. We just got home from church. We were changing clothes to go grab some lunch."

Lauren looked at Jonathon. Almost twenty years of marriage had taught him to read his wife's expressions. He patted Tallon on the shoulder. "Let's go, son. Lauren, we're going to eat. We'll bring you and Grant something when we come back."

Lauren turned to Grant. "Are you in a hurry?"

Grant agreed to stay through lunch. After securing lunch orders, father and son left for Aunt Jenny's Restaurant. Lauren and Grant sat down on the couch and began to catch up on each other's lives. Like Suzanne Pattie, Lauren was able to follow Grant somewhat on the Internet. Lauren educated her brother on Jonathon's career and her recent employment. She then provided him the life histories of Brent and Tallon. Brent was in college at the University of Southern Mississippi, and Tallon was the star soccer player for the Ocean Springs Greyhounds. After Grant educated Lauren on his career and his recently-severed relationship with Samantha, the conversation turned to the reason for Grant's presence in Mississippi.

"So, little brother, what finally brings you to Mississippi?"

Grant adjusted his sitting position, looked toward the window, then back at Lauren. "I came to see Brandon Smallwood."

Lauren's mood became solemn. She looked at Grant with intense lines in her brow. "I read in the *Greene County Herald* that they were having a benefit for Brandon. I guess it was yesterday?"

Grant had been so busy dealing with Brandon's death that he had forgotten to ask Jade about the benefit. "Yeah, it was yesterday."

Lauren looked at Grant with a serious, but gentle, expression. "What's wrong with Brandon? I knew he was released from prison, but I had not heard what happened to him."

As Grant was preparing to answer Lauren, he noticed that

she looked more like their mom as she had gotten older. "Brandon died yesterday. He had cancer."

Lauren's face displayed the gravity of Grant's statement. "Oh, no! I'm sorry, Grant. I know he meant a lot to you."

Grant thought of Lauren's statement. Brandon did mean a great deal to him, but Grant had neglected his friendship for so many years. "His mom, Ms. Elsie, called me a couple weeks ago and said Brandon wanted to see me, so I came. It was hard watching him die."

Lauren stared lovingly at Grant. "Grant, I spent several years angry at you. I wanted to blame you for what happened. Over time, I realized that nobody is to blame. Daddy was depressed, and he ran. I love him just the same, and I miss him. But it's not your fault. It's not anybody's fault. It took several years for me to learn and accept that fact. Daddy just never got to a place where he could be happy without the approval of the whole world. I still feel sorry for him when I think about it." Lauren paused as she watched Grant staring blankly into the floor. Lauren put her hand on Grant's knee. "I've hoped and prayed for years for us to reconcile. At first, I was too angry. Then, pride prevented me from contacting you. But..." Lauren began to cry again. "But I know Daddy would want us to be close again."

Lauren's words caused tears to stream down Grant's cheeks. "Lauren, I miss him so much." They both embraced and shared their tears. As Grant held Lauren, he recognized that he had missed his big sister more than he ever realized. After their embrace, Grant looked at Lauren. "Dad left me a letter, Lauren. He wrote it before he died. Sheriff McInnis has been holding it for me. He gave it to me Thursday. Dad wanted me to tell you that he loved you and Mom very much."

The sound of car doors slamming indicated their lunch had arrived. Grant and Lauren would share a few more memories before joining Tallon and Jonathon in the kitchen. The reunited family would visit for the next two hours. They laughed often. As the conversation moved along, Grant realized how much he and Tallon had in common.

Grant looked at the clock. It was almost 5:00 p.m. "I need to get going. I'll be speaking at Brandon's funeral in the morning, and I have to prepare."

They all stood and walked him to the door. Lauren walked him to his vehicle and hugged him once more before he got into the Range Rover. "Grant, I'll be at the funeral in the morning. I want to be there for Brandon and to support you."

Grant closed the door and rolled the window down. "Lauren, I've learned so much about Daddy since I came home. He is still loved and respected there. Brandon will be buried next to him."

Lauren, blinking away the tears which had seeped back into her eyes, spoke. "I think that is where he needs to be, Grant. Please be careful. I'll see you in the morning."

Grant drove the hour and fifteen minutes back to Greene County with the final piece to his reconciliation puzzle. He was overcome by a feeling that he had never experienced before. Grant had finally made peace with his daddy, his sister, the place he called home, and, most importantly, himself. Grant had never felt this way before. He was truly happy. His pain was gone. On his drive back toward Greene County, the sky seemed bluer, and the trees seemed greener. He looked at himself in the rearview mirror and smiled. He pondered: so this is what forgiveness feels like?

It had been a busy afternoon at Nana's house. Word had spread throughout the community that Jade had been attacked on Friday by Danny Narbo. Jade was able to tell Nana the details before the neighbors began arriving to check on her. Nana cried as she thought of how close Jade had come to being assaulted. She admonished Jade for not telling her sooner. As was the custom for Jade, she put others' needs before her own, and she elected not to say anything until after Brandon died. Jade assured Nana that she was okay and that Reverend Mimbes had made sure Danny Narbo would think twice before attacking anyone ever again. Reverend Mimbes was now a local hero.

Grant had texted Jade and told her he would be there around 6:30 p.m. It was now 6:00 p.m., and Jade was trying to rush Sheriff Coaker along before Grant arrived. Jade wanted to tell Grant without the presence of the sheriff. Sheriff Coaker had driven out to check on her and also to inform her that Danny would not be granted bond. Just prior to Danny's attack, the attorney general's office and the sheriff had finalized the investigation of two other instances of sexual assault by his deputy. Danny had stopped a young college girl on Highway 98 near McLain. When she refused to go with him to the sheriff's office, Danny pulled her from the car, took her to a wooded area, and raped her. Danny was also charged with the repeated sexual assault of a local girl who was incarcerated in the county jail. Judge Eaton denied bail for Narbo, finding that he was a sexual predator and did not deserve to be released. Judge Eaton was especially furious that the former deputy committed the crimes under the cover of his trusted badge.

Sheriff Coaker had been gone for less than five minutes when the Range Rover turned into the driveway. Jade was sitting on the front steps waiting on Grant while Lad and Max were playing on the porch. Grant got out of the car and walked to the steps. He was smiling, obviously happy to see Jade. They hugged, and Grant kissed her. "Jade, I've spent the afternoon with my sister, Lauren, and her family. They're coming to the funeral tomorrow!" Grant finally noticed the worried look on Jade's face. "What's wrong, Jade?"

Jade walked to the front door and opened it for Lad and Max to go inside. She then walked toward Grant, and she began to cry before she could make it back to him. They embraced. Jade turned her head sideways and rested it on Grant's shoulder. Wondering what had happened, he was staring at the background behind her.

They sat down on the front steps as Jade told him the entire story. Grant's demeanor began with shock. Then it changed to anger as he got up to pace in front of the steps. At that moment, he wanted to destroy Danny Narbo. As Grant was dealing with his anger, he looked at Jade sitting on the steps. She looked weak and vulnerable. She had held this in for two days to deter his distraction. He walked over to Jade and knelt down in front of her. He then cupped her face in his hands and looked into her blue eyes. "Jade, I don't know what I would do without you." Grant embraced her, and they spent the next hour sitting on the steps holding each other's hand and talking.

Using her walker, Nana walked to the door. "Jade? Y'all want something to eat?"

They both turned to Nana and indicated that they were not hungry. Jade then looked at Grant. "Grant, please put this out of your mind. You need to focus on the funeral tomorrow. Danny is in jail, and he's not going anywhere."

Grant looked at Jade. "Can I sleep on your couch tonight?"

Jade smiled. "Sure, you can. But it's not necessary. Have you prepared what you'll say tomorrow?"

Grant looked into the distance. He then took out his cell phone, and he noted the time was 8:30 p.m. "No. Things have been so hectic I haven't. I tried to think through what I would say on the way back from Ocean Springs, but I have a mental block. I'm beginning to panic a little."

Jade put her arm around his waist. "You'll do great, Grant. I'm so happy that Brandon knew before he died that you would be speaking at his funeral. It brought him peace."

While Jade prepared Lad for bed and got him to sleep, Grant sat on the porch alone. As he sat on the steps, he reflected on Elsie's March 16 phone call. He had no idea that her call would be the key which would open two doors: one to his past; the other to his future. Grant relived in his mind his days in Greene County since his return on March 20. He smiled as he thought of Sheriff

McInnis and his new friends: Edwina, Johnny, Pete, and Robert. He thought of Reverend Mimbes and Reverend Clark. He thought of the genuine quality of the people here, both black and white. Grant reflected on his own imperfections, and suddenly he realized that he was just like them. He was far from perfect, but he did the best that he could. Tomorrow morning he would be Brandon's advocate. He would stand in front of his hometown, and he would deliver the message with which Brandon had entrusted to him.

After everyone went to bed, Grant lay on the couch encapsulated by darkness. As the illuminated clock above the television welcomed midnight, Grant faded into a deep sleep. He had never gone to court without a meticulous game plan for every facet of the trial prepared days in advance. Tomorrow's eulogy would be the most important speech of his life. Yet, as sleep overtook him, words could not be found.

chapter forty-seven

THE ROOM BEGAN TO RECEIVE THE FIRST signs of daylight. Grant opened his eyes, blinking them in an attempt to determine where he was. He turned his head to the left and remembered that he had slept on the couch at Jade's. He pulled himself up and sat on the edge of the couch rubbing his eyes. He glanced at the clock which read 5:48 a.m. The pit grew within as he realized what day it was. In a little over four hours, he would be speaking at Brandon's funeral. The butterflies in his stomach were wide awake as they reminded him that he was not prepared. After a few moments, he slipped on his shoes and headed for the door. He backtracked to the kitchen and left Jade a note that he would see her at the funeral.

Grant decided he would go to his room at the Grand Avenue Inn to get ready for the funeral. After he showered and shaved, he sat down at the small desk in his room to prepare his remarks for the funeral. No matter how hard he tried, the words evaded him. He became mad at himself for waiting so long to prepare. His cell phone chimed indicating that he had received a text message. He picked up his phone and looked at the text. It was from Jade. "Grant, I'm thinking of you. You will do great today!"

Grant pressed reply and typed, "Thanks, Jade." He pressed send and realized that he was in trouble. He feared his words would not be sufficient. He anguished over why he had agreed to speak at the funeral. Why did he? He was not one that knew how to comfort people. He agreed to speak in a moment of weakness. He simply could not say no to Brandon. And now at 7:00 a.m., he was ill-prepared. Grant decided to slip on some jeans and put his suit in the Range Rover. He would take a ride and dress at the church. Grant needed inspiration. And he only knew of one place that he might receive it. The cemetery.

Elsie was dressed for the funeral by 7:00 a.m. She spent Sunday receiving visits and phone calls from people expressing their condolences. Pamela Ricks, who was also to sing at the funeral, drove out to Elsie's Sunday afternoon and fixed her hair. Pamela and Shannon Courtney ran a beauty salon in Leakesville. One or both of them sang at most of the funerals and weddings in and around Leakesville. For the first time in years, Elsie had a new dress to go along with her brand new hairdo. Elsie attempted to wear the costume jewelry Jade picked out for her, but she elected to forego any jewelry. It just did not match the sorrow she was feeling.

Greene County schools were out for spring break. For some reason, spring break in the local school system was always later than most Mississippi schools'. Elsie's coworkers from the cafeteria brought breakfast for the Smallwoods. They arrived at 7:15 with a crockpot full of grits, a pan of fried sausage and bacon, at least three dozen scrambled eggs, and two Tupperware bowls filled with homemade biscuits. They brought jelly, syrup, blueberry muffins, orange juice, milk, and a large pot of coffee. The ladies formed a line on the front porch and fixed the plates for the Smallwoods. Lester taught the children to stick their fingers gently inside a biscuit in order to make a hole, then fill it with syrup. He and his brothers used to eat their biscuits that way as children. Being home reminded Lester of those days.

Elsie elected not to have the traditional wake the night before the funeral. Brandon's casket would not be opened anyway. However, she would be at the casket at 9:00 a.m. to receive visitors. Elsie's insecurity over entering First Baptist Church had passed. She recognized by now that they were her neighbors, too. After all, Terry Lowery and Scharlotte Bounds attended there. Terry and Scharlotte visited Elsie on Sunday to inform her that the benefit had raised a little over $44,000, including the $25,000 designated for the home improvements. The funeral had already been paid for. Counting the donated labor for the home improvements, the benefit would exceed $50,000. Elsie was overwhelmed.

After the ladies from the cafeteria fed the Smallwoods their breakfast, they cleaned up and dispersed in order to get ready for the funeral. Everyone was gone except Lester, his wife, his five boys, Larry's two little girls, Ernie, and Elsie. Lester walked up and put his arm around his mother. "Momma, the people around here have been mighty good to us." He kissed Elsie on the cheek. "I know Brandon appreciates it, too."

Elsie looked at Lester. "I know they have, Lester. Brandon knew it, too. It made things easier for him." Elsie paused and then began walking back inside the house. "I guess we better get things together and go to the church. Brandon's waiting on us."

As Grant pulled onto Cemetery Road, it was much different. The road was cut, raked, and cleaned. The limbs that had hung wildly over the road had been neatly trimmed to avoid scratching a vehicle that would traverse the two-path road. When Grant pulled into the opening which housed the cemetery, his eyes could not grasp what they saw. The wild-looking old cemetery was beautiful. The grass was cut, and each grave and headstone had been individually manicured. The greatest artists in history could not have captured the beauty of the old family burial ground. As Grant stood at the gate leading into the cemetery observing the handiwork of Johnny, Pete and Robert, the El Camino pulled up.

The three friends got out and quietly walked over to Grant. Grant looked at his new friends with appreciation. "Men, I don't know what to say. It's incredible." Grant's eyes returned to the cemetery. Brandon's grave had been dug, and it was waiting his arrival. Johnny, Pete, and Robert looked at each other not knowing what to say. They had worked all day Saturday and Sunday on the cemetery. They decided to ride out to make sure everything still looked the same as when they left the place at dusk the day before. Their work was their contribution. They had no money, but they gave of themselves. Grant turned back to look at the men who were uncharacteristically quiet. Grant walked over to shake each of their hands. "Johnny, thank you. Pete, thank you. Robert, thank you. This is amazing. Brandon thanks you, too."

Pete and Robert looked at Johnny as if they were waiting on him to say something. Johnny's nasal voice finally spoke. "Mr. Hicks, you reckon me, Robert, and Pete can go to the funeral?"

Grant looked at Johnny. "Why, certainly. Anybody can come."

Pete and Robert again looked at Johnny as if to say that he had forgotten something. Johnny perceived the hint and spoke again. "Mr. Hicks, we ain't never been to no church. Well, Pete has, but me and Robert ain't never been. We ain't got no church-goin clothes."

Grant looked at Pete and Robert, then back at Johnny. "Guys, y'all can wear anything you have." Then a thought crossed Grant's mind. "But, if you like, I have plenty of clothes at the Inn if you want to try them on. You're welcome to anything I have." Grant pulled his room key from his pocket. "I have already showered, and my clothes are in my vehicle. Y'all make yourselves at home." Grant handed the key to Johnny. The men shook Grant's hand and left.

Grant walked to the bench at the base of his daddy's grave and sat down. It was now 8:00 a.m., and he still had no prepared remarks. He would sit there for the next hour thinking of the words he would say, while intermittently talking to his dad. Grant slowly walked to his vehicle at 9:05 and drove toward town. His greatest fear was failure. And even that fear could not dislodge the words needed for his speech which was now an hour away.

The crowd began lining up in the sanctuary of First Baptist Church at 8:30 a.m. The Smallwood family arrived just before then. Reverend Clark was waiting for them in the parking lot. First Baptist's pastor, Dr. Jimmy McLendon, led them to his office and welcomed them to First Baptist. He told the Smallwoods how honored the congregation was for their decision to allow them to host the funeral. He informed them that the church would be serving the Smallwoods and their family and friends lunch after the funeral in the fellowship hall. He prayed with them and then left to give Reverend Clark time to prepare Elsie and the family for the funeral. At 8:45, Reverend Clark led the Smallwood family to the sanctuary to begin receiving those who wished to pay their respects.

Grant was astounded at the number of cars parked around the church when he arrived at 9:25. The church parking lot was full, and the empty grass field across from the church was overflowing with mourners. Grant spotted Reverend Clark's truck and double-parked behind it. He grabbed his suit, shirt, and shoes and walked into the back entrance of the church. Grant found an empty Sunday School room where he changed clothes. He looked at his cell phone. It was 9:40. Time was rushing by. When he walked out of the Sunday school room, he found Reverend Clark looking out of the door leading to the parking lot.

Reverend Clark was relieved to see Grant. "Morning, Grant. I was beginning to worry about you." Grant did not have a look of confidence. "Are you okay, son?"

With a distressed look, Grant responded, "I can't do it."

Reverend Clark paused. "Grant, you'll know what to say. I've prayed for you. Let me give you some advice. The first funeral that I ever conducted, I was up all night, scared to death. I was only twenty-one years old. An old preacher told me just before the funeral to remember that the family was hurting. That I did not need to use fancy words. Just get up there and let them know that it's okay to mourn. Then say some words to give them comfort. Nothing fancy. Just speak to the family." Reverend Clark paused, but Grant did not respond, so he continued. "Grant, Elsie and her family love you. Yesterday, they told me how honored they were for you to be here. Son, they don't care so much as to what you say. Your being here says enough."

Grant looked at the reverend with a child-like innocence. "I'm going to put these clothes back in my vehicle and then sit on that bench by the playground for a few minutes. I can't come into the sanctuary until it's my time to speak. I'll be too nervous."

Reverend Clark looked at his watch. It was 9:46. "Okay, Grant, Pamela Ricks will sing first. After I speak, then Pamela, Bill Walters, and Shannon Courtney will be singing 'It is Well With My Soul.' Reverend Clark pointed in the direction of a door leading into the sanctuary. "You'll need to come in that door. The musicians will be singing from the other side of the church, and they'll be sitting in front of the other door when they are finished."

Reverend Clark began to walk back into the sanctuary. Grant stopped him, "Reverend, are you sure I can do this?"

The wise minister gave him a confident smile. "Son, there is no doubt in my mind that you not only can, but will."

Grant had just sat down on the bench when he heard the familiar voice of Sheriff McInnis. "Hello, Grant." Upon entering the sanctuary, Reverend Clark had mentioned to the sheriff that he might need to encourage Grant.

"Hey, Sheriff," Grant replied, glancing only slightly in the revered man's direction.

The sheriff walked over to Grant and put his hand on his shoulder."Grant, I know this is hard, but it's nothing compared to what our friend endured. Brandon will help you through this. Just remember the strength he displayed."

Looking at the sheriff, Grant shook his head. "I know, Sheriff. I know. It's just hard." Grant then looked at the time on his cell phone.

The sheriff released his hand from Grant's shoulder. "Grant, there's been a lot of forgiveness since you've come home. But there's one thing left to do." Grant looked into the sheriff's caring eyes as the older man pointed at the church. "Those people in that church need to know that they're forgiven, too. And Brandon trusted one man to tell them that. Just speak from your heart, son."

The sheriff slowly limped back toward the church. It was 9:54. When he entered the sanctuary, he went to Jade. "Go to him, Jade." Jade handed Lad to Nana and walked out of the sanctuary. The sheriff managed to tell Reverend Clark to delay a few minutes before starting the service.

Jade meekly walked to the bench and sat down next to Grant. "Hey, you."

Grant looked at Jade and slightly smiled. "Hey, Jade."

They could hear the pianist and organist playing as the start of the service was imminent. Jade grabbed Grant's hand. "Grant, you better get in there so we can start the service. Edwina is sitting between Johnny Newbill and Pete Ball acting like she has the pneumonia." Grant smiled as Jade continued to try to relax him. "And if I'm not mistaken, Johnny has on the same pair of Prada shoes that I remember seeing at the auction a couple weeks ago."

Grant leaned up and grinned. "Yeah, I gave them the key to my room."

Jade then laughed. "And Robert Coxwell has on a pair of chinos, but I keep thinking about that clopper thing Pete mentioned." They both laughed. It was now 10:01, and the pianist and organist had stopped playing. "Grant, you'll do Brandon proud. You always have." They heard the beautiful voice of Pamela Ricks begin to fill the air. Jade stood and began walking toward the church.

Grant turned to look at her as she walked away. "Jade?" She turned around, and Grant thought he had never seen anyone so beautiful as Jade at that moment. "Jade..." Grant paused briefly. "I think I love you."

Jade smiled. "I think I love you, too, Mr. Hicks." She then walked around the corner and entered the church. Grant stood and made his way inside the church to the doorway he was to enter as Pamela Ricks finished her song. Grant sat in a folding chair and cracked the door to the choir loft in order to hear Reverend Clark.

The well-rehearsed minister had been sitting in a chair behind the pulpit. Grant watched through the crack in the door as he stepped to the pulpit. Grant could see him from the waist up. His coat was a little too big. Perhaps it fit him at one stage in his life, but as the reverend aged, his body began to get smaller, and the coat that had once fit perfectly now hung loosely on his aging frame. Grant noted the furrow that ran the length of the back of the old preacher's neck. His hair was slicked close to his head. The preacher was reaching for something. He started stacking the items on top of the pulpit.

"Good morning. Elsie, Lester, Ernie, family, friends, and neighbors, I count this a high honor to stand before you today."

Reverend Clark's words were slow and deliberate. "On behalf of the Smallwood family, I want to first thank you all for being here this morning." The preacher's head swivelled as he looked at the crowd and then back at Elsie. "Elsie, there is no doubt that this community loves you, your family, and Brandon. I don't recall ever seeing a crowd this large for a funeral." Grant cracked the door a little wider. He tried to get a glimpse of Elsie, but he could not. "Folks, on behalf of the Smallwoods, thank you for the love shown them over the last several days. The food, flowers, visits, and phone calls have been much appreciated. Elsie also wanted me to thank you for the love shown them through your generosity at Saturday's benefit, the largest and most successful benevolent effort in the history of our beloved county. We are indeed a blessed people to call this place our home."

The preacher looked down at the pulpit, then up again at the crowd. "I will read you Brandon's favorite Scripture in a moment. After that, we will have a word of prayer. This morning's service is a little different than is customary. When I'm done, we will have another song. Then Brandon's dear friend, Grant Hicks, will bring the eulogy. I will bring a very short message at the gravesite to conclude the service. Again, friends, thank you for your neighborly love."

Reverend Clark lifted a small New Testament Gideon Bible from the stack on the pulpit. "Brandon entered Parchman in August of 1989. The Gideons visit Parchman every September to distribute these little New Testaments. We're all familiar with the wonderful work of the Gideons. When Brandon returned home sick, I began to visit with him and Elsie. I noticed this stack of Bibles in the windowsill of Brandon's room." Reverend Clark opened one of the New Testaments. "This Bible was given to Brandon on September 23, 1989. This was the first one Brandon received." The reverend put the Bible down. He picked up another Bible. "This one was given to him on September 21, 1994." Reverend Clark put it down and picked up yet another Bible. "This was the last one Brandon received before he was released. It is dated September 14, 2007, just a few months before his innocence would be revealed."

The preacher opened the Bible. "In every one of these Bibles stacked on this pulpit, Brandon had underlined these words from Romans 8:38-39. 'For I am persuaded, that neither death, nor life, nor angels, nor principalities, nor powers, nor things present, nor things to come, nor height, nor depth, nor any other creature, shall be able to separate us from the love of God.'" Reverend Clark closed the Bible and returned the New Testaments to the shelf on the inside of the pulpit. "Folks, we know Brandon's story. Elsie, family, friends, we should all take comfort in knowing that Brandon understood that nothing, absolutely nothing, could separate him from God's love. Let us pray."

The nervousness that had receded slightly as Grant listened to Reverend Clark returned with a vengeance. He stood and began to pace. He finally accepted the fact that he had no idea what he would say. But say it he must. The prayer ended. Pamela Ricks, Shannon Courtney, and Bill Walters began to sing that old hymn written by Horatio Spafford. In the sanctuary, as the second verse began, Reverend Mimbes, who was sitting midway from the front of the sanctuary, rose to his feet and began to sing along with the trio. Tyrone Burley stood next. Before they would reach the chorus, the entire congregation was standing, singing in unison the comforting words written by a man who had suffered so much. Grant paused to listen. As he listened to the words, they brought him comfort. Brandon was his friend. Except for the family, he knew him better than anyone there. In 1989, he wanted so badly to have someone, anyone, to speak up for Brandon. It was twenty-one years later, and Grant realized that day had finally come.

After the song ended, Grant could hear rustling as the multitude returned to their pews. His hand was on the doorknob, ready to turn it, open the door, and enter the sanctuary. He closed his eyes and allowed his body to relax. Reverend Clark was glaring at the place where the door was to open. Jade was holding Lad and, too, looking at the door. Elsie was staring at the casket, not sure what was to come next. The crowd sat solemnly with some of them beginning to get uncomfortable. Did someone forget what was to be next? Grant Hicks was not anywhere to be seen. Had he decided not to come? Against the backdrop of corporate mourning and collective curiosity, the door slowly opened, and Grant entered the sanctuary, walked up the steps leading to the pulpit, looked at Reverend Clark, then turned to face the crowd.

The appearance of the native son was indeed impressive. He wore a dark blue Armani suit with a tiny pinstripe. His slip-on Gucci shoes sparkled. He wore a light pink tie with his white dress shirt announcing its splendor. Pete Ball leaned forward, looked around Edwina, and whispered to Johnny. "Johnny, he looks like a movie star."

Edwina cut her eyes at Pete, and just above a whisper barked at him. "Shet up!" Pete remembered Edwina's apparent sickness, so he covered his nose and mouth and leaned back watching her from the corner of one of his eyes.

Grant scanned the crowd. The pews were packed. People, mostly men, were standing against the walls. Folding chairs had been placed in the center aisle, leaving enough room for the casket to pass when the service was over. Each chair was occupied. A group of people was crammed into the foyer. Grant slowly began to see familiar faces. His eyes connected with Reverend Mimbes' who gently nodded his head at Grant. A few pews behind him, Grant's eyes met Judge Eaton's who was sitting with Felix Bufkin. As Grant's eyes made their way to the front of the sanctuary, he found Lauren, Jonathon, Brent, and Tallon. Sitting in front of them was his mom; her husband, David; Grant's secretary, Linda; and Linda's husband. On the same pew on the opposite end sat Ryan and Suzanne Pattie. Grant's eyes were making their way to the left front of the sanctuary to find Elsie, and he discovered Jesse Bolton and the hospice staff sitting on the fourth row reserved for family.

The third row was occupied by Jade, Nana, Lad, Sheriff Mcinnis, and Elsie's co-workers. The second row was taken by Lester's wife and Elsie's grandchildren. Grant's eyes finally met Ernie's, then Lester's, and lastly, Elsie's.

Grant grabbed the edges of the pulpit, gripping them tightly. He stared into Elsie's aching eyes. "Ms. Elsie...." The lump in Grant's throat appeared so quickly that he could not contain it. The tears rushed forward. Grant, wanting to hide, knelt behind the pulpit, crying uncontrollably. Lad escaped from Jade's lap and ran to Grant. The child embraced Grant tightly. Grant stood hugging Lad as Jade walked up on the platform to retrieve him. Grant's tear-filled eyes met Jade's. A dry eye could not be found. Reverend Clark had held his tears the longest, but even he could not stop his tears after witnessing the essence of brotherly love demonstrated by a child.

Grant pulled a tissue from the box sitting on the ledge of the pulpit. He wiped his eyes. Before he could began talking, Elsie spoke through her tears. "We love you, Grant."

Grant shook his head in affirmation to Elsie. "I love you too, Ms. Elsie." Grant finally looked into the crowd and slowly began:

> *I believe it was Mother Teresa who said, "If you judge people, you have no time to love them." My dear friend Brandon was indeed too busy loving people to judge them. Brandon taught me, and all of us, so very much. As I look across this sanctuary, it is evident that he taught us to love. Some of us for the first time. For others, it was a revival of sorts, as our heartstrings were tugged by the innocence and kindness of our friend.*
>
> *I know I have received a lot of credit for standing by Brandon when it was indeed difficult to do so. It is credit that I do not deserve. You see, I started kindergarten with Brandon. At first, my classmates and I were all alike. But, as we grew older, we all began to develop our identities. Brandon was perceived as a weakling by my classmates and me. I stood silent as many times my friend would get picked on,*

have his lunch spit upon, or his books knocked from his hands. I stood at a distance knowing it was wrong, yet I did nothing. So you see, I deserve no credit. Brandon is the only one that demonstrated strength, and he is the only one who deserves a hero's praise. Ms. Elsie, family, I am so very sorry for not standing up for Brandon all of those times that I knew I should have.

Elsie nodded at Grant as if to say, "It's okay, son, I forgive you." Grant looked at Lester, Ernie, and then back at the crowd as he continued:

On the day before Brandon's trial was to start, I visited him for the last time before he would be convicted and sent to spend almost twenty years in prison for a crime his spirit was incapable of committing. By that time, I was angry. Angry at the circumstances, angry at the fact that, except for Sheriff McInnis and Brandon's family, no one believed him. I became bitter as I watched public opinion convict Brandon before the first witness was sworn in at his trial. Yet, as I lamented the circumstances surrounding my own anger, Brandon never showed the first hint of animosity. Even then, Brandon encouraged me. I remember him defending my dad as I was angry at him for not representing Brandon.

Grant paused and his eyes slowly looked into the hurting and repentant eyes of a people that he once vowed never to see again.

Today, we have the benefit of hindsight. And we can look back in time to 1989 with 20-20 vision. It is crystal clear that Brandon was as innocent as a newborn baby. Brandon was convicted by ignorance, prejudice, poverty, cowardice, and outright hatred. None of which can ever be rationally explained. Brandon was convicted by a judicial system that was then, and still remains, more accessible to the rich than to the poor.

As I stand before you today, I can tell you that I have never met another human being with the capacity to love and forgive as our friend Brandon. Personally, he helped me to finally release the lingering pain in my own spirit that had for so long gone unforgiven. Pain unforgiven, folks, robs us of any semblance of joy or peace. And, friends, Brandon understood your hurt, too. And he never stopped loving you or this community.

I had absolutely no intention of ever coming back to this place. When Ms. Elsie called my office on Tuesday, March 16, to tell me Brandon wanted to see me, I told her I would let her know by the following Friday. The truth is, Ms. Elsie, I was not planning to come back. I was going to be a coward and have my secretary, Linda, call and tell you that I could not come. Again, as you can see, people, I deserve no credit.

But I did come back. And, I spent some precious time with Brandon. He not only taught me how to forgive, he also taught me how to accept forgiveness. I shall never forget that day when Jade, Sheriff McInnis, and I went to visit Brandon. Brandon had learned of the benefit you were planning for him. He was so excited. While we were there, Brandon looked at the sheriff and said, "They have forgiven me, Sheriff."

Grant began to wipe the tears from his face that had returned without warning. Sheriff McInnis pulled a handkerchief from his pocket to wipe his eyes. After a moment, Grant looked back at the crowd and continued:

You see, Brandon thought we needed to forgive him. Why? He had done nothing wrong. But he felt responsible for the hurt this community experienced and the guilt that was raging within. People, that is a level of love which I cannot understand. The day Brandon asked me to speak at his funeral, I will always remember his words. He said, "Grant, I know I'm dying. I don't know when. But it will be soon."

Grant's tears returned once more. The crowd was absorbing every word spoken. They came for Brandon and to hear the words Grant was about to speak.

> *Brandon then looked at me with the compassion that was beyond human capability and said, "Grant, I want you to tell the people that come that I have forgiven them." He then concluded by asking me to tell you that he loved you.*

The crowd was quietly crying as the guilt slowly began to lift from its collective spirit. Grant paused again before concluding his remarks. Grant spoke to Elsie first.

> *Ms. Elsie, on behalf of everyone here and the many neighbors and friends that could not be here, we thank you for sharing Brandon with us. He has taught us so very much. He has demonstrated unconditional love for his neighbor. And, he has been patient with us as we have learned to love, to forgive, and to receive forgiveness. He is indeed a hero.*

Grant slowly looked at the crowd, making eye contact with many of the people. He then concluded:

> *Folks, I'm not a religious person. However, I know there is a God. I have never quite understood religion. In particular, I have been confused by the denominational conflicts that are out there. I know enough about religion to know that in an effort to be right, we sometimes forget the big picture. And when we do so, people fall victim to prejudices that should not exist. We tend to want things placed neatly in a box where they are easy to understand and easy to explain. I stand before you today with twenty-one years of education, and yet all that education cannot innoculate me from the hatred that prejudice can infect my soul with if I am not careful and ever vigilant to guard against it.*

Some people are born ahead of their time, it seems. It's like God sends them in to storm the shores of humanity in order to pave the way for future generations to understand how to treat them. History is filled with such people. Rosa Parks refused to sit at the back of the bus; therefore, Reverend Mimbes can today sit in First Baptist Church as a welcomed neighbor and community leader. I believe Brandon was such a person.

Folks, Brandon's pain is gone. And he wants ours gone, too. The greatest gift we can give Brandon today is for us to accept his forgiveness, love one another, and be keenly aware that God will be sending other pioneers into humanity. And when we discover them, let's follow Mother Teresa's lead and love them first. Then, we will have no time to judge them.

With his eyes retreating to the coffin, Grant spoke his final words to Brandon.

Good-bye, Brandon. Thank you for being our friend. And thank you for being my best friend. I love you, Buddy.

After Grant concluded, he turned to look at Reverend Clark who stood and led Grant off the platform. The funeral director then instructed the friends to please rise. Grant followed the beloved pastor down the center aisle to exit the church. The funeral director then instructed the pallbearers to follow behind. The casket was slowly rolled down the crowded aisle. Elsie, being held tightly by Lester, quietly cried as they walked behind the casket. The remaining family members followed Elsie and Lester. The coffin was placed in the hearse as the grieving family watched from the doorway.

After the doors to the hearse were closed, Elsie, Lester and Ernie were led to one of the black funeral home Cadillacs that would follow Brandon to the cemetery. Reverend Clark and Grant were directed to a separate Cadillac that would follow immediately behind the hearse. Sheriff Coaker led the funeral procession behind the sheriff's office and onto Lafayette Street before turning right onto Main Street which would lead them out of town.

Grant sat quietly looking out of the car window as the Cadillac rolled through town. They passed the courthouse. Grant noticed a few of the county employees standing along the roadway to pay their respects. Cars and trucks were lining each side of the road with some of the occupants standing beside them. They then passed the junior high school and approached Ward's. The sign at Ward's read, "Good-bye, Brandon. We love you." Grant noticed the staff and customers at Ward's standing along the street. People were standing along the roadway in front of Piggly Wiggly. Grant smiled as he pondered how proud he was of his hometown.

The funeral procession left Leakesville en route to the Hicks Family Cemetery. Grant looked over at Reverend Clark who was gazing out his window observing the respect being shown by Brandon's neighbors. Grant had come home. As he reflected on his life, he finally realized that he did love this place. He loved the people here. Imperfect, yes they were–as was he. But they were his neighbors. They were his people. Grant turned to look behind him at the stream of cars following Brandon. He then looked ahead at the hearse which carried Brandon and muttered, "Dad, I'm bringing you our friend."

THE END

epilogue

THE GREENE RURAL NURSING CENTER had never seen this much excitement. It had been six months and a handful of days since Brandon's funeral. Elsie's house was remodeled, and for the first time in her life, she has central heat and air–and a utility room! She returned to work at the school cafeteria, and Lester and his family made the drive up at least two times per month to visit her and to visit Brandon's grave. The town seemed to be more relaxed in the days following the funeral. Danny Narbo pled guilty to his crimes, and now he was serving his time at Parchman. The Greene County Wildcats' football team was undefeated and had finally beaten the George County Rebels after a long dry spell. All seemed well in Grant's hometown.

After the funeral, Grant spent his remaining time off from work in Leakesville. He managed to buy the "old place" where he grew up. He allowed the Seals to retain a life estate so that they could live out their remaining days there. Grant was able to buy it for less that way, and the Seals were able to access their money while staying in their home. Grant rented a condo in Orange Beach, Alabama, for a week and took Jade, Lad, Nana and Max for a vacation. When Grant returned to work at Rimes & Yancey in Atlanta, he had a new attitude. He still had the incessant fire that drove him to work, but he left at noon most Fridays to drive to Greene County to see Jade.

Becky Berry and her staff had the nursing home decorated immaculately. The personal care facility had never hosted a wedding before. It was October 10, 2010, Michaels Hicks' birthday. Jade chose the date, and Grant willingly agreed. The staff and the residents were all dressed in their Sunday best as Brother Clark, Grant, and Ms. Elsie walked out of a side door and to the front of the room. Grant grew to love Lollis Clark, and now he called him "Brother Clark." Grant's best friend, Brandon, was gone. Elsie was honored to accept Grant's request to stand in the place of her beloved son as Grant's best man.

Edwina wore a deep purple dress which was splendidly complimented by jewels and flowers, some matching, some not. But nothing radiated more than her smile. As Edwina walked down the aisle between the wedding guests, Grant grinned as he recalled the last time he had seen Edwina smile this big. She had been on the casino's billboard along Interstate 10 grinning from ear to ear. There was no doubt who would be the Maid-of-Honor. Edwina was Jade's best friend.

Developmentally, Lad had practically caught up with children his age. He was talking more, and as he carefully walked down the aisle as the ring-bearer, Grant became excited about the adoption. Ladetrus was soon to be a Hicks! Grant had given Max to Lad; there is indeed something special about a little boy and his dog.

Mary Ball began to play that familiar tune which announced the entrance of the bride. Family and friends stood. Sylvia and

Lauren smiled at Grant as they wiped tears from their eyes. Sylvia had her son back and Lauren her brother. And as a bonus, they were soon to have Jade and Lad.

Grant began moving his head as he watched for his bride to come into view. Just around the corner, and out of view of everyone, Sheriff McInnis hugged Jade and told her he loved her. Jade told him he was officially the daddy she never had. The sheriff, with his cane in his right hand and Jade's right arm holding to his left, slowly walked down the hall and around the corner.

Jade was stunning. She wore a simple, straight white dress. Her eyes sparkled as she gazed at Grant. The crowd was whispering at how beautiful she was. With a feeling only a father could experience, the sheriff gave her away and sat down. Brother Clark performed a beautiful service. At the conclusion of the ceremony, he proudly introduced the guests to the new couple: Mr. and Mrs. Michael Grant Hicks! The familiar bluegrass band began to play at the reception in the common area of the nursing home where the wedding was held.

The Range Rover was awash with soap announcing that the occupants were "Just Married." The tin cans were tied neatly behind the vehicle, as per local custom. Grant and Jade hugged everyone en route to the SUV. Grant was the picture of the complete man as he strode to the driver's side, after having made Jade, Nana, Lad and Max comfortable in the Range Rover. He waved good-bye to the crowd one last time.

Grant drove south on Highway 63 past the sign which indicated he was leaving Greene County. A few short months ago, he had reluctantly entered his home county for the first time in almost twenty years. He turned left onto Highway 98 heading toward the Alabama line. He smiled as he passed the sign that simply read *Auction*. He wondered where his extension cord was. They made it to Interstate 65 and headed north toward Atlanta. Grant looked at Jade who smiled at him with her beautiful, endearing dimples. He then glanced out of his window at a vacant baseball field and thought of his dad. For a moment, he smiled as he imagined a younger version of himself pitching to his daddy who was kneeling behind the deserted home plate.